Legend of the Emerald Rose

Legend of the Emerald Rose

A NOVEL

LINDA WICHMAN

Kregel Publications

Legend of the Emerald Rose: A Novel

© 2005 by Linda Wichman

Published by Kregel Publications, a division of Kregel, Inc., P.O. Box 2607, Grand Rapids, MI 49501.

Scripture quotations marked KJV are from the King James Version of the Bible.

Library of Congress Cataloging-in-Publication Data
Wichman, Linda.
    Legend of the Emerald Rose: a novel / by Linda Wichman.
        p.   cm.
    1. Arthurian romances—Adaptations. I. Title.
PS3623.I26L44 2005
813'.6—dc22   2004027839

ISBN 0-8254-4109-9

Printed in the United States of America

05 06 07 08 09 / 5 4 3 2

To my confidante,
midnight plotter,
character-driven schemer,
and passionate dreamer.
Hey, Fran,
I finally found it . . .
the rainbow connection:
the lovers, the dreamers,
and me!

In loving memory of
Francine Ann Ciske
November 11, 1955–May 6, 2001

Acknowledgments

TO MY LORD AND SAVIOR Jesus Christ, in whom all things are possible. You gave me the desire of my heart, and I'm forever grateful.

To Gary, my lover, best friend, and knight in tarnished armor! Thank you for more than thirty-three years of love, patience, encouragement, living with a dreamer, and for the guy's POV.

To Chad and Janell. You got stuck with a weird mom who wrote because I could do no other. There's more of you in what I write than you'll ever know.

Andrea and Travis, my children's godsends, you are more than special. You are blessed.

In remembrance of William Keither. The creative seed he nurtured in a shy sixth-grader has bloomed.

Char, my oldest girlfriend and sister of artistic gifts, isn't God amazing?

Joan, Pat, and Faith—twenty-plus years of objective and subjective critiques, yummy food, tears, joy, and, most of all, unconditional love.

Andrea Boeshaar—for a writer-agent relationship sparked by friendship, united by loss. Thanks for believing in the Creator of the intangible supernatural, and me.

Jill Nelson, God dropped you into my life when I needed a critical eye and a warped sense of humor. His timing is awesome.

To Steve Barclift, Paul Ingram, Janyre Tromp, and everyone else at Kregel for taking a chance with this dreamer.

To Becky Durost Fish, you have encouraged and enlightened me in the craft, and in doing so, became a blessed friend.

To my son Chad, whose artistic hands created and sketched the Isle of Wind's Haven, just as I imagined.

To Linda Windsor and Donita K. Paul for your generous endorsements and friendships.

To the marvelous, Spirit-filled writers of ACFW, you are inspiration, sounding boards, and prayer warriors.

To Cindy for faithfulness.

To Ruthie for prayers.

To my extended family and friends, thank you for hanging in there.

To Jaybird, Dave, Rick, and Vicky, who may not always understand their oldest sibling but love her just the same.

Nathan, my first grandchild, you keep me young at heart.

Destin, your unconditional love for Jesus will forever own my heart.

Dad, I'm so thankful you're here for me.

Hey, Mom, you were right—I can write.

Pronunciation Guide

AS A READER, it's frustrating to stumble over ancient words in fiction. That said, only a few Celtic, Briton, and Gaelic names and words have been used, most of which should be familiar to fantasy and historical readers. If not, this guide will help.

WORD	PRONUNCIATION	DEFINITION OR DESCRIPTION
Ayris	Air´es	ancient lost civilization
bracchae	'bra' k	loose-legged breeches
burn	burn	creek, stream
caer	kare	Welsh for fortified home, castle
Caithest Uais	Kay thesst Uä´is	fictitious cousin of Colla Uais, king of Ireland
Can un Scye	Kane un Sky	Celtic name meaning "cane of sky"
Demesne	di man'	a possession of land, or estate
Eire	âr´ _	Ireland
Galahad	Gal'| had	son of Lancelot
Guenevere	Gwen´ev ear	high queen of Isle of Might
Hengist	Hin´gest	historical invading Saxon king
Iona du Maur	I oh´ n| do Mar´	cousin to Queen Guenevere

WORD	PRONUNCIATION	DEFINITION OR DESCRIPTION
Isle of Might		Britannia and Caledonia
Lancelot du lac	Lance´| lot do lak	Lancelot of the lake
loch	lock	lake, body of inland water
Merdyn	Mer´ din	Merlin's Druid name
Mordred le Fey	Mor´dred le Fay	son of Morgause
Morgause le Fey	Mor´gauze le Fay	sorceress/half sister of Arthur
Niamh le Fey	Neeve le Fay	half sister of Morgause
Perceval	Purs´eh val	knight of the Round Table
Rayn	Rain	princess of Isle of Might
scion	si´on	Gaelic for son
Shadoe un Hollo Tors	Shad´ow un Hol´low Tore	Celtic name meaning "Shadow of the hollow hills"
talisman	tal´ez mun	amulet believed to hold magical powers
Tor	tore	a high craggy hill, mountain
Tristam	Tris´tum	knight of the Round Table
Villeins	vil´inz	occupants of a village
Uther	You´ther	Arthur's father
Vortigern	Vort´i gern	historical Romano-Briton commander
winnock	win´ek	Scottish for window

Introduction

THE FIFTH CENTURY A.D. saw the gradual collapse of the Roman Empire and, with it, the expansion of Christianity. Yet most of humanity remained entangled in paganism, separated from God by a great chasm. Thus arose superstitions and legends of great men who had crossed that divide and achieved immortality and a restored relationship with God. A man so regarded was Merlin un Hollo Tors. A poetic bard, genius, and superior warrior, Merlin became the first emissary of the Isle of Might as well as a teacher and an advisor/negotiator in Britannia and the larger world. Addressed as the Merdyn, he was perhaps the most misunderstood man of the Dark Ages. His unique abilities were dubbed sorcery, magic—but were they really?

His appearance in our world is cloaked in mystery, and no one records recollections of Merlin ever being a child or a young man. Pagans claimed he was their enchanter, the offspring of an incubus of the air and a virtuous young woman. Merlin himself asserted he was a descendant of Joseph, son of Jacob, and endowed with unique gifts of discernment and foresight by the God of Israel as well as the ability to converse, upon occasion, with God's angelic legions.

With Merlin came a jeweled talisman, the Emerald Rose of Avalon, a symbol of his people's faith in the triune God, Jehovah. The talisman had been forged for Merlin's greatest ancestor, Joseph, who served as governor to an Egyptian pharaoh. The circular bronze and gold amulet held twelve diamond points. Each diamond represented a tribe of

Israel descended from Jacob's sons. Set within the heart of the talisman was an emerald of evergreen color, signifying God's everlasting sovereignty over Joseph's descendants.

For generations, members of Merlin's noble lineage served as high stewards (political advisors) to emperors and kings. It became the duty of Merlin's forerunners to designate a righteous king and bestow upon this king the Emerald Rose of Avalon.

Respected for his wise instruction and peacekeeping stratagems, Merlin un Hollo Tors became high steward to Uther Pendragon, high chieftain of the Britons of South Wales. Once word of Merlin's political ingenuity reached the Roman Senate, his council was oftentimes sought by its members.

During the span of his life, Merlin witnessed the grandeur of the Roman Empire and its inevitable fall. Once the Isle of Might was no longer under Rome's guardianship, conflict there ensued among rival chieftains for control, leaving Britons who wanted to maintain a Roman way of life to fend for themselves.

With King Uther's health failing, a desperate cry for leadership arose. Thus Merlin engaged a reluctant Romano-Briton warrior to take up the challenge. This man was Lucius Artorius Castus, commonly known as Arthur, son of Uther Pendragon. Arthur remained one of Merlin's greatest achievements. From the moment of Arthur's birth, a bond grew between them that no man would ever sever. Under Merlin's tutelage, Arthur learned of his own Jewish heritage and received Jesus Christ as his Lord and Savior.

Unlike his father, Arthur had no design to be king but every desire to ensure peace among the peoples. In all, he fought a dozen campaigns across the Isle of Might, manning the fortresses of Tintagel, Cadbury, and Camelot in Southern Caledonia. If Arthur had ever boasted (which he didn't), it would have been of his love of command and his accomplishments as a warrior, not of his rule over men. Upon the death of Uther, the chieftains set Arthur on the throne as high king of Britannia and Caledonia.

Arthur's fervent love for the Isle of Might kept peace between the

Britons, along with the Celt and Pict clans—a peace certain Britons abhorred. Challengers arose and Vortigern, a former Roman officer, was one such usurper. Once Arthur took residence at Camelot in southern Caledonia, Vortigern dismissed Arthur as a threat and declared himself emperor, going so far as to invite the Saxons to leave their home countries and ensure Vortigern's conquest of the Isle of Might.

When news reached Camelot that Vortigern intended to attack Arthur's southernmost holdings, Arthur led an army of Britons, Celts, and Picts to block Vortigern's advance. The battle was brutally long, ending only when Vortigern fell under Arthur's sword. Still, the war was not won. The Saxon tribes invaded full-force and with a new commander, Arthur's traitorous son, Mordred Pendragon.

Legend has it that Mordred, Arthur's illegitimate son, had been conceived when Arthur's half sister, Morgause, a druid priestess, used a love potion to seduce him. But her plans to become Arthur's queen were shattered the day Arthur took young Guenevere as his wife. Hungry for power, Morgause vowed that her son Mordred would rule, no matter the cost. With domineering influence Morgause groomed Mordred for the throne, knowing he could only succeed by defeating his father and pressing a victor's claim before the tribal chieftains.

Merlin foresaw Arthur's death in battle against Mordred and warned the king of his son's treachery, advising Arthur not to engage in battle against Mordred's legion of Saxons. Although the king acknowledged his son's betrayal, Arthur sought to mend his tattered relationship with Mordred and refused to believe that his son would slay him in cold blood. Merlin and Arthur argued fiercely, and rumors of an alliance between Merlin and Mordred poisoned the land.

At that point, Merlin appeared to vanish from history and another's manifestation began. This account is of that apprentice who succeeded him and sought to uphold a vow Merlin made to Arthur and Guenevere Pendragon—an oath that would forever alter the course of history. Thus begins the chronicle of Shadoe un Hollo Tors—son of Merlin— and the Emerald Rose.

Somewhere, sometime, someone wrote, legend begins where truth ends. . . . Or is it the other way around?
—CAER TINTAGEL,
Southeastern Britannia

'TWAS KNOWN BEFORE the Isle of Britain's history was put to quill that the bard Grat-Telor was as olden as the hollow tors of the Isle of Might. A crown of moonstone hair framed his cockle features, and though his vision was clouded, his brown eyes sparked with mischief and wisdom.

That dayspring, as always, he sat on an oak stump within view of the ruins of Tintagel, playing a sweet melody on his lyre, his arthritic fingers miraculously never missing a chord. His audience, a gathering of impetuous young lordlings, languished about, waiting for him to speak.

One youth finally urged, "Please, Grat-Telor, amuse us with the legend of King Arthur and Merlin."

Weary, the bard was not impressed with their thirst for diversion, for he did not relate fables, as was the custom of other bards, but truth alone. Setting his lyre aside, he rubbed his weathered palm across the haft of an ancient staff and deliberately scanned their eager faces. *Mayhap, one of these lads will be the righteous king.* His desire for this to be so caused him to draw a breath and sigh. "And why wish you hearken to the reminiscence of an old singer of tales?"

"By virtue that you recount with such passion, we almost believe it true," replied a freckle-faced stripling who sat separate from the others.

Grat-Telor eyed this particular youth, and then scowled at the lad's faithlessness. "Almost? Mayhap I need tell it so well that you will believe, aye?"

Willing nods honored Grat-Telor.

His gnarled hands embraced the haft of the staff, and thereupon he rested his gray-bearded chin. "Then indeed, lads, I have a tale for you about the legendary Emerald Rose of Avalon, a talisman passed on from the High Steward Merlin to King Arthur, though Arthur Pendragon and Merlin un Hollo Tors are not the innermost characters. First, however, I shall expound about a land called Ayris, from which Arthur's and Merlin's forefathers came."

All but the freckle-faced youth looked confused. "I've heard about Ayris, Sire."

"Have you now?" Grat-Telor sat upright, hearing his backbone creak.

"Aye, 'twas in the Mediterranean Sea and likened to Caledonia's southwest isle of Arran. Is that so, Milord?"

The bard shut his eyes to savor another's memories. "Aye, in some regards, but 'twas farther away. Always warm, always balmy. The colors brilliant, especially the birds, dragons, and—"

"Dragons? Were they as evil as folklore proclaims?" another lad chirped.

Murmurs erupted as the lads scrambled closer to Grat-Telor's sandaled feet.

"Evil?" the man mused. "Hardly. Least not the ones of Ayris. Just because something looks fierce doesn't mean it's bad. Similar to people, there are good and evil dragons. Highly intelligent creatures, they are. On Ayris, dragons were protective and loyal to the clan. They guarded the royal family. Why, it is how King Arthur's surname *Pendragon* came to be. Alas, the dragons of Ayris vanished when . . ." Grat-Telor felt their wide-eyed stares. He rolled his shoulders back and cleared the emotion from his voice. "'Tis another story, that is, aye?"

They nodded agreement.

"Where was I? Ah, yes. Two vital families dominated Ayris. Merlin's family was a shoot of Ephraim, blessed son of Joseph. King Arthur's lineage rose from the tribe of Judah and house of David."

"But the tribe of Judah never left Israel," the same freckle-faced lad injected.

Impressed, Grat-Telor eyed the youth. "You have been taught a bit for a lad of your winters. True, but a cluster of Judah's descendants remained among the ten tribes. The tribes of Israel disobeyed Yahweh, the one true God, and they were punished with defeat in great wars. When the tribes were captured and scattered by the Assyrians, God lead those of Ephraim and Judah who believed the seers to a safe, fertile island, where a soft, steadfast breeze blew from heaven. With time, the inhabitants called that isle *Ayris,* which means 'air of God.'"

"And did they bring the faith of Yahweh with them?" posed the freckle-faced lad.

"Aye, clan Ayris became abundantly blessed. They gave all glory and honor to our Lord God. They had wealth, engaged in commerce, and sailed the world. Because of their obedient love for Yahweh, he bequeathed the Merdyn's forefathers and his offspring with gifts of foresight, the Breath of Eden, and other abilities not oft known among the sons of Adam."

"'Twas a special blessing, these inborn memories?" The same youth now stood, as if to draw attention.

Annoyed by the boy's constant interruptions, his peers shot him disparaging remarks and glares.

"I like an inquisitive nature, lad. So do not fear asking questions, any one of you." Grat-Telor's firmness rebuked the rest. "I will do my best to answer."

They each nodded respectfully.

"Aye, one of many gifts the chosen of Ayris inherited. Those of Ephraim's who had righteous hearts became stewards or magi and they held high positions of influence, while from the house of David came great godly kings like Arthur, who ruled with compassion and wisdom. Furthermore, Yahweh endowed them with a unique comprehension of science that even Greece and Rome did not possess."

"Science?" another piped up with a bold smile.

"Aye, the wisdom of Yahweh's universe swelled within our magi." Tipping his head, he squinted at the azure sky and gestured heavenward.

"Merlin's great-great-granda foresaw a time when mankind will soar among the clouds like the great eagle."

"You mean we'll grow wings?" another quipped.

The bard guffawed and gripped his sides in mirth. "Not exactly. We'll fly in iron chariots designed with wings."

Excited voices vibrated the air.

He had their attention. "For centuries, Ayris flourished and erected libraries of knowledge deep within the caverns of their tors. They taught God's love and were titled 'peacekeepers' among the nations. Merlin's forefathers served as steward-counsel to the royal families of Ayris and advised the kings on political matters of state.

"But a time came when clan Ayris grew prideful in their gifts and turned from Yahweh and took credit for comprehending the science of the stars, wind, sea—the equations of this vast universe. They declared that the anointed gift of foresight was similar to their inherent memories and longevity, as if in their blood. They complimented themselves for their good fortune and spiritual gifts. So Yahweh ordered the sea and the brume of time to descend upon Ayris and conceal it from mankind's eyes."

"Why didn't God destroy it like Sodom and Gomorrah?" one boy ventured.

"King Uther was Aurelius's great-great-grandscion."

Another boy asked, "So King Uther, sire of Arthur Pendragon, was of Ayrisian seed?"

"Aye, unlike Merlin, Uther had no inherent memories of his proud birthright, nor did Arthur. Apparently God divided the gifts so that no one Ayrisian possesses them all. Thus, the knowledge Arthur learned came from Merlin's lineage, mayhap God's means to keep their clansmen dependant upon one.

"Originally, the Ayris clan settled the western shores of Britannia and an isle named Wind's Haven before God's wrath descended upon Ayris. In time, they traveled southeast and settled Cornwall, where Uther became a great warrior and king. 'Twas here at Caer Tintagel that Arthur was conceived and born. Do you all know of Uther's sinful union with the married Duchess Igraine, who later became his wife?"

Heads nodded. Voices raised, and then simmered.

"Aye, that union produced Arthur," one lad responded. "After Arthur's birth, King Uther insisted Merlin take Arthur away, safe from those who would have seen him dead. Thus, they went to Caledonia. It was there Arthur grew into manhood."

"Aye. The rest is history." Grat-Telor rubbed his arthritic hands. "Even after he returned to Tintagel and became high king, Arthur sensed God drawing him back to those stormy shores that his ancestors once called home. There, he embraced the customs of the Romano-Britons and initiated peace between the Celts, Irish Scotti, and Picts. Arthur's inborn leadership led him to govern the northern lands of Britannia and Caledonia. His mastery of governing has become an inspiration to all mankind.

"So now bestow me vigilance, young sirs, and I will transport you to the darkest hours following Arthur Pendragon's death. A time when chivalry scarce endured, but the love of a reluctant enchanter and a most unlikely princess rescued this blessed Isle of Might. Yea, listen to the legend of the Emerald Rose."

THE LEGEND

Oh, isle of bright Pendragon might,
Gaze upon these vermilion shores
Of scattered limbs and sightless souls.
Behold yer noble Arthur's slain;
Avalon hast claimed her own.
'Yea, the hoary dragon of Satan's loins
Seizes bondage to your isle
To duel the Almighty Fisher of Men,
And the world defile.
Heaven's mist veils Splendor Lost
To shield the blossom rare.
This rose of emerald Briton hope,
Shall placate the Celts' despair.
Yea, he the endmost of Ayris blood
To fulfill the promise told,
Must prick his flesh upon the briar,
To claim the Emerald Rose.

—THE STEWARD CHRONICLES,
Shadoe un Hollo Tors

Chapter One

456 A.D.

NORTHWESTERN SHORES OF BRITANNIA

"Duck!"

The blunt blow sent his short sword flying from his grip, but twelve-year-old Shadoe's response to that warning delivered him from the battle-axe's lethal blade. The Saxon warrior cursed his miss and moved to swing again. Like a well-choreographed dancer, King Arthur Pendragon pivoted and wielded Excalibur, slicing the man's neck muscles and spinal column clean through. The astonished expression of the Saxon's beard-matted face seared itself onto Shadoe's memory. A moment later, the man's head toppled to the boggy sod before his body fell forward.

"Keep your back to mine, lad!" Arthur smacked his fist between the bony shoulder blades of his armor bearer. Before Shadoe could respond, the king caught up Shadoe's sword and shoved its peat-caked hilt into his hand. "I mean you to outlive me, Apprentice."

The youth smiled and, for a heartbeat, he held the passionate gaze of his high king's green eyes. "Aye, Milord, but," he yelled over the combat's din when Arthur rushed to engage more enemy warriors, "how can I keep my back to you when you don't stand still?" Shadoe gave Arthur chase, diving and swerving between quarter staves, spears, swords, battle-axes, horse hooves, and falling bodies. At such a harrowing time, Shadoe un Hollo Tors rejoiced for his limber build.

From out of the mists, Mordred Pendragon charged through the fray on horseback, wielding his scarlet-stained sword at anyone in his wake, even his ally Saxons and Jutes. Wearing a sardonic smile, his striking face was splattered with fresh blood. Mordred truly was Satan incarnate.

Too late to stop, Shadoe stumbled into Mordred's path. As Mordred charged him, Shadoe did what he did best. He ducked. The swoosh of a near miss burned his right ear. A horse's hoof cleared his head. Short sword in hand, Shadoe flipped over backward and landed upright on his feet. Mordred reared his snorting steed and glanced back. Their gazes met—Shadoe and Mordred, first cousins but fighting on opposite sides. Mordred laughed, and then charged off.

Drenched with blood and sweat, Shadoe dove behind an outcropping of rocks and took stock. Mordred could have slain him but hadn't. Why? The clash of metal and wails of warriors overrode that question. Shadoe had lost sight of Arthur. He spotted Perceval and Tristam, who watched each other's backs. A short distance away, Cai and Geraint did likewise. Such was the honor code of Arthur's knights of the Round Table.

Leaping onto a rock, Shadoe rejoined the combat with a prayer on his lips, "Father God, protect me. Protect Arthur and—"

Shadoe was slammed facedown into the bog. He glanced up to see an enemy's quarterstaff plunging toward him. Shadoe grabbled for the haft of his short sword and rolled over, evading the enemy's weapon. The bloodstained staff rose again in the hands of a young Jute. A direct blow to Shadoe's skull would be fatal.

"Skewer him, Shadoe!" Lancelot's voice rang out. With the hilt of his sword, Lancelot rammed the warrior's back ribs and sent him sprawling over Shadoe.

His sword's haft braced against his stomach, Shadoe thrust upward. The blade pierced the youth's stomach and exited his back. The Jute screamed. Blood trickled from his mouth and nostrils before his weight slid to Shadoe's hilt. Shadoe struggled to push the young man off.

Lancelot du Lac jerked the Jute's lifeless body off Shadoe's blade.

Offering a gloved hand, Lancelot drew Shadoe to his feet and gave him a brief look. "For your first battle, you are doing well, scion of Merlin."

At the mention of his father's name, Shadoe flinched. "I try, Sire."

"So where's our high king, Apprentice? You're to have his back this day."

"I lost him, Lance. He went—" Shadoe swerved as Lancelot delivered a deadly blow to one Saxon, then another.

Shadoe held his own against a Jute before driving his blade through the man's heart. Before long, Shadoe guarded Lancelot's back. Despite his worry about Arthur's whereabouts, Shadoe fell into a comfortable rhythm with Lancelot. Minutes later, Shadoe saved the Silver Lion from an incoming spear. Pride squirmed into his heart, and with it, newfound confidence. Mayhap war wasn't hell after all.

∞

War was *hell!*

Arthur was dead!

Anguished wails echoed across the battlefield—an altar saturated with sacrificial blood. Celts, Picts, and Britons rent their clothes and cried to the heavens over the loss of the Pendragon. A slate gray mist shrouded the gory carnage, but nothing could conceal the wretched stench of death. Arthur Pendragon's armor bearer, Shadoe un Hollo Tors, knelt beside his dead master. With blood-coated hands, he held tight to Arthur's battered helm. His gaze never wavered from the ashen features of his sovereign lord.

An exceptionally large man, Arthur Pendragon lay on his back, clutching his sword Excalibur. A sleeping giant, Shadoe had often called him, for despite Arthur's lofty height and breadth of shoulders, there had never been a man of gentler heart.

Absently, Shadoe wiped dirt from Arthur's jaw and pushed the unruly auburn hair off his king's forehead. That noble brow was no longer tension-creased but masked in youthful virtue. Arthur's fiery green eyes were forever sealed. Shadoe grieved, for he would never again feel those confident jewels of light gaze upon him.

Oh, to hear his rich voice shouting orders, bursting forth in laughter, and humbling itself in prayer. Oh, Arthur. Shadoe gripped the gilded helm tighter. *Why didn't I foresee this day? Why didn't God spare you and take me? Why didn't I have your back?* Shadoe's brow knit low and tight. Grief, guilt, and ire slashed him through.

The brutal siege assailed Shadoe's mind, and the events that had led to this tragic morn misted his eyes. It had been a momentous day, when from all corners of Britannia, including the farthest regions of Pictland, chieftains of every tribe rose to support Arthur. Not since before Rome's desertion had there been such loyal unison on the Isle of Might. With support of the clans, Arthur organized a series of campaigns against the Germanic invaders. The current battle had lasted three days. Once more, Arthur's troops were victorious, and Mordred had been restrained. Only in the aftermath did the high king's men discover Arthur himself had been mortally wounded.

Shadoe's reflections came full circle. Multiple versions of Arthur's death heated the stagnant air. Had it been a Saxon? Or had the seasoned warrior taken an ill-fated step and fallen upon his blade? Having witnessed Arthur's final contest, Shadoe and Lancelot knew neither premise was true, but they had vowed to their dying Pendragon not to reveal that nineteen-year-old Mordred had slain his own father.

Through grief-veiled eyes, Shadoe gazed at the dust from the retreating Saxons and Jutes. The Britons and Celts had pushed them south from Arthur's lands. But for what prize? How long before Mordred stormed Hadrian's Wall again? How long before he marched on the innermost summer realm of Camelot? How would Lady Guenevere defend her people? Of an army more than two thousand strong, nine hundred Celts, Romano-Britons, and Picts had perished. From the head count, another two hundred men were wounded and many missing. Fortunately, the enemy's loss was greater. Still, Cai, Geraint, and four other brave souls of the Pendragon Round Table had perished.

Shadoe knelt, waiting for a miracle, waiting for Yahweh to return their high chieftain to life. How could God allow this? Arthur had been a godly man. What would happen to his peaceful kingdom of Camelot? *Jesu help us,* Shadoe prayed heatedly, *Arthur is . . . was Camelot!*

Chapter Two

"'TIS TIME."

The familiar baritone dragged Shadoe up from his well of despair, and he swept the back of his hand across his wet eyes and glanced at the sun. Nearly two hours had passed.

"Aye, Lance." He stretched, setting down Arthur's helm, and gazed upon the tall Normandy warrior known to all as the Silver Lion.

"Bedivere was to have fulfilled this final oath to Arthur. Alas the young knight's wounds—" Lancelot choked with sentiment.

"Nay!" Shadoe struggled to deny the gravity of Lancelot's words. Rage twisted his belly. Bitter bile scorching his throat, Shadoe pummeled his fists against his brow and wept. Gentle-hearted Bedivere. They'd been like brothers! *Oh, God, how can you tear another loved one from my heart?*

Lancelot du Lac clenched Shadoe's shoulder. "Bedivere shared your faith, Shadoe, so you must believe he resides with Arthur in God's kingdom." Lancelot's voice deepened with conviction. "Our high chieftain is dead. We must be about our final duty to him."

"I will not leave him!"

Lancelot shrugged a burly shoulder. "Perceval, Tristam, and Galahad will escort his body to Lady Guenevere at Caer Camelot."

"But the Celts want to take him down into Cadbury to cross over to Avalon, while the Picts wish to cremate him."

Lancelot shook his white blond head in firm denial. "Curse their pagan hearts! Arthur will have the burial of his Christian faith."

Shadoe lifted a brow at his friend's adamant tone. While raised druid, Lancelot had never taken a stand on what he believed, although in recent months he seemed to have been influenced by Arthur's conviction of faith in the Christ.

"Besides," Lancelot sighed, "Guenevere will want to see him and . . ." His voice trembled before he extended his arm, freshly marred from battle. "Now hand me Excalibur," he ordered.

Shadoe's limbs felt heavy as iron. When he reached for the weapon atop Arthur's body, he froze. Excalibur was different from other swords. This was the sword of kings, the sword of clan Pendragon. Its silvery blade was unlike any other—the exact age of the weapon still unknown for it had been handed off to several generations of high kings. According to Merlin, the blade had been hammered from the fragment of a fiery star that had fallen from the heavens. The blade never corroded, never chipped.

Unlike the popular Roman short sword, Excalibur remained grand in every aspect. The razor-edged metal itself was longer than a warrior's arm and designed for a large man—for Arthur. The gold dragons, intertwined on the hilt, always seemed threatening, the haft too broad for Shadoe's young hands. Something else restrained Shadoe: Arthur's blood, not even dried, painted the argent blade.

To Shadoe's relief, Lancelot took up the sword and wiped it clean on the dew-drenched sod. Then the warrior shot out a hand that Shadoe accepted, staggering to his feet. They embraced, and he felt a quake in the man. He'd not seen the knight cry but knew Lancelot grieved. Lance had lost brethren of the Round Table and, more importantly, a man who'd been like blood kin—Arthur Pendragon.

Rubbing his jaw, Lancelot du Lac looked upon Shadoe as if taking inventory. The knight scowled. Shadoe cringed. He didn't need Lancelot's critical gaze to know what the seasoned warrior saw: a long-legged stripling with, in Lancelot's perfectionistic estimation, little hope of ever being a knight. Shadoe's blue tunic was torn and blackened from the pitchy peat bog; his breeches were in no better wear. Even in chain mail, he looked elfin beside the other warriors. Yet at age twelve, he had shed his first blood, taken lives. The bile rotting his empty belly gave a constant reminder of what his young eyes had beheld.

Shadoe was taken back when Lancelot softly said, "I regret the tragic circumstances that have taken place here, lad. War being what it is, there is no romance in its brutality. Only sorrow."

Shadoe felt Lancelot's concerned gaze and sensed the knight about to broach a sensitive subject—the tragic loss of Shadoe's father. But two battle-worn chieftains approached, the Pictish king obviously absent.

Caithest Uais, Celtic king of the southwest, halted, and after bending a knee before Arthur's body, stood and addressed Lancelot. "Sir Lancelot, we give thanks that the gods have granted us this reprieve, but Mordred will return."

Caithest glanced at Shadoe, who met the king's troubled gaze with a challenge. Caithest shifted his bulk to one foot, rubbed his braided black beard, and turned back to Lancelot.

"I have consulted the chieftains," he hedged. "Our gods reveal that Mordred dines with the Adversary. We are defenseless against such evil. The fact that your great God, Yahweh, did not save Arthur bears witness of what awaits if we tarry."

Lancelot's eyes narrowed. The muscle of his strong jaw flinched. Knowing what was coming, he stood unable to prevent it. "You are deserting us."

"Nay, not in our hearts." The Briton king Can un Scye shook his head. "We do what we must to save our people. The voices of the wind say Mordred rides south to invade my lands. Moreover the Saxons and Jutes continue to arrive in fleets, trampling our fields, burning our villas, and stealing our livestock. We must defend our homelands before all that was Britannia is nevermore."

"Aye," Caithest snorted. "'Tis dreadful the Pendragon is dead, but with the august enchanter, the Merdyn, vanished or dead, my men refuse to battle Mordred on Caledonian soil or any other soil."

Ire fueled Shadoe's battle-weary limbs with renewed strength and urged him a step closer to the Celt. "But Mordred was browbeaten by our numbers!"

Caithest glowered. "It is not the beast Mordred we most fear, but his mother is indeed another creature. We fear her hellish magique. She has defiled the druid ways and sleeps with the monarch of Hades. Merlin's Jesu was a great champion against the priestess Morgause le Fey. Without him or Arthur, we are vulnerable against such a union of iniquity. Furthermore, even as we speak, the Irish Scotti invade my kingdom and steal my people into slavery. I must return."

"You'd let Mordred take the throne?" Shadoe charged the kings, who marched off.

Halting, Can un Scye answered regretfully, "'Tis the last thing we want, Apprentice, but unless there is another heir and a righteous one at that, Mordred is Arthur's successor."

Caithest looked over his shoulder. "Take solace. For if the Merdyn's foresight is true, there is another Pendragon. Moreover, we kings of Britannia will never acknowledge Mordred as Pendragon without a high steward's public sanction. Pray to your Jesu to defeat Mordred, for if not, we will pay homage to that scion of an incubus." The kings turned and disappeared amidst the throngs of horses and men.

Shadoe's mouth opened to debate, but Lancelot's firm grip turned him around. "Let them go, Apprentice."

"What of Camelot and our people?" He looked one last time upon Arthur while a soldier placed the Pendragon flag over his king's face.

"We'll prepare for the worst. First we must reach Loch Lady and preserve the Pendragon's legacy." Lancelot tramped off across the battlefield.

Shadoe tried to keep up with Lancelot's long-legged stride, but in fear of recognizing a lost friend, he dodged mutilated bodies without looking, hampering his pace. It took a few yards before he matched

Lancelot's gait. Shadoe gulped air, and then charged, "You expect me to believe anything my da foresaw? If not for Merlin, Arthur would be alive, as would Cai, Geraint, and Bedivere."

"Arthur refused to heed Merlin's counsel not to fight Mordred," Lancelot protested.

"You took Merlin's side on the matter?"

"Aye. And Arthur did not listen to me, either."

Shadoe shook his head. He wanted to believe in his father's innocence, but present evidence proved otherwise. Yet why would Merlin betray Arthur, who in Shadoe's mind had always been first in his father's affections? And if Merlin had fled, why had he not taken Shadoe along? Shadoe would not have left, of course, but he'd have liked the option. He'd been at odds with his father for some time, and although his heart now burned with regret and loss, anger won out. "Once Merlin could have stopped the wind, commanded the seas. He could have stopped this battle. He could have saved Arthur's life but didn't."

They paused where their horses were tethered, and Lancelot shot Shadoe a troubled glance. "Aye, the august enchanter, the Merdyn, could have indeed conjured a spell and saved Arthur. But not the new Merlin, not this follower of the Fisher of Men. I admit my druid blood rages at that fact, but my heart knows Merlin would not turn against your Jesu . . . even to save our beloved Arthur or any other lost brothers of the Round Table. For that I respect him."

"I, too, love Jesu, but regardless, Merlin betrayed us!"

"You knew him best, Apprentice. Do you really believe that's possible?"

"It was my da's counsel that turned Mordred against Arthur. Does that not vex you?" He drew the reins over his horse's head.

"If there's validity to his conspiring with Vortigern and Mordred, then yes. But Mordred turned his heart against Arthur long before your father interfered. Besides, if Merlin chose Mordred over Arthur, he'd be here declaring Mordred the new chieftain of the Pendragon clan, and . . . ," he paused, "I'm sorry, Shadoe, but your da's still not to be found."

"I know." Shadoe tried to temper his emotions. He'd tried not to think of the rumors that enveloped Merlin's disappearance. Gripping the reins, he swung onto the saddle and directed his mount to stand beside Lancelot's.

"We've searched everywhere, identified most of the bodies," Lancelot stated.

Shadoe watched Lancelot remove a black fleece mantle from his saddle sack.

The knight handed the cloak to Shadoe. "Although there was no sign of shed blood, we found this on the shoreline boulders. Mayhap the tide carried his body out to sea." The warrior's lips pressed tight with speculation. "Arthur said Merlin stumbled and fell off the cliff while they argued about Mordred."

Inhaling the familiar scent of the mantle, Shadoe expelled a breath. "I saw him, Lance. He didn't fall."

The knight maneuvered his stallion closer to Shadoe. "What?"

Shadoe tried to contain the bile flaming his throat and the tremor of his voice. "It was not as Arthur described. I saw it happen. I rode to the cliffs, found them in dispute and shoving one another about. I'd never seen them so fierce."

Lancelot grunted. "'Twas not the first time, Shadoe. They'd been at odds much of late."

"This was different." He glanced off to where the cloud-shrouded cliffs had vanished like his father. Shadoe's jaw trembled, but he refused to weep. "When Da spotted me, our gazes met and . . ." He shook his head, trying to push the memory away. "He took a deliberate step back and leaped."

Lancelot's gauntlet-sheathed hand grasped Shadoe's bony wrist. "Forgive me, Shadoe. I've been unduly harsh on you. No child should have to watch his parent perish."

"Don't pity me." Angry shame overwhelmed him, and he jerked free. "My father knew his actions, knew he was deserting me and everyone else for another of his righteous causes."

"Deserted!" Lancelot whirled back. His right brow tugged up in his customary expression of dubious thoughts. "You speak as if he's still alive."

Shadoe rolled his shoulders. "Do you believe he's dead?"

"I'd rather not, but you saw for yourself."

Shadoe turned his war-horse back onto the Roman highway. "Aye, I thought to see him jump, Lance, although I've learned that when it comes to my da, what is seen is not always reality. What I do know is that he vanished before me."

"He often did that. One moment he was there; the next he was gone."

Shadoe's tattered heart turned cynical. "Aye, my da, the august enchanter, the Merdyn. The pagans believe he transformed into an eagle and flies to Avalon as we speak. Mayhap they are right."

"Curse your druid ancestry, Shadoe. Your Yahweh's Spirit bestowed on you the hidden sight. Obviously you have doubts about his death. What really happened to Merlin?"

"If I had the foresight of the Merdyn, I'd have foreseen, as did he, Arthur's demise. Instead I saw nothing, know nothing; it is the same with my father. What I want and what is no longer matters."

Shadoe's heart failed to accept his father's death, let alone suicide. He would have sensed a separation. For despite their differences, he and Merlin had a powerful father-and-son bond based on faith in the great I Am, Yahweh. For some unfathomable reason, Shadoe had believed he would share his father's last moments on this earth—and not from a distance. As close a kinship as he had with Lancelot, he withheld his suspicions. Even so, Shadoe felt Merlin had betrayed him.

As they rode toward Caer Camelot, Shadoe sensed the mounting rage in Lancelot's heart.

"Best you pray Merlin died, for if not, I'll be responsible for his next death!"

Shadoe held his tongue.

"And just what happened to the Emerald Rose of Avalon? Arthur wore it always, and we saw him collapse during his duel with Mordred.

Your cousin had no time to steal the talisman, because Bedivere charged him the moment Arthur fell."

Shadoe didn't argue. To the Celts, Britons, and Picts, the Emerald Rose signified the legal high chieftain of Caledonia and Britannia. Even if Mordred had managed to filch the ancient Pendragon amulet, it meant nothing without the Merdyn. Merlin was high steward, and he alone could designate the future leader. Arthur's firstborn or not, Mordred would have to wipe out the Britons and Caledonians to take the throne without the high steward's blessing. Even Mordred wasn't foolish enough to try that. Or so Shadoe hoped.

But what if Merlin was no longer among the living? What if Shadoe's ire was without cause? He snuffed back tears and sought to focus on the present.

Lancelot seemed to perceive Shadoe's thoughts. Reaching across, he patted Shadoe's forearm and said with fervor, "Forgive me. My threats are nothing more than the hot air of a battle-worn warrior. This has been a sorrowful day for all, Apprentice. And if your father is dead, my heart grieves. Nor need you be brave on my account. I know the pain of losing one's parents, especially at such a young age."

A single tear tracked Shadoe's cheek. He squashed it and sat soldier-like in his saddle. "If I am brave, it is for my God and my clansmen. As you said, we've a duty to fulfill. We must return Excalibur to our Lord Jesu from whom it came. If not, Camelot will cease. Peace will end. We must keep our promise to Arthur and in doing so fulfill the destiny of the Pendragons."

∽

The riders galloped the narrow causeway of earth and stone that connected the mainland to Wind's Haven and their home, Caer Camelot. They must forgo breaking the news of Arthur's death to Guenevere until they had completed their task. Shadoe accompanied Lancelot to the loch, where they knelt in prayer, calling upon God to receive the sword of the Isle of Might. For hours they kept vigil until, overcome by exhaustion, they slept.

Shadoe awoke with a start. A peculiar quiet embraced the glen. The thunder of the falls hushed. He looked over to find Lancelot aware of the mystical transformation.

Beyond the treetops and cliffs, the sky exploded with light, and the men shielded their eyes. Suspended over the water stood a gigantic being arrayed in fiery ivory garments. Speechless, they fell to their knees.

The stranger said, "Fear not, good sirs. I am a herald of the triune God Jesu Christ. He has heard your prayers. Now hear his command. 'Until the Pendragon and the endmost of Ayris unite, this sword of righteous might shall be consummated to stone, and all who seek the blade for sinful means shall find the bleak embrace of a watery death.'"

The next moment, Excalibur shot free from Shadoe's hand and rested in the angel's grip. The Celtic stone materialized and hovered over the still waters. Lifting Excalibur above his head, the angel drove the sword into the heart of the rock. The Celtic stone sank into the loch at the base of the falls, and the fiery brilliance of the angel faded.

The staccato beats of Shadoe's heart made him bolt upright from the ground. Before his pulse could stabilize, an anguished cry sounded above the rumble of the falls. Pushing to his feet, he drew his blade and trampled across the straw grass like a wild boar. On the boggy banks, he found Lancelot, his arms raised to the late-day sky. Shadoe went to the knight and bent a knee.

"Excalibur is gone." Lancelot dropped his hands to leather-clad thighs and shook his head with astonishment.

Shadoe glanced toward the churning mist of the waterfalls. "Aye, prophecy has been fulfilled."

"Your faith is like a rock, Apprentice." He rose, and Shadoe stood with him.

"My God gives me faith, Lance."

Lancelot braced his tremulous hands on Shadoe's shoulders. Shadoe met his friend's wide-eyed gaze and recognized something he'd never seen in the warrior's eyes: fear.

"Your God is a mighty God. Never have I seen such a thing as this fiery being that took the sword."

"He was an angel sent by Yahweh. What we saw is sacred. Few people, even believers, ever see the spiritual realm."

"Until now I doubted your God's existence. No longer. I give Yahweh my heart and soul!" Lancelot's face broke into a smile of joy Shadoe had never witnessed. Before he could protest, the large knight embraced him and planted a kiss on his cheek. "All glory and honor to God Almighty!" Lancelot proclaimed as he released Shadoe.

"Aye, the angels of heaven rejoice each time someone comes to faith."

"They do?"

"Aye, Jesu is our Shepherd and when one of his sheep is lost, he searches for it. You, Lance, are the lost sheep that has been found and brought to God's flock."

"And you have the wisdom of your father, Apprentice."

Shadoe felt blood sting his face. "Nay, Da said wisdom is gleaned from maturity. But I do have the faith of a child." He offered a smile.

"And I pray you keep it. Now we must pledge that the sword remain hidden from Morgause and Mordred." Lancelot removed his stinger. The knight turned his right palm face up and sliced an incision from which his blood streamed. He offered the stinger to Shadoe. With a hitch in his breath, Shadoe did likewise. The men gripped each other's hands.

As their blood mingled, Lancelot declared, "By all that is sacred, I swear upon my blood that no matter the cost, I will reveal to no man the location of Excalibur or the miracle witnessed here today."

Shadoe matched the knight's indomitable expression with his own. "And I vow to my Lord and Savior Jesu Christ our covenant of blood shall never be broken."

❦

Dusk was nigh; wisps of crimson spattered the summer skyline. At the ancient oak coppice, the riders dismounted and approached the sanctuary. Inside its rib-arched walls had rested the ancient Celtic stone from which the seventeen-year-old Arthur had removed the sword. Smoldering incense countered the pungent spit of wall torches and signified the grotto was occupied. Pronounced silence bristled the flesh of Shadoe's backbone. His hand fastened to the hilt of his sword as he plunged ahead of Lancelot to the barren altar. A crucifix lay on the earthen floor along with the toppled candles. The red sandstone slab upon which the crucifix and candles once rested was no longer in sight.

"Our Celtic stone is gone," announced a soft voice from the shadowy recesses, "as is my beloved Arthur."

Shadoe recognized the woman's joyless tone. Both men pivoted to see the beauty struggle to rise from a bench only to waver like a flickering flame. Lancelot snatched her up before she toppled. He drew her into his arms and tenderly swept her ebony tresses from her pale, tear-marred face.

"My Lady!" Shadoe knelt beside her, and his heart contorted with agony. "We meant to tell you ourselves." He struggled to find words to console her.

Guenevere took his unsteady hand and drew it to her cold, wet cheek. "I know. But Yahweh told me first, he did." She turned her head toward the bare altar. "His pledge to my husband was long foretold. 'When stone and sword join as one, so shall I claim, Artorius my scion.'"

Shadoe searched her grief-reddened eyes and found her humble acceptance of Arthur's eternal passage. "Do you think God weeps over our loss?"

Leaning against Lancelot, Guenevere drew Shadoe to herself and answered with a tremulous voice, "Aye, Apprentice, for there's no deeper sorrow than when divine love weeps."

Chapter Three

CRIES OF THE DYING cut like jagged steel through Shadoe's heart. Chaos reigned rampant throughout Camelot. Those who had been fortunate enough to avoid the deadly plague now fell victim to Mordred's warriors. On the mainland and the Isle of Wind's Haven, the Saxons had ransacked and torched the villages. Black soot permeated the air like an inky fog.

Shadoe knew Guenevere had taken refuge in her apartments. He suspected she had fallen prey to the deadly plague because she had remained hidden behind the guise of layered drapery the last few months. During their visits, they had prayed for God to deliver them. His lady's unshakable faith gave Shadoe the strength to carry on.

His affection for Guenevere as complex as was their relationship, Shadoe revisited the intricate pattern this godly woman had woven about his heart. In childhood, his love toward her had been for the mother he'd never known, then that of a sibling, and in time, that of youthful infatuation. Through all these phases, Guenevere never wavered in her love for him. When Mordred's troops charged the walls, Shadoe found himself at odds with his queen. She commanded he leave with the rest through the secret passageway and into the safety of the hollowed tor upon which Camelot stood. Shadoe swore he would flee, but his love and concern for his mistress restrained him.

With his stabbing sword unsheathed, Shadoe secured the landing outside Guenevere's apartments. Shortly, Mordred would mount the serpentine stone ascent, and Shadoe would be ready, or so he prayed. Despite the cool weather, sweat tangled his hair, trickled down his ribs. Fear filled him. He pressed his trembling spine to the oaken door and became privy to a fierce exchange between Lancelot and Guenevere.

"'Tis over, Guen. Come with us while there is time."

"I'll not leave my home or people," Guenevere's stubborn voice returned.

"Most of your clan are dead from Morgause's cursed plague, and those who chanced to survive have laid down their arms."

"Arthur would not have surrendered." Her voice trembled with emotion.

"Nay, but he had the wisdom to know when to retreat."

"Allow me dignity, Sir. I've ever reason to live. Now do as I ask, nay order!"

As if mindful of Shadoe's eavesdropping, their exchange ceased. Alarmed, Shadoe flung open the door to find Guenevere alone and the hidden passageway closing. His queen drew her stinger and spun toward the open portal. Shadoe made a quick assessment. Not even Guenevere's younger cousin, the Lady Iona du Maur, was present. This made no sense, Shadoe thought, scanning the empty apartment; the cousins were inseparable.

"My Lady, where's Iona?" He strode into the dimly lit room.

Lowering her dagger, Guenevere sighed. "Safe." Her relief flashed to indignation. "As you should be. I ordered you to depart hours ago, I did!"

"I'll not go without you, Guen. You are family, my sovereign."

"I am but a bondservant of the living God, I am."

"And I am your bondservant." He smiled into her cobalt eyes, seeing the shimmer of tears but knowing she would not shed a one in front of him.

"'Tis a most disobedient servant, you are." She presented her back, assuming a stiff pose of impatience.

"And you are as stubborn a mistress as I have ever served." He walked around and grinned into her stern countenance.

"I am the only mistress you have served." She tweaked his cheek.

Oh, how he loved their banter, although now mere camouflage for the tragedy they shared. Shadoe found her expression confident but her eyes were darkened by circles of fatigue. Hard to believe she was but twenty-two years old. She appeared to have aged another dozen years these past months. Arthur's death had shattered her, and Mordred would ruin not only her willful Celtic-Pict nature, but her beauty as well.

Despite their age difference, Shadoe had yet to know of more passionate and devoted lovers than Arthur and Guenevere. The rumor of her and Lancelot's affair disturbed him, yet he dared not ask her for the truth.

His gaze drifted over her tall, slender form. *She looks like high queen,* he mused, noting Guenevere no longer wore her favorite faded blue tunic and loose-legged bracchae. Instead, she had donned a cloud-white silk palla that draped a scarlet red, pleated tunic accentuating her feminine curves. Two gold brooches held the palla in place at her shoulders, and her usually free-flowing hair was pinned high, falling over her right shoulder in a long ebony braid. For finery she wore an ornate torc neckpiece of braided gold designed by Celt craftsmen. Guenevere had dressed for company, Shadoe soberly concluded, unwelcome company. Mordred!

The tapestry that billowed from the draft of the passageway distracted his gaze.

"Where's Lance?" He clenched his jaw, concluding Lancelot had left his queen to defend herself. His features flushed with antagonism.

"'Tis not how it looks." The habitual shake of her head caused her waist-length black braid to bounce. "Lancelot obeyed orders. As will you. I'll be along shortly, I will."

"Nay, we must go!" Shadoe dashed to the wall and flung back the tapestry concealing the hidden stone panel.

When he turned about, Guenevere hotly contended, "No loveless brat drives me out of my home without a fight." She brushed past, pushed ajar the panel, and directed him into the safety of the dank cavern. "You forget Arthur taught me well, he did." She pulled the six-inch stinger from her waist belt and flipped it with expert ease. "Now go."

"But—"

"You are the future high steward, Apprentice."

"One needs a teacher to be an apprentice, Guen. My mentor chose desertion over love and duty to his family and clan."

"I know you don't understand the Merdyn's actions. If I could . . ." She looked away.

"What?"

"Nothing," she reassured him. "Remember each of us are the Creator's apprentices." Guenevere captured his hands and pressed the warmth of her lips to his battle-bruised fingers, then gripped them. "All that has come to pass, 'twas long foretold. The morn of my beloved Arthur's death, I went to the chapel to pray, and the stone of Scone, our Celtic stone, vanished before my eyes, it did. I don't know what you and Lancelot did with Excalibur. But surely as Jesu lives, I know the stone and sword are one again."

Withholding comment, Shadoe wiggled free of her tender clutch.

She lifted a delicate shoulder. "You, Shadoe un Hollo Tors, hold the source to Camelot's future and the clan Pendragon."

Shadoe gaped, doubting her emotional stability.

"You think me daft, Apprentice. But your destiny will be revealed to you. Now, if I don't meet you on the Dragon's Back, go with the others to Tintagel, but don't return here until God instructs you. And Shadoe, whenever you are afraid or have doubts . . ."

"Aye?" He looked into her loving gaze.

"Even when the Adversary's demons attack, trust Yahweh. Be still and know he is God." She turned, and the tapestry fell into place.

Hunkered within the dank obscurity that led to freedom, Shadoe could not obey his queen. Who would defend her? Where were Galahad, Tristam, Perceval, and Iona? Rage infused Shadoe's heart and soul. Even Lancelot had abandoned her! How could Lancelot leave the woman he professed to love to die alone? How could God?

After Guenevere returned to the other side of the chamber, Shadoe stepped back inside and slipped behind a stone pillar. He watched Guenevere extinguish the floor lamps. Only two wall torches were left lit. She drew a stabbing sword from behind her bed of straw and tossed a coverlet of otter's fur over it for concealment. In abandoned submission, she collapsed on the rush-strewn floor and called out to her Lord and Savior, begging his will be done, that those she loved be kept safe from harm's way. Shadoe closed his eyes and silently joined her prayer. Only Guenevere and Jesu knew why she chose to fight a battle she would no doubt lose.

From outside her apartment, hostile voices ended her vigil. The door hinges splintered, and the door crashed to the floor. Guenevere rose to face her nemesis, Mordred Pendragon. Behind him, Saxon warriors bore axes and swords.

Shadoe's gaze riveted on his queen. Guenevere stood fearless, challenging the younger man's intrusion into her quarters. Her right hand concealed the stinger tucked beneath the belt of her bodice.

While Mordred seemed spellbound by her beauty, Shadoe saw the flames in Guenevere's eyes. Flames of life, invincible faith, that made her stand against this fierce enemy. Moreover, he noticed what only close acquaintances would: the vertical vein in the midst of her brow throbbed dangerously.

Shadoe experienced revelation. This was not the last fight of a dying woman. This was a woman who had every intention to live and who had a purpose. Guenevere was wasting time to allow Lancelot's escape. Why?

"Even when defeated, you're beautiful, my fair Guen," Mordred growled, as he stalked closer. "I am surprised that, knowing what I desire, you have not taken your life."

"Suicide is a sin in Yahweh's eyes. I trust him to place his angels between me and my foes."

"Angels? I see no one to defend you, least of all angels," Mordred mocked as he removed his mantle of deep purple and advanced.

Brazenly, he toyed with a tendril of her black tresses and then skimmed the widow's peak at her forehead with his fingertips. Shadoe could almost read his evil cousin's mind. Aye, she was an unusual beauty, and the pronounced hairline only enhanced her mystery. With the back of his hand, Mordred caressed her freckled ivory cheeks, and slowly descended to the long arch of her slender neck, where her pulse beat like that of a lamb being led to slaughter. "I do hope you put up a fight, for I'll enjoy you that much more."

Guenevere stood gallantly silent. Mordred yanked the palla off her shoulders, exposing the milky white of her bare arms and shoulders, but she defied him with an icy glare.

Shadoe scowled. *Why don't you fight, Guen? Draw your stinger!*

He could no longer hold back. When Mordred directed Guenevere to her bed, Shadoe, intent to slay Mordred, charged forward with his Roman sword. Before he could strike, the Saxon lunged upon him and they both fell to the floor. Shadoe's head struck the rough stones with mallet force, pain fired through his temples. He heard Guenevere's war cry as she pulled out her stinger. Chimes echoed in Shadoe's head. His vision blurred as he struggled beneath the weight of the larger man. Helpless, he prayed for Lancelot, Tristam, Perceval, and even young Galahad to come to their rescue.

Guenevere fought Mordred as he tore the sash from her gown and discarded her stinger. "Oh, My Lady, do you think this will deter me?" Pressing her to the straw mat, he muttered his lustful intentions and pawed at the swell of her tunic-covered breasts. Within seconds, curses burned from Mordred's lips, and he leaped off the bed, dragging Guenevere to her feet. No matter what had deterred Mordred, Shadoe breathed relief.

God had intervened.

Guenevere was safe.

Trying to focus on the cause of Mordred's fury-imbued features, Shadoe realized their voices had become an inaudible echo. Mordred shook his fist at Guenevere's bodice and the milk-drenched scarlet fabric covering her bosom. Shadoe understood all too well.

Guenevere had given birth!

Impossible!

"Where's the babe?" he thought to hear Mordred demand of her.

Guenevere offered that feline smile Shadoe admired. Until now he'd not feared for her life since Mordred desired her. But something had changed drastically. The loathing in the prince's eyes was for Guenevere alone. He appeared possessed.

Fetching the gold-handled stinger from the floor, Mordred towered over Guenevere, holding her steadfast gaze as he toyed with the jagged blade in his hand.

In an effort to snatch the stinger, Guenevere lunged at him. To Shadoe's horror, Mordred plunged the knife into her belly, twisted, and withdrew the stinger dripping with blood. He stepped back. Guenevere gripped her midsection and went down on her knees.

"Oh, my Jesu!" she cried out.

In a burst of fury, Shadoe shoved free of his captor and ran to her. Guenevere collapsed in his arms. "My Lady," he choked out and gazed upon his dying mistress.

With trembling fingers, Guenevere brushed his unruly dark locks from his brow and gave a brave smile. "My sweet apprentice, you are here with me?"

He nodded.

He could hear.

His attention lowered to the fatal gash in her belly and the flow of blood that even Merlin would not have been able to stop. Mordred had seen to that. Shadoe found Mordred apathetically watching the intimate exchange between the living and dying. His eyes were glazed as if he were not even aware of what he'd done. Still, his methodical actions seemed to contradict his expression. Wiping the stinger's blood against Guenevere's white palla, Mordred spit on the blade, cleaned it, and then slipped it into his waist scabbard and chuckled. For the beat of a breath, Shadoe imagined it was Morgause le Fey's laugh.

He loathed them.

"Promise me?" Guenevere's white tapered fingers encircled Shadoe's wrist.

"Anything, Guen." Tears streaked his face as he held her head in his lap and stroked her ebony tresses back from her ashen countenance.

"To live?"

Blinded by tears, he nodded.

"To forgive?"

This was a difficult request to honor, but he agreed.

"Don't desert the Isle of Might or . . . God's ordained destiny. . . . Ne'er desert the living God, Jesu Christ."

"I swear, My Lady."

She gasped, her lovely face etched with pain. "All's well . . . for I've eternity with Jesu and my godsend, Arthur." Clutching his sleeve, Guenevere insisted, "Your duty is clan Pendragon. Protect Emer . . . Rose. . . ." Guenevere drew a final breath and fell gently against him. Holding her tight, he rocked her just as she had rocked him when a child. Violent sobs shook his body as he realized he'd failed to protect his queen.

The moment of silence was desecrated by a shriek from the chamber's threshold. Hastening into the room, the witch demanded of Mordred, "What have you done?"

Mordred stumbled back. His blue eyes flickered with confusion as his gaze shot from the dead Guenevere to the attractive petite woman in front of him. "I–I slew the wench."

"You're mad!"

The prince touched the stinger at his waist in distaste. Then as if he had a moment of clarity, he vehemently accused his mother, "Nay! The voices told me you wanted her dead!"

"I wanted her alive." Morgause le Fey dropped to her knees and examined the lifeless vessel. Shadoe possessively pulled Guenevere's body closer.

"The whore gave birth," Mordred growled with a sickening shudder.

"Of course she did!"

"You knew?" he asked in a hurtful tone.

"I suspected. Where has the babe been taken?" She glared back at her son.

"What difference does it make? I am firstborn of the Pendragon, and he's dead! I am high chieftain of Caledonia and soon Britannia!"

"You fool! This dead Pendragon has a living progeny! Which means you have a blood rival. What were Guenevere's last words?"

"She muttered about Shadoe being responsible for the Pendragon," said Mordred.

Morgause cursed in Celtic and glared down at Shadoe.

Feigning to be unmindful of their exchange, Shadoe continued to mourn.

Morgause's face smoothed into a mockery of motherly concern. "Shadoe?" she asked in honeyed tones.

He leveled his iron gaze upon her but did not reply. She crouched before him and looked unconvincingly compassionate upon Guenevere's peaceful face. "Shadoe, dearest, you know despite all our family problems that you are still my youngest sister's child. I have always loved and cared for you. I am relieved to find you unharmed."

Mordred snorted, and Morgause shot him a piercing look, and then refocused on Shadoe. "Nephew, it is crucial to all our futures that you be honest with me. Guenevere had a bairn. I wish for the child to be properly cared for. Who took him, Shadoe, and where are they going?"

Cradling Guenevere, Shadoe's head pounded fiercely. Morgause appeared to weave in front of him. *I must concentrate.* In the span of Arthur and Guenevere's marriage, she'd remained unfruitful. If there was a bairn, Shadoe doubted Arthur had sired the child. That left one other. Lancelot! Rumors of their affair had permeated the air for several years. For Guenevere's sake, Shadoe would not betray the possibility. If Mordred and Morgause believed a Pendragon rival existed, Shadoe had an edge.

"I'll tell you nothing, harridan!" He cursed and spit in her face.

Wiping his spittle from her cheek, her open palm raised to strike and then lowered. Morgause snagged her lower lip between her even pearled teeth and tossing her head of strawberry blond hair, she closed her eyes and sighed out.

Shadoe knew she was regrouping. He didn't care.

"Shall I slay him, Mother?" Mordred stalked forward.

Shadoe heard the scraping of metal against leather as Mordred withdrew the stinger from its scabbard. No doubt, he was going home to Jesu!

Standing, Morgause looked from Shadoe to her son. "Nay, you've ruined enough."

Shadoe's breath hitched. He'd been reprieved, but why?

Her icy stare returned to him and melted. "Besides, he is of my sister's womb and the Merdyn's loins. He's also the enchanter's apprentice. We've need of his powers."

Shadoe remained on his knees, feeling nothing but the silky tresses of the dead woman resting in his arms. He could not accept that the Supreme Creator could allow this godly woman to be murdered. Everyone he loved had been slain by his vile aunt and cousin. Blind rage coursed through his veins and scorched his heart as he realized he was but inches from Guenevere's sword beneath the otter's skin. Easing Guenevere's head from his lap and onto the floor, he grasped the hilt of the stabbing sword.

A vengeful howl seeming to come from someone else exploded from the pit of Shadoe's soul. He glimpsed the stunned expressions on his cousin and aunt as they looked from one to another, then at the Saxons for the source of this rage. Before anyone could act, Shadoe struck! His vision still blurred, he missed his objective, Mordred's heart. The sharp blade sliced across his cousin's forearm, severing his left hand at the wrist.

Mordred gaped as his hand dangled from threads of tendons, and blood spurted across the rush-strewn floor. The young man wailed. Clutching his detached hand, he buckled to his knees.

For a moment Shadoe thought to see a mother's concern in Morgause's eyes before she tossed him a rag and huffed, "Wrap it tight, fool!" She ordered a Saxon, "Take him away. See to his needs."

Morgause riveted her brilliant blue gaze on Shadoe, who had been subdued by another Saxon. He struggled until the warrior kicked him in the midsection. Shadoe collapsed, dropped his head, and gasped for air. The Saxon gestured to strike him again.

"Enough!" Morgause intervened.

The Saxon complied, grabbed Shadoe from behind, and yanked him to his feet, holding him painfully tight.

Pressing a ragged, sharp-nailed finger beneath his chin, she forced his head up and stared into his hate-filled gaze. Her generous mouth pursed in contemplation. "I'm impressed, scion of Merlin. You have your father's strong sense of fealty and your mother's tenacity. A precarious combination if not handled with forethought. Your cousin might lose his hand, but you, sweet lad, could be dead, and what would that gain you?"

"I would be with my loved ones in Paradise," he growled and jerked his chin upward, disengaging from her poisonous touch.

"Bah! You don't believe that gospel prattle! You've too much Celt stock in you. Your birthright is of the old religion, Shadoe. My wee sister, Niamh, gave birth to you. You know the truth of her conception, aye?"

Shadoe had no intention to engage in irrelevant talk, but he was not ignorant of his heritage. "Aye. I know the tangled web of deceit and bed switching."

"King Uther, disguised as my father Duke Gorlois, seduced my mother Igraine, thus siring Arthur that night."

Shadoe rolled his eyes. "Yes, well, before that your aunt High Priestess Nivian, lured your father Duke Gorlois into her bed," Shadoe mocked.

"Lured him?" Morgause cackled. "Hardly. My father wanted a scion. My mother, Igraine, had born Gorlois only daughters: Morgan and myself. So with Igraine's blessing, he entered into an arrangement with my aunt Nivian—the contract being that if she bore him a scion, she would become his high steward, his advisor in all political matters."

"I know all this! Nivian bore a girl child, Niamh, my mother, your half sister."

"Aye," Morgause beamed. "A pretty wee bairn, only a month before Arthur's birth. Moreover with Gorlois slain in battle by Uther's warriors, it no longer mattered except to Nivian."

Shadoe sought to contain his anger and pain. "Get to the matter, witch!"

Catching up a ripe apple from Guenevere's fruit dish, Morgause brought it to her lips and nibbled. "Want some?" she offered, passing the apple beneath his nose.

He snuffed with disgust.

She shrugged. "Most folks assumed my mother Igraine forgave Uther for the murder of her husband. Never! She and Nivian plotted their revenge for years. Nivian took me under her wing, and when Niamh was of age, she taught your mother the veiled rituals and, most importantly, the magique. All those years we'd been waiting to avenge our father's murder, and it began with Uther's death." The witch smiled.

"Now Arthur is dead and his queen." Her calculating gaze settled on Guenevere's lifeless shell. She trailed her tongue across her lips and snickered just loud enough for Shadoe to discern. "My scion thinks he acts on his own! He hasn't the backbone to kill, let alone attack his own father or this strumpet. I honor the demons that dwell within him."

She turned back and stared into Shadoe's grief-moistened eyes. "So you see, nephew, all has come full circle! Niamh seduced Merlin for one reason—you! You are not just Celt and Briton, for the blood of the gods courses through you. Merlin was no ordinary man. Like his granda before him, Merlin was the august enchanter and possessed conjuring that common man can never imagine. You have those powers. You are the enchanter's apprentice."

"I'm sorry to disappoint you, Auntie, but my father was no different than anyone else—nor am I."

"Bah! The gods have revealed the truth to me."

"You're right—I am Celt. But I follow the living God, Yahweh. The old ways are false religions designed by the Adversary to condemn souls and keep them from salvation."

"The old ways are strong with magique."

"Aye, magique from the bowels of the abyss. The druid gods are but a guise for your thirst for power. The fallen angel, Satan, the Adversary, is your god."

"Aye, so he is." Morgause winked and gave a triumphant smile. "The fact you see what common folks do not is proof of your heritage. Clearly, before the Merdyn died, he transferred his abilities to you."

"He gave me nothing."

"He gave you life!"

"Yahweh gave me life, Morgause, just as he did you and all of creation."

She waved off his statement of faith and paced the bedchamber, her gown sweeping up dust from the rushes. "I am a great seer, and my predictions come true. I've seen your future, Shadoe. Fear rules your heart, and pride will harden it. Soon you will turn against this so-called Redeemer of yours."

"Never!" he bellowed, causing the lone Saxon to snap Shadoe's head back and hold him painfully tight.

Morgause sneered. "I am fond of you, Shadoe. You are druid. Just like your mother, Niamh, you hold the secret to forces you can't fathom. Combine that with Merlin's gifts and you could command the winds, tame the seas! Look deep into your soul, Shadoe un Hollo Tors. There's a reason you did not die at Arthur's side and then survived the plague I cast upon your beloved Camelot. I protected you. Don't you see I care for you, Apprentice? You are the scion I wished to have."

"You have a scion, if you consider that blood-sucking cretin human."

She sighed and nodded. "Alas, Mordred was not born with either his sire's intelligence or with my influence over the druids. But you have the blood of the august enchanter and a druid high priestess."

Her voice softened beguilingly. "If we could strike a bargain? If you'd tell me where Arthur's progeny is, you and I . . . would be invincible!" She giggled like an impetuous girl. "We could conquer nations. We could—"

"Rot in Hades!" he snapped. "I'll never strike a bargain with you, Morgause le Fey. I'll not talk."

The conviction in his voice was so stalwart that the exquisite features of the priestess turned repulsive. Snorting, she ordered the Saxon, "Take him to Belizar. Mayhap sitting in the bowels of hell will refresh his memory!"

Shadoe tried to conceal his shock but failed.

The witch snickered. "You are acquainted with Belizar? Why of course you are. It was Arthur's peace offering when he failed to wed the mother of his firstborn." She poked a finger against the swell of her firm bosom. "'Tis a shame you never came to visit. Belizar is not grand like Caer Camelot, but it does have its amenities . . . such as Hell's Gate, which the Adversary provided." Her voice lowered for effect. "I've had the pleasure to subject a few of my enemies to that inferno. We devised a cage. When it is lowered into the pit, its floor springs open, and the prisoner is dropped onto the searing-hot base. If the heat doesn't kill you first, breathing will. Of course, that's because I cast a spell on the air." She chuckled.

Shadoe scoffed. "There is no demonic magique about Hell's Gate. My da said the intense heat comes from the sulfur springs that run parallel to the pit, and the victims die from the fumes of the sulfur burning their lungs. But of course, you are not clever enough to comprehend the sciences. Nor can you read Greek or Latin. But you can add. One man and one woman in love can create life. And by all that's holy, if it was Yahweh's will that Arthur sire a child through Guenevere, then there is indeed progeny, and God will protect the bairn at all cost. Which means you, dear Auntie, are ruined!"

Morgause struck fast. Her nails clawed a deep fiery gouge down his cheek. Shadoe felt blood trickle from the rising welts.

"I tried, Shadoe. Really I did." Her voice held a tremble, and her eyes shimmered with regret. "But you have made your choice." With that she swept away from him, and with all the animosity of her son, she ordered the Saxon, "Take the apprentice away!"

"No!" Shadoe fought fiercely to stay with his dead queen. A blow from the hilt of a sword turned his world black.

She slips into my restless dreams
Enchantress of neither present nor past.
But morning breaks and she escapes
Eludes my very grasp.

—THE STEWARD CHRONICLES,
Shadoe un Hollo Tors

Chapter Four

SHADOE SAT HUDDLED in his dark, dank corner of Belizar's prison. He sought to force back the storm at the base of his skull. During his eighteen-month incarceration he'd endured many headaches, most due to hunger, but several identical visions helped keep him sane. Strange, when he submitted to the dream, the pain vanished, as did the headache. Tonight was no exception.

The enchantress appeared: luminous eyes green as highland moss, dark as emerald jewels; hair like crimson flames; and voice like the seductive call of a siren. She was his godsend, and he knew her like he knew himself. He'd never felt such oneness with anyone as he did with this nameless woman. She stood on the opposite shore of Loch Lady, beckoning him. When he walked toward her, Excalibur rose from the depths of the loch and advanced on him as if an invisible hand wielded the mighty blade. No matter how Shadoe tried to elude the sword, it remained between him and his beloved.

Desperately, she called to him, "My godsend, if we are to stand together, you must master the sword of kings, or we can never be one as Yahweh ordained. Our oneness will unite Camelot and free you from your demons."

Despite her petition, desperate fear held him prisoner. Even his tongue would not respond.

"Then I must do it alone, I must," she asserted. Reaching out with both hands, she embraced not the jeweled haft, but the fiery, sharp-edged metal. Agonizing pain stressed her beauty as the blade sliced into her palms and fingers. Scarlet blood trickled and then flowed like wine into the pristine

waters of the loch. His enchantress cried out and tried to free herself, but Excalibur soared through the air and held her captive above the loch.

For a breathless moment, Shadoe met her terrified gaze. And then, to his astonishment, her expression turned into one of peaceful acceptance. "Unlike you, my godsend," she said confidently, "I do not fear death, for 'tis only the beginning of an eternity with my Lord Jesu."

Before Shadoe could intervene, his enchantress and Excalibur vanished into the icy vapor of the loch. "No!" he screamed as the mists turned black and silent with death.

Awakening with a jolt, Shadoe realized he was still in his cell. As always, he tried to rationalize the vision. *Surely, she's an illusion of my imagination, and in any event, what does Excalibur have to do with my winning the hand of this beautiful woman?*

His only answer—guilt.

Shadoe had broken his promise to Guenevere to live. Still, would it not be better to die bravely at the hands of Mordred as Guenevere had than to serve this spawn of Lucifer?

Over the preceding months, Mordred had tortured Shadoe and demanded to be told the locations of the Emerald Rose of Avalon, of Excalibur, and of Guenevere's child. Not having prior knowledge of Guenevere's pregnancy, Shadoe answered honestly that he did not know where the babe was. He gave the same response concerning the Rose of Avalon, unless one considered Merlin was wearing it when he plunged to his death. Neither Morgause nor Mordred accepted Shadoe's denials.

Were it not for the druid priestess, Shadoe suspected he'd have been dead within days, but Morgause held an invisible rein on her progeny. Mordred, however, personally orchestrated his prisoner's regular, regimented torment. Shadoe was cut and branded with blades that were fired to a crimson blaze like the flames of hell. Only when near death did he confess the location of Excalibur, nothing more.

While Mordred attempted to retrieve Excalibur, Shadoe rotted at Belizar. In the interim, Belizar's prison overflowed with Celts, Britons, and border Picts whose worst crimes were stealing to feed their families.

Shadoe prayed for rescue. Clan Pendragon, including Lancelot, seemed to have deserted him. But Shadoe convinced himself that, aside from having no solution to the impregnable puzzle that is Belizar, Arthur's faithful few also assumed that Shadoe, like Guenevere, was dead.

After months of failure to retrieve Excalibur, Morgause offered Shadoe freedom and riches if he agreed to reveal the secret to releasing Arthur's sword from the Celtic stone. The remorse he felt at having revealed the sword's location pained him so immensely, he refused to divulge anything more. Hence, he would become a permanent occupant of Hell's Gate.

Within moments of being delivered into the pit, Shadoe's sandals began to disintegrate. His feet blistered. He recalled Guenevere's words, "Be still and know he is God." A peace that surpassed all understanding enveloped him. Shadoe decided to die like the son of the Merdyn. He glared up at Mordred through the stinging sulfur. Morgause stood silently at her scion's side.

"What's wrong, Apprentice?" Mordred feigned surprise. "Can't conjure your way out of this mess, can you?" He then proclaimed, "Oh, that's right! You're no more an enchanter than was your spineless da. A Christian you are. No druid magique to free you, only your Jesu. He seems to have deserted you just as he did my da and Guenevere."

Biting back the pain in his limbs and lungs, Shadoe remembered Guenevere's request, and he cried out, "I forgive both of you!"

As if moved by Shadoe's words, the priestess's trembling hands cupped her mouth.

Mordred snickered. "This is your last chance, weevil, and only on my mother's behalf is it offered. Pledge us your fealty, and you'll be free save for a few blisters. The honor and wealth we'll bestow upon you will hastily cure your wounds."

The spirit of God flooded Shadoe's heart, and he prophesied, "Hear me, Mordred Pendragon and Morgause le Fey. Within the week, the blood of innocent bairns will stain your hands. And in your last breaths before death, you will know the living, triune God. But before one of you can call upon his blessed name, his judgment will consume you, and the eternal fires of Hades will be your final reward!"

A haunting silence proved the effect of Shadoe's prophesy, especially on Morgause, who waved a pagan sign of reprisal before she hoisted her skirts and hastened away.

When Mordred did reply, his baritone wavered. "I fear neither your curse nor your Jesu, but if there is a hell, you will know its flames before me."

When Shadoe said nothing, Mordred strutted off, his mocking laughter ringing in the air. Above him, Shadoe heard the outraged voices of the prisoners who had become his comrades. Their pleas would not save him.

As his throat and limbs began to blister, he prayed, "Dear Lord, I deserve death for betraying your honor. I beg forgiveness! Oh, sweet Savior, deliver me from this inferno. Take me home . . . with you."

Blinded by the sulfuric fumes, he wheezed for air. His knees buckled, but he didn't hit the searing ground. A bolt of light breached the yellow sulfur mist, and a hand reached for him. Desperate, Shadoe accepted, feeling unnatural strength in the hand that clenched his own.

A moment later, he buckled on the earthen floor above the gate, panting for air. When a hand touched his shoulder, Shadoe's blisters and pain vanished. Stunned, he looked up to find a strange entity before him, the being's face so gloriously illuminated, it was impossible to look upon. Shadoe knew he was in the presence of an angel, more importantly the angel who'd taken Excalibur. The angelic being transformed into a young man, and Shadoe was able to see his face.

"I am your guardian Tomas. God sent me to rescue you, Shadoe un Hollo Tors. Follow me. Stay within the realm of my light, and you will not be heard or seen."

Astounded, Shadoe obeyed. As they entered the prison block, not one of the prisoners took notice, but Shadoe could see and hear their tortured presence. A muscle-bulked guard beat a man Shadoe recognized to be one of Arthur's soldiers. Shadoe pleaded with Tomas, "Please, Sire, free these men. They've committed no crime against God."

"We are not to interfere. God alone knows their destinies. Trust him. He will not forsake any man who calls him Lord. You are a witness to that truth."

Tomas's words gave Shadoe little comfort. When they started to take the stairs, he fled the safety of the angel's light. Shadoe attacked the guard, ramming the beefy man's head against a wall. When the guard collapsed, Shadoe took his keys. Quickly, he freed the abused man and began to unlock the cell doors.

"Halt!" Tomas's furious voice shook the stone walls.

The ring of keys seared Shadoe's palm, and he dropped them.

One of the prisoners snatched up the keys and opened the cells. Men and boys charged the stairs, attacking the guards. From overhead, alerted soldiers stormed through the corridor, cutting down the fleeing prisoners and leaving the bodies in their wake. One moment Shadoe was in the midst of the bloody siege, the next he stood within the ring of light, unable to move.

Tomas pointed at him accusingly. "You have gone against the will of the Lord God Almighty. The blood of these innocent souls is on your head, Shadoe un Hollo Tors."

Before Shadoe could answer, he stood at the top of a knoll, staring down at Belizar and the mayhem he had ignited. Soldiers encroached upon the moors and woodlands, and the howls of Mordred's hounds pierced the cold night air.

The whinny of a horse drew Shadoe's attention to the steed pawing the ground less than a yard away. He mounted the gift horse and glanced back at Belizar. Although the angel was no longer visible, Shadoe heard Tomas's command: "Flee, Shadoe un Hollo Tors. Your life depends upon it. God abides with you, but his favor shall not return until you seek his forgiveness and bend a knee to his will."

Anger enveloped Shadoe. Bend to his will! "Hear me, God of my fathers. You freed me and left the others to die. Why?" He looked into the midnight sky but received no response.

Dangling between youth and manhood, Shadoe was frightened and shaken over his miraculous escape. His faith should have been restored; instead his heart hardened against his Redeemer. Yahweh had taken away all he had ever loved: Merlin, Arthur, and Guenevere, even Caer Camelot. There was nothing left for him in Caledonia or Britannia. Turning his back on the Isle of Might, Shadoe did as Tomas ordered; he fled and never looked back.

Through the virtue of this child
And fervor of her youth,
These dried bones
Taste the living waters,
And find mercy's truth.
 —THE STEWARD CHRONICLES,
  Merlin un Hollo Tors

Chapter Five

471 A.D.

THE ISLE OF WIND'S HAVEN

"MER, TELL ME OF MY knight in shining armor," asked the lissome girl, tramping behind her mentor through the craggy meadow of sun-tinted heather along the shores of Loch Lady.

Merlin un Hollo Tors stooped to uproot a golden cluster of herbs, and scowled at the delicate, set chin of his ward. "Name the plant, lass!" He shook the bouquet at her.

"Whist!" she murmured in an apathetic tone. "'Tis Woad. And after proper treatment the leaves produce a blue dye that—"

"Excellent." He plopped the plant into an overflowing basket and hastened on to his next objective. "Before sunset you will plant these in the herb garden and on the morrow practice the six healing potions of herbal lore."

"Aye, as always." She snatched the basket from him, giggled, and sprinted off before he could find another plant. Her faded green tunic and bracchae of russet melded with the lush woodland landscape.

Merlin chuckled at her evasion of study. In truth, today his heart was not in the sciences. The afternoon grew late, with little time for them to share. He had tried to keep this day as normal as possible, but no day with Emerald Rose Rayn was normal, and he would dearly miss her.

Wetting his finger, Merlin tested the moderate mid-summer zephyr that rustled the beechwood. Her back to him, Rayn knelt on one knee, distracted by a gray squirrel. With the sudden stealth of a predator, Merlin shot his staff directly at her back. A slight vibration charged the air. Rayn dodged the flying projectile, snatched it mid-air, and hurled the staff back toward him with deadly accuracy.

Merlin snared it single-handed. His palm burned. *Excellent reflexes, lass,* he mused. But as was the Merdyn's way, he withheld praise. "You almost lost your head, Princess."

"Nay! I'm faster than ever. Even Da says so. Why can't you?" she countered.

As blood blisters erupted on his leathered palm, he snapped, "Because adulation is overrated. All that matters is that you defend yourself well. Now we've but an hour before day-glow fades. Back to your studies."

Her hands braced on slender hips, the maiden stood her ground, and the squirrel trustingly scrambled onto her shoulder. Rayn's gift with animals amazed Merlin; then again, so did her tenacity.

She puffed wisps of auburn curls out of her green eyes, but the tendrils refused to obey. "Milord Mer, this very day I've identified thirty-two plants and herbs along with their medicinal values. I wish to rest."

"Rest! There's much to learn about nature, about God's wondrous creation."

"Even God rested on the seventh day. Let's talk a bit, aye?" She stroked the squirrel's wiry tail and mischievously winked at Merlin.

"'Tis not the Sabbath, Rayn. And do you never weary of my tales?" He strove to elude her enchantment and willingly failed.

"Nay, Sir, you talk so well I almost believe it so." She settled upon the toppled oak, where they often took respite and patted the spot beside her.

Merlin drew a labored breath. *Ah, Princess, you pose upon that log as if 'tis yer throne and this glen yer kingdom. If you but knew the truth of it.* Of late, Merlin had tutored Emerald Rose Rayn with urgent abandon.

Each heartbeat counted, especially this day. Vigilant of her playful interaction with the squirrel, he desired to be attentive to the child she still was and the woman she'd soon become. He'd failed the others. He could not afford to fail this precious one, this future emerald rose of the Isle of Might.

Propped on his staff, the aches in his lower back made up his mind. "Mayhap, I will sit a mite . . . but I assure you that I weary of this old man's prattle. I'm quite dull you know."

"Nay, Mer, never. You are more pleasurable than Da and my uncles, who only speak of battles, hunting, fishing, and Jesu."

He snorted. "We speak often of Jesu, so why is it less enjoyable with them?"

Rayn reached into her pouch and pitched a handful of crumbs to the peaty earth. The squirrel leaped down and gorged its cheeks. "Because you tell me of his life and the miracles he performed . . . and of Noah, Joseph, Moses, King David, Esther, and Ruth—all things Da knows naught of." She gulped air after her long discourse.

Merlin released a humbled sigh. "Such splendid tribute from a wee maiden."

"I know," she said with frank humility and hooked her arm within his.

Rayn burrowed her nose into his thick woolen sleeve. Merlin felt her inhale like a young pup sniffing its master's scent and hoped she memorized the smoky cedar fragrance of his black mantle. He knew she trusted him above all others, even though his once proud title of Merdyn had become Mad Mer.

After he had feigned his death, Merlin dwelled with the tattooed Pict tribes and then had wandered the highlands and northern islands of Caledonia clad in animal hides and his cloak. He even spent time on the ancient isle of Eire. Rayn had never seen that side of him and, though others had considered him balmy, she thought him the sanest man to ever live. Merlin prayed it would remain so. He caught her observant eye, knew she was pondering something serious, and winked with an inviting smile.

"Is surely good fortune that those of Ayris blood live longer than most humanity."

Merlin chuckled. "You think I am ancient, aye?"

Rayn rocked her cap-donned head up and down. "Da says you're older than the hollow tors of Caledonia."

"Now that *is* old." He snorted and fingered his white beard.

"Really, Mer, I don't think of you as ancient. You certainly don't look over fifty seasons, even though Perceval swears you to be a hundred-forty. You are handsome and as spry as any young man, you are."

"With such a honeyed tongue, young woman, you could fleece a Greek merchant of his last gold piece."

"I do not bestow compliments freely, Mer, but when I do, they come from my heart, they do."

He slipped his arm about her willowy shoulders and hugged her tight. "And your praise is truly welcome, my Princess."

She smiled back and pecked a kiss onto his leathery cheek.

Merlin gently thumped a hooked finger against her head full of dreams. But his tone darkened. "'Tis a great burden to be the end of your kind. Most of all, not to leave progeny and instead witness the demise of one's bloodline."

Rayn fingered the Emerald Rose of Avalon, a medallion in the shape of a twelve-pointed star, which swung from a thick gold chain about Merlin's neck. He touched her graceful long fingers as she held the medallion up to the sunlight. He knew that when the emerald at the center of the diamond points captured the light, the talisman emitted a startling green glow and grew warm to the touch. Merlin waited for her reaction. As if singed, she let go, but he noted she schooled her features. Rayn appeared unmoved by the experience.

"And this, the Emerald Rose of Avalon, is the symbol of the high kings of Ayris?"

"Aye," he answered, compressing his lips.

Rayn breathed out and turned from the talisman as if the amulet was cursed.

"Do not fear, child. There are no powers of enchantment in these cold stones."

Rayn looked back into the luminous jewels of the amulet that signified the virtue of the Ayris legacy. Merlin had once explained to her that prior to Uther's coronation he had worn the amulet as Merlin did now. Seventeen years later, following Uther's courageous fall in a battle against invading Irish Scotti, Merlin had placed the legacy of Ayris around young Arthur's neck. Rayn had been told that in accordance with Ayris customs, the high steward retained the Emerald Rose of Avalon between successors.

Although he tried not to show it, her inquiry stirred heartache within Merlin. He assumed Rayn knew the gossipmongers' version of how he'd sired a son, but they rarely discussed that subject. Plagued with guilt over Shadoe, Merlin avoided the issue at all costs. Rayn had remained sensitive to his heart and rarely pried—until now.

"Pray tell me of my godsend, my knight in shining armor."

Merlin felt as if she'd plunged a dagger into his heart. If she'd had any idea what she asked of him, she wouldn't have. "I'd prefer not," he said with a finality that should have ended the matter. "We will discuss political strategies and concentrate on the present state of—"

The girl's generous mouth curled into a well-practiced pout that had a beguiling effect on men. Merlin grimaced. She'd heard his foretelling a dozen times, yet still pursued the matter.

Merlin considered the reedy female whose luminous green eyes sparkled with inquisitive mischief, eyes that would quickly seduce a man. For the present he preferred the innocence of a freckled, dirt-smudged face, an oversized russet tunic and breeches cinched at her diminutive waist, and the muddy toes she jabbed into the spongy green moss. Atop her head, a tattered felt cap concealed her prized possession.

"You make a comely boy. Now let your hair down, lass."

She glanced about the open field and said in a conspiring whisper, "Oh, Da will be furious, he will."

Merlin grunted with indifference. "We are hidden from your father and the world, precious jewel. It is time you look and behave like the creation God made you. You are beautiful like your mother. You are an Eve and should be proud."

"Oh, but I am proud of my womanhood, Mer, surely I am." She removed the cap and the blue ribbon that bound her braided tresses. "It's just that Da's so protective of late."

"And rightfully so."

However reluctant, she released the sun-kissed curls of auburn, and they spilled about her shoulders and waist, dispelling any doubt as to her sex.

"Lancelot had best recall I am your mentor, and I will let no harm befall you. It is also difficult to discuss matters of the heart when you look more like Adam than Eve."

Rayn spit into her palm and applied the moisture to gritty cheeks, and then rubbed her tunic sleeve across her spit-polished face. Moistening her lips with the tip of her tongue, she pinched each of her cheeks, heightening the natural rose tinge of her freckled features. "Better, aye?"

"Where did you learn that?" Merlin gawked.

"I saw a woman in Ayr do it. Is it a sin, Mer?" She rolled a shoulder and looked ashamed.

"Nay, it is no sin." He suppressed a chuckle. "Aye, Rayn, you are forever enchanting."

"And my future love will think me enchanting, aye?"

He settled his weary bones against the bald limb of the log. "He will indeed. Why, *my enchantress,* he will call you."

As if partaking of a conspiracy, she leaned close. "And is my knight in shining armor tall, regal, and comely like you, Milord Mer?"

"You are too good to my threadbare soul. I know not what I shall do without you when I leave."

Rayn nestled against him and planted a kiss upon his whiskered jaw. "You promised we'd not talk of such matters, least of your exodus."

He watched her eyes mist over, and when her lower lip quivered, Merlin had not the heart to admit his departure was imminent. "That we did, Princess." He tenderly arranged her silky tresses about her shoulders, and his thoughts flew back to Arthur. In his youth, the girl's father had possessed the same hair color of autumn leaves.

Ah, if your parents could see you, he reflected, setting his gaze on the widow's peak of Rayn's hairline. *For you are blessed with both their attributes.*

"Mer?" She cocked her head as if to ask where his thoughts had strayed.

He shrugged off his musings. "Umm, in regard to your godsend, well, I do not recall stating his armor gleamed. You must remember his sinful humanity. In all honesty, his leathers are weather worn and his armor is tarnished around the edges."

"Aye, nothing spit and polish will not fix."

"And some help from Jesu, of course."

"Of course," she answered heartily.

"Rayn, do you know what a knight really is?"

She bobbed her head. "Da says only Camelot has knights and that it is a very old title that originated in Ayris. It means 'a man of honor who solely serves God and his sovereign.' Men like Da, Tristam, Perceval, and Galahad."

"Aye, it would be wondrous if there were more knights in this world. Mayhap one day. In the meanwhile, understand knights are flawed beings just like us."

She crinkled her nose. "Are you implying my godsend is not a knight?"

He frowned at her perceptiveness. "I'd say that your expectations and reality might not be the same. In addition, most young women your age are wed, but you must be patient and trust God. Your godsend will come when the full bloom of womanhood is upon you. But I doubt you'll recognize him; in truth, you will probably dislike him and he you."

"Nay, Mer. I'll know him, and we will be friends first off!" She squeezed her eyes shut and expelled a dramatic sigh. "For he will fall headfirst in love with me, he will."

Merlin groaned and rolled his weary eyes. "Oh, I've no doubt he will fall headfirst for you—quite literally I suspect."

Rayn's gaze returned to her mentor.

"You will pray for him more than you do now and wonder why you bother, for he will be proud, defiant, and tenacious." He frowned into her attentive gaze. "Much like yourself, Emerald Rose Rayn." Exasperated, he muttered, "And God help anyone who must referee your clashes."

"What?" She offered an expression of puzzlement.

"Nothing, Princess." His voice deepened, his eyes fastened on her. "You must help him overcome his demons for they will make it difficult for him to commit to those he loves . . . especially Yahweh."

"You never said that before, Mer, about his lack of commitment to our Lord Jesu."

"True." His brows meshed. "Because although the journey will be laborious, I pray God will use you to lead your knight back into the arms of Jesu."

"I no longer like this knight you've conjured me, Mer. Too much work, he is."

Merlin cupped her firm-set chin and held her gaze. "Nothing worth having comes easy, fairest child. In all honesty, I imagine he will think you an ocean of work as well."

She folded her arms across her chest with an audible, "Humph! I am not work, Sir. I am a delight. You've said so yourself."

Merlin drew in a breath and let it out slowly. "Yes, you are. You are also pampered and at times self-righteous. That is more the fault of we who've nurtured you. As for your godsend, he is intelligent, levelheaded, and courageous. Most of all, he has a heart many will covet, but to you alone will he give it." He pushed to his feet and stretched, feeling the increasing aches and pains of his hundred and thirty-seven years. Staring longingly at Caer Camelot, he asked, "Promise me one thing, Princess?"

"Anything, sweet Mer." She looked shaken by his serious tenor.

He needed her to answer what his heart longed to hear. While he contemplated his request, Rayn slipped off the timber and tramped alongside him as they returned to the foot-worn path that wound down to the sea and the causeway to Camelot.

"Trust him."

"My knight?"

"Aye."

She nodded obedience.

"Even when you have cause to doubt him, trust him."

Again she agreed, although he sensed her doubt about where these promises might lead.

"Now, I must confess that what I've foretold are more my aspirations than those God decreed, so trust God and speak to him. He will always answer. Also remember that sometimes his answer is no answer at all."

She frowned, obviously finding his words a riddle. "I pray daily, Mer."

"Aye, you are a devoted prayer warrior, Rayn. Your faith will be tested. Remember the Fisher of Men rules our destinies."

"I will." She smiled, revealing a flash of white teeth against wine-colored lips.

"And Princess?" He shot her a keen look.

"What, Sire?" She engaged his serious countenance.

"I want to verify that the hoaxers who claimed to be Arthur and Guenevere haven't returned to Caer Camelot."

She picked up a stone and flung it toward the surf. "Not since you evicted them. Although they were kind to me, they were."

His lips curled into a grim smile. "Looks can be deceitful, Rayn. 'Twas not kind to fool you into believing they were Arthur and Guenevere. You know that our king and queen are with Jesu in heaven?"

"Of course, Mer. Anyway, that was quite long ago. I've nearly forgotten."

"Good." He pressed a finger to her freckled nose and grinned when she crinkled it beneath his touch.

"Besides, as long as I have you as my best friend, I need no one else, not even Arthur and Guenevere."

Merlin opened his mouth to reply, and then shut it. He had performed a ceremony, exorcising the imposters, and there was no reason to believe the demons were not vanquished to hell. He had more pressing issues. The inevitable drew nigh, and each moment it grew less easy to contemplate. He realized how much Rayn needed him and he needed her. Yet another obligation demanded attention. God had been tugging his heart for some time now. He had no choice. He must leave.

As they descended to the rugged shore of the Irish Sea, Merlin inhaled the salty breeze. Rayn discarded her sandals, tossed them overhead and then giggled when he snatched them midair. She smirked over her shoulder. He winked and encouraged her to race ahead. At her intrusion, scavenging seagulls took to the air. Her arms outspread, she dashed into the brisk surf and chased the tide, not escaping getting splashed.

Merlin watched her frolic. His heart longed for what he'd never again see, smell, or touch in this earthly realm—Emerald Rose Rayn Pendragon, Arthur's progeny.

Better this way for us both. Ah, she is the greatest of my accomplishments, better than Uther, Arthur, better than . . . how I failed you, dearest Shadoe. Blessed Jesu, help my scion."

Tears of shame and regret bathed his face as he cried out to God. More minutes had passed than he should have allowed. After he drew a ragged breath, Merlin dried his face and called Rayn to his side.

Dancing with the sea, she seemed oblivious to his command. Merlin could have touched her thoughts but felt no need. He knew what occupied her daydreams. What direction her knight would come from—north, south, west, east, land, or sea? No doubt she'd ask him if the subject arose. It would not.

A heartbeat later he stood in the tide, and Rayn still dodging the breakers collided with him. Merlin steadied her, snatched her wrist, and escorted her back to dry land.

"Sire, must you always do that!" She stomped her wet feet against the sandy turf.

"Do what?" He released her once they were tramping across the sand dunes.

"Whist! Disappear, and then appear out of nowhere." She hobbled along as she slipped on her sandals, and crouched to lace them up her calves.

Merlin snorted. "Mayhap you need be more alert, aye?" he suggested, with a mischievous smile beneath his beard as he trod on. Breathless, she caught up and managed to match his long determined strides.

"But I know of no one who does such mysterious acts as you do, Sire."

"You mean slight-of-hand tricks?" Not missing a step, he tossed the herb basket high into the darkening sky. It vanished, only to materialize in Rayn's wide-splayed arms.

With a loud gasp, she secured the herb-filled basket and stated with astonishment, "You truly are the august enchanter, you are."

"Once mayhap. Now I am an old Christian bard telling stories of lost enchantment to an audience of one." He turned and winked. "And a most attentive audience she is."

Against the fading sunlight he caught Rayn's affectionate smile as she said, "And I'm forever grateful to be your audience, Mer."

Drawing her to his side, Mer pressed a kiss to her forehead and smiled. They hiked the causeway that separated the Isle of Wind's Haven and Caer Camelot from the mainland. Once ashore, Merlin gazed past her to the walled fortification of the Romano-Briton hamlet Ayr, where she and her father resided. He drew a labored breath and looked upon her innocent visage, imprinting it on his memory for all time. He led her to where a copse of trees merged with the waterfront.

"I have a gift for you." He ducked beneath the tree's overhang and returned with a covered cage. "You know I've tended him several months now." Merlin removed a tattered cloth. "His left wing is almost healed." He hoisted the twig-framed cage, revealing a young male eagle.

Rayn expelled a loud gasp. "Oh, Mer, he's beautiful, he is!"

"He needs more attention than I can give. I hope you don't mind."

She accepted the gift. Elation colored her cheeks. "Of course not. You know how fond I've become of him. We should name him."

"That I leave to you." Merlin smiled upon the fledgling predator.

"Now I can go hawking with Da."

Merlin frowned. "Nay. Once this great bird is healed, you must release him. If you manage to build a bond of trust, he'll return of his choosing. Never make a prisoner of what Yahweh created to be free. Understand?"

"I think so." She tipped her head at the golden-eyed bird and then at Merlin. "You are leaving me now, Mer?" Her voice quavered.

"You are an astute apprentice, Rayn."

"Apparently not astute enough to foresee this." Her voice quivered and her eyes misted, but she tempered her emotions as he'd taught her.

"We all have different gifts of the Spirit, Rayn. You are just discovering yours, but I sense you possess a gift of diplomacy that will impact many lives as well as your descendants. Jesu said, 'Blessed are the peacekeepers for they shall be called the sons and daughters of God,' as shall you, Princess."

Rayn didn't seem to hear his prophecy. "Does Da know of your departure?"

"Nay. He would fight me on this. I have an important matter to resolve before I pass into God's kingdom. Here." He gave her his staff. "I taught you how to defend yourself with it so it is only proper that the staff of Aaron be yours."

Accepting the ancient wooden rod, Rayn's large eyes widened. "You never go anywhere without it!" She looked up and met his intense gaze. "You won't be back?"

He drew her into his arms and pressed his lips to the crown of her head. They clung to each other a long while before he stepped back and looked into her misting green eyes. "'Tis my heart's desire to return, but if not, Princess, we shall meet in the sky with Jesu. Until then, remember me with a charitable heart."

"I shall keep you in my heart always, Mer," she uttered through a sob.

"And you in mine, Emerald Rose Rayn." He swept her a bow, and then retrieved a bundle and walking stick from the bushes.

When he took up his lyre, Rayn cried desolately, "I shall never again hear the mystical strum of music flowing from your fingers, your rich ballads of romance or joyful praise to Yahweh, will I?"

Merlin put his hand to his heart. "From here my songs will always sing to you. You need only listen. Whenever you need me, just open your heart, and I will come to you."

She gave a feeble nod and swiped her tears with the back of her hand. "Yahweh goes with you, Merlin un Hollo Tors."

Straightening, Merlin smiled and turned, but not before emotion misted his eyes. As he stepped onto the causeway between the mainland and Wind's Haven, a dense brume encompassed him. Merlin vanished.

Some folks might think it odd that when Merlin departed, he turned back toward Wind's Haven and Camelot. Rayn did not think it so. Was he not the august enchanter, the Merdyn?

Chapter Six

THE SHORES OF WESTERN ITALY

The rhythmic strum of a lyre echoed through the underground maze of stone hollows. From a centralized fire pit, smoke billowed upward like spirit breath, wound through the vast stone canopy to the slumbering world overhead. Still this mystical place quaked with the anger of reality beyond this dream-place. Boulders crashed. Dust strangled the air.

A black wolf pup scrabbled across the tremulous cavern floor and huddled at Shadoe's feet. Setting aside the instrument, Shadoe patted the submissive pup's head, and then knelt before a straw-covered stone slab on which lay a timeworn man too weak to rise. Not any man, this was.

Stretched out beneath a fig tree, Shadoe un Hollo Tors tossed about on his bed of sod, struggling between the vision and reality. Over the years he'd experienced many such dreams, so vivid that they blurred the line between the waking and sleeping worlds. This dream had come consecutively for nigh onto a week. Tonight it was stronger, more compelling than the last, and Shadoe sensed he'd not be rid of it until he saw it through. Without a doubt, a higher authority had visited this vision upon him, and whether its origin was of heaven or hell, Shadoe pondered as he yielded to its seduction. A tremor rocked the earth, but he remained captive in another realm while dream and reality melded.

"The mount is about to explode. We must go!" Shadoe insisted, bending to scoop the old man off his straw pallet.

"Nay! God calls me home but has answered my prayers and brought you to me. When you leave, take Echo." He shook from a raspy cough, and gestured to the four-month-old she-wolf. "Like you, she's alone. She'll be a faithful companion."

Shadoe ignored the simpering pup. "This is but a dream, Sire, and this cavern a memory of my youth."

"Often Yahweh speaks to us in dreams, Apprentice. You would not come to me, so I've come to you with our Creator's intervention."

"Nay, I saw you dive off the cliffs to your death!"

"And you believed what you saw?"

The muscles of Shadoe's jaw twitched. "Nay. So why did you deceive so many—deceive me?"

"Too much at risk. I had to fabricate my death and make certain there would be witnesses. I didn't expect you to be among them."

"Then Arthur knew you weren't dead?"

The bard nodded. "At the last moment he tried to stop me!"

"'Tis why you fought?"

"Aye."

"Why didn't you let me know?" he demanded.

"To protect you. Would you have come sooner, Apprentice?"

Shadoe looked away. "I'm no longer your apprentice, Sire. I'm a man."

"And a strong, handsome lad you are." The bard's fragile fingers clutched the younger wrist until Shadoe turned and met his mahogany gaze. They were the eyes of a wise man that had seen more of life than most. Shadoe looked into the seasoned face, beyond his impotent body and the unsteady hand that held Shadoe's own sturdy grip. His guard vaporized. He experienced compassion toward this man who for the most part had been a stranger to him.

Dream or not, emotions Shadoe had long sought to bury roiled to the surface. He glanced about the cave in which the bard had chosen to live out his last days. Most would have questioned living in this dank desolate place. Not Shadoe. This hollow was exactly what he had expected of the Merdyn.

"Your contempt for me is righteous, Apprentice. I wish that you could forgive me, but if not, at least forgive yourself."

Blood charged like hot oil through Shadoe's veins, and he bolted to his feet. "Of all the ludicrous, priggish remarks! Forgive myself! For what?"

"For hardening your heart against love."

"You, who placed more value on political agenda than on human life, dare lecture me on love!"

The bard closed his eyes as if accepting Shadoe's judgment. "I admit I was not a paragon, so glean from my mistakes."

Stalking the dusty quarters, Shadoe tossed back his cloak, seeking to regain his composure. His feelings were raw, ready to erupt. Yet a more immediate explosion was in the making just miles away. Actuality invaded his fantasy, and although the quakes had ceased, he wished to be gone from this cavern and the threat of Mount Vesuvius. Whether this was dream or reality, he must convince the bard to leave.

Shadoe stared at their silhouettes on the cold earthen walls and struggled not to press the issues that had alienated them all these years. Old wounds festered. Arthur Pendragon had been Shadoe's rival, and even with Arthur's death so long ago, Shadoe experienced the bitter battle for his father's heart.

Another cough jolted the trembling bones of the bard, and Shadoe turned to find him spewing phlegm and blood. Shadoe took up a rag, lowered to one knee, and wiped the elderly man's mouth. Look at him! Shadoe rebuked himself. He's dying! The least I can offer is a truce. "You need rest, Sire." Shadoe offered him water, which he refused, and then tucked another fur coverlet about his frail shoulders. "Let me take you to a safe place."

"Nay." He shook his head. "It is my time."

"This is but a delusion," Shadoe argued.

The bard interrupted, "Is it? Hear God's foretelling. With my departure, among the ashes a violet shall bloom, and your life will have new forging. As a child you knew the light from the darkness. Walk with the Scion's light. 'Tis a gift from Yahweh."

"I walk alone, Sire."

"Aye, hear the words of the prophet Isaiah, 'Who is among you that feareth the Lord, that obeyeth the voice of his servant, that walketh in darkness, and hath no light? Let him trust in the name of the Lord, and stay upon his God. Behold, all ye that kindle a fire, that compass yourselves about with sparks: walk in the light of your fire, and in the sparks that ye have kindled. This shall ye have of my hand: ye shall lie down in torment.'"

The truth of the bard's words sent a shudder of fear through Shadoe. Truly he had chosen to make his own light, to walk alone. And truly he was in torment.

"You, my scion, walk in shadows; 'tis why you were so christened."

"You have foreseen my future?" Shadoe could not quell his concern.

"Yahweh revealed your life struggles to me, nothing more. Until you turn toward his light again and obey him, you will suffer without hope." The dying man motioned him closer. "Take my neck chain."

Shadoe hunkered down and slipped the heavy necklace from beneath the bard's tunic. The sight of the amulet stained his face with ire. "In thunder's name, the Emerald Rose of Avalon!"

Shadoe stared with loathing at the gold talisman suspended from a gilded chain. The formidable dark emerald surrounded by twelve diamonds drank rays of firelight giving it an ethereal quality.

"'Twas my duty," the old man said.

"Duty! Thousands died because of this cursed jewel!" Fury charged through Shadoe's being.

"Aye, and now 'tis your responsibility, Apprentice."

Shadoe gaped in horror. The last thing he wanted was the Emerald Rose, let alone the duties it incurred. Possession of this ancient amulet meant trouble.

"I assure you the talisman holds no powers, good or evil."

"This amulet's legend has reached the farthest lands, Sir. And like most pagans, the druids idolize the Rose, believing it holds mystical powers."

"Do you?"

"Nay." Shadoe scoffed. He'd witnessed druid mysticism and its bloody rituals. He also knew that, despite the fishwives' exaggerations, his mentor had long turned his back on the seduction of druid beliefs.

"Be on guard with Mordred."

"I've no intention to get within sight of him."

The bard drew a deep breath, his wizened face shadowed with resignation. "You have no choice."

"I have many choices, Sire. First, never to return to the Isle of Might, and second, to destroy this cursed jewel!" Shadoe motioned to toss it into the fire pit. "It does nothing but bring out the worst in men."

"Nay!" The old man struggled to stop him. "'Tis your heritage! The amulet has as many legends as it has names. The oldest, most revered being the Rose of Sharon. There is only one truth: it is a symbol of a people's faith in the triune God, Jehovah. The Rose was forged for your greatest of ancestors, Joseph scion of Jacob, who served as governor to the Egyptian pharaoh. There was one other gift bestowed unto Joseph, a rare blue diamond called the Blue Angel. 'Tis said to be buried in a tomb the Egyptians erected for Joseph."

Shadoe's eyes widened at this news.

The bard waved his limp hand as if to dismiss the subject. "The Emerald Rose is always to be shielded by one of your seed. Sometimes the least likely will be chosen to possess the Rose, for God alone will choose that guardian. What's important is that you, Shadoe un Hollo Tors, are one of Yahweh's chosen."

"I am?" he asked in astonishment.

"Aye." The bard managed a stately smile. "God scattered the tribes of Israel across the face of his earth, but Caledonia and Britannia is where he destined you and your scions to be. Listen to God, Apprentice. He will speak to your heart as to whom you should serve. To those who know the truth, he who wears the Emerald Rose of Avalon is high steward to whoever rules the Isle of Might. The high steward alone can appoint Arthur's successor. Since Aurelius, Uther Pendragon was the first true high chieftain of the mighty isle, and then followed his reluctant successor, Arthur.

"A time will come when there will be a drought in your progeny and the patronymic of steward will not be acknowledged. Still kings will emerge from your lineage, great ones. And one day, the world will know the surname of Steward."

Shadoe struggled to absorb the gravity of his heritage. "Why didn't you tell me this before?"

The bard looked upon Shadoe with death-clouded eyes. "'Tis the way of Yahweh, of our people. You needed to taste the greatness of his creations in this world. You were too young to understand or appreciate the blessing of your heritage and your destiny. No longer."

Angry defiance fueled Shadoe. "I am not you, Sir, nor do I desire to be high steward."

The bard snorted. "Do you think I wanted the post God assigned to me? Bah! I fought him fervently until, broken and convicted by the Holy Spirit, I yielded to his almighty will. It was not until I committed my life to him that I experienced boundless compassion and blessings unlike anything I had ever known." He reached up and trailed the withered leather of his right hand along Shadoe's tense jaw. "I feel your stubborn nature, Shadoe. We are alike."

Shadoe eyes narrowed in denial.

"God will use your tenacity for his purpose. Because I invented my first death, Mordred was unable to secure a covenant with the major tribes. Even that pagan Mordred fears and respects the legacy of Ayris and unknowingly respects Yahweh. Without the Emerald Rose of Avalon, he can't appoint a high steward. 'Tis why the clans dismissed his claim of Arthur's crown. The day young Arthur drew Excalibur from the Celtic stone, God forged his destiny, and so shall it be for his successor."

"Aye, Arthur was the greatest strategist and warrior in Caledonia and Britannia, but he never officially accepted the high kingship."

"He didn't have to accept what was his by blood. Desperate times call for desperate dreams . . . even of things that never were."

"Aye and thus the prattling fishwives have buried the truth," Shadoe groused.

"Few choose to remember truth, especially when their lives are at risk for speaking so."

"I remember Arthur's humility. Such a reluctant hero, let alone king. He was the one leader the clans truly respected. Like them, his veins flowed with Celt and Briton blood."

"And Ayris blood." The bard smiled. "As does yours, scion. Ah, Arthur successfully compelled our enemies to coexist in peace."

"With your guidance," Shadoe stated, certain this dying man was the real peacekeeper of the Isle of Might. "There is a vast difference between acquiring unity with words and compelling it through war."

The old man smiled but continued as if he feared he'd not enough time. "Most of all, Arthur lived his life for the Christ and died defending his faith. Even his foes respected him. Most of his allies are gone. Mordred's design is to slay those who still believe in the code of the Round Table and the unity of the clans. If he succeeds there will be no need of a high steward and peacekeeper on our blessed isle, for slaughter will wear the crown and despair rule the land. 'Twill be generations before the clans unite as one. This I have foreseen."

A rumble shook the cavern's foundation, and Shadoe reached for the old man.

"Nay, Apprentice. If God be merciful, he will take my spirit home." His dull eyes took on a brilliant gleam and he smiled.

"Nay!" Shadoe protested.

"Please. Will you now honor my last wishes?"

Shadoe felt himself wavering. He may not have always liked his mentor, but he did love him. At the bard's urging, Shadoe leaned closer.

"However absent a parent I was to you, please, just once, call me Da?"

Shadoe's years of ire mellowed. Love forged his heart. "What are your wishes, Da?"

A thin smile cracked his father's parched lips. "Find Arthur and Guenevere's progeny."

"Progeny! Your mind is weary."

The bard gave Shadoe a look he'd long come to resent—superior, wiser, all knowing. "You were with Guenevere in her last moments of life. You know she bore a bairn."

Shadoe scoffed. "If there is a child, 'tis not of Arthur's loins."

"So all were meant to believe for the child's protection—shielded by the Silver Lion."

"Lancelot?"

"Aye. He protects this jewel of the Isle of Might. God willing, the Pendragon will breathe life into that desolate land. Use all I've taught you—all you've learned—to guide the young warrior and defeat Mordred and those who would pillage our land."

A tremor shook the cavern; debris crashed around them. Anxiously Shadoe insisted, "I am no seer or high steward."

His father shook his white-crowned head. "Nor was I. At last as a simple bard I joyfully die. One day you will as well. God Almighty crafts your providence. Eventually you will discover that destiny is a process not an event. Your years in Arthur's court and in Greece and Rome have prepared you for such a day. You are a scholar of politics, science, and war. There is none better suited—"

Shadoe was stunned by Merlin's knowledge of his wanderings. "I am a sword for hire, Da, among other occupations you'd detest."

"Aye, it is said your hand in a man's money pouch is faster than a cobra's bite. And that you and Galahad are equals with the sword."

The nerve of Shadoe's jaw-line quavered. "Galahad is more suited for this role."

"Galahad has his own destiny."

"As always, you withhold information from me! Not unlike when you were accused of aiding Vortigern and plotting with Mordred. Why did you not defend yourself but instead allow the realm to believe you were a traitor, a coward?"

"To protect the realm."

"And what of me, Da? Do I mean nothing to you?"

"You are my life, Shadoe."

Shadoe wanted desperately to believe his words, but too much had passed between them, too many lies and too much bitterness. "You only sought me out because of your debt to Arthur."

"Nay. You and his seedling are Caledonia's last hope. One day when you are full of the Creator's light, you will know the depth of my love." As if summoning the remnants of his strength, his voice gained momentum. "Until you can reach into yourself and know God's truth as well as the night knows the stars, you will be vulnerable to the Vortigerns and Mordreds of this world.

"Far too long I accepted the pagan title placed upon me. August enchanter, indeed! Magique, bah! Yahweh granted me grace and the gifts of His Spirit—and despite what the world would believe, I did not turn from him. Nor, Shadoe, did I turn from you.

"Hear me, scion. You needed to achieve the self-reliance that comes with years of experience in the world. That is why I let you believe I'd died. You've learned much, but there is more. You must love unconditionally, give totality to others, no matter the cost. You must be in this world, not of it."

Shadoe's nerves grew taut, but he held his father's gaze. He didn't want to hear another word about God, yet he decided that no matter what was asked of him, his father would die in peace.

The bard drew a deep, quavering breath. "If I was called the august enchanter, then you will be called the last enchanter, Shadoe un Hollo Tors. Let them call you what they will. They will know you by your walk, your deeds. They will see Yahweh in you. For works without faith is folly. Faith must motivate deeds of goodness." He exhaled a labored moan. "One thing more. Vow that you do not fall victim to the wiles of worldly women."

Shadoe felt discomfiture warm his cheeks. He knew the pleasures of women and wasn't pleased with the vow of chastity his father sought to secure from him. "Not even in love?" he hedged.

A smile touched the elder's face. "True love is a gift from God, and if the woman's love is genuine, you are blest. But if you are seduced by one who serves the Adversary, you must pay the price as I did." His eyes glowed with bittersweet memories. "Even so, my regrets are few, for I have you, my scion."

Shadoe needed to know what his father had always refused to discuss. "Tell me of my mother, Sire, of Niamh le Fey. Does she still live?"

The bard pressed his fingers to Shadoe's forehead. "Forgive her, pray for her. . . . My fault. I loved her more than God, fell prey to her enchantment, to eyes that sparkled like sapphires, Yahweh forgive me."

"Then she is alive? Where?"

Waving off Shadoe's questions, the old man tried to rise, but mortality held him prisoner, and he begged, "Please, Abba Father, a few moments more?"

Heaven conceded.

"Yahweh has provided you with a godsend, scion. Vow to remain chaste until you are one with God's chosen."

However reluctant, Shadoe nodded. "I pledge that from this day forth I will abstain when faced with carnal temptations, Da."

The bard smiled. "Now, as our fathers before us, I give you my blessing and ask that you return to Wind's Haven. Find my chronicles, for they hold the truth of Arthur and the summer realm of Ayris . . . the translated Gospels. . .

"What chronicles . . . what Gospels . . . where?"

His father did not explain. Instead he spoke in rapid gasps as if sensing his last breaths. "Mephistopheles' heel has been dashed, yet there remains one spawned by an incubus . . . Morgause. She controls Mordred's hand. He's but a puppet . . . not his fault . . . mine! The seventeenth year of Arthur's death draws nigh, and twenty-five years prior he freed Excalibur from the stone. You and Arthur's progeny must finish the task Arthur and I failed to complete. Defeat Morgause."

"That's madness!"

"Nay," the bard wheezed. "Morgause is of Ayrisian seed . . . of the traitorous incarnates who escaped God's wrath upon Ayris."

"Morgause is Ayrisian?"

"Aye. She must never know. Her powers come from the Adversary. So protect the Pendragon. Join forces . . . free Excalibur from the stone. The sword belongs with the Pendragon as does the Emerald Rose of Avalon with you. To this day, Morgause believes that by possessing Excalibur and

the Rose she will acquire the powers of a goddess and put down the up-
surge of Christianity on the Isle of Might. Thus the pagans will exalt her
and Christians will believe God turned from them."

Shadoe leaped to his feet, his features clouded with torment.

His father groaned. "Aye, take heed. You have choices, but Yahweh has
chosen you. You, the endmost of Ayris blood, must hear his voice and
obey. Trust Jesu to protect you and to subdue your foes!"

The expiring man clutched his heart, his last words a labored whisper.
"Go home, my scion . . . face your demons. . . . God will guard you as he
guarded you from the sulfuric fumes of Belizar."

Shadoe was stunned into silence. His father knew of Shadoe's demons,
of Belizar and Excalibur! Had God revealed Shadoe's sins to his father?

The bard clenched Shadoe's wrist. "I love you, scion." He gazed off into
the distance as if acknowledging an invisible presence. "Ah, you have been
eternally patient, Friend. I am ready. . . ."

Shadoe glanced about but found the cavern empty save for the wolf
and his da. A tranquil smile unlike anything Shadoe had ever seen illuminated the bard's waxen countenance, and for a heartbeat Shadoe
glimpsed a younger man much like himself. The bard's hand relaxed on
Shadoe's wrist. His eyes shut, and he slumped against the straw pallet.

Shadoe clutched the dead man's shoulders, shaking the limp vessel of
his father. "Don't, Da! You can't die! There's much we—"

As if in response to his grief, the cavern quaked and rocks hurtled down
around him. The granite base split open. Fire spewed forth, licking Shadoe's
sandals. Earth and stone heaved, bringing him down onto the raging surface. His face cut and bleeding from sharpened teeth of stone, Shadoe
pushed to his feet. The temperature intensified. With an audible whimper, the wolf-pup leaped the gap of molten rock into Shadoe's arms. His
father's harp teetered on the edge of the expanding crevice. With Echo in
tow, Shadoe vaulted over the fiery pit. He caught hold of the instrument's
wooden neck, and rolled free of the hellish inferno. The tremors intensified, and the crack made a circular path around the bard's deathbed, separating father and son.

"No!" Shadoe's desperate scream died on a wave of violent tremors sent by the demons themselves. Flames ignited the fur coverlet over his father's body, and the sarcophagus began to sink into hell.

Heaven intervened. The cavern roof cracked open, revealing a firmament of glimmering stars as the volcanic pressure shot upward, bearing the sarcophagus and bard up through the hilltop toward God's embrace.

Strangling for air, Shadoe fled through the cavern passages and out into the fresh sea air. He scurried up the side of the tor, and from there watched the fire's wind carry his father out over the sea, where he vanished.

Across the bay, the summit of Mount Vesuvius exploded. A black cloud of ash smothered the air. Although he did not know why, Shadoe sensed that the fury was dying. The earth ceased its thunder, and dawn seduced the night. From nearby came the song of a lark, and a stream of apricot-tinged light sluiced through the black rain of ash to rest at Shadoe's feet.

Excited, the wolf burrowed her nose in the blanket of cooling ash and unearthed evergreen stems and a violet patch. Dazed, Shadoe dropped to his knees and stared at the miraculously budding flower. He fingered its delicate blue petals, and then crushing the violet in his hand, he wailed his loss to the silent spring morn.

"Merlin!"

Hands shook Shadoe. Strange voices called to him. He opened his eyes to find himself prostate on the lurching ground.

"Hurry, Sir," a villager urged in Latin. "We must leave before the mount explodes!"

Shadoe shot to his feet as citizens ran for boats on the seashore while others fled with their oxen-drawn wagons loaded with provisions. He felt disoriented, then remembered. He was in Italy. Miles away Mount Vesuvius spewed its fury while hot veins of lava flowed into the Mediterranean Sea.

Shadoe snatched the reins of his skittish horse and tried to dislodge the realism of his fantasy. It was a dream! Mounting the black Arab, Shadoe galloped out of the village and northward along the shoreline, putting miles between him and harm.

He turned to look at the sea. In the distance, on the island of Capri, flames erupted as underground geysers spewed into the pewter gray sky. He had never been to the island, yet . . . *Impossible,* he thought, as he splayed his fingers to find the remnant of a violet-colored blossom pressed into his palm. Dropping the flower as if scalded, Shadoe kicked his heels against the horse and rode hard, denying the truth of his vision until a whine from his satchel disconcerted him.

It was another good mile before he halted to inspect the source of the high-pitched noise. Reaching back, he unlaced the leather satchel to find a black wolf-pup looking up at him. A muscle along Shadoe's neck pulsed; his heart accelerated. "I'm trapped in a nightmare!" Tentatively, he petted the warm soft fur of the wolf-pup. The creature licked his hand with a sloppy tongue. "Then mayhap not." Shadoe tucked the pup back inside the bag and pulled his mantle over his head as cover from the falling ash.

He became conscious of a weight about his neck. Reaching beneath his tunic, he fingered a neck chain. When he clutched the star-shaped medallion, his hand burned and he let go. Miles away, the roar of Mount Vesuvius receded; save for the sea's thunderous waves, all was deadly calm. Shadoe blinked against the storm of ash and became aware of how alone he had been most of his life—by choice. In his heart, Shadoe knew Yahweh had never abandoned him. He'd abandoned Yahweh.

"Vision or not, if you want my attention, Lord, you have it. But if you expect me to submit and trust you, well . . . I'll not make promises I don't intend to keep." Shadoe waited for God's hand to smite him. When nothing happened, he released a painfully held breath. The irony of the situation made him grunt and acknowledge the Almighty Fisher of Men. God's allowance for him to live meant he'd have to execute the promise he'd just made to his father, thus fulfilling the deferred promise he'd made years earlier to Lady Guenevere. Like it or not, Shadoe knew he was succumbing to God's will, but one thing remained certain: he'd not surrender without a fight.

In passion's flame
Arthur forged this precious jewel
To claim what Yahweh long ordained
And dub Lancelot the fool.
Behold no hearts were set to rest
Nor joyed in Guenevere's shame.
Thus, only with eyes of emerald fire,
And beauty of the purest rose
Shall Splendor Lost once more reign.
—THE STEWARD CHRONICLES,
Shadoe un Hollo Tors

Chapter Seven

473 A.D.

THE FIRTH OF CLYDE, CALEDONIA

SHADOE HAD FOUGHT the homecoming. Aye, he did. But his conscience and his honor—what was left of them—at last forced the decision.

Nigh unto the first anniversary of Merlin's death, he sailed from Gaul to Britannia. Even before he stepped ashore, he had conversed with Britons who confirmed the accounts that engrossed the courts of Rome and beyond. Mordred Pendragon had joined allegiance with the Saxons and ruled most of northern Britannia.

Shadoe's ardent hope to find Arthur Pendragon's seal yet on the grand fortress of Tintagel was crushed. Mordred's stamp of ownership was clearly visible by the Germanic settlements of the Angolii and Saxons scattered among the beautiful Roman villas of the southeastern coast. He thought this would change as he journeyed farther inland. It didn't. Saxon settlements were everywhere. As he traveled west, Shadoe witnessed the devastation to the Britons and Celts who resisted the Saxons.

Donning armor, Shadoe kept his weapons within reach at all times. Along his travels, he acquired pertinent particulars, one about the Saxon High King Hengist, who had ridden with Vortigern seventeen years ago and now ruled the southeast region of Kent, Britannia. Hengist had joined forces with Mordred and intended to ride against the Scotti and Picts, but their first plan of action was to crush the Briton and Celt dissidents in the lowlands of Caledonia. At that news, Shadoe's heart sank. Mordred was trouble enough without an ally like Hengist.

Shadoe made the treacherous journey toward the western shores of Britannia and up into Caledonia. To his dismay, he found the Saxons had managed to obtain strongholds in the mid-lowlands of Caledonia. Bad enough Mordred had taken Tintagel; King Hengist now held the Pendragon's third stronghold, the great fortress of Cadbury tor.

The Saxons' most recent attack had scattered much of the Briton population. Some had moved north, hoping to elude the invaders. Furthermore, the chance that Lancelot still lived seemed slim. The Silver Lion would choose to die fighting the Saxons rather than surrender or make peace with them.

Guilt can make even the hardest of men break, and although Shadoe hated to admit it, he had begun to buckle. He hoped his return would put an end to the nightmares from his imprisonment in Belizar and quiet the ceaseless nagging of his father's voice, requiring him to fulfill his promise. He also hoped this tiny obedience would set to flight the other strange dreams that continued to possess him, such as the one of the phantom enchantress hovering over Loch Lady.

Despite the odds, he would make a reasonable effort to locate Lancelot as well as Arthur's hypothetical heir and be gone within two months. Shadoe had already made arrangements to board a ship after that time and sail off to wherever the winds took him—anywhere but this place where the ghosts of his past were too real.

Two hours past dawn of a clear day, with Echo loping at his side, Shadoe galloped onto the western shore of Caledonia where the Isle of Wind's Haven at last hovered on the horizon. A strong sense of security embraced him as he dismounted, and for the first time in weeks, he removed his chest and back armor plates and helm. He strapped the heavy weaponry to Destrier's saddle. The horse snorted, and Shadoe comforted the disgruntled Arab. "Do not worry, lad. Soon as we make camp, I'll relieve you of that burden. Hopefully, we'll enjoy some freedoms, aye?"

Shadoe dismounted Destrier and allowed the stallion to graze the sweet meadow grasses of Wind's Haven. Shadoe and the wolf set off on foot. An hour later, they cleared the highest peak of the rugged tors. Though the object of Shadoe's search remained out of sight, he heard the rumble of the waterfall.

Securing his scarlet mantle over his shoulder, Shadoe stretched. The muscles of his shoulders flexed taut beneath his timeworn jerkin, while he rubbed a callused palm across the planes of his face and three-day beard. A breeze stirred the hawthorn trees, and the breathtaking vision of the secluded island expanded all around him. To the east, he saw the mainland and the Briton city of Ayr on its shore, which he had side-stepped. True to the isle's name, a steady breeze prevailed, and even in this wooded glade, Shadoe inhaled the salty scent of the sea.

In reality, Wind's Haven was bridged to the mainland by a natural causeway that, long neglected, would in time surrender to the sea. Therefore, most considered Wind's Haven the isle it would one day become. Shadoe closed his eyes, remembering what had been. Once, Arthur's mainland demesne had stretched far as the eye could see. Although not a large realm, it had been noteworthy and secluded by the hazardous seas on the west and on the southeast by the boggy moorlands where few men dared venture.

It had been years since Shadoe had traveled past Hadrian's Wall to the western shores of Caledonia and his childhood home, even longer since he'd stood upon this ridge of Wind's Haven. It seemed more beautiful than memory, mayhap because he possessed the appreciation of a man's eye. This was an enchanted place, and for the moment, Shadoe felt his heart soften. Here the sun shone brighter, the sky beamed bluer, the clouds floated whiter, and the forest and meadows of heather grew greener than anywhere on earth. He recalled Merlin's words that, besides Ayris and Eden itself, this islet remained as pure as when God first created the world.

Shadoe distinguished the outlines of fields, now abandoned by the villeins who had once harvested them. Villas, crumbling from long neglect, sat beyond the walls of Camelot. The Isle of Wind's Haven, deemed enchanted by pagans and cursed by Christians, had remained uninhabited since Arthur's and Guenevere's deaths. Leastwise, few folks dared cross the sea-swept causeway, let alone spend the night. Most believed demons walked the island, searching for victims to possess.

The grand thought of having Wind's Haven to himself split Shadoe's face into a grin. "Superstitious fools, they don't know what they're missing."

In the distance, swirling mist indicated the abundant hot springs that dotted the island. Ahead of him, the thunder of the falls beckoned. With Echo trailing behind, Shadoe followed the swift-flowing burn until he stood near the perimeter of the falls. Sheathed in slippery green moss, the high falls cascaded over a series of stone ledges and pockets. From there it spilled into the churning depths of the loch that nurtured another course of rivulets before flowing out to sea. Because the burn was fed from several warm springs, the waterfall was not as frigid as the deep waters of Loch Lady. The warm waters merging with the cold loch caused a constant surreal mist at the base of the falls. As a youth, Shadoe had spent many an afternoon splashing in the burn and the shallow pools of the falls. The memory reminded him that he desperately needed to bathe.

"What say you, lass?" he called to Echo above the roar of the falls. "We scrub up?"

Echo whined at the very suggestion.

Chuckling at his reluctant companion, Shadoe hiked down to the second level of the falls. From here it was a straight decent into the loch. Beside a water-carved stone pool, he unhitched the sword from his waist. And then he spotted her. She stood in another pool below with the steady spill of water behind her. Shadoe pressed back where he could not be seen and peered at the splendid creature. His heart began to beat madly.

Her back to him, she wore a white chemise that clung to her slender form and stopped just above her knees. Shadoe watched her untie a blue ribbon that released her halo of sun-drenched auburn hair. Securing the ribbon about her diminutive waist, the enchantress shook the ringlets free and became cloaked in a mist of frosty red. She lifted a small phial and poured oil into her palms. Resting one foot on a rock, the beauty caressed the length of her left leg and repeated her actions with her right leg. Shadoe gulped as he pondered her long shapely limbs.

Echo leaped onto an accessible ledge and sniffed the air. Shadoe saw the wolf's ears perk and the fur along her spine rise. Echo lowered to her haunches with bared fangs and emitted a low growl.

"Hush!" Shadoe tugged the wolf to his side as the woman began to sing. "Listen."

If a wolf could look disgusted, Echo succeeded. She plopped onto her tummy and rested her muzzle on outstretched paws.

Although the rumble of the falls drowned her lyrics, the enchantress's melody plagued Shadoe's memory. Desiring a better view, he leaned out farther. Despite his efforts, the swirling mist and her long tresses shielded the beauty of face he felt she possessed. As if hypnotized, Shadoe watched while she giggled and splashed about in the pool. It was the music of youthful innocence, and he pondered the reality of his unearthing. Clearly, the woman thought to bathe in privacy, and although he acknowledged it indecent, he could not look away. When she stretched a long slender leg over the pool's edge, fierce passion pounded at the vow of celibacy he'd made to his father.

Without warning, a winged darkness with the screech of a raptor soared overhead. The predator swooped toward the enchantress. Though he knew his warning would go unheard, Shadoe stood and yelled. Astonishingly, the bird of prey perched an arm's span from the beauty, and she bent to caress its feathered head.

"Humph!" Shadoe gaped at the exchange between the enchantress and a golden eagle. He was jealous. *Oh, to feel her caress!*

"Look this way," he silently commanded and crept farther onto the slick fringe of moss. His feet dislodged a few stones, which clattered into her pool.

The eagle took flight, and the enchantress turned, looking upward. Even from his distant perch, Shadoe perceived the tender blossom of her mouth, the rose-fire that flushed her alabaster complexion, and the glint of bright eyes. In a single heartbeat, Shadoe pledged, whether she was angel or demon she would be his bride.

Before he could react, Shadoe heard the predator's shriek mingled with the snarl of his wolf, then felt the eagle's talons score his shoulders. The blow drove him to the ground. He staggered to his feet in an effort to throw off the powerful bird. Echo leaped, but her fangs claimed only feathers for reward. The wolf's botched rescue sent them into the pool, and then over the cliff to flounder in the void between earth and heaven.

Shadoe plummeted toward the waters of Loch Lady. A flash of burnished hair was his only glimpse of the enchantress during his wingless flight, though he managed to wave on his way past.

The icy grip of the loch closed over him, dragging him deep. He recalled the unfortunate souls who'd drowned swimming this close to the falls. He struggled in an effort to break free, to swim upward, but the current overpowered him. The force of the falls merged with the depth of the loch and pummeled his body. For a suspended period, he endured. Shadoe had never been a strong swimmer; now that disadvantage tore the air from his lungs and the strength from his limbs.

Tranquility embraced him. Shadoe opened his eyes, imagining he would see the face of death. Instead, he found himself floating in a cold world bereft of light save for the luminous silver object before him. Reaching out, he caressed icy steel that sliced open his fingertips. Bewildered, he watched his blood mingle with the wintry waters. He slid his hand over the jewel-studded hilt to grip the sword and free it from the prison of stone. Piles of bleached sticks littered the flat rock. Only when Shadoe's dulling mind spotted numerous skulls did he realize the sticks were actually human remains. Despite this, a strange seduction commanded him as he recognized the significance of his find. Excalibur!

Shadoe tugged the sword's hilt, but the blade held fast to its jail-stone, as did his hand, which froze to the sword. Try as he might, he could not free himself from the jeweled steel and realized this was how the others had died. It must be his final whimsy, but Shadoe fancied the enchantress swam toward him. When she grasped his imprisoned hand, the sword and stone separated for a heartbeat. There was un-natural strength in her delicate hands. The enchantress pulled him free from Excalibur and farther into the dark void of the loch.

Shadoe hung limp in death's embrace and looked at the specter that held him. Her burnished tresses floated behind her like a wedding veil, and even in his waning moments, Shadoe pondered whether or not she claimed air for existence.

My auburn-haired angel is the enchantress in the loch! Clinging to her, he ascended swiftly. Sunlight burst overhead as the loch spewed him forth. He gasped, but no air filled his agonized lungs. While the enchantress held his head above water, he saw Echo paddle toward him. Shadoe's clarity of the event became more muddled when Echo's powerful jaws clamped about his wrist and the wolf dragged him through the water. He envisioned the enchantress swimming along-side him, her breath on his cheek the only warmth he felt. He heard her pants of exhaustion as she yanked him up an embankment to a bed of straw grass, where he collapsed. Air was still denied him until her hands thumped his upper back and caused him to cough and spurt forth water. Echo's wet muzzle prodded him as the enchantress rolled him onto his back.

Shadoe forced his eyes open to see this mystical creature the pagans called the Lady of the Loch. He focused on the long wet strands of auburn that brushed his cheek and chest, the wet chemise that clung to gentle curves, her slender ivory neck that met a delicate-boned chin, her concerned eyes. Their color eluded him as she dropped her gaze. He tried to rise, but she pushed him back to the grass.

"Rest sir," her airy voice commanded.

Shadoe's lips parted, but exhaustion dulled his tongue. He faded into oblivion.

⚭

Emerald Rose Rayn knelt over the outlander, shivering and panting. She examined his bloody, slashed fingers and muttered disgust as her suspicions were confirmed. Another fortune hunter's greed had almost cost him his life—and hers.

"You foolish cur," she spat in Celtic, bandaging his hand with a strip of her hair sash.

When she had finished, she shoved his drenched cloak aside and swept the hair off his face. Her rage dropped to a simmer. Several days beard framed a strong jawbone, while a section of wet dark hair fell across his sun-bronzed forehead, giving him a waggish appeal. Wisps of white hair above his ears revealed him a man of maturity. *Ah, he's quite pleasing,* she admitted, *but still a mule's behind!*

She pulled at the short leather strap about her neck and removed her stinger from its sheath. Holding the dagger over him, she felt safer with her situation. She'd use it if she had to, she resolved.

Her gaze returned to his face. Although there were signs of beard growth, it was obvious the man shaved his facial hair, which meant he was not Anglii, Saxon, or Irish Scotti. *Mayhap he's Welsh,* she surmised, *or Briton.* Her eyes rested on the cleft in the center of his noble chin, and her fingers itched to trace it.

Overhead, the eagle swooped down and perched on a stony out-crop. She looked up and addressed her wild, feathered friend. "So, Mer, what was he doing up there, aye?" She glanced toward the waterfall.

The young eagle chortled and tipped its head cockeyed as if examining the strange wet creature.

"I agree, Mer, only an idiot would dive the falls and wave in passing no less. He was so confident he'd retrieve Excalibur, he was. Humph!"

She jabbed a finger at the stranger's chest and received a guttural groan in response. Rayn jumped and tightened her grip on the stinger.

When he failed to awaken, she relaxed. "Well, I've news for his unworthiness, Mer." She rested on bare knees and proceeded to wring the water from her hair. "'Twas the Creator who ordained Arthur to free Excalibur from the Celtic stone and God who reunited sword to stone when Arthur died, so did the Merdyn proclaim. Why, the whole Isle of Might knows it to be so, it does. What confuses me is why he's still alive. 'Tis a first, I'm sure."

Mer seemed to agree and ruffled his feathers while Rayn bent over the man for closer inspection. By the look of him he was no clansman. Although his clothing showed wear, the sewn pieces were of the finest leathers and wool. Next to catch her gaze were the sheathed stabbing sword and the dagger forged from Roman steel.

"Thunder! A cursed Roman!" she hissed.

It had been nearly a century since Rome had forsaken Britannia, leaving the Britons, including those who resided in southern Caledonia, to fend for themselves. Despite the passage of time, like most Britons, Rayn's feelings for Rome remained anything but cordial—even more so because of her love for the Isle of Might.

Rayn experienced strong foreboding about the stranger, as if worms crawled inside her belly. She didn't like him, yet felt a duty to remain until confident he would live. Being Christ-like often didn't set well with Rayn.

Mer flapped his wings and took to the air.

"Smart bird," she groused, trampling down the high grass around the man to allow the sun's warmth to reach him. Seated again, Rayn relived the terrifying moments beneath Loch Lady as she'd attempted to rescue this outlander. A thought rose foremost in her mind's eye. When she had attempted to break his tight grip on the sword's hilt, for a split second, she'd sworn the sword released from the Celtic stone. Surely, it was her fanciful imagination. In all her years of swimming in the loch, Rayn had never touched the sword of King Arthur. She considered it sacred. The bleached bones scattered about the Celtic stone were witness to the heavenly enchantment placed upon the sword.

The questions remained: Who was this outlander? Why had he, above all the others, survived the rune? Rayn touched his neck. His pulse beat steadily. Still he did not stir, although his chest continued to rise and fall. Inquisitiveness tempted her eyes to rove beyond his muscular chest to his flat stomach, slender hips, and long powerful legs. Rayn had been reared by men and was familiar with their shape, but she'd never examined one with this sort of personal interest.

To her surprise, her cheeks smarted with heat, and she hastily prayed, "Heavenly Da, forgive me, but this Adam of yours is astonishingly fashioned!" Pleasant sensations pulsed through her, and guilt convicted her it was best to leave. A warning growl from behind froze her in place. Slowly, Rayn turned her head toward the wet creature she had assumed to be a dog. In reality it was a black wolf, now advancing upon her with bared fangs. Wolves were uncommon on Wind's Haven, but Rayn reasoned the animal had ventured over with the outlander. Calling on her natural way with God's creatures, she offered her open hand to the wild animal.

"Your master's fine, he is," she spoke with soft reassurance.

The wolf appeared soothed by Rayn's voice, lowered its head, and approached submissively. Relieved, Rayn caressed the wolf, and watched it crouch on the ground between her and its unconscious master.

She sensed another presence. Gazing across the waters, Rayn spotted the woman on the opposite bank. Shrouded by mist and draped in a gown of pale blue stood the Lady un Loch. The lady's attention was upon Rayn. There was an ethereal quality about the lady. As a youth, Rayn had felt apprehension toward her. No longer. Rayn waved, and as was their relationship, the lady nodded. Rayn thought to inform the lady of her find but realized the enchantress already knew. The veiled woman was always cognizant of events on Wind's Haven. No doubt after Rayn left, she would inspect the outlander.

Sailing the air currents overhead, Mer shrieked. Rayn glanced at the sun's position. She'd been gone too long. She must return before her father sent someone after her. Returning to the loch's bank, Rayn glanced back at the handsome outlander. She shivered, sensing they would meet again. It was no coincidence she had saved his life. As always, her Lord Jesu was in control. Rayn just wished she knew what he was up to.

"Glory knows," she muttered heavenward. "I'm not always thrilled about your plans, and . . ." She glared at the comatose man. "I still don't like him!"

⸜⸝

Shadoe struggled between dream and reality. A sweet voice spoke his name with such familiarity that he racked his mind to recall the bearer of that gentle voice. His eyelids fluttered open to behold a beauty, or so he imagined, as her face was hidden behind a white palla that revealed eyes of the brightest azure he'd ever beheld. Shadoe reached out, but his illusive enchantress vanished as he sank back into an abyss of unconsciousness.

Insects buzzed near his ears and stung his face. Shadoe awoke to find himself alone except for Echo, her hind paw scratching her ear as she snapped at the aggravating sand gnats. A shadow fell across him as Destrier trotted over and nudged him. Judging from the missing patches of grass, the Arab stallion had been grazing awhile.

Shadoe leaped up and checked the satchel that hung from Destrier's saddle. His money purse and possessions were undisturbed, and his cloak had been draped across an outcropping to dry. Befuddled, he looked up at the midday sun and pondered the missing time. The last he recalled was an eagle ripping at his back. Flinching, he flexed his sore shoulders and examined his dry, shredded cloak. He realized that had the powerful bird wanted him seriously harmed, it would have succeeded.

His memory returned in confused patches. He felt unsure what had been real and what had been dream. The glimmer of a jeweled hilt passed his mind's eye, causing him to shudder.

He addressed the yawning she-wolf. "So, Echo, did you rescue me or were you assisted?"

The young wolf licked Shadoe's hand in playful jest. "Ah, if you could talk," Shadoe said. "And I suppose you retrieved Destrier and the beautiful woman is no enchantress but human."

Hope tinged his last statement. Echo stretched and rolled in the grass, her sign that she wanted to be petted. Shadoe stared at the loch, trying to understand what had happened. He suddenly recalled the melody the enchantress had been singing. Guenevere's song. A love song Arthur had written for his wife. Only those intimate with the Pendragons ever had the privilege to hear Guenevere sing. *Then who's this mysterious siren, and what is she doing on Wind's Haven?*

The question forced Shadoe to recall the past he preferred to forget. As the winds crested and the sun's warmth faded, he felt less inclined to dismiss the misty memory of the sword at the base of the waterfall, let alone the Lady un Loch. Though reared as a follower of the Fisher of Men, he at times felt the lure of the old Celtic ways and the dark powers of the druids.

"There's logic for everything, Echo. Even this." His attention riveted on the sky blue ribbon bandaged about his two left fingers. "I'll be!" He slipped the bloodstained fabric from his hand and held the ribbon to his nostrils, inhaling a scent of honeysuckle even as he felt the tight ache of his injured hand.

Shadoe examined his wounds and found them deep but clean. "How?" he asked. "Nay, but a sharp rock! A sword would be rusted, but then Excalibur was no ordinary sword and . . ." He didn't want to speculate. Safer not to think about angels and demons or, more importantly, Yahweh.

As Shadoe gazed across the loch, its waters reflecting sun and sky, he realized this was the very spot he and Lancelot had prayed before they released the sword to the waters. He'd not uttered a prayer to God in so long, he didn't know how to start—nor would he now. To pray meant he loved the one living God, Jesu. Worse, it meant commitment, a word that had become foreign to him. Shadoe left Loch Lady and did not look back.

Chapter Eight

CAÉR BELIZAR

TERRIFIED, MORGAUSE LE FEY awoke with a jolt from her slumber. Her eyes darted to the closed door of her chamber. *What foolishness! The guard is right outside. Close your eyes. Sleep.* She could not. Her gaze fastened on the sill of the narrow winnock as if expecting an intruder there, though her tower chamber was a hundred feet above the ground. Edgy, she surveyed her moonlight-drenched apartment.

An ethereal silhouette suddenly blocked the moon's glow. Morgause stared at the horrible apparition, denying its existence, yet knowing it to be real. As the rag-donned creature lumbered toward her, Morgause leaped from the bed and recoiled against her chamber wall.

The hag bent over and picked up a long black feather from the winnock's sill. "Molting are we, sister?" her gentle, feminine voice derided as she let the vulture's feather drift to the floor. "Do you still do a wolf and human? Humph! After all these years, I would think shape shifting had drained the marrow from your bones . . . or have you made another bargain with the Adversary?"

The hag clutched a mantle of tattered, layered veils about her head to conceal her face. Morgause knew the disgusting deformity that lay beneath them.

The hag's words cut into Morgause like jagged razors. "Whose soul this time, sister? Mayhap your own scion's? Is that what you wagered for your magique?"

"Be gone!" Morgause commanded, loathing the tremor of her tongue.

The softer voice goaded, "He's returned, sister. The child you coveted, the child of my womb and Merlin's loins has come to fulfill his destiny and end yours!"

"Nay! I'd have foreseen his return."

"Oh, Morgause, you have feared him since his birth and with good cause. When he was but a child, you tried to lure him to the ancient ways but failed because of his God."

"You asked me to teach him our beliefs and the ways of the druid."

"I have denounced all paganism, sister. I once believed the druid faith represented the balance between good and evil, but we used its incantations to benefit our selfish desires for revenge."

"It was you who wanted to destroy Merlin," Morgause reminded her.

"Aye, I was full of vengeance toward him when he took Shadoe from me. But all he wanted was to protect our scion from the evil that corrupted my heart. The day you sentenced Shadoe to Hell's Gate, you sealed your fate and freed me from mine. But like me, you can be redeemed. Call on the name of the living God. Call on the Christ and live for eternity!"

Morgause gazed upon the disease-eaten flesh of her youngest sister and shuddered with revulsion. "You call what you've become living?" She recalled the fatal day so long ago when Niamh learned that she and Mordred had tortured Shadoe, and then condemned him to Hell's Gate.

Long known as high priestess, Niamh le Fey's influence with the druid-practicing Celts and Picts reached far greater than Morgause's. In fear of her sister's reprisal, Morgause had Niamh abducted and abandoned on a leper colony off the Mediterranean Sea. For years, Morgause believed her sister to be dead. Then three years ago, at Caer Tintagel, she awoke to find this phantom from her past hovering over her as she did tonight at Caer Belizar. Not only had Niamh survived, but she had also converted to Christianity. Better she were dead, Morgause wished, despising the guilt Niamh's presence caused her.

"I cast the scourge of leprosy upon you. And all the time you rot, you proclaim your love and forgiveness toward me. Where is your compassionate God, wee sister? Why hasn't he healed you as you insist he did others? I'll tell you why!" Morgause grew bold and strutted closer. "Because he can't! The Adversary is more powerful than the druid gods, than your God, Jesu. The Prince of Air, Angel of Light, rules this world. The day you rejected him, he took your youth and beauty and gave it to me!"

Niamh coughed painfully, and hoarsely stated, "What you possess is mere illusion. Look upon me. See the reality of your transgressions. See who you really are!" She detached the veils and turned her face into the moon's light.

Morgause shrieked, but no one heard for the terror froze in her throat.

Replacing the veils, Niamh limped toward the winnock, and then turned back toward Morgause. "I accept the cross given me. This decaying body is but a jar of clay for my immortal soul, and I rejoice to know that however brief my days, I have eternity in paradise. You ask why God has not healed me? I do not know his ways. My faith is sufficient, Morgause. The faith of a mustard seed is all that's needed to be saved from an eternity in the abyss."

"Look what your faith has bought you, Niamh." Morgause recalled how their competitiveness had once bonded them in a morbid way. She wanted that back. "We can be together, wee sister. Renounce the Christ, and you will have your beauty, your health, and wealth beyond measure."

Niamh shook her veiled head. "You do not understand. God could release me from this molding flesh anytime. Furthermore, all I need do is ask him."

Settling back on her bed, Morgause gawked at her sister's conviction. "If it's so simple, why haven't you?"

"I have. But I asked that his will be done, not mine."

"And this is his will?" Morgause gestured to Niamh's withered hand, which only had two digits left.

Niamh smiled. "You are afraid, Morgause, but 'tis not me you fear, aye? You sense the Spirit of the Creator within me. He brought me to you. I've come to remind you of pending issues."

"Then on with it." She waved her hand, trying not to look at Niamh, for it disgusted her so.

"Remember, it was two days before Arthur's seventeenth year when he freed Excalibur from the Celtic stone. It has been foretold that in the seventeenth year of the Pendragon's death the rightful heir shall free Excalibur and rule Camelot."

Morgause looked down to find her limbs quaking. "I know the significance of this year; it is for this purpose I've returned with my scion, Arthur's firstborn." Her voice strengthened with conceit. "Mordred shall take the sword from the stone. He will rule as Pendragon!"

"Mordred tried and failed! He's a coward who sent others to their deaths beneath the icy waters of Loch Lady!"

Morgause could not deny this but argued, "He is older and braver."

"And apparently no wiser. Neither of you heeded the words the Merdyn spoke before Arthur went into battle against Vortigern."

"Bah! Merlin was forever spouting predictions. Of which one do you speak?"

"That the Endmost of Ayris blood shall return to the Isle of Might to fulfill the promise long foretold." Holding her cloak over her face, Niamh limped closer. "Long before the fall of Ayris, our Celtic ancestors foresaw the offspring of that great civilization join with our blood-kin. And we know Shadoe un Hollo Tors is the last male descendant of Ayris."

Morgause pulled away, gagging from the stench of her sister's rotting flesh. "Nay! Mordred is the only living descendant, he is the Pen—"

Niamh did not back down. "Is he, sister?" She circled Morgause. "Or is that what you had Arthur believe, what you'd have Mordred believe?"

"You have no proof!"

"I need none. I have been a part of our family's reprisal against the Pendragons since I was old enough to talk. You taught me to hate them as well to desire to be one of them. I remember how you chased Arthur, but he rejected your advances.

"Still, your first passion was Merlin. Your dark heart lusted after him, desired his powers, his bairn. You wanted to be Arthur's queen as well. To achieve that, you needed Merlin on your side. So you lured him—"

"Are you implying I bedded Merlin?" Morgause's tone held incredulity. "And for selfish gain?"

"I don't need to imply. Merlin told me. When his heart was turned from Yahweh by your enchantment, you shared his bed. You swayed him to pressure Arthur to marry you and unite the Celts with the Romano-Britons. When Arthur refused, you drugged him with a lust potion. Thus when he awakened, he found you naked in his arms. What he didn't know was that you were already with babe—Merlin's.

"Mordred is no more Arthur's scion than I am! I regret I allowed your tongue to corrupt Arthur. I regret many things and will no longer let you deceive the innocent, including Mordred. Pitiful Mordred. By now, the potions with which you've poisoned him all these years have weakened his mind and his ability to reason."

"You think anyone will believe you? Bah!" Morgause swept boldly forward, her glare penetrating Niamh's veil. "Mordred has known the truth for years . . . and that to be the scion of the Merdyn is more forcible than being of Arthur's loins. He is the endmost of Ayris, and it is he who will rule Camelot, rule this Isle of Might, and one day the world!"

Niamh scoffed. "Take heed, sister. The prophecy also confirmed a virgin would conceive the endmost of Ayris blood. You were not pure when you slept with Merlin." She appeared to smile beneath her veil. "I was. Thus my scion, Shadoe un Hollo Tors, will join alliance with the Pendragon conceived of Arthur's seed and Guenevere's womb. Together they will be Britannia and Caledonia, they will be this Isle of Might!"

Morgause went rigid with shock as her sister's ominous words took root. "Nay, the bairn is dead!"

"The Adversary cannot destroy the child Yahweh protects. True, you and Mordred slew hundreds of innocent babes, but the Adversary never had one of those children's souls, nor does he possess the heart and soul of the legitimate living Pendragon."

Morgause huffed, "It would seem this Pendragon is nothing without your scion."

"That is where you are mistaken. The Pendragon has the faith, strength, and wisdom of Arthur and Guenevere, as well as a warrior's heart. You would be wise not to underestimate this progeny. So be thoughtful, sister, before you pursue your selfish designs for Arthur's realm. For what are you profited, if you shall gain the whole world, and lose your own soul?"

Before Morgause could answer, a cloud skirted over the tower, and darkness swept across her chamber floor. A moment later the moonlight returned. Niamh le Fey had vanished.

Chapter Nine

FOR NEARLY A WEEK, Shadoe remained on the craggy shores of Wind's Haven. Still, he did not venture to the ruins of Arthur's fortress until last. When it was barely dawn, he hiked the nature-encroached Roman highway toward the gates of the formerly magnificent fortress. Splendor Lost. Summerset. Camelot. Over time, the stone caer had acquired many titles. Of the few Roman structures north of Hadrian's Wall, none could compare to the awesome magnificence of this once proud keep, its singular design found nowhere else on earth. Someday, mayhap, Shadoe mused, a genius architect might reinvent Ayr's advanced blueprint. Now even as the sun crested the sea, slivers of light refracted from the towers. Lined with marble, those towers, aglow with sunlight, had been capable of blinding attacking enemies. The Picts, Scotti, and Saxons had never overthrown Camelot, not until that fateful day Shadoe had yet to forget.

Viewing the fifteen-foot-thick walls, Shadoe felt a pang of regret pierce his breast. The caer had long been abandoned. A tangled mass of overgrowth barred access to the outer courtyard, and the ancient oak and iron gate was barely visible beneath sheets of ivy. Although tempted to enter through one of the ancient underground passages, fear restrained him. Some phantoms were best left undisturbed. Likewise other ghosts he'd rather not encounter. He was not sure what he had thought to find on Wind's Haven, but he had hoped to fulfill his quest here. It had been years since he'd carried on a conversation with God, let alone out loud, but the familiar setting caught him off guard.

"All right, Lord," he confessed. "This is my first attempt since Merlin's death. As expected, I've found no Pendragon heir, no sign of human life on this isle, let alone at Caer Camelot. That, of course, you already knew." Still, he had glimpsed the enchantress for whom he'd earnestly searched. And he'd found Excalibur. He longed to return and free it, but his brush with death remained too fresh. Mayhap, like Arthur, the great sword was not meant to rise again.

The truth about Arthur Pendragon had long been cultivated into myths of dragons, druid magic, and his death—slain by the swords of his own traitorous knights. His real heroic death—in battle against Saxon invaders and Mordred—lie buried beneath legend. Now Merlin's madness about a living Pendragon heir would be added to the fledgling legend. Misery enough that bards sang of Arthur one day returning to reign over the Isle of Might.

Reaching into his satchel, Shadoe retrieved the talisman that spanned the width of his hand. The instant sunlight touched it he was temporarily blinded by the brilliance of gold and jewels. The star burned hot. He muttered an obscenity. "Are you cursed as legend says?" he asked, half-expecting an answer. None came.

He longed to toss the amulet into the sea. Something restrained him. Mayhap guilt for not being steadfast in his search of the Pendragon. If such an heir had existed, Mordred no doubt had eliminated him. Shadoe eyed the sparkling diamonds and flawless emerald at the heart of the gold star. "You could bring a hefty price," he reasoned, knowing full well Merlin would haunt him the rest of his days if he disposed of it. That was no pleasant prospect. Reluctantly, he eased the necklace over his head, slipping the Rose beneath his jerkin. To his surprise, it felt cool, and he chuckled in relief, his superstitious nature dissipating.

For a moment, Shadoe thought about his father's private chamber deep within the soul of the tor upon which Camelot stood. Surely like the deserted halls of Camelot, the contents of the crystal cavern had long ago deteriorated. Besides, there were only two ways into the deep caverns: one through Camelot, the other behind the waterfall of Loch Lady. After his recent encounter with death, Shadoe decided the memoirs of his father were not worth the risk.

Disgusted at the past that was forever gone and at his lack of conviction, Shadoe mounted Destrier. With Echo taking the lead, he turned away from Caer Camelot. His heart heavy, he did not look back. Shadoe left Wind's Haven intending to trek southeast and sail back to Gaul. At the last minute he felt an urgency to visit the hamlet of Ayr on the mainland shore across from the Isle of Wind's Haven.

As he approached the inland bay and shipping port, he saw but two foreign vessels in dock. Furthermore, there was no sign of the once prosperous fishing trade. At the outskirts of the municipality, he was alerted to the depressed atmosphere. The sun seemed lusterless, the sky pewter gray, the clouds murky, and what few colors existed were muted. The fields were unattended, and livestock wandered without supervision.

En route, he passed a ragtag peddler. He pulled his cart heavily laden with wares, the left wheel's axle in need of repair. When Shadoe met the dealer's hollow-eyed gaze, the man abandoned his goods and dashed into the sparse shrubbery as if in fear for his life. The closer his approach to Ayr, the more folks Shadoe encountered. All made a wide path around him, and not one person made eye contact. Not until he had passed by did he hear their low whispers, whispers of fear. Something was strangely wrong.

Though at first optimistic, Shadoe accepted that he would not find the Ayr of his youth, but he was unprepared for the devastating reality. A once proud monument to Roman civilization, Ayr, the prominent city of Romano-British culture, had gone to the devil. The grand villas, once brightly painted, were colorless, their roof tiles broken or missing. Previously framed winnocks were now gaping holes, and the wooden doorways held rotting animal hides. Moreover, the gardens, at one time full of colorful blossoms, were overgrown with weeds and littered with garbage.

It was a fact of history that, after Arthur's death, the treaty with the tribes of Britannia and Caledonia had collapsed. Thus the increasing invasions from the Irish Scotti and the Saxons had left the Briton citizens in violent turmoil. Shadoe had seen the horrific results traveling to Ayr, yet he had somehow imagined the demesne of Camelot would have miraculously survived. But Ayr's outer fortress walls were neglected, huge sections of timbers missing. That no one had attempted to rebuild the defensive barriers proved more depressing. It was as if the inhabitants of Ayr had accepted their fate. They no longer cared.

Still, a feverish excitement choked the air, and that wasn't all. The stench of human waste overflowed the neglected Roman sewer system. Gagging, Shadoe was forced to hold his breath while he and Echo dodged the increased traffic. Despite the city's horrid conditions, milling bodies revealed Ayr was inhabited and still a trade center of the western coast. Voices carried on the air along with the comforting fragrances of baked bread wafting from the ovens. Further inside the unmanned walls, smoke rolled skyward from a smithy's fired forge. A large-boned ironsmith was mending a sword blade. The song of metal on metal rang clear in the damp spring air. Shadoe halted while the sweat-drenched man expertly turned the crimson red blade on his anvil. Shadoe tipped his head in greeting.

The craggy-faced ironsmith paused, hammer in mid-stroke, his dark eyes laced with terror. "Err isna a blade, Me Lord . . . truly it isna. Just a plow's tongue I be fixin'," he hedged.

Realizing the ironsmith's eyes were fastened on Shadoe's armor and weapons, he nodded reassurance and rode on. He felt the man's anxious gaze bore into his back. The familiar chime of Ayr's large bell snatched his attention, and the citizens moved like herded cattle in its direction.

Riding cautiously into the heart of the city, he noted the tattered rags most of its inhabitants wore and the strange absence of youth. Countless eyes sent cautious looks his way, but no one approached him. The largest gathering appeared near the heart of the city's main throughway, the community well. The ancient stone foundation raised five steps from the center of the hamlet's square. Here, folks came not only to fill their urns with fresh spring water but also to converse. When public announcements were made, the ancient bell above the well would ring as it now did. The bell's clang ceased, only to be replaced by disconcerted voices in heated exchange.

"I tell you they're all dead!" exclaimed one woman. "Slain by Mordred's Saxon hellhounds."

"Nay, I canst believe that!"

"Well, 'twas a foolish plan, those old hermits spying on Mordred's camp, and worse tae make soldiers o' fishermen and herdsmen. Our men folk have no experience in the art o' war. Aye, we best pay the tribute before the Saxons burn our villas as well."

"Tribute with what? Mordred has stolen our best crops, livestock, and boats. He takes our men as well. I hear King Hengist rides with him."

"Hengist! His lands are in southern Britannia. What brings him this far north?"

"Rumors say 'tis tae wage war against the Scotti and Picts, not us! 'Tis Mordred we should fear."

"I knew his return would bring bloodshed! Arthur should have slain Mordred when he slew Vortigern."

"Aye," an older man bellowed, "we canna accept this fate. We'll attack."

"With what—pitchforks?" The wrangling continued.

Shadoe urged Destrier farther into the crowd, drawing attention with Echo alongside him.

"Look there!" a hag called out.

"God be merciful. Galahad has returned. . . ."

Shadoe jerked around, expecting to see Galahad behind him as middle-aged and elderly men, mothers and children rushed him. ". . . and with a wolf!"

A scraggly bearded, toothless man clamped onto Shadoe's leg.

"Milord, is it really you? Rumor had it you'd been slain in the south by the Jutes!"

Shadoe tugged free of the stranger and rode to where other citizens gathered around a motley band of warriors, some on horseback, most on foot. The wounded also waited. The remnants of Ayr's defense had returned, and what he beheld was not promising. Only a handful wore armor, and those who did were lucky if they had a chest plate; none had back plate or helm. A dozen at best had shields. The others wore the traditional bright Celtic paint across their faces, arms, and legs, bright colors muted with blood and mud.

Shadoe urged Destrier forward, and the crowd parted like the Red Sea. Above them an eagle circled, and then perched upon a nearby rooftop overlooking the assembly. Shadoe stared at the large raptor, and scratched his jaw, recalling the golden eagle that had attacked him. The clamor of the crowd reclaimed his attention.

Near the well, a slender young warrior leaped off of a laboring, dapple-gray war-horse. After removing his battered helm and armor, he tugged a Phrygian felt cap over sweat-plastered hair and acknowledged familiar faces in the gathering. The warrior seemed to have the interest of the citizens and villeins. A leader no doubt. From his perch atop Destrier, Shadoe noted the young man's confident long-legged stride, which carried him up the steps of the well. Caked blood stained his tunic and breeches, and his soiled facial features were barely visible beneath the blue paint that streaked his face.

At the base of the well, two men in hooded cloaks stood on either side of their leader. At that moment, a woman wearing a yellow palla of fine woven linen strode forward and embraced the warrior. The dignified lady turned and heatedly chastised the older companions. By her actions, Shadoe assumed she was the warrior's mother. There was something familiar about this petite, dark-haired woman with noble bearing. Even though he could not discern her low tones as she berated the men, for unknown reasons Shadoe felt drawn to her.

When the warrior raised a gloved hand, the crowd ceased its murmuring, the irate woman included. Shadoe was mildly impressed by this leader's formidable and commanding presence.

"My fellow Celts and Britons . . ."

Shadoe frowned. The warrior's soft-pitched voice revealed he still wavered between youth and manhood.

The lad continued. "I return with grim tidings. Our men fought bravely, but many fell to Mordred's army, they did."

Wails from grievous wives and mothers thickened the air.

"What of the Silver Lion?" One man called out above the sobs.

"Aye, is his leg holding him up?"

Shadoe stiffened. Silver Lion! What were the odds?

Silence followed before the stripling said with an unsteady voice, "The Lion is a captive of Mordred Pendragon."

Greater wails scorched Shadoe's ears.

One man shouted, "Then we'll free him!"

"How?" countered another.

Many agreed.

Some bickered.

Shadoe looked at the pathetic assembly. They couldn't defend themselves, let alone attempt a rescue. Even worse seemed the possibility that the Silver Lion they referred to was none other than Sir Lancelot. Shadoe frowned, his memories of Lancelot's cunning ever vivid. What chance was there that the legendary warrior lived within view of Camelot's ruins? If true, the Pendragon might also be near. The moment Shadoe thought of the Pendragon, the Rose felt uncomfortably warm against his chest. *My duty to Father is nearly complete.* He attempted to slip into the background.

"Sire?" The toothless man singled Shadoe out. "We know you are eager to rescue your father. Let us help? We'll fight to the death, we will." Cheers of unity rose from the crowd.

The warrior at the well shot a look across to Shadoe. Their gazes locked, and for an instant Shadoe thought to know those eyes. The man leaped down and brandished a large fighting staff, and then approached Shadoe with long, disciplined strides. "You there!"

"'Tis him, Lady Rayn," the toothless man insisted.

Lady? Shadoe stared at her blood-soiled tunic and muttered, "Hardly."

"Aye, Sir Galahad has returned to help, he has!" another villager cried out.

The mannish-clad girl peered up at Shadoe with suspicion. "You're not Galahad!" she proclaimed with confidence, though her features paled beneath her battle grime.

"Nor do I claim to be." Shadoe chuckled.

"He's no doubt a Saxon infiltrator. Toss him into the well." The scrap of a girl pinned him with an accusatory gaze.

Shadoe attempted to turn Destrier away, but dozens of hands dismounted him. He hit the earth with a painful thud but came up swinging and sent three men sailing through the air. Beside him, Echo growled, hackles raised and fangs bared. Shadoe didn't blink when his Arab stallion pawed the earth, and then charged the incoming swarm. When Lady Rayn's weary warriors surrounded him, Shadoe tossed them off, and drawing his sword, advanced on her with Echo at his heels. "I am no spy!"

"An outlander, you are," she charged, not backing down.

The dark silhouette of the swooping bird distracted him. "Not every outlander is a spy." He slammed his fist in another Briton's face and kicked him aside. The eagle dived low enough that Shadoe tucked his head. Echo leaped as if to claim the flying predator for lunch, but missed.

"Then worse, you are a bleeding Roman!" She spit into the dust and challenged him with a glower of disgust. The crowd supported her with jeers. She advanced.

Shadoe had never met such a brazen maiden. He was slightly impressed and greatly annoyed. "Wrong again." He stepped closer, his sword aimed at her heart. "One more guess and you lose." His lips curled into a sneer.

"Whist, you fight like a Celt, you do." She braced her quarterstaff in self-defense.

"Because I am!" he growled in Gaelic and closed in on her. Dust danced between them. The girl did not retreat but waved aside those villagers who charged Shadoe with pitchforks.

"No one comes to Ayr by choice, Sir."

"No doubt." Shadoe's voice thickened with disdain as he lowered his blade, keeping a cautious eye on those encroaching his space. He glanced skyward to find the predator bird nowhere in sight. "I seek the Silver Lion."

Angry voices shrilled.

"Silence!" Rayn set her quarterstaff upright. "Let him speak." She addressed him, "Who are you?"

"Shadoe un Hollo Tors." His gaze shifted to the familiar staff she gripped.

"Un Hollo Tors?" she mocked. "There is but one who bears that given name, and you're not he."

"No, I'm not the Merdyn." He looked her straight on and challenged her with a smug expression.

The dark-cloaked men approached and stood on either side of the female warrior. The noblewoman followed, still jabbering.

"The august enchanter has been dead seventeen winters or more," one man snapped from beneath his hood.

His threat did not divert Shadoe. Towering over the girl, he tipped his head until his lips almost brushed the tip of her soot-greased nose. "He died one year and three months ago in my arms."

"Nay!" She shook her head and stumbled back against one of her companions. The noblewoman rushed over and drew the stunned girl into her arms. Curious, Shadoe strolled forward, but the larger man barred him access and emitted a barrel-chested growl. After a few moments, the girl shook free of her companion and glared into Shadoe's eyes. Despite the tremble of emotion to her voice, her derision was undeniable. "Whist, you expect me to believe you are the scion of Merlin un Hollo Tors?"

"Believe what you will. Tell me where the Silver Lion can be found," he hotly demanded, "and I'll take my leave."

Angry shouts ignited the crowd, and one of the robed men stepped between him and the girl Rayn. The younger of the two men and the noblewoman whispered to her.

Glaring at Shadoe, her approach remained frosty, "Follow us!" She stalked off with the other man.

Shadoe had had enough. He'd find Lancelot on his own. He mounted Destrier and turned the agitated steed away. Echo joined him.

She turned and called out, "Do you not seek Lancelot du Lac?"

Shadoe glared down from his saddle. "Yes. Where is he?"

"Obviously not here," she snorted.

"I can see that!" He wanted to bruise her behind.

"He's held prisoner at Caer Belizar."

Shadow felt bile rise in his throat. "So what would you know of the man?"

"Everything. He's my da, he is."

"Humph!" He cantered behind the foursome in the direction of a modest, thatch-roofed villa.

Before he could ponder the situation further, the air shrilled with the cry of the eagle. All eyes shot heavenward, and the assembly grew vocal as if the bird alerted them to some impending doom. Another breath later, the ground shook with the thunder of horses' hooves.

"Saxons!" a woman cried out.

Someone ascended the well wall and struck the bell.

A regiment of fierce-looking horsemen galloped into the square, their blades drawn as their leader called out, "We seek the one named Rayn du Lac . . . and the others who slaughtered women and children at our encampment."

"The lying snake!" Rayn charged toward the mounted Saxons. Her companions raced to stop her. As she sped by, Shadoe alighted Destrier and swept her to him. Pinning his hand over her mouth, he ordered, "Quiet! Unless you want to die!"

Rayn hit and kicked as he dragged her behind a villa and into an alleyway. Her friends followed. Her teeth found the soft leather below his thumb, and Shadoe cursed. Angered, he jerked her slender frame against his chest and heard her breath burst from her lungs.

One of the armed Britons slipped back to retrieve her mare, while the other insisted with a low, raspy voice, "You must leave, Rayn." He pointed to the cavity in the northern fortress wall a hundred feet away. "And you, Sir Shadoe, escort her."

Shadoe rolled his eyes and snorted. With one arm about her diminutive waist, he sucked the blood she'd drawn from his palm and spit it out. The brat continued to squirm and sputter Celtic that burned even Shadoe's mature ears.

The second armed man ignored Rayn's antics and addressed the noblewoman. "Stay out of sight. I'll be back." He merged into the crowd and left Shadoe with his arms full of the squirming fireball.

The dark-haired woman in the yellow palla addressed Rayn. "Now, sweetness, you know he's right. You must go while you can."

"Not you, too!" The ragamuffin tussled with Shadoe and breathlessly inquired of her female companion, "You . . . you really believe this imbecile is Mer's scion?"

The noblewoman's tensed features softened as she assessed Shadoe. "I see a favor of Merlin about him." She paused. "Only if he answers correctly will I believe he is Shadoe un Hollo Tors." He felt her challenging gaze.

"As a boy, Shadoe had many pets."

"I had one. A bear cub."

The noblewoman's lips curled up, until Rayn huffed, "Whist! Anyone could know that." Then she nailed him in the left shin.

Pain shot through his calf. "Blast it! What do you want from me, blood?"

"It could be arranged," she snarled, writhing harder.

"Was the cub male or female?" Iona prodded.

"A lass!" Shadoe glared.

"And did you have any mishaps with the cub?" The noblewoman continued as if Rayn were no more than a pesky fly.

"Several." He scowled, trying to contain the slippery minx. He had no idea someone so small could be so strong.

The noblewoman narrowed her brown gaze. "I'd like a specific example."

"Mercy!" He racked his mind. "Aye. It was my duty to keep her out of the food pantry. I failed. She made a mess. Guen and Iona were so angry, they drizzled honey on me and let the cub lick me clean—with an audience, no less. While fleeing the rambunctious cub, I slid and fell into a pile of dung." He felt the brat giggle against him.

"Iona laughed so hard she began to cry," Shadoe continued. "Aye, Iona was almost as pretty as Guenevere but five seasons my senior." He scrutinized the woman as intently as she did him. "I fancied her until she dubbed me—"

"Honey?" she suggested.

"Nay." He arched an inquisitive brow. "'Twas Puwee."

"Aye!" she exclaimed, clapped her hands, and leaped in the air.

"I do not believe this. Ow!" Rayn sputtered as Shadoe tightened his grip beneath her ribs and jerked upward, silencing her.

"Lady Iona du Maur?" He labored harder to keep the feisty worm in tow. "Glory, I feared you'd died at Mordred's hand."

"I escaped with Lance and the others." Iona smiled. "Aye, he's Puwee, he is." She reached around Rayn and tweaked his blue-shadowed cheek.

"Glory, I loath that!" He flinched.

Iona's bonnie smile grew wider. "Ah, he hasna changed." She grinned at Rayn and asserted, "Aye, I've no doubt."

"Well, I have!" Rayn tagged him hard in the ribs with her elbow.

Pain shot through Shadoe. He dropped her so fast she hit the ground, grunting with pain and shock. Shadoe dismissed her with a curse.

Destrier pawed the earth and snorted. Shadoe caught the reins, ran a comforting hand down the horse's damp neck, and said in a soothing tone, "Quiet, lad." He glanced about, noting Echo was nowhere in sight. If the wolf was smart, she'd fled—something Shadoe wished he himself had done. From the edge of his vision, he saw Iona peering around the corner of the villa wall. Leaving Destrier, he rushed over and clamped onto her forearm to pull back. The woman shrugged him off and gestured to two children stranded in the dangerous thoroughfare. "We must get them!"

Before Shadoe could snatch hold of her again, Rayn raced out into the dangerous skirmish. A curse burning his lips, he withdrew his sword and tore after her. Dodging skittish horses and armed Saxons, Shadoe ran to the older child, Rayn to the younger. He scooped up the youngster in one arm. With the other, he thrust his blade into the back of a Saxon who tussled with Rayn as she swept up the toddler. Sidestepping horse hooves and clashing swords, Shadoe and Rayn fled back into the haven of the alley.

After speaking softly to the youngster, Rayn handed the child to Iona but made no gesture of appreciation for Shadoe's gallantry. Instead she stood in full view of the town square.

"Rayn, come away from there!" Iona insisted. She took the child from Shadoe and then sung softly to the little ones.

In a few long strides, Shadoe yanked Rayn behind the villa. "You are gallingly dull-witted!"

"And you are a mule's rear." She swung a closed fist at his jaw, but he ducked and unceremoniously dragged her farther into the alley before letting go.

Rayn rubbed her wrist and glared up at him with admirable defiance. Shadoe experienced a perverse pleasure in her challenge. He ignored her and strained to hear over the pandemonium in the streets. The Saxon commander ordered his men, "Search the villas; then torch them. Leave none standing until you find the one called Rayn!"

"Demon's dung! I'm not going to hide while my clansmen die!" Rayn drew up her quarterstaff and shifted to step around Shadoe.

His patience expired, Shadoe snatched her wrist and single-handedly shoved her against the exterior defense wall. "You will do as told," he growled, and yanked the staff from her grip so fast and hard, he felt her flinch.

"I despise you!" She glared into his eyes with loathing.

"The feeling's mutual, brat."

"You're nothing like your father," she countered.

"How would you know?"

Her lips twitched before she smiled. "Because I knew him better than you ever did."

A stinger to his heart would have been less painful. "What I wouldn't give to put you over my knee and—"

"Enough!" Iona hissed as she came alongside them. "We don't need to be found out, now do we?"

"Iny, make him release me." Rayn sent a pleading look to the older woman.

"Only if you promise to behave," Iona insisted.

"Aye," Rayn muttered like a chastised child.

The noblewoman nodded, and Shadoe reluctantly complied.

Rayn wrung her wrist and put her back to them.

Shadoe scowled at Iona, who merely shrugged. "She really has a good soul, Shadoe."

"Oh . . . she has one?"

Iona clucked her tongue, and turned her attention to the frightened children.

Around the corner and less than three hundred feet away, the skirmish escalated. Shadoe didn't have to see the bloody battle to know what was happening. Brave Britons and Celts were attempting to defend their homes. Shadoe struggled with conscience. He was an expert swordsman. He should be fighting instead of babysitting a half-pint wildcat.

A few minutes later, the air crackled and flames shot skyward as Ayr was set on fire. Battle cries burdened the smoke-hazed air. Women wailed. Children cried out. Shadoe knew the innocent were meeting a bloody demise at the end of a Saxon's blade. He could bear it no more.

Brandishing his sword, he headed for the main street just as the female warrior drew her stinger and single-handedly wielded the six-foot staff like a deadly weapon. *So, the brat intends to fight, does she?* With the wounds she inflicted on him still aching, he decided to let her.

Iona blocked his way. "Please, Shadoe, get her out of here?"

"I don't like her," he groused and glanced past Iona at the torched city.

"And I love her," Iona insisted, searching his eyes. "Besides you owe me, Puwee." She winked and, with kids in tow, fled down the back alley away from the impending danger.

"Hey, wait!" he called out, only to be distracted by Rayn's warrior cry.

Her quarterstaff in midair, Rayn was about to charge into the street, but Shadoe lashed out, snatched her into his arms, and turned to toss her onto Destrier's saddle.

"They can't die because of me!" she protested, swinging her staff at his head.

"Glory, but I detest smug gallantry." He yanked the stinger from her right hand.

"How dare you imply . . ." Her fist pummeled his face.

Shadoe snatched her forearm, jerked it behind her, and then hissed, "Imply that you are not the sole reason these barbarians slaughter everything in sight?" He matched her glint with his own.

Rounding the villa with Rayn's mare, one of her cloaked comrades argued, "He's right, maiden. Your surrender will not stop this massacre." He pulled the staff from her hand and slipped the weapon into the leather sheath of her saddle. Shadoe released her only to have the older man counter her defiance with paternal patience. "Trust me, Rose Rayn. Go with him." He nodded to Shadoe.

"And you . . ." The raspy-voiced man clenched Shadoe's arm. "Protect her, Apprentice Enchanter."

"What the—" Shadoe yanked off the hood that had camouflaged the man's features. The ruddy complexion, the thatch of fading blond hair engrossed Shadoe's gaze. "Sir Tristam, you old boar, I should have known that voice!"

Tristam nodded with a twisted smile.

When the other man dropped his hood, Shadoe dumbly acknowledged, "Perceval?"

The younger of the two knights slapped Shadoe affectionately between the shoulder blades.

"Wait! You know this man?" Rayn gaped.

"Aye, Mistress. He is Merlin's scion . . . and best you trust him. Now take advantage of this chaos and ride. We'll meet near the causeway at sun rest."

Begrudgingly, Rayn hoisted herself onto her dapple-gray mare.

"Where's Iona?" Perceval looked anxiously about the alley.

"She fled with some children." Shadoe swung himself into his saddle and gripped the reins.

"I should help her!" Rayn pointed her mount in the direction of the alley.

"We'll find her." Tristam tossed off his cloak to reveal a full suit of Roman armor. "Go now. The mercenaries are closing in." Before Rayn could contend, he slapped her mare's haunches and sent her galloping off.

"Listen up," Shadoe asserted. "I've one goal. To find Arthur's rightful heir."

"Then keep that filly in sight." Perceval tipped his head in Rayn's direction.

Navigating his stallion about face, he balked at his old friends. "You can't be serious!"

Perceval winked.

Tristam grinned.

"Wait! Don't answer that!"

Growling a curse, Shadoe put his spurs to Destrier's flanks and tore off.

The knights turned their attention toward the raiders. Perceval glanced back with further advice for Shadoe, but Tristam stopped him. "Do not weary yourself, friend. Too late it is."

Perceval sighed as they brandished swords to defend their fellow citizens. "Then it has begun," he said with acceptance.

"Aye," Tristam added and sliced into the belly of a charging Saxon. "And God be merciful to all who survive this test of faith."

"Especially those two." Perceval dodged a burning arrow and nodded in the direction of the two riders. "I don't know which of them needs our prayers most."

"Somehow . . ." Tristam huffed, put down another Saxon, and slit the warrior's throat, "I think we should pray for the apprentice."

As they became surrounded, Perceval put his back against his friend's. "Aye, he hasn't a clue to the hell she can make of his life." His sword clanged against that of a foe's. "Nor of the heavenly bliss."

Tristam chuckled and drew the buried hilt of his dagger from a mercenary's ribs, then turned his sword on another.

"'Twill take a godly man to tame that shrew," Perceval said between gasps. His Celt brother shoved an adversary into his ready blade.

"Then pray Merlin tutored his apprentice well."

"And I suggest we pray that we live to see it unfold."

Tristam rolled his eyes, and they prayed in unison for all to hear: "To Jesu the Christ be the glory and the honor, to Jesu our lives entrust."

Chapter Ten

SHADOE BARELY KEPT pace with Rayn's furious gallop through the woodlands and bogs. She obviously intended to lead him on a fool's chase—whether to elude the Saxons or himself, he wasn't certain. She turned and headed down to the shoreline and passed the neglected shipping piers.

Destrier now glided across the unfamiliar surf and sand, and it took Shadoe's firm hand to keep the Arab from overtaking the smaller, powerful charger Rayn expertly rode. She changed course again to gallop across the deteriorating causeway to Wind's Haven. Shadoe wondered what she thought to accomplish by this escapade, considering he knew the island better than anyone.

∽

After Rayn pounded onto the isle's stony shore, she reined in her mare and glanced back. Her adversary was tightening the gap. Flustered, she gulped a breath, sank her heels into the horse's flanks, and tore off again. *Glory!* She should have gone straight for Belizar, where her father was held prisoner. Trouble was, she didn't know the route. She also needed supplies and hadn't expected the enchanter to hold his own. Heading up the steep bank toward the tors, Rayn headed into the dense pines, intending to reach her destination without Shadoe un Hollo Tors underfoot.

She rode some distance and at last reached the hidden passage into the highest tor of Wind's Haven. Once inside, she sat silent upon her winded mare, awaiting the thud of hooves on the soft forest floor. When she heard not even the chirp of a bird, she allowed the young charger to trot the familiar dark maze of passages. Ten minutes later, Rayn felt confident she had lost Shadoe. She hoped he hadn't been foolish enough to enter the caverns. Odds were not favorable that he'd find his way out. Evicting him from her thoughts, she reined within a stone's throw of the hollow's south wall, illuminated by a sputtering wall torch.

Rayn dismounted and watched the horse canter to its manger of feed. Only then did her warrior senses alert her. The torch was already lit! Rayn pivoted about, wielding the long wood staff with the expertise of a swordsman.

"Hey, you're going to hurt someone!" a male voice charged.

Rayn leaped back. The phantom moved within the shadows, the contours of his face indistinguishable. "That I'll do, you foul vermin!" She swung the tar-sealed staff at his chest. He shot out an arm and blocked her attack, but she slammed his right shoulder and sent him off balance, giving her the advantage. A deadly growl was the only warning before the wolf leaped between them, fangs exposed, and haunches arched.

"Drop the staff, Princess," the man gruffly commanded. "Echo eats anyone who threatens my health, even with a stick."

Rayn ignored the wolf's warning. "Shadoe un Hollo Tors!" She flipped her staff upright between her hands, careful not to further upset the riled creature.

"Thanks." Shadoe patted Echo's head. "Good girl."

"Whist, don't patronize me!"

Shadoe chuckled. "I meant the wolf. You, on the other hand, are indeed bad." He jerked the staff from her grip so fast that her palms burned.

"Ow! Give it back."

Shadoe dismissed her demand and examined the steel-hard wood staff. "You handle yourself well, Princess."

"It's lighter than a sword, it is," she muttered warily.

"But just as deadly. The Picts are experts with the staff, and you seem to be as well, Princess."

It had been nearly three years since anyone had used the endearment of *princess* toward Rayn. Her heart lurched, recalling this outlander's adamant pronouncement that Merlin was dead. She shook off her melancholy and focused on Shadoe. "I can defend myself."

"No doubt," he said, flexing his bruised shoulder.

Rayn felt concern for his injury but refused to display sympathy.

"It's a mite large for someone so small."

"I'm used to it," she defended, disturbed by his interest in her weapon. Despite the poor lighting, she could see the deliberation on his face.

"It's very old," he said more to himself than to her. He traced a finger over the Hebrew inscriptions carved into the upper half of the staff. "How did you acquire this?" he demanded.

His insolence provoked her. "Give it back!" she challenged.

"Answer me," he demanded, his timbre unyielding, his tempered gaze cold as stone.

She eyed the staff and pondered how right he looked holding it. "You won't believe me." She shrugged her indifference.

"Try me," he ground out.

"'Twas a gift, it was."

His dogged glint prodded her.

"Merlin . . . ," she murmured.

"Merlin what?"

". . . gave it to me," she said with rigid jaw.

"All right." He tossed the staff to her, and she caught it in a fluid motion.

"You believe me?" She set the staff upright and gaped at him.

"Aye."

"Just like that?"

"This is the Merdyn's staff, so unless you're lying about how you came to own it, this discussion is finished."

"I don't lie." She stared at him, wondering why she felt the need to defend her claim to what was hers. Mayhap, because he claimed to be the son of the great sage. Hunkering down, she gestured Echo to come.

Shadoe shook his head. "I'd not do that. You just threatened me. Wolves have good memories."

"I know." She set her gaze on the beautiful creature.

Echo dropped her head and charged Rayn.

"Echo stop!" Shadoe intervened too late.

Rayn fell back, giggling, while the large wolf licked her face.

Stunned, Shadoe leaned against the damp stonewall. "'Tis a first!"

Rayn hugged the wolf and leaped to her feet. "Animals can sense whether or not a human is threatening or scared." She smirked with the realization she had one up on this enchanter.

"Aye," he responded, eyeing her suspiciously. "Then again, the druids also have ways with creatures of the wild."

Rayn laughed. She liked that he felt leery of her. Still, any comparison with the druids was not considered a compliment. "I follow the Fisher of Men, Enchanter. Any gifts I have come from Yahweh."

"Are you saying there are more?" He stepped closer as if to inspect her.

Flustered by his proximity, she gestured toward the wall torch. "How did you arrive before me, aye?"

"This was my home . . . once." He shrugged taut shoulders and advanced, scratching his chin as if puzzled.

"Of course," she muttered, pressing against the cavern wall. There were but a handful of men still knowledgeable of the island's underground maze.

"I found human remains along the Dragon's Back." He gestured behind them.

Rayn's eyes widened. "No one but Arthur's chosen knew of—"

"That entrance?"

"Aye," she whispered with awe.

The light flickered across his face, revealing a confident smirk that confirmed why she could trust and still dislike him. His egotism boiled her blood. She rubbed the pulsing vein in the center of her forehead. This same man had tried to steal Excalibur. Her trust wavered; her dislike elevated.

"Why would anyone be silly enough to believe they could enter these cursed hollows and get out alive?" he remarked.

Stepping clear of him, she rolled a shoulder. "Legends of treasure can bring out the worst in men, Sir." *But that you know.*

He scratched his blue-shadowed jaw and gestured about them. "Seems I missed something during my absence. Just what treasures are hidden here, Princess?"

Rayn could not believe his audacity . . . pretending to know nothing of the treasured sword . . . unless he did not realize it was she who had rescued him from the hilt of Excalibur at Loch Lady. "Whist, cease calling me *princess*. And legends are based upon rumor, Sir, and rumors upon supposition." She strolled boldly around him toward the wall torch.

"You sound like the Merdyn," he bellowed, following on her heels.

"Then you compliment me, Sir."

"By a hair's breadth," he groused.

She spun about and glared at him.

He glared back.

Words perched on her lips, uncharitable ones at that. How could such a striking man be so outrageously rude? How in glory's name could he be Merlin's son? He was nothing like Merlin! Rayn knew first-hand that God had a sense of humor. Nevertheless, if Shadoe un Hollo Tors was God's idea of a joke, she wasn't laughing. Not certain who won the stare-down, she removed the torch and turned the wall's bronze mounting counter-clockwise.

"Now what?"

"The tide will be in shortly, and I need provisions, I do."

"And your point is?" He lifted a brow of annoyance.

"When Mordred left Camelot, he cut the dikes and aqueducts that controlled flow of the sea beneath the causeway. Hence 'tis submerged at high tide, which is less than an hour from now."

"You are enlightening, Princess."

"So many have said. Once again my name is not *princess*. 'Tis Rayn."

"Well, you act like a highborn. All posh and mighty, giving orders; even Tristam, Perceval, and Iona submit to you. No doubt Lancelot does the same, aye?"

Rayn pivoted and looked fiercely into his insolent expression. "Listen here, Sir Windbag. I'm no highborn. I am the daughter of Sir Lancelot du Lac, one of the greatest warriors to ever pay you heed. Whatever respect my companions allow me is due only to their honor for my father. We are family. As for Iona, she has been mother, sister, and best friend to me. I love her, Tristam, and Percy, I do. And despite your perception, no less honor do I give them, and you should do likewise, you should."

"There's no way you can enter Belizar and escape alive."

Taken aback by his wide turn in subject, Rayn gawked at his cavalier response. It took a moment for her to regroup. "Well, there's one way to find out, isn't there?" When she heard him swear, she offered her back. The wall slid across the floor, revealing a narrow passageway. As she entered, Rayn noticed that, although Echo did not hesitate to follow, her master held back.

"Are you coming, Enchanter?"

He snarled something disrespectful to God.

"What do you fear? Surely not me."

"Hardly." He stepped into the gloomy passageway. "I loath tight places."

"But you grew up here."

"Doesn't mean I liked it."

She halted in her tracks. *Ah, he wasn't as poised as he portrayed. That made him likable.* Rayn didn't fancy that. "Do you know where we're headed?"

"Aye, and I don't care about that, either."

"You're a strange man, Shadoe un Hollo Tors."

"At least I'm not dull-witted."

"I prefer tenacious." She laughed softly and tramped the dark serpentine passage up into the mountain.

The music of Rayn's mirth caused Shadoe to pause. She lifted the torch and glanced back. For a moment they stared into each other's eyes. It was a most bewildering exchange, and Shadoe wished to know what she looked like with a freshly scrubbed face. Her eyes were definitely not the sapphire-blue of his enchantress but instead the deepest hue of emeralds he'd ever beheld.

Rayn broke the spell. "The war room's entrance is just ahead." She took the lead.

He nodded, and although the corridor was damp, he felt unusually warm. Shadoe distracted himself by noting the obvious lack of spider webs or bats. The passage was used a lot. That disturbed him.

Minutes later, Rayn set the torch into another wall mount, lit a taper from its fire, and slid ajar an opening to reveal a dark chamber. Soon she had lit enough terra-cotta oil lamps to give the room a soft glow. Echo squeezed passed them into the war room. The hair along her hackles rose on end. Growling, she backed out and sat close to Shadoe at the threshold.

The animal's behavior alerted Shadoe. His breath hitched in his throat. His pulse quickened. The innate discernment he had not experienced in years washed over him. "You're sure no one else is here?"

Rayn seemed to accept the wolf's odd conduct. "Not living anyway."

Wary, he arched a brow at her before patting the anxious wolf's head. Echo refused to enter, panting as if frightened. Although he didn't like Echo's reaction, Shadoe strolled about the large chamber in an effort to dismiss the regenerated spiritual sensors he wished he no longer possessed.

"The inner keep is in total disorder save for a few chambers such as this," Rayn explained as she lit more lamps until the room warmly brightened.

The additional light seemed to lessen the spiritual discomfort Shadoe felt. He ambled over to the Round Table, its granite surface layered with dust and debris. He recalled how gossipmongers had twisted the truth about this war table.

For truth, King Arthur's Round Table was not round. While carved from stone, the famed table was long and narrow. The phrase *knights of the Round Table* identified the knighted chieftains and officers of King Arthur's realm who met in a round, or gathering, to discuss military issues and strategies. Plenty of rounds, though, had consisted of plain old revelry.

Shadoe approached the ornate wall cabinet and opened the squeaking door. Surprise burned Shadoe's lips, but he tried to remain calm as his gaze took in the familiar rolled parchments that occupied the shelves.

Lifting a scroll, he blew off the dust and carefully opened it. "Mercy! These are Arthur's defense strategies. I'd thought Mordred would have taken anything that wasn't nailed down."

"Da said Mordred left in a hurry and never returned." Rayn's full lips curved into a smile. "The caer may be tarnished from neglect, but everything is as it was, as it should be."

The finality of her voice unsettled him. Respectfully, he replaced the scroll, shut the cabinet's door, and scowled. "The splendor of this once great keep is forever lost, Lady Rayn, and is why the pagans call it *Splendor Lost.*"

Rayn crossed her arms over her chest and spoke with powerful conviction. "Nay! There shall come a time . . . if for only the flash of an angel's wing . . . Camelot shall . . ."

Quirking a brow, he looked at her. "Shall what?"

Despite the layers of bluish lye, dirt, and blood, her cheeks deepened in color. She turned from him. "Forgive me, Sir. Sometimes I get carried away. I've a romantic heart, I have."

Shadoe smiled to himself. *A romantic heart? Who'd have thought the boyish-clad brat contemplated such whimsy?* He shifted his attention and strolled to the high-rise chair where Arthur once sat and discussed battle strategies with his men. He felt Rayn's fixed gaze. Lazily he dragged his fingertips along the worn arms of the oaken chair and the insignia of Arthur Pendragon carved into its high, straight back. Bittersweet memories assailed him. Shadoe's eyes watered; his brow tensed. The muscle along his jaw quivered, and he turned away but feared Rayn had glimpsed his sentimental reaction. As a desperate distraction, he brushed the dirt off the seat.

"Don't you dare!" Rayn called out.

Shadoe swiveled his head in her direction. "Dare what?"

"Sit there!" Her staff lifted in threat, she stalked toward him as if to engage in battle.

He straightened to find her coral lips drawn tight, her green eyes blazing with rage. He was amused and intrigued. "That, Princess, I would never do."

"But you were—"

"Cleaning it," he explained. "After all, this is the seat of the greatest Briton warrior ever known. I was merely showing my respect." He placed his hand about hers that held the staff in attack position and slowly but forcefully set the weapon in a vertical line at her side.

Her eyes fastened to where his larger hand gripped hers, and her stern countenance softened like rain. "I'm sorry. It's just—"

"Aye." He let go. The urge to swipe the soot from her cheeks was overwhelming. Meanwhile, his fingers itched to tug the cap off her head. Frustrated, he changed gears. "I'm surprised the caer hasn't been ransacked." *Remember, she's a child and a brat, no less.* He turned from her hypnotic green gaze.

Rayn cleared her throat. "Aye, a strange thing happened after Arthur's death. Rumors of a curse broke out among the clans, especially after Mordred lived here and nearly went mad, he did. Within months, he abandoned Camelot. To this day, he insists Arthur and Guenevere haunt the keep. The locals accept it. Even the Saxons fear this place."

"But you don't, aye." He eyed the provisions and bedding that lined one of the walls along with a large clay urn of oil.

"I find peace here. It's more home than any place I've ever known."

Shadoe gave an absent shrug. "As a child I used to hide under the table and . . ." Reprimanding himself for reminiscing, he strolled toward the outer door.

"I have no time to conduct a grand tour, Sire." She returned to her business of stuffing a satchel.

"Don't need one." He could still find his way about blindfolded. He turned and scowled at her rushed actions. "So do Lancelot, Perceval, and Tristam stay here, too?"

She glanced up, her brows meshing with contemplation before she replied, "Aye, sometimes. 'Tis the last place Mordred or his Saxons would venture."

"Apparently Mordred's more insecure than ever." Shadoe snuffed a breath with contempt.

Her green eyes narrowed and flashed in anger. "His insecurity caused the deaths of many a bairn after Arthur's and Guenevere's demise. 'Twas said more than two hundred perished . . . their wee hearts pierced . . . or their throats slashed by the sword. Aye, the man is the Adversary's spawn, he is!"

Shadoe latched onto the archway as his heart hammered painfully. "I didn't know," he admitted.

"That's right. You'd fled," she said it so adamantly that he wondered who else knew of his past transgressions.

"Mordred's mother, Morgause, prophesied Guenevere had birthed a child, and then placed the infant in safekeeping. It is believed that the bairn bore Arthur's blood-seal. Mordred gathered all the male infants under the age of one . . . within a three hundred mile area. He examined them for the mark of the Pendragon."

Nausea stirred Shadoe's intestines; his knuckles whitened. "But none bore the mark?"

"Nay." He detected a quiver in the young girl's voice. "But that didn't stop Mordred from slaying them in case Morgause had been wrong about the blood-seal. I'm told the wails of the mothers were heard throughout all Caledonia and Britannia, they were. Oddly enough, 'tis said Mordred had been forewarned by a magi or enchanter that he would one day commit the atrocity. Mordred declared that he intended to see prophecy fulfilled. So the filthy dog did."

Shadoe barely retained the bile burning in his throat. The last thing he needed was to retch in front of this haughty female. Yet hearing his prophecy had come true nearly undid him. *All those innocent babes dead because of my foresight! Mayhap, if I'd not told Mordred, mayhap. . . . Grace, glory, and love, why?* His hatred toward Mordred intensified. "I assume he gave up his search?"

She shook her head and resumed packing. "Nay. He left for about ten years; five years ago he overtook Tintagel. Three years ago, we lost Cadbury. Then eight months ago he started moving northwest, plundering everything in his path. For the present, he has taken up residence at Belizar. The latest news is that he inspects all males between the ages of seventeen and twenty-one. Fortunately, he is not killing them this time, just enlisting them into his service. Of course, their other choice is death."

Rayn stopped packing. A black void spiraled through her, causing her breath to hitch in her throat. The sickening hatred permeated every nerve of her being, but she knew somehow that it wasn't her own. She tried to shake off the sinful passion, and her glance was drawn to Shadoe. He quickly looked away. Still, she caught the whiteness about his drawn lips, the tremor of his strong jaw.

His wrath was directed toward Mordred and more . . . guilt. For what? Rayn knew Shadoe had undergone many atrocities at Mordred's hand. How he must despise the prince. What she didn't understand was how she'd just shared this stranger's black heart—or why.

"Be grateful to God that you survived, Shadoe un Hollo Tors. According to Da's sources, Mordred curses you for his failures. He believes you escaped Hell's Gate because you are the Merdyn incarnated and speak to Lucifer and his demons under the guise of a Christian."

"Humph!" Shadoe scoffed and turned back to her. "I've no link with Lucifer—or his demons, Princess."

She stood and, flexing her sore shoulders, addressed him. "Merlin spoke about you and of his love affair with Morgause's younger sister, a druid priestess. So why should I believe you are not druid or some other pagan enchanter? You are, after all, of Merlin's loins and the womb of Niamh le Fey."

Shadoe closed the distance between them and gripped Rayn's upper right arm. "Then you believed the fishwife tales about her demonic nature?"

She struggled to wiggle free, but he held firm, his fingers digging into her flesh. "Aye. I did."

"Then you indeed have reason to fear me, Princess."

"Unhand me!"

He glanced at his hand on her arm and immediately released her.

Rayn stepped back and rubbed her sore arm, delivering a scathing look his way. "We are all vile, hopeless creatures, Sir. But when we seek God's forgiveness, his grace transforms us into redeemed creatures."

He scrubbed his hand over his face and growled, "Redeemed or not, thanks to my da, I never had a chance with my mother."

"I am certain that back then, the Merdyn had good cause to keep you from her. From what I know of Niamh le Fey at that time, better off you were."

"'Tis easy said when you know your mother."

"And you're swift to assume, Sir. I never met my mother. She died giving me life. You, at least, have the chance to meet yours, you do."

"She still lives?"

Rayn gave a reluctant shake of her head. "By all that's sacred, Sir, Niamh le Fey is dead. But your mother lives and has become a new creature in Christ Jesu."

"A believer! Does she reside close by?" His eager tone amazed her.

Closer than you think. "Do you desire, then, to meet with her?"

He seemed taken aback by her curiosity. "I'm not sure . . . I didn't expect . . ." He dragged splayed fingers through his dark locks.

When his stony countenance softened with uncertainty, Rayn began to warm toward him, although she did not intend to get too comfortable. With the enchanter's comely looks wearing on her resistance, she glanced away. "Now you understand my apprehension about which God you serve, Sir."

"If it's of consolation, I serve none."

"Aye, I assume you have no bond with my Lord Jesu."

"That obvious?" he asked lightly.

"Upon conversion to our Lord Jesu, believers receive gifts of the Holy Spirit, they do."

"And I'm to believe that Merlin told you I am a godless man?" He smirked.

Rayn blushed. "Nay. Merlin told me that as a child you walked in God's light, but he feared since you left Caledonia you'd rebelled against God. Besides, Christians are known by their fruits while yours, Sir, have withered and died."

"I thought Christians were to be humble, non-judgmental . . . and above all," he added with a bite of sarcasm," non-condescending, brat."

Rayn flustered at the well-deserved slam to her conceit. "You are right, Sir. Sometimes I speak my mind. That is not always in the best interest of the soul I'm trying to save."

"Nor was I aware that you had the ability to save souls."

"Nay! What I mean is . . ." She met his baiting gleam and realized she was no contender for winning this round of wits. Her pride spoke instead of God. Rayn needed to seek the Lord's council and above all get away from this confounded man. "I'm sorry, Sir Shadoe, but we haven't time for a religious debate. Mayhap another time, aye?"

"I look forward to it." He winked, agitating her so much that she switched the conversation and her attention.

"I am grateful for you helping to free my father, Sir."

"Free him!"

She turned back. "I assumed that's why you're here. You are looking for Lancelot?"

"Aye. But you're addlebrained if you think I'm going to Belizar."

Rayn's jaw clenched, her eyes became fused with rage. "Your escape from Belizar is legendary! Why all these years later Mordred still curses you. You are the only man to survive Hell's Gate and—"

"And I intend to keep it that way, thank you."

Rayn sensed emotion bleeding beneath his tempered voice. *Is it fear or anger?*

"Sir, I beg your aid," she pleaded with pouting lips and tear moist eyes. For a heartbeat she imagined him beginning to succumb.

"Nay!" he bellowed, startling her. "I spent more than a year in that inferno, and for nothing, not even Lancelot, would I return!"

"I see." Her voice steeled. She squared her shoulders and presented her back to him.

"You do know how to reach Belizar?" he inquired more gently.

"Nay, but Perceval and Tristam know the route."

"You expect Tristam with his lame back and Perceval with his bum arm to travel that distance?"

She turned and scowled before she remembered he knew the former knights of the Round Table and their chronic ailments. "I expect they will do what's necessary to free my father."

"Aye, even if it kills them," he stated cynically.

"I couldn't stop them if I tried," she countered. "Lancelot, Perceval, and Tristam are the only surviving knights of Arthur's league. You, better than anyone, know that they were once chieftains in their own realms, but have sacrificed all. Their loyalty to each other is foremost, it is."

"You enjoy trying to make others experience guilt, don't you?" He extinguished all but two of the terra-cotta lamps.

"Guilt is a result of sin." She tried to hoist two overloaded satchels while a third sat on the floor.

Shadoe snatched the satchels from her and tossed them over his broad back as if they were full of feathers. "And if God hadn't allowed Adam and Eve to sin, we wouldn't be in this predicament."

"I thought you didn't believe in the One," she challenged.

"Even the Adversary acknowledges God's existence."

"We all have free will, Sir. His gift of salvation is meant for everyone, but many choose to reject him. For he is not willing that any should perish, but that all—"

Shadoe's grunt warned her to silence. Snatching up the other provisions, she followed him out of the war room with Echo eagerly in the lead.

As she began to close the secret panel, a masculine voice whispered, "Rose Rayn?"

She froze as the familiar gossamer image floated above Arthur's chair.

"Sire!" she acknowledged.

Another voice, enticingly feminine, beckoned, "Please, my child, stay awhile."

"Nay. I must go." Rayn fought the seductive desire to reenter the room. Fresh perspiration beaded her forehead. Even as she stepped into the passageway and sealed the door shut, Rayn heard their pleas. When she dropped her satchel and leaned against the door, the thudding of her heart against her ribs blocked all sound. A bright light loomed in front of her. Rayn was startled to find Shadoe leaning over her.

"Mercy! You look as though you've seen a ghost," his tone was condescending, but concern etched his rugged countenance.

"O' course not!" She snatched up her belongings and squeezed past him.

"Confounded brat," he muttered and glanced back at the war room door. Shadoe teetered on the edge, feeling drawn to the closed chamber, but his defenses reared up just as did the hair on the back of his scalp. He had no desire to know who or what was behind the door, and he quickly fell into step behind Rayn. Shadoe didn't know what unnerved him so. One thing remained certain: Rayn was not honest with him.

Then again, he was not honest with her.

Chapter Eleven

SHADOE AND RAYN trudged the passage in silence and returned to the cavern. Her mare still at the manger, Rayn wondered where Shadoe had secured his steed. At his master's whistle, the black Arab trotted out of the darkness.

"'Tis well trained, he is . . . and a beauty." She frowned. *Whist, what a lame remark, Rayn.* She stroked the stallion's heavy black mane and avoided Shadoe's alert stare.

He muttered and started to swing the satchels onto the saddle.

"Nay, I'll take them."

"Fine, fine." He dropped two bags and returned to his horse with the third.

Dumbfounded by his lack of chivalry, her gaze rested on the satchels at her feet. "It's obvious we don't trust one another." She watched him hoist the bag containing grain and dried beans onto his horse and then tie it down.

"That we agree upon."

So is this the closest he'll come to saying he'll help? At least she hoped that was his intention. She loaded the provisions onto her mare's back, then swung herself onto the Roman saddle and reined the horse about.

With Echo in the front, Shadoe rode up beside her. "Let's go before we're stuck overnight." He tossed her the torch and galloped out of the cave and into the maze of passages, leaving her in his dust.

"Demon's dung!" Rayn galloped after him, exiting the way she'd entered. Minutes later she arrived in the ebbing light of dusk. Shadoe was nowhere to be seen. *Blast! The cur's ditched me and taken our reserves, no less.* Riding hard, she descended the steep terrain of the forest and headed for the waterfront.

The tide surged in.

The causeway flooded.

Strong frigid waves crashed against her mare's withers, making it difficult to cross. At last on shore, she looked back at Wind's Haven, wondering what that fool thought to accomplish by staying behind. "He truly is rabble," she muttered loudly.

"And you give new meaning to the word *slow*, Princess."

She reined in her horse to find Shadoe trotting over to her. The black stallion appeared neither damp nor fatigued. "How did you . . . ?"

"Wind's Haven was my home." He sneered and urged Destrier eastward.

Rayn flinched. Hate was a sin, but her dislike of this man intensified—mayhap because she thought of Wind's Haven as *her* home, and she coveted the intimacy that Shadoe had with island and caer. He'd literally plummeted into her realm. Now if she could just devise a way to get rid of him.

"I suggest we get some hard riding in before nightfall," his husky voice interrupted her scheming. He indicated the setting sun.

"Not without me, you won't!" A voice boomed behind them.

The two turned in their saddles to find Perceval trotting up the beach.

Rayn berated herself. She'd become so absorbed with the irksome enchanter that she'd failed to notice Perceval's approach. *Heavens, we might have been ambushed. Whatever is wrong with me?*

"Percy," Rayn's voice held an authority that brought Shadoe's head around sharply. "You must stay and organize the tribes for Lancelot's return."

Perceval scowled. "Tristam is doing so as we speak, and Iona's helping with the children. The Saxons burned more than half the village before they left. Tristam has his hands full. As for me, I am sworn to protect you, Lady Rayn, and not even your mulish defiance will keep me from my duty."

"But what of the others who pledged to ride with us?"

"Three were killed, nineteen wounded. What few are left chose to stay in case of another raid. They've families to protect."

"I understand. But we must rescue Da." Rayn sighed.

"And we will." He looked to Shadoe. "And what of you, Shadoe. Do your ride with us?"

"Aye." He glowered at Rayn. "Whether we have twenty men or three, there's little chance we'll come out alive, let alone with Lancelot."

"Yahweh will not give us more than we can bear," Rayn said confidently.

"Amen!" Perceval smiled at her.

"Correct me if I'm wrong, but I don't believe God's Word supports your statement."

Rayn and Perceval gawked.

"He's got a point, lass." Perceval rubbed his jaw. "Otherwise we wouldn't need God."

Rayn glared at Shadoe's smugness.

"Besides, Belizar is now the Prince of the Air's domain, not God's," Shadoe said.

"Jesu crushed Satan's heel when he went into hell," Rayn admonished.

"Mayhap, but there's a good reason the Christ hasn't visited Satan these past five hundred years. It's bloody hot in hell. I know. I've been there!"

Rayn's lips parted to denounce his sacrilegious words, but Perceval glared at her through the ebbing daylight, and she held her tongue.

"Here." Perceval tossed Shadoe a dark brown robe. "You're safer undercover." He drew his own cloak about his shoulders.

Catching the hooded mantle, Shadoe muttered his thanks, reined Destrier, and then galloped southward.

"His faith is frail, brother." Rayn glanced at Perceval.

"Aye, he is torn between the two worlds of his parents."

"And he just found out his mother lives."

Perceval's ruddy complexion paled at her remark. "You told him?"

"Aye . . . he'd a right to know. Why didn't Merlin tell him?"

"To protect him, lass. Like Morgause, Niamh walks in darkness. After all these years, she's returned to our isle. The wretched creature searched for Shadoe with a vengeance, and now that he's back, she will do whatever is necessary to gain his allegiance."

Rayn nodded. "She's no longer druid, and she is his mother. I've learned from you and Da that the ties of blood-kin are mightily strong."

"I harbor no ill toward Niamh, Rayn, but I saw what she did to Merlin, and I'm not convinced she's received our Lord God. There is a reason people shun her. You would be wise to do the same. Niamh is Morgause's sister. That alone makes her dangerous. She is also a leper!

"As for Shadoe, it's not entirely his fault that his life has been tragically twisted. Merlin chose duty over fatherhood and denied Shadoe a mother. Arthur and Guenevere were more family to him than anyone. Aye, by returning here, he has many demons to confront, and helping us free your father is the least of them." He drew a long breath.

Rayn felt pity for the tortured man who rode at an easy gait ahead of them. She'd treated him unfairly, but then he did not exactly strive for civility. "God be merciful to him."

"Aye, upon all of us may Yahweh's blessed mercy rain."

∞

It was far into evening before they made camp. Shadoe said little, confusing Rayn more than ever. When he spoke at all, he addressed Perceval. She wondered what she'd said to antagonize him, not that Shadoe hadn't done his share of offending. Even after she snared four rabbits and put them on a fire spit, he held his tongue . . . until he burned it on his first bite.

"Demon's fire!" He snatched up his water skin and doused his mouth.

Perceval laughed and settled against a tree's trunk with his share of rabbit. "One can never say Rayn doesn't cook her meat well done."

Rayn turned and smirked at Shadoe. He glared until she turned her attention to the fire, but she sidled a glance his way.

"Have you noticed we're being followed?" Perceval spoke through a mouthful of food.

"Aye." Shadoe wiped a hand across his wet jaw. "Since midday. Probably bandits." He picked at his charred meat.

"I saw no one." She regretted admitting her lack of alertness. Once again, she wondered why she was distracted. What irritated her more was how both men dismissed her blubbering blunder.

"How many did you count?" Perceval looked at Shadoe.

"We're outnumbered three to one." Shadoe tossed a piece of rabbit to Echo.

"Percy," said Rayn, casting surreptitious glances beyond the firelight, "why haven't they attacked?"

"No reason to bother two beggars and a lad," he replied. "Still, Shadoe here has a sizable bounty on his head."

"For escaping Belizar?"

Shadoe chuckled. "That's the least of my problems." He drained his hot mead, and lifted an inquiring brow at her. "Tell me, Princess, just what are Mordred's worst fears?"

Rayn crinkled her nose in suspicion. Why, after hours of silence, had he chosen to address her now? She was more than confused; exasperated best described what she felt. She knew more about Mordred Pendragon than Shadoe un Hollo Tors.

"I'm waiting." His flat mouthed expression tested her.

Rayn diverted her gaze to the crackling fire. "That loyalists to Arthur still exist and are willing to challenge him. But then, Mordred has managed to wipe out everyone except our wee clan and the Briton Caledonians." She realized where the conversation was heading. "But Mordred knows you are the Merdyn's scion."

"Aye." Shadoe gave a satisfied nod. "Even to this day, the ways of the Britons and Celts remain the same. Tradition is foremost. The ancient ways don't die easily. In order to gain unconditional hold of Arthur's realm, Mordred needs to have Merlin's legal heir in the post of high steward. He needs me. The last time he asked, I refused."

She felt a glimmer of hope. "Then you acknowledge your tribute to the Pendragon?"

Shadoe scoffed. "I give my loyalties to no man. Mordred had a problem with that and apparently still does."

"So do I," she muttered beneath her breath and poked the fire with a stick until embers drifted skyward.

"I was loyal to one Pendragon, and he's dead, Princess," Shadoe's tone had darkened.

"But what of his clan? Do they mean nothing to you?"

"You need people for a clan to exist."

"And just who do you think occupy Ayr and Wind's Haven?"

"That handful of ragamuffins is an actual clan?"

"Aye!" Rayn came to her feet and stalked toward him. "They may be few and the last of their kind, but they are loyal to the Pendragon crest, they are!"

With a rabbit thigh in hand, Shadoe closed the distance to lean over her. "Loyal or not, you need a living kin to carry on the Pendragon bloodline. Thus, you haven't got a clan . . . least not Pendragon." He leered into her fiery green eyes.

"He makes a strong point, Rayn," Perceval admitted.

"Exactly whom do you side with, aye?" Rayn glowered at Perceval.

"At this late hour, neither." Perceval yawned and stretched. "Well, we must set a watch for the night." He cleared his throat and looked from Shadoe to Rayn.

Rayn refused to step down.

As if dismissing her, Shadoe turned and tossed the thigh to Echo, who greedily devoured the rabbit. "You rest, Percy. I'll take first stand."

"I'll take second," Rayn injected. "Unless you've a problem with that, Enchanter?"

"Only with you calling me *enchanter*."

"So what would you prefer, since you've rejected your heritage?"

"Shadoe will suffice."

"As you wish, Sir Shadoe." She threw him a mock salute, and retrieved a change of clothes from her satchel.

"And what do you think you're doing?" Perceval asked in a fatherly tone.

"I won't sleep in these filthy rags another night." Rayn pushed to her feet and snatched up her staff.

"I advise you wait till dawn." Shadoe arranged his bedding across from her. "No telling what those thieves might do."

"They're no doubt setting camp. Nor did I ask for your counsel." She motioned to tramp off toward the stream.

"My Lady," Perceval intervened, "Shadoe's counsel aside, you haven't slept in two days. I'd feel better if you were refreshed with sleep before bathing."

"I appreciate your concern, Percy, but I sleep better clean, I do." Rayn's tone softened toward her friend. Not waiting on his approval, she marched past the men and into the woods.

"Stay with her," Shadoe ordered Echo. The wolf bounded after her.

Hearing the animal behind her, Rayn scowled but did not look back.

Chapter Twelve

"SO WHO DIED and made her queen?"

At Shadoe's comment, Perceval nearly choked on his meat. "Umm, I admit Rayn is accustomed to having her way, friend, but her heart is godly."

Shadoe hunkered down before the fire, and then scrubbed his hands over his face and through his hair. "She's curdled cream and deserves to be put over someone's knee."

Perceval chuckled. "Aye, she's a mite headstrong, but finding someone willing to take on the task of spanking her is another matter."

"Well, I'd like to." Shadoe met the sparkle in Perceval's eyes. "Confound it, man," he snapped, "she's trouble. The brat has no right being in the midst of warriors' work."

"She has more right than either of us," insisted the redheaded knight. He removed his chest plate and set it aside.

"What?"

"I mean she has Pict blood in her veins, Shadoe. You know Pict women are held in equal station with men."

"Aye, I do. So her mother was Pict?"

Perceval nodded. "Aye, Pict and Celt."

"I didn't say I don't respect her; it's just that she acts like she's experienced the horrors of battle," he groused. "As if she knows what it's like to slay another human being."

"You saw the blood on her clothes?"

"Aye, what of it?"

"'Tis blood spilled doing warriors' work."

Shadoe's brows rose. "She's slain?"

"Yes . . . to defend herself and those she loves. Although you won't see her display her emotions, she suffers the same anguish any man with a heart suffers after shedding another man's blood. I've seen many men pay dearly for underestimating the strength in that willowy feminine frame of hers. And her knowledge of strategic warfare—let's say she's inherited her da's intellect, she has. Rayn's smarter than most men I know, including scholars."

A warrior. Who'd have guessed? Then again, there's nothing feminine about the brat. Maybe a slight sway when she walks. Okay, a distinct sashay. That aside, she can handle herself, especially with the staff.

Shadoe massaged his sore shoulder. He'd yet to see her wield a sword, but he recalled the blood crusted on her blade. Though the sword was large enough to do mortal damage, it had been designed for her smaller grip and frame. Now as he closed his eyes, it didn't take much to visualize Rayn ramming her blade in a man's belly. A chill blasted the length of his spine, and his eyes flew open. Shadoe's regard for Rayn heightened, as did his respect.

"Aye, she has a warrior's heart, Shadoe, and chose to fight the evil Mordred and the Saxon's spill upon our land. Lancelot's done his best. But with Galahad gone more than present, and Rayn's having no mother figure, grumpy old soldiers have nurtured her. True, she's never worn a gown and lacks the charms of womanhood. She needs guidance, but Tristam and I are hardly experts in those delicate matters. We're most thankful Iona returned when she did."

Shadoe met Perceval's drawn look. "Who was Rayn's mother?"

The older man looked away. "That is not for me to say."

Shadoe grew annoyed. No one seemed willing to give him a direct answer to anything of importance. "Despite what the fishwives say, Lancelot was no womanizer. I venture to guess there were but two women in his life: Galahad's mother, Lady Elaine, and of course

Guenevere, who—!" The revelation coursed through his veins like lava. He shot to his feet. "Blessed Avalon! Does the brat know?"

"Know what, man?" Perceval glanced toward the burn behind the trees.

"Look, Percy, I thought you and Tristam were fooling about her being the heir to Arthur's throne."

"Did you now?"

Shadoe rubbed his beard-roughened jaw. "I was but a lad, but I remember the nasty affair! Just how old is this brat?"

"Seventeen years this autumn's eve."

Shadoe did his math and bellowed. "Ah! That's about right. Guenevere died five months after Arthur, which means ... Rat's breath! You're serious!"

"Aye. Lancelot fears for her safety as it is. Can you imagine what Mordred and Morgause would do if they knew the truth?"

First Shadoe had needed to absorb the fact that this officious youth was female; now he was to accept that she was Guenevere's daughter? They didn't look anything alike. Then again, he hadn't seen her with a clean face, or without her hair bound and covered. His mind wandered where it shouldn't. What exactly lay beneath her baggy-fitting tunic and breeches? Feeling heat warm his face, he waved a hand in her direction. "Shouldn't you check on her?"

"That could prove hazardous," Perceval stated with conviction.

Shadoe grinned.

"Besides, your wolf is with her." He shrugged his burly shoulders.

"I haven't quite decided whether or not Echo approves of her."

"Rayn has an unusual way with animals, especially wild ones." The knight lifted his sword to clean it.

"Aye, better than with people," he groused. "It is hard to believe she's Guenevere's child. I mean she's so uncouth."

"Then your memory of Guen is shaded."

"I think not."

"Was not Guenevere opinionated, fiery, and hard as nails when needed be? Mule headed comes to mind. Not to mention she could wheel a sword against the best, and curse up a mighty storm when her dander got stirred."

"Aye. Two weeks after the honey-dung incident, Guen caught me raiding the honey barrel. While lecturing me on wasting God's nectar, she made me drink a large quantity . . . at one time." He gagged and shuddered. "After which, I vomited. I haven't been able to eat honey since, thus ensuring the honey stock remained intact."

"Ah, you did have your share of sweet moments." Perceval chuckled.

Shadoe huffed from the memory of that undignified experience, but a smile tugged his lips. "That was one of the most daunting days of my childhood. I never doubted her authority again." Shadoe's smile faded away. "So after all these years, what the rumor mongrels spoke is true. Lady Guenevere and Lancelot were lovers."

Once again, Perceval looked in the direction Rayn had gone. "If that's what you believe."

"You just told me that she's Guen's bairn."

"Aye." Perceval took up his sword and sharpened the blade on wet soapstone.

"Thus Lancelot is her father." Scratching his chin stubble, Shadoe settled beside Perceval, who remained silent. "Then why doesn't it feel right?"

"It shouldn't." The man began to hum.

"Only because it goes against what I was raised to believe is right and wrong. I knew there was a point when Arthur neglected Guenevere and she turned to Lancelot for comfort. Half the kingdom knew of their indiscretion . . . including Arthur. Many were surprised at his response, they way he hastily attempted to restore his failing marriage. He took full responsibility for the affair, as I recall. My heart never accepted that Guenevere and Lancelot could commit adultery, but to think that their indiscretion continued. . . . Then again, they were human like the rest of us." He rubbed his brow in agitation. "Yet before Guen died, she pledged her oath of love to Arthur." He met Perceval's sober countenance. "The fact is Guenevere was barren for years until her dalliance with Lancelot."

"Aye."

"You're going to make me drag it out of you, aren't you?"

"Let's just say, I need to know if you are the same Shadoe un Hollo Tors I knew long ago. If not, this conversation goes no further."

"None of us are like we were, Percy. Life changes people."

"I speak of your heart, Shadoe. I strongly sense it has hardened like this stone." He drew the blade across the smooth surface faster and faster.

"That I won't deny. Yet it doesn't mean I am no longer a friend to you, or to Tristam or Lancelot. Just don't ask me to promote a rebellion I believe is not only hopeless, but nearly twenty years too late, and based on the mendacity of this brat being Arthur's progeny."

"Your father sent you on a quest, Shadoe. Do you intend to see it through?"

"'Tis why I'm here."

"Yes, but your heart is not . . . nor is your soul. Which brings me to another matter. Do you still possess the gifts of the Spirit?"

"You refer to the gifts of discernment and foresight?"

"Aye. As a child you spoke with God's angels, or so Merlin told us. And like your father, you acknowledged these abilities by giving God the glory. If that be truth, Shadoe, then your spiritual gifts, however dormant, dwell within you."

Perceval seemed to finish, but continued his disquieting probe. "But if you never received the Holy Spirit and rejected the Fisher of Men, your gifts are not of the Father but from the Prince of Air and Light." He paused. "So whose gifts do you possess, Shadoe un Hollo Tors?"

Shadoe's blood heated in his veins, and he clenched his fists. "I have no powers, Sir, neither of heaven nor hell!"

Perceval didn't look surprised. "So I assumed, or you would have discerned Rayn's lineage, including her destiny. What worries me most is whether you ever accepted God's free gift, my friend. Your immortal

soul may be in dire jeopardy, yet you do not seem the least bit both-
ered by that damning knowledge."

Shadoe withheld comment.

"It's my hope that you are indeed God's child, Shadoe un Hollo Tors,
who like a careless lamb has wandered off the path of righteousness. I
pray our good Shepherd leads you back into his fold." Perceval returned
his sharpened sword to its sheath, yawned, and then eased down upon
his earthen bed.

Shadoe was grateful the knight did not pursue the issue concerning
his lost gifts, let alone his soul. *Lost lamb indeed!* Although curious as
to what Perceval hinted at concerning Rayn's destiny, he preferred not
to know. But he did want an answer to her birthright. "So what is the
truth to the girl's true namesake?"

"Do you really desire truth, Shadoe?"

"Aye."

"Then heed God's voice, lad."

Shadoe scowled. Perceval sounded too much like Merlin: riddles and
insinuations but not one honest answer. Mayhap the truth was too
hard for Percy to accept. "Then I assume you have no further need of
me after we rescue Lancelot?"

"That's for God to decide."

Shadoe flinched at the finality in Perceval's tenor. Evidently, Perceval's
relationship with Jesu had deepened over the years. Shadoe almost
envied him . . . almost.

"I may be younger than Lancelot and Tristam, but I'm ten years
your senior, Shadoe, and need rest. A word of advice, though. Don't let
the brat soak too long; she might catch cold. And when she's sick, she's
a foul whiny creature, she is."

Shadoe frowned and shoved to his feet. "It'd serve her right." He
glanced over his shoulder. "Then you trust me?"

"I trust Rayn to care for herself . . . even against the likes of you."
Perceval yawned deeply.

"Somehow that isn't the answer I sought." Shadoe flinched when he saw the smirk on Perceval's lips as the hermit knight stretched out on his straw mat and went to sleep.

∽

Once at the stream, Rayn faced the fast flowing current and dipped her sword and stinger until both weapons were free of the crusted blood. As she watched the dried blood liquefy, her belly began to knot and rumble with nausea. Afterward, she peeled down her soiled tunic, braise, and breeches, pounding them against a rock and praying for the blood of her enemies and comrades to be washed downstream. She scrubbed until her wrists hurt and her fingers were numb and raw. She burst into tears, sobbing over the life's blood that stained not only her clothes but also her heart and soul. Pleading God's forgiveness and peace, she dried her tears and laid her clothes on the bank, then dove into the icy burn . . . to forget.

Whoa! These were not the hot springs of Wind's Haven, and the frigid waters caused her to wash furiously. Within minutes, though, she began to enjoy the refreshing water. Rayn had not intended to scrub her bloodstained clothes tonight, or even bathe. She'd have fallen asleep upright had Shadoe not been present. But she needed to be away from the apprentice enchanter and hoped by the time she returned he would be asleep. Then with a stab of dismay, she remembered he'd volunteered for first watch. She realized that she was so exhausted she hadn't thought straight.

Rayn was amazed she hadn't collapsed from fatigue hours ago. No doubt Shadoe's annoying presence kept her alert. Now that she'd scrubbed her face, she wondered how she would prevent him from recognizing her. So far he hadn't given her a second glance, and he had been semiconscious when she'd rescued him. She preferred he not know it had been her at the loch that day or that she'd dragged him ashore. Shadoe thought her no more than a pesky insect. She'd like to keep it that way.

With the river shallow, three feet at its deepest, Rayn was partially submerged. Once the moon's glow subdued, she would make for shore where her wool chemise hung on a bush. She would not tempt the fates and be caught naked, especially by Shadoe. Although cold, the water felt delightful against her aching limbs, but if she soaked any longer, she'd go numb.

On shore, Echo paced like a watch hound. Rayn found the sight amusing. When she laughed softly, Echo growled as if ordering her to leave the babbling burn.

"I'll come when ready, I will."

Echo placed a paw in the water, and then retreated.

"Too cold, huh?" Rayn splashed water at the creature.

The she-wolf didn't want to play, and Rayn turned about as a cool breeze invaded the warm night air. Pewter-spotted clouds blanketed the moon, and Rayn waded into shore. Her chemise was gone! She looked left, then right, only to find Echo had fetched her garments and was dragging them toward the camp.

"Echo!" she called softly. The wolf just turned and wagged its tail. *Traitor!*

⬦

Shadoe poked at the fire. Although Rayn was just on the other side of the trees, he concluded she had overextended her pleasure time. When Echo's wet muzzle nudged his leg, he found a puddle of clothes at his feet. "What in—"

He snatched the garments and his sword and jogged toward the burn, berating the wolf. Her playful leaps, though, assured him that Rayn was not in danger. "Show me where she is." He followed the wolf to the brook.

Moon glow trickled through the clouds to reveal Rayn hunched in the water, her long tresses adorning her shoulders. For a moment Shadoe could only stare at the fan of fiery hair afloat in the water. *Blessed mercy,* he thought before remembering this was Guenevere's daughter.

"Looking for these?" He sought to maintain an air of calm he did not feel.

"That . . . beast stole th-em!" she stuttered.

Shadoe waded toward her.

"Nay!" She raised a hand of protest.

"Then get out!" He tossed the chemise at her. When she snatched it midair, he turned around, impressed by her dexterity.

She dressed, and then plowed through the water so fast he barely saw her. The words that sprang from her blue lips amazed him. Quite unchristian they were; some he didn't recognize. Possible Pict curses? He drew a breath and attempted a straight face. He failed.

"Take that wet thing off!" he demanded, following on her heels.

"Nay! Fetch me dry clothes!" Rayn reached for her staff.

Shadoe snatched it away.

"You're an ungodly cretin!" she accused, and then charged him, butting her head into his muscle-packed stomach. Her aim was accurate and hard enough to draw a grunt from his lungs and stir his dander. Shadoe swung her into his arms and up over his shoulder. "And you're a piggish brat!"

Rayn hit and kicked, but Shadoe held fast, hauling her to camp. Her loud ranting awakened a sleep-drugged Perceval.

"Here!" Shadoe tossed Rayn toward Perceval's lap, but she twisted in his arms as he let go, and landed on the sod.

"Whist! You dull-witted snail!" she blustered and pushed to her knees, then massaged her backside.

"Best warm the tatterdemalion's bottom before I toss her back in that icy burn," Shadoe growled to the hermit, then chafed his bruised stomach muscles.

Perceval gawked at the shivering package of tangled wet hair. Hastily, he draped his sheepskin about her and began to rub her down.

"'Tis no bairn, I am!" She yanked free and snuggled beneath the wool coverlet.

"Aye, even a child knows when to come out of the water," Shadoe jeered, fueling the fire.

Perceval guffawed.

Shadoe tried not to laugh, but the sight of her snarled, wet hair and quivering chin amused him.

When Echo ran over and curled up against her, Rayn shook a hand of protest.

"I wouldn't refuse her," Shadoe suggested. "Echo doesn't share her fur with just anyone."

Rayn conceded.

As if unruffled by the incident, Perceval mumbled, "Will you be alright?"

"Aye," she said with chattering teeth. "I've swum deeper, colder water than that wee burn."

Holding a smoldering stick, Shadoe turned from his crouched position before the fire. "And just where might that be?" He stared into her green eyes peering out from beneath the sheepskin.

She glared, and presented him her back. For a moment, he appraised the wet ringlets of auburn that had escaped her wrap. *What are the odds? Pretty high, if she frequents Wind's Haven.* Still, Rayn had managed to keep her face from his view, so she might as well be dirt caked. Perhaps morning's light would reveal her features, yet he could not recognize what he barely recalled.

Perching against a tree, Shadoe realized that if he had his foresight, he wouldn't be second-guessing such foolishness. *I wonder what kind of commitment God would demand to allow me to see with my mind's eye?* He drew a quick breath. No doubt a commitment he was not ready to make.

∽◯

Perceval hung Rayn's wet garments to dry and observed the courtship banter. The emotional and physical attraction between Rayn and Shadoe was so intense it made him weary to watch them. It also made him smile. He doubted either of them realized what was happening.

Many couples willingly fell in love. These two were blatantly defiant, and neither questioned why. Perceval knew. They were intellectual equals and emotionally matched. If he didn't know better, he might assume they were each other's godsend.

How long since he'd seen such fierce passion between a man and woman? *Ah, Arthur and Guenevere,* he recalled with fondness, and then returned to the present. This blossoming love affair could not be played out. Although she didn't know it, Rayn's destiny rested with another.

Besides, Shadoe has chosen to walk his own path, not God's. I must make sure Rayn and Shadoe do not fall in love. The future depends upon it! Bowing his head, Perceval called upon God to give him the strength to do what must be done—no matter the cost.

Chapter Thirteen

CAER BELIZAR, NORTHERN BRITANNIA

LANCELOT WAS unceremoniously deposited onto a rough earthen floor. Blindfolded, gagged, and bound, Lancelot du Lac had been dragged by three fully armed Saxons through an archway and into a dank chamber. Grunts of good-riddance emitted from his escorts as they shoved him to the ground. When he hit the filthy rushes, he encountered animal bones, other disgusting things, and unless his nose misled him, dog excrement.

Barely able to lift his head, Lancelot discerned the presence of two figures and their fiery exchange of words. A moment later, something swept past him: the disquietingly familiar scent of lilac.

"What the . . . !" a gruff voice demanded. "I ordered he not be harmed. He's got twenty years on you men. Remove the gag and blindfold. Let him speak!"

The filthy rag was jerked free and the blindfold as well. Lancelot swallowed several times to regain moisture in his parched mouth. Even with their hands on his bindings, his captors hedged. "But Sire," a Saxon insisted. "This old man slew four men and mangled seven others. He's dangerous."

"Of course! He's one of the mightiest warriors on this godforsaken isle. He is Sir Lancelot du Lac." Then, as if having second thoughts, he added, "Leave his hands bound for good measure."

Lancelot's eyes adjusted to the hazy lighting of the smoldering wall torches as he took a defensive stance. The armed Saxons moved in, weapons aimed at him.

"Enough," the gruff voice ordered. "Stand back. Let him breathe."

Lancelot turned and glared. A younger man stood with muscular, leather-sheathed legs slightly parted, his hands braced behind him, assessing Lancelot with a casual eye. The arrogance of the man was undeniable. "Mordred!"

"Aha, you remember me, Lance," Mordred stated with a sneer.

"Aye, and it is *Sir* Lancelot to you."

"Not brother Lance, as your Christian friends call you?"

"You're not Christian, Mordred."

"How would you know?"

"Because you share the company of dogs." Lancelot tipped his throbbing head toward the Saxon guards.

"Now that's not Christlike. Your Jesu kept the company of thieves and tax collectors, did he not?"

Lancelot straightened and towered over Mordred. "He was among them, yes, but he neither condoned of nor engaged in their sinful deeds."

"But he loved and forgave them." Mordred circled like a vulture.

So, Mordred baits me, testing my faith. "God loves all mankind. It is sin that he detests."

"But does he not forgive as well?" Mordred leaned in closer for the kill.

"Only if a man is truly repentant will he be forgiven."

"Then I am truly sorry for having slain your beloved Guenevere, Lancelot. If God can forgive me, I'd expect you could as well."

He felt the mockery of Mordred's feigned confession. Contempt overpowered him. "That is where I fail my God miserably, Mordred. I am not Jesu, and only he knows what is truly in your heart. I can only speculate about the state of your heart and will not forgive what I doubt you regret."

"Such a pity." Mordred sighed, removing a gold-handled stinger from the leather scabbard at his hip. He toyed with the sharp blade.

Lancelot's eyes fastened on the weapon's delicate engraving—a dragon and rose encircling the hilt. Guenevere's! When he looked up, he found Mordred amused by his sickened reaction.

"I always did covet your pretty queen, so when I couldn't have her, I settled for this. Such an unfair exchange, but . . . something is better than nothing, aye?"

Refusing to submit to the man's sarcasm, Lancelot lowered his eyes. The ill expression he wore changed to surprise when he noted Mordred's missing left hand. Lancelot's lips twitched, and he experienced satisfaction, wondering who he should thank for disfiguring this disciple of evil.

"Guenevere would be too old for me now," Mordred continued. "Better she died young and beautiful. Besides, she tried to kill me, you know. Oh, you weren't there, were you? Nay, you'd run off with your gutless knights and left your beloved to die with that sniveling child, Shadoe."

Lancelot lunged for Mordred. Three sets of hands caught him and slammed him to the floor. The aging warrior cursed his lack of self-control.

Mordred waved the stinger at him. "I'm pleased to see that despite your creased face and thinning hair, you've still the tenacity of youth."

"I should have slain you years ago." Lancelot was jerked back onto his feet, but the guards held him in place.

"That would have indeed changed things, aye? Arthur might even be alive. But you were too late to rescue him . . . or mayhap you realized that with Arthur dead, sweet Guenevere would be yours."

"You spawn of Lucifer!"

Mordred burst into laughter. "Lust has it merits, as does the guilt you still wallow in, my friend. Which brings us back to why you were sneaking about my encampment at Hadrian's Wall." Mordred stepped in front of Lancelot, pressed the tip of his dagger beneath Lancelot's jaw, and sliced deep, drawing blood. "No doubt you assume if you avenge Arthur's and Guenevere's deaths, you can make atonement for your sins."

"Jesu Christ atoned for my sins at Calvary, Mordred. All I need do is repent and believe on him."

Mordred snorted, although his tone seemed reflective. "Ah, if life were that simple."

"It is," Lancelot confidently replied, pondering the flicker of confusion in Mordred's eyes. As much as he hated the man, he felt pity for Mordred the child, lost in sin.

Lancelot's captor stepped back, his expression one of confusion and bewilderment. "If I thought for the briefest moment this God nonsense held merit, I'd pursue our conversation. The once headstrong Sir Lancelot seems to have acquired a peaceful discipline. But that could be attributed to good wine and beautiful women. Ah, you have had your way with the ladies, Lance."

Lancelot shut his eyes and tried to steal his emotions from Mordred. Those wild, womanizing days still haunted him. He could only give glory to God for changing his heart and his ways, but he doubted Mordred would understand.

"I learned a lot about the fairest gender from you," Mordred smirked, "especially how to seduce them . . . the way you seduced Guenevere. So were her lips as sweet as Arthur said? And her body . . . her long, sensuous legs and her bosom so full and—"

"You'll gain no ground ruining Guenevere or Arthur. You slew two people who loved you without measure and moreover forgave you." Lancelot shot a steely look at the younger man and saw the strangest thing in Mordred's face. Hurt. Perplexity. For the length of a breath, it seemed someone other than this heartless murderer was looking at him.

Mordred turned away and asked in a quieter, more sincere tone, "It is said that Lady Iona du Maur is in residence with you. Is this true?"

A mask of indifference slipped over Lancelot's features and into his voice. "She is dead to you, Sir. Has been for years."

"Is she still beautiful?"

"Aye, last I saw of her." He remained evasive.

"And are the two of you wed?" Tension darkened his tone, and he stepped round to face Lancelot.

Lancelot's brows arched, and his gaze narrowed suspiciously. "Iona has long been a gracious friend, Mordred. As to the state of her availability, she never wed."

"Never?" He appeared startled.

"Nay." Lancelot's suspicion intensified.

Relief marked Mordred's countenance.

"You could have any woman you want, Mordred. Yet you are not married and have no heirs, least not legally acknowledged."

"What is your point, sir knight?"

Lancelot wondered himself. He noted a vulnerable side of Mordred not seen in years. Only one person had ever penetrated Mordred's cold heart, and that woman was Guenevere's cousin Iona du Maur. He decided to see if that was still the case. "We all knew Morgause despised Iona. I honestly think your mother was jealous of her. If memory serves, after you slew Arthur, Iona rejected you and chose blood-kin over you. I suspect you hate her for that decision. No doubt you seek revenge against her." He stared Mordred straight on.

The Pendragon imposter stepped closer and spoke softly as if for Lancelot's ears alone. "I have always loved her, Lance. Still do. I just want to know if she is well . . . if she is content."

Lancelot had no reason to believe anything Mordred said, but the emotion that laced the man's words rang true. Still, Lancelot gauged his response. "She is healthy and at peace with herself, Mordred, which is more than I can say for you."

Mordred's smile watered. A muscle along his jaw flickered. Lancelot had struck a nerve. Mordred stepped away, an icy hardness killing the momentary warm gleam in his eyes. Lancelot knew any hope of reprieve had vanished.

"Why were you spying on my legions?" Mordred demanded.

"No man owns the wall. Not even you, Mordred. You and your Saxon mongrels have forged a bloody path across Britannia and

Caledonia. I came to see if the rumor of your return to Camelot held merit."

"You could have just knocked and asked." He snickered.

"Some habits are hard to break."

"Well," Mordred chuckled, "I intended to look you up, anyway. Rumor has it you were dead along with the rest of Arthur's Round Table."

Lancelot continued to stare.

"As for Camelot and the Pendragon clan, there really is no demesne left. I rule much of this Isle of Might, and my legions sacked Ayr more than a month ago. I captured most of your able-bodied men, and I'm making soldiers out of them. Thus there's not much left to your Pendragon clan but women and bairns."

"There are more clans to confront than you think."

"Aye, I know of the minor kings, but without leadership, they will fall." Mordred shrugged.

"We're talking tens of thousands yet to conquer. You act as if you're swatting flies." Lancelot's fingers had gone numb, and he strained against the ropes.

"Act?" Mordred scoffed. "I assure you, Sir Knight, defeating the clans will, indeed, be as easy as swatting flies. I have great allegiances, Lance. I intend to use them. The Anglo-Saxons and Jutes are close to conquering this isle, and I have their superstitious blessings to be high king of northern Britannia and Caledonia . . . at least for now. Thus, I need a caer worthy of such greatness."

Mordred met Lancelot's eyes with a smirk. "Not that Tintagel isn't grand, but I need a fortress to occupy when I visit my western kingdoms and the lowlands." Mordred gestured at the dark, dreary present surroundings. "Needless to say, I've been away from Caer Belizar too long. It has gone to the dogs during my absence. All in all, rather disgusting. Alas, even in its glory days, this timber frame could not compare to the bright charm of Caer Camelot . . . or as the Caledonians now call it, Splendor Lost."

"You've two-thirds of Britannia under your thumb, Mordred. What do you want with us? We have nothing but quarreling Picts and raiding Scots to deal with. My people survive day to day; they have nothing you need."

"Ah, *my people*, you say. You still cling to the leadership of your noble lineage, Lancelot, even if it's to rule nothing but the most pitiful of mankind."

"I asked what you want."

"Tens of thousands more to bow before me. 'Tis cause, is it not?"

Ire heated Lancelot's face. His lips thinned with contempt; his nostrils flared.

Mordred roared with mirth before his eyes slanted dangerously. "In all honesty, I loath this dank, barren land and its icy sea. I prefer Rome, but its empire has many problems that I shall shortly eliminate. Soon I will be emperor."

The man is mad. Lancelot restrained a chortle of ridicule. "So?" he ground out.

"You old fool! You think I've forgotten? That I don't know about the prophecy concerning Arthur's successor, of the power and wealth that lies beneath Loch Lady? Nor think that I've abandoned my quest for the Emerald Rose of Avalon and its mystical powers. When I left Caledonia, I went with the sole purpose of returning with an army and enough power to take what's mine! I am Arthur's firstborn and intend to have my legacy!"

"You are the fool! You lost any right you had to the Pendragon name the day you rode with Vortigern against Arthur. You're nothing but a bloodsucking vulture."

"Look at me, Sir! Look hard."

He did. Thick auburn hair crowned Mordred's handsome head. His features were flawless, save for the center cleft in his jaw, which made him only more distinguished. His blue eyes flashed confidence, and the nostrils of his Briton-Celtic nose flickered with each breath. All this atop a muscular, lean frame projected an image of masculine beauty and strength, the image of high chieftain. Lancelot shut his weary eyes and shook his head.

His lack of words expanded Mordred's ego. "Aha! You see my father. You see the man you called friend. I am Arthur's scion, and I will be high king of Caledonia, Britannia, Gaul, and Rome."

Lancelot grinned, for there was something else he saw in the man's countenance. Something he'd long suspected and had been confirmed in a brief encounter with Niamh months before. "Just because you put henna in your hair does not make you Arthur's scion. But that cleft in your chin does remind me of someone. Someone who had access to your mother's bed before Arthur."

Mordred paled and failed to avoid Lancelot's confident gaze.

"I wonder how the Saxons would feel if they knew you are not the Pendragon but an imposter and, in fact, the scion of the Merdyn. You are Mordred un Hollo Tors. Of course, I assume you already know the truth, and if I do, others do as well."

Livid, Mordred stalked to within a few feet of Lancelot. "It makes no difference to the Saxons who spawned me. Arthur and Merlin were both descendants of Ayris. What matters is the Saxons are superstitious and believe the legends of Ayris. Furthermore, my reputation of leadership precedes me. The people long for the Pendragon's return, and as I am the only one, 'twill not matter."

"Think again," Lancelot muttered.

Mordred eyed him warily. "Speak up if you've something to say, or I shall be delighted to slice out your tongue."

"I simply suggest you not underestimate the clans who remember your brutality. You will never be freely accepted as anyone worthy of Arthur's throne." Lancelot held the man's threatening gaze until Mordred looked away.

"Worthy!" he spat. "Just who among your peasants is? Or do *you* intend to fill Arthur's sandals?"

Lancelot gave a humble sigh. "I have not been ordained by God for such high calling, but I will do my best to make certain that you do not succeed."

"I could slay you and be rid of your petty threats, Lance, but I will prove

I have honor and wait until we are on the battlefield. As for my birthright, it is of some relief to know I did not slaughter my own sire. I must say, although at first disappointed, I now consider myself better for it—to be scion of the high steward, to say nothing of inheriting his powers."

"These powers you speak of are from God and are gifts of the Spirit . . . gifts you do not possess."

"I speak of my forefathers, of the blood gifts I was born to wield."

Lancelot scoffed. "You truly don't understand, do you, Mordred? Yahweh blessed your ancestors with special abilities, and he can just as easily take them away. I doubt you possess anything but a cold, aching heart."

Mordred set his acid gaze upon Lancelot. "I'm not talking about invisible powers, Lance. I refer to the immense force of Ayris found in certain objects. My stepfather never appreciated the power he held in his hand, but I do. And with Excalibur and the Rose, I shall rule."

"There is no power in the amulet or the sword."

"That is a lie, and you know it!" Mordred hissed. "I've seen its magique, as have others. Merlin knew their powers and used them to his gain."

Lancelot held his tongue. It would do no good to defend Merlin. Mordred practiced sorcery, sacrificed to pagan gods, and believed what Morgause would have him to.

A knock on the door drew Mordred's attention, and he motioned the soldier to open it. A handsome, stocky built man stood at the threshold. His clothing and manner alerted Lancelot he was not only of Germanic blood but a chieftain.

Mordred sauntered over and offered his hand to the warrior king only to be dismissed. Lancelot glimpsed Mordred's bruised expression. Lancelot did not recognize this man who found no favor with Mordred, but that alone was reason to like him.

"Lord Lancelot, I presume?" he said in Greek.

Lancelot nodded, his facial features revealing surprise at the man's formal tongue. The chieftain extended a hand of greeting.

Lancelot shrugged and answered in Greek. "I am unable to return the courtesy, Sire."

"Release him!" the chieftain barked at the guards in their Saxon dialect.

They obeyed without a glance Mordred's way.

Mordred stomped forward and argued, "How dare you override my commands, Sir!"

"Don't forget that not only your mercenaries, but these Saxons, are in my service, not yours." The chieftain glowered.

Mordred paled.

Rubbing circulation into his wrists and hands, Lancelot felt his poise return. So the Saxon legions were not under Mordred's leadership as the fishwives rumored. But seeing Mordred be brought down a few notches held little comfort, for when this noble Saxon departed, Mordred would exercise his frustrations on Lancelot.

The Saxon introduced himself. "You probably don't recognize me, Sir Lancelot du Lac, but I remember you. When I rode with Vortigern against your high chieftain Arthur Pendragon, you honored me with this." He turned his face sideways and traced a deep bleached scar from his jawbone down his neck and to his collarbone.

For Lancelot, the memory came sweeping back—a young, wild-eyed Saxon screaming in a foreign tongue, bent on killing every Briton, Celt, and Pict in his wake. Lancelot crossed that warrior's path. He'd been certain he'd left the young man for dead.

Lancelot squared his sore shoulders and straightened. The last Saxon he had expected to find in Caledonia was the infamous ruler of Kent, King Hengist. Although he felt no affection for this invader, he did respect him. "My Lord." He dropped his head in homage.

"You remember?"

Lancelot lifted his head. "Aye, King Hengist, your conquests precede you."

"As do yours, Sir Lancelot du Lac." He offered his hand, and Lancelot accepted.

Mordred growled his disgust.

"You were, and I suspect still are, a worthy opponent."

"I try," Lancelot quipped.

The room's lack of lighting made it difficult to distinguish facial features. Retrieving a torch, Hengist held it over Lancelot, and then frowned at his freshly battered face. The Saxon gestured Mordred to his side. "This is not acceptable! This man is a champion, and you dare humiliate and beat him when he's defenseless. I would not do that to a chained dog! Have you no honor?"

"That's where you and Mordred are different, King Hengist." Lancelot vocalized his thoughts only to meet Mordred's threatening gaze.

"So it seems," the Saxon acknowledged grimly.

Mordred forfeited his patience. "King Hengist, you forget you are my guest."

The king looked hard on the younger man. "And you forget whose assistance you seek to fund your petty war, Prince Mordred."

Lancelot tried not to smirk. Mordred was not as financially sound as he portrayed. Lancelot wondered what Hengist wanted from Mordred in exchange for his services.

A guard entered, marched over to Hengist, and spoke quietly to him. "I am needed elsewhere, Sir Lancelot. But I will return as there are issues of the utmost importance I wish to discuss with you."

Mordred kept silent until the prince departed. Before he could speak, a vulture glided past him and vanished into the darkness behind Mordred. Lancelot's spine tingled. The heady scent of lilac filled the hazy air. Lancelot knew a malevolent presence had entered the chamber, and he asked God to send his angels.

Emerging like gossamer mists from the shadows, a petite, veiled woman came to stand beside Mordred. She gazed upon Lancelot with the same cobalt eyes her son possessed. "Time has been kind to you, sweet Lance. You are still stunning to look upon." Her sensuous voice caught him off guard.

"I would extend you the same compliment if I could see your face, Morgause le Fey."

She laughed softly. "I doubt my appearance would make any difference to you. You refused my affections when I captured every other man's, including Arthur's. But I assure you . . ." She dropped her veil. "The gods remain generous to me." She brazenly slipped off her cloak, revealing a sheer gown that left little to the imagination.

Lancelot blinked in bewilderment. True, the lighting was dim, but by all that was sacred, she appeared even younger than the last time he'd seen her. Why, she didn't look a day over sixteen. Impossible! She was beautiful!

Stepping closer, Morgause drew a long, delicate finger along his close-shaven jaw and pressed upward, closing his gaping mouth. "Oh, Lance, how I've missed our entertaining spats. 'Twas like making love with words, but wouldn't you rather feel my love?" She took his hand and pressed it to the moist softness of her lips.

Lancelot became lost in the depth of her shimmering blue eyes. Lust scalded his blood, lowering his defenses; then the Spirit of God rescued him. Lancelot jerked his hand away, freeing himself from the arousing touch and seductive gaze.

"So good to see you are still human," she taunted. "The fishwives said that you, Tristam, and Perceval had pledged your allegiance to the Fisher of Men. That you abstain from the carnal pleasures of this world."

"And I'd heard that you were dead," he hissed. "Such a pity the gossipmongers were wrong."

She giggled like a young girl, but to Lancelot it sounded like a hag's cackle. "Dead? Nay, I shall outlive the lot of you, sweet Lance."

When she struck an alluring pose, Lancelot thought he glimpsed desire in Mordred's eyes. Lancelot felt sick to his soul. "What do you want, hag?"

She pouted. "What I've always wanted. What Arthur denied to our scion, the title of high king."

"Don't make me laugh, Morgause. Arthur never denounced Mordred's birthright. But had he known the true means of Mordred's conception, that Merlin was your scion's real father—"

"Bah! Arthur never intended to put Mordred on the throne." She gestured to her son.

"Then why did Arthur treat him like a prince and give him lands to govern?" Lancelot didn't give her time to respond. "Because he expected Mordred to prove his worth, which he did not. He squandered his gifts, neglected his fields, and abused his slaves. Even his clansmen and their families fled. Your scion did not then, nor does he now, deserve to be called Pendragon."

"I am Pendragon!" Mordred strutted forward and slapped Lancelot across the mouth.

Lancelot's head snapped back, and he tasted blood. Still he growled, "You are nothing but this beldam's puppet, Mordred." His retort caused Mordred to step back.

Lancelot glared at Morgause. "Just as your beauty is but an illusion, Morgause, so is your quest for the legacy of Ayris . . . for it is a legacy of the heart, and you have no heart."

Morgause's bright blue eyes darkened like black onyx. Lancelot felt pain pierce his chest. Gasping, he toppled to his knees.

Ruling over him, she snarled, "My powers are no illusion, old knight, nor is the agony you feel. Surely you are aware that life has been seeping from your veins for some time. My spirits have revealed what I've long suspected. You are the key to the Pendragon."

He lifted his head, and in his pain, he saw the diabolical creature Morgause really had become. She seemed to hunch over and shrivel before his eyes. Most of Morgause's prized golden hair was replaced with bald patches. Flesh hung loose from her bones. Her creamy white complexion transformed to a pasty gray. Deep pox marks scarred her skin, and puss oozed from ugly boils. Her nose became fleshless and beaklike. Her lips cracked and blackened, while her beautiful blue eyes became sunken hollows from which demonic yellow orbs peered out.

Closing his eyes, Lancelot drew a breath. His lungs burned as if on fire. He told himself the torture was not real and prayed for deliverance.

"Taste the flames of hell, Lance. Breath the sulfur."

"What do you want?" He peered through watering eyes and grimaced. "Arthur and Guenevere's scion."

He managed a bowed smile. "There is no scion."

"Liar." Mordred put his small worth into the exchange.

"Silence!" Morgause snapped back.

"Nay!" Mordred argued. "My men spoke of a youth who has influence over the Celts and Britons. I've sent soldiers to Ayr to find him. His name is Rayn."

"You fool! We're not looking for some pimple-cheeked child! He'd be seventeen years by now. A young man fashioned after Arthur's likeness, tall, handsome, with hair the color of autumn leaves or black like the midnight sky."

Mordred groused, "Well, they said he was tall and slim, but barely grown and had freckled features."

Morgause redirected her gaze at Lancelot.

More demons attacked him. Lancelot buckled, crumbling to the floor.

Morgause gracefully lowered to one knee and touched his agony-drawn face. "So, Lance, what of this boy who accompanied you? Not Arthur's scion, umm?" She snapped her fingers and stood. "We'll know soon, won't we?" She set her diabolical gaze upon him, and the misery intensified.

Lancelot never ceased his prayer and met Morgause's confident gaze unafraid. The Holy Spirit burned bright within him. Morgause took an unsteady step back. She knew who challenged her and had no choice but to retreat. God intervened. Lancelot's pain vanished.

Morgause looked away as if to hide her loss. Her voice held a slight tremble as she lied, "Be thankful I released you." When she turned back, her beauty had returned. "Now who is this Rayn?"

"She's my daughter."

A Saxon dragged Lancelot back to his feet as he caught his breath.

"A daughter who fights like a warrior and commands legions?" Morgause turned her head and considered him.

"Aye, the times are dangerous. I've raised her to defend herself like a Briton knight. As for her nature of authority, well, she is a headstrong child, always has been." He knew Morgause was able to discern truth from falsehood, and he stared straight at her, hoping he passed inspection.

Her red lips curled upward in silent triumph. "So you haven't been so faithful to your vows after all. Who's the mother?"

"It matters not," he challenged. "She's been dead for years." Once more he felt Morgause probing, and he prayed for the Spirit to protect him.

"So it would seem."

"This can't be!" Mordred groused, stalking toward Lancelot. "The woodland spirits said Arthur's child still lives! So if Lancelot doesn't have him, who does?"

Morgause seemed to consider her son's inquiry, and then glowered at Lancelot.

Mordred's dark gaze followed.

Lancelot forced himself to remain calm, confident. God had delivered him before and would do so again if it was his will. One problem remained. The only way he'd ever leave Belizar alive was to not give them what they wanted.

Chapter Fourteen

"AHH-CHEW!" RAYN sneezed and swiped her leaking eyes with the tattered edge of her sleeve.

Leading the way, Shadoe grunted his lack of sympathy. She was thankful that so far he hadn't rubbed her illness in her face. She didn't want to look at Perceval, who rode abreast of her. She felt miserable enough.

The aggravating Shadoe un Hollo Tors had occupied her thoughts a good share of the night. The rest she'd spent praying to the Lord Almighty to protect her father and to bless their rescue attempt. Since her first encounter with the young enchanter, she'd spent too much time dwelling on him, and she pleaded with God to give her peace. In short, the sleep she desperately needed she never got, and now her head felt like a ripe melon about to burst.

If I could just sleep a few minutes, I'd—

A firm hand tugged her forearm. Rayn jolted in her saddle and stared into Perceval's concerned features.

"My Lady, are you feeling well?"

"Of course." She tightened her grip on the mare's reins.

"You were asleep." His burnished brows meshed in that familiar way that stated he was short on patience with her.

"I was not!" Rayn felt shame further warm her fevered cheeks.

Before she could speak further, Shadoe came alongside her. "You'll ride with Percy."

"I will not!" she hissed, making certain the hooded cloak she wore concealed her face.

"She's holding us back, Percy," Shadoe asserted.

"Aye," the knight confirmed. "I have but one good arm and doubt I can hold her and control my horse at the same time."

The men locked gazes.

Rayn didn't like what she saw. "I'll stay awake, I will," she said with a tight jaw. She sat high in the saddle and glowered at Shadoe's approach.

"You need rest." His voice held no leeway. He snatched her off her mare and onto his lap. "And we need you alert in a few hours."

"Nay!" Rayn twisted in his arms and slugged his sinew-tight chest. She sent a frantic look to Perceval. He frowned and shook his head.

Shadoe clenched her wrists with one hand. "Don't worry, maiden. I prefer my women awake and willing, not to mention with meat on their bones," he murmured, releasing her wrists.

Rayn gasped at his insult but got no help from Perceval, whose brows were still meshed in annoyance. "Shadoe's right."

"Percy!" she gasped in disbelief, but his innocent expression suggested he hadn't heard Shadoe's remark.

Perceval took her mare's reins, and then tossed over her staff. "Here. In case he gets frisky, which I doubt."

Catching the staff, Rayn witnessed an exchange of winks between the men. Despite having her staff and dagger, she felt uncomfortably vulnerable.

"Don't I have a voice?" She planted herself rigidly between Shadoe's leather-clad thighs and sat arrow straight, maintaining the barest contact with him.

"Aye." His breath burned hot against her cheek. "And I suspect sleep is the only time you don't."

Rayn's elbow found its target, and he flinched.

"So much for niceties," he groused. "Hold on!" He put his heels to Destrier's flanks and galloped off, leaving Perceval in their dust.

A good mile later, after making his point, Shadoe eased Destrier into a trot. Within minutes of riding across the flat grasslands, the rolling motion seduced Rayn. Somewhere in the misty landscape of dreams, she found refuge in the strong arms of an imaginary knight and the coolness of his hand against her hot brow.

Rayn nestled further into her fantasy lover's arms and grimaced. Every muscle of her body ached. Her head pounded fiercely. She wished this part of her dream would vanish. When she broke into an uncontrollable cough, she awoke to discover she was indeed in a man's arms. Shadoe's. Jolting upright, she would have toppled save for his swift reflexes. He snatched her waist and pulled her firmly against him.

"Whoa!" he ordered Destrier.

Spooked, the stallion reared up.

With steeled expertise, Shadoe commanded the reins and juggled Rayn.

Not impressed, Rayn sunk her teeth into his wrist. "Let go!"

Shadoe did.

Rayn encountered the ground face first.

Sprawled on her belly, Rayn lifted her muck-drenched face and spit mud. She glared at Shadoe, who, still in his saddle, stroked Destrier's mane to console the horse. Rayn's anger surged when Shadoe engaged Perceval's stunned expression.

"Guess she's awake." Shadoe smirked.

"You bumbling oaf!" She spit mud.

"I'm not the one eating mire, brat." Alighting, Shadoe chuckled.

Perceval offered Rayn assistance, but she brushed him off and rose to her knees. "'Tis fine, I am." The trees spun around her, and she felt sick to her stomach. When she staggered forward, both men caught hold of an arm and carted her to a nearby tree. After plopping her against the trunk, Shadoe examined his left wrist. He sucked blood from the puncture and spit it out as if he'd been bite by a snake. "You little viper, you drew blood."

"And the taste of you makes me want to retch," she whined, clenching her waist.

"Enough!" Perceval growled. "Rayn, you've a fever and must rest. Belizar is over that ridge." He pointed to the line of pines. "We must decide if we are to enter before nightfall or wait until morning."

"I suggest neither." Shadoe stepped back, pulled out a faded blue ribbon, and wrapped the bite mark.

Rayn gawked at the familiar ribbon, then looked back at the trees, hoping her expression didn't betray her. *No doubt about it, I'm going to vomit!*

"What are you talking about?" Perceval inquired of Shadoe, brow furrowed in suspicion.

"There's no escape from Belizar."

"But you did."

"'Tis fabrication. I did nothing." His voice softened. "An angel freed me."

Rayn and Perceval stared at him, wide-eyed.

"Now it's you who speaks fabrication," she squeaked as her voice faded. "You who admit to believing in nothing, let alone God, expect us to believe an angel freed you?"

"I never said I don't believe in God," Shadoe snarled.

Rayn scoffed. "Bah, next he'll have us believing he sees dragons!"

"Actually there was the time—"

"Well," Perceval broke in, "I don't know 'bout dragons, but the last time I saw Shadoe, his faith in our Lord God was strong if not greater than my own. Besides, 'twould explain his escape from Hell's Gate."

Rayn rolled her eyes. "He's afraid is all." She gripped her midsection as nausea pressed against her ribs.

Shadoe dropped to one knee and glared into her watery gaze. "Aye, I am. And best you are afraid. Fear keeps us alert. Keeps us alive."

"I haven't time to be afraid, Sir, or ill. Mayhap my father is dying as we speak, he is!"

"Nay, I'm quite alive, daughter."

Stunned, Rayn staggered to her feet while Shadoe and Perceval drew their swords to defend her.

"Da!" Rayn called out to the familiar voice.

"Aye." An exhausted Lancelot stumbled out of the trees, leading his unsaddled horse.

"Lancelot?" Perceval held his sword between them and glanced about the woods for Saxons.

"I'm alone and unarmed." He lifted his arms to show his sword, lance, and stabbing knife missing.

Rayn stumbled around Shadoe and Perceval and into her father's open arms. "Oh, Da!" she cried, reaching up and touching his bruised, lacerated face. Lancelot kissed Rayn's forehead and face, and she kissed him back. He embraced her so hard she thought she'd break. "We thought you'd been captured." She gasped for air.

"I was," he admitted. He sent a suspicious glance Shadoe's way. "Would seem Mordred believes I'm of more value alive than dead."

"At least for the time being." Perceval sighed and gave Lancelot a brotherly hug.

Embracing him, Lancelot nodded. "Aye. Best we leave before he changes his mind. Then again, I don't think it was entirely his idea to set me free."

"What are you saying, Da?" Rayn questioned.

"The Saxon King Hengist was present. I suspect I owe him my life."

"What?" Perceval looked stunned. "His tribe settled in southern Kent. Why would he venture this far north?"

Lancelot shrugged. "We know Mordred has Saxon support. Now we know who it is. Hengist wanted to talk to me alone, and I'm sure I would have found our conversation of deep interest. But Morgause got rid of me before it could happen." He brushed his soiled hand across Rayn's hot cheeks, and his smile dropped into a frown. "Blessed stars, you're ill, child."

"I'm better now that you're here, Da," she said with conviction.

Lancelot leveled his gaze on Shadoe, who acknowledged him with a reserved nod. Shadoe appeared edgy. Did her father not recognize him?

"By all that's sacred!" Releasing Rayn, Lancelot strode over and addressed Shadoe. "Welcome home, Shadoe un Hollo Tors. You're more than a foot taller, you are!"

Shadoe extended his hand. "Thank you, Sir Lancelot, it's good to be back."

"You traitorous murdering cretin!" Her father's fist flew.

Shadoe dodged too late.

Lancelot struck his jaw.

Shadoe went crossed-eyed, then toppled.

When Shadoe hit dirt, Rayn gasped. She must be dreaming. Her father was alive and had just punched her nemesis. She was so deliriously overwhelmed, she wanted to vomit. Bending over, she did.

∽◦

"I can't believe you let that jackal into our lands!" Lancelot lectured Perceval.

"And I can't believe you claim to be a follower of the Fisherman, yet fail to forgive Shadoe."

"More than a hundred men died in Belizar because of his cowardly heart!" He knelt next to Rayn and pressed a wet rag to her warm brow.

"They would have died anyway," said Perceval from where he knelt at Rayn's other side. "No one enters the dungeons of Belizar and leaves alive."

"He did!" Lancelot hissed.

"God sent an angel to deliver him."

Lancelot balked. "You expect me to believe that?"

Perceval sighed. "No less than you expect me to believe that you and Guenevere were never familiar."

He glanced to where Shadoe was still sprawled, out cold. "'Tis a low blow, Percy."

"Aye, so was your fist to his straw jaw."

Lancelot flexed his right hand and bruised knuckles. "Well, 'twas a wild guess that his chin was as weak as when he was a stripling. He never could take a direct hit."

Perceval snorted. "I'm more upset over your anger at Shadoe. He made mistakes. We all have. I strongly sense Shadoe's need for forgiveness, as well as a desire to become part of clan Pendragon again. He has no one, Lance. Surely we are partially responsible. We wrongly accused the Merdyn of betraying Arthur, and then during Shadoe's most desperate hour, we did nothing. Had not God intervened, Shadoe would be dead."

Lancelot argued. "We had no proof that Shadoe survived Mordred's invasion of Caer Camelot. How could we have known, then, that he'd been captured?"

"Then how did Mordred learn of Excalibur's location? You didn't tell me of yours and Shadoe's spiritual encounter until after Mordred offered a reward to anyone who could free Excalibur from the loch. Tell me, friend, how would you have responded under torture?"

"We made a blood vow, Percy, to take that knowledge to our graves. And I would have. Shadoe is a traitor in every respect!"

"Lancelot's right. I betrayed him and clan Pendragon."

Lancelot looked over his shoulder at Shadoe.

"You were barely a man," Perceval defended.

"I make no excuses." Massaging his battered chin, Shadoe approached Lancelot.

Lancelot shot to his feet and strode toward Shadoe, pinning him with a lethal glare.

Perceval stood and stepped between them to intervene the feud. Shadoe motioned him aside. "I can handle this myself, Percy." He came within a few feet of Lancelot. "Sir Lancelot du Lac, I did not, nor ever will, possess the noble heart of a knight of the Round Table. But I have returned to fulfill an oath to Lady Guenevere and to my father. Once those vows are complete, I will be gone from Caledonia and from your sight."

The years of Lancelot's hate at the betrayal surged forth. He glared into the taller man's intense features. It was like looking into the face of a young Merlin, although Lancelot had not known the Merdyn as a youth, but it affected him greatly. His heart hammered so fast that he thought it would burst. Everything Perceval said was true. Shadoe had been no more than a child when he was captured, tortured, and according to good sources, thrown into Hell's Gate. Still, here he stood alive and with enough courage to confront the one man who had every right to kill him. What if Yahweh had freed Shadoe and brought him home? Lancelot glanced at his sleeping daughter, knowing she was the reason for Shadoe's return. However painful, it was time Lancelot fulfilled the promise he'd made to Arthur.

"Sire, you have every right to cut me down," said Shadoe. "If that is your choice, be quick about it." Shadoe presented the hilt of his sword to the former knight as if to accept his fate.

Lancelot met Perceval's anguished look and recalled Jesu's words to Judas during the hour of his betrayal, "But woe to that man who betrays the Son of Man! It would be better for him if he had never been born." Lancelot aimed the blade at Shadoe's heart. "I thought I'd forgiven you, Shadoe un Hollo Tors, but God has revealed the coldness of my heart. If he can forgive my iniquities, surely I can do the same for you. Now can you forgive me as well?" He turned the sword's hilt to Shadoe.

Accepting his weapon, Shadoe slipped it back into his waist sheath and met Lancelot's sincere gaze. "There is nothing to forgive, friend. Your acceptance of me is more than I ever hoped for."

Putting out his hand, Lancelot smiled. "Welcome back, Shadoe un Hollo Tors, and this time, I mean it."

Both men shook hands. A bellow exploded from Perceval, who rushed over and clasped the men's shoulders, drawing them together. "Wait 'till Tristam sees this! Glory to God, the Round Table is once more complete."

Shadoe paled.

"What of Galahad?" a trembling voice inquired. Three sets of eyes lowered to where Rayn had managed to perch upright against the tree trunk. Her features were flushed, but she seemed alert. "It's been months since we sent for him. Something is amiss."

"Mayhap when we return to Ayr, there will be news," Lancelot offered in reassurance, then noted the curious expression on the enchanter's face. "Shadoe, you and Galahad have crossed paths over the years. When did you last see him?"

"Aye, in Rome two years ago."

"Oh, Da, that's the newest account we've heard since he left. I worry for him so."

"Galahad is quite capable of taking care of himself," Shadoe stated. "I've had firsthand experience with his swordsmanship."

⤙⤚

Rayn struggled to her feet. *Wishh!* A spear nearly grazed her neck. Dropping to her belly, she heard curses as the men drew their weapons. She spotted her staff two yards off; it could have been miles for how ill she felt. Their horses bolted as unknown men invaded the camp, swords drawn, and axes and spears raised in the air. The colorful painting on their faces identified them as Scotti. Heavens, why were they attacking? For the most part, the Caledonians were at peace with the Scotti. Rayn had no time to reach a conclusion. When she looked again, Lancelot was blocking attacks with her staff, while Perceval and Shadoe fought with swords. Echo had another man on the ground, tearing at the attacker's throat.

A Scotti brandishing an axe spotted Rayn. She rolled behind the tree and whipped out her stinger. Rayn leaped to her feet and flung the dagger into his midsection. She sped into the open to engage the next Scotti.

"Rayn!" Lancelot called out.

Rayn looked toward her father, and the world began to spin. Overhead, Mer screeched, then dove at a Scotti. The Eagle's strike sent the man sprawling on his back, and his spear fell to the ground. Mer clawed his face with razor-sharp talons. Rayn snatched up the Scotti's spear and looked about but could not focus.

"Get her out of here. We'll meet in Ayr!" Lancelot ordered Shadoe.

At the Scotti's blood-curdling wail, she flung the spear at him and he toppled over—but not from her botched strike. Shadoe pulled his sword out of the man's back. The next moment the earth rose to meet her.

Rayn's world went black.

Chapter Fifteen

THE ROCKING MOTION had returned, and Rayn drifted in and out of consciousness. Each time she tried to awaken, a cool hand pressed against her, and she nestled into the possessive arms of her phantom knight.

In her dream, the air smelled like sweet rain. Explosive cracks burst inside her head. She awoke startled. Disoriented, Rayn looked around the vast moorlands and the encroaching wall of gray, fringed with jagged spears of white light. When another thunderclap cracked the air, she jolted in the saddle. The arm that held her waist tightened, and she twisted about to find Shadoe staring down at her.

"It's just thunder, Princess." His tone was pleasant.

Rayn's warrior pride reared up. "I do not fear storms. Where are my father and Percy?" She looked around frantically.

"Not far behind."

"You left them?" Rayn cradled her throbbing head.

"Your da ordered me to get you safely away."

"When did you start obeying anyone?"

"I've always been respectful of my elders, especially your father."

"Well, I was doing just fine."

"Aye, until you passed out face down."

"I'm better now. Turn back!"

"There are miles between us. . . ." He motioned to the murky gossamer sky. "And a storm approaches. We'll take shelter in that tor."

He indicated a cresting summit with a craggy face and a broad overhang of bush. Minutes later, he rode Destrier along the outcrop of rock then reined his steed to a stop.

Before he could escort her, Rayn swung down off the horse and stretched her sore limbs. Shadoe removed the stallion's reins and gently patted its hindquarters. "This is home tonight, Destrier."

Thunder rolled overhead, and she jolted. "Shouldn't you tether him?"

"Nay, especially not during a storm. Trees are often struck by lightning." He turned and looked at her. "Thought you knew that."

"I know lightning hits trees, but . . ." She gestured at Destrier, then looked away flustered.

"He won't run off, if that's your concern."

She shrugged, uncertain what she had meant. She was babbling. Rayn heard the familiar screech of an eagle and hoped Mer wouldn't show himself. She smiled, recalling the eagle's assistance during the raid. Not wanting to give Shadoe a link between her and the raptor, Rayn raised her hands as if stretching and used the opportunity to motion Mer to keep clear—trouble being, Mer never listened well. To her dismay, she caught Shadoe's studied surveillance. The enchanter rolled his eyes and smirked but did not refer to Mer.

"Follow me. There's a cave a ways up this rock." He tossed her a satchel as he swung his saddle and cloak over his shoulder and proceeded to scale the bush-draped cliff. Mountain climbing being second nature, Rayn scaled the wall with ease. Sixty feet later, Shadoe swung himself onto a ledge and then offered Rayn his hand. She ignored him and hoisted herself onto the shelf. Shadoe shot her a smile of approval, then gestured to an aperture in the bare-stoned rise.

"After you." He made a sweeping bow and stepped aside, allowing Rayn to duck and scramble through the four-by-four-foot opening. Inside, the cave expanded to between ten and twelve-feet wide. *At least we won't be in each other's faces.* She crawled into the musty darkness.

Shadoe tossed his saddle inside, smacking Rayn's backside.

"What the—" She cursed in Gaelic and turned to glare at him.

"I'll collect kindling before the sky opens," he called, already out of view.

Rayn huffed. She didn't know why she behaved so wretchedly but hoped it perturbed him. She liked doing that. Besides, she felt dreadful and feverish. *This is one horrible cold!* She wished she had her horse and most of all her sack that held healing herbs.

Shoving Shadoe's supplies aside, Rayn stood upright and slammed her head. "Ow!" She pressed onward into the darkness, relieved to find a spot where she could stand. The ebbing sunlight visible from the chasm would vanish once the storm hit. Feeling safer near the light, she returned to the cave's mouth and settled on the hard, dry floor.

Shadoe made two trips before the spring gale broke. Inside, his expression curious, he arched a brow at her. Rayn pondered what was wrong. A curl tickled her cheek. She froze. The tendril had escaped her cap, and she shoved it back in place. When she looked up, Shadoe had turned away. She hoped the lack of light concealed her hair color.

Using his flint, Shadoe ignited a twig and held its flame near the ceiling. The smoke snaked along the cavern's roof before being sucked up through a crack. Beneath the crevice he built a fire just big enough to restrain the chill that would come with nightfall.

"Don't know how long before this updraft changes, but we'll have a fire for a while."

Shivering, Rayn nodded. When the fire disturbed a batch of bats, she glanced up as they dove over her head and out the cave.

"Well, well!" Shadoe said in an admirable tone to her lack of fear.

"Good Sir, considering we just slew murdering Scotti, bats aren't about to ruffle me. More important, I'm worried about Da and Percy. Do you think they got away?"

"Of course." He foraged through the satchels.

"You sound quite confident for someone who doesn't believe in Yahweh."

"Uh-huh." He took out a cloth-wrapped bundle.

"You're a conceited insect, you are!"

Shadoe opened his find and presented her half. "How did I offend you this time, brat?"

"In your arrogance that my father and Percy are on their way home."

"Forgive me if my faith in them is greater than yours. I've seen those two stand up against a band of twenty and walk away without a scratch. And since there were only ten Scotti, I'm sure they fared well."

Why does he twist everything I say and then dub me the skeptic? Rayn burned.

"My trust in their abilities is the utmost, Sir, but that doesn't mean I don't fret over them."

"Mayhap you should trust God more." He guffawed.

To refrain from spewing something ungodly, Rayn examined the chunk of dried leather. She fingered it several times then frowned.

Shadoe set his teeth into the brown strip, tore off a slice, and chewed. When he saw her reluctance, he urged, "It's salt pork and quite tasty."

"Really," she muttered with disparagement, while the growling of her stomach brought the object past her lips to her teeth. It was an effort to tear the meat apart, but she succeeded, and then chewed. Two minutes later, still chewing, Rayn admitted it tasted like salty meat. *But will I live long enough to swallow it?* Just when she realized she needed water to wash it down, Shadoe offered his goatskin. Accepting it, she tipped the full skin back and swallowed. A delicious sweet juice wet her mouth, but a few gulps later she suspected it was fermented and gave it back. She did not handle well anything fermented, nor did she believe in drinking spirits. She sneezed again and wiped her sleeve across her dripping nose.

"There's enough for both of us."

Stop being nice! "Thank you, Sir, but I'm fine, I am. What type of brew is this?"

He sent her a curious look. "I suppose you've never consumed anything other than distilled rye or cider. It's a fruit called plum from Spain. I brewed it last year."

"The Merdyn used to brew wine." Rayn reflected, a smile tugging her lips.

"He still did that, huh?"

"Aye, the first time we met I came across him bent over a cauldron in the wood. I thought him a druid priest concocting a ceremonial potion. He was cooking grapes he'd brought from Gaul. I never understood how he transported grapes that distance without them rotting—"

"When was that?" He removed his cloak and armor and laid them out to dry. Rayn noted his damp tunic. Her attention fixed on the ripple of muscles against the wet shirt as he tugged the blouse free of his leather leggings. When she'd failed to answer, he turned back and settled down across from her. She felt his discerning gaze and cleared her mind of her flustered thoughts.

"Forgive me, Princess, but I am curious about my father's time here. How old were you?"

Assured by his inquisitive tone, she rested against the cold stone wall and folded her arms. "I was almost seven years wise. We had just come from Tintagel where we'd lived since my birth. We stayed at Camelot for a while, but Da said it was too large to keep up alone. So we moved into Ayr and visited Camelot regularly—at least Tristam, Percy, and myself—and still do." She had Shadoe's attention.

"And?"

"'Tis when I met your da. He was so gallant and oh so tall. Although well seasoned with age, Mer is . . . was very handsome. My first infatuation." She blushed at the memory. "Being but a child, I decided that whomever my godsend would be, he had to be as handsome as Merlin in his experienced years. Men turn more handsome with age, they do."

"Really?" Shadoe arched a speculative brow and hunkered closer to the heat of the crackling fire. He chaffed his hands and waited on her.

Rayn stifled a cough. Just thinking about Merlin's gentle heart warmed her. "The Merdyn was kind to me, he was. We met almost every day. We'd sit on the petrified log by the loc and—"

"That fallen oak is still there?" His brows waggled with keen interest.

"Ahh. Like a rock it is, now. No doubt it shall be there forever."

Shadoe smiled warmly and held her gaze until she glanced away.

Snagging her lower lip, she pondered why he bewildered her so and that she liked when he smiled at her.

"I saw Camelot through Merlin's eyes: the sights, sounds, smells, people. Oh, it must have been a place of grand splendor in its day." She looked to Shadoe for affirmation.

"Aye, but that splendor's lost." He seemed to reflect, and then cleared his throat.

Rayn was intrigued by the forced composure that strained the handsome lines of his face. *What are you thinking, scion of Merlin? Dare I assume to see sentiment in your eyes, remorse?*

"Then you knew he was the Merdyn?"

She gave a negative toss of her head. "Not at first. He was simply Mer. I knew there was something mystical about him . . . something wondrous." Hugging her chilled arms, she spoke with childlike enthusiasm. "He taught me to dream dreams and that all things are possible if one believes in God. Every day with Mer was an adventure. A fantasy, it was."

Rayn glimpsed a longing in Shadoe's eyes. A sigh slipped past his lips. "Aye, I remember we once . . ." He donned a mask of indifference. "Did Lancelot know about Merlin?"

"Nay. Mer made me promise to tell no one he was on Wind's Haven. He feared that he'd be forced off, and his only desire was to live out his days there. I agreed because I was selfish. I loved your da and wanted to keep him to myself, I did. Eventually, my da found us out." She winked.

"Three years later," she continued. "Oh, 'twas a nasty affair, it was. Why I feared Da would kill Merlin. Da accused him of betraying Arthur to Mordred all those years back. Fortunately, Perceval and Tristam arrived, and after several hours of negotiating, they came to a truce. What was said behind those doors I know not, but somehow Merlin convinced Da and the others he was no traitor. He had faked his death to protect Arthur's lineage, not destroy it. From then on, the Merdyn became my mentor, my best friend, he did."

When Rayn hesitated, Shadoe gestured with his hand for her to proceed.

Although her head throbbed and her throat ached, she obliged him. "During the long stretches when Da, Percy, and Tristam were fighting distant enemies, I stayed with Mer. Once, I asked if he'd like me to pray for him. He replied, 'Aye, pray that my prodigal scion returns home.'"

Agony marked Shadoe's face, but he said nothing.

"Mer told me he loved you, he did. That he'd abandoned you by allowing you to believe he'd died. He chastised himself for not being able to free you from Belizar, for he'd fled to Gaul and didn't know of your imprisonment until after you'd escaped."

Shadoe's eyes darkened. The muscle at his cleft jaw twitched. He turned his head and stared at the black sky.

∞

"Don't stop now, Princess. It's intriguing to hear someone else's version of those missing years," he muttered sarcastically.

She cleared her throat. "About two years ago, he left. I was the last to see him and foolish enough to believe he would return. I was wrong. I just can't believe . . ." Her voice clotted. "You were with him. Did he suffer?"

"Nay, not much."

The silence that separated them was a blessing and a curse. Soft sobs emitting from the brat reaffirmed Shadoe's suspicions. Rayn had clung to her belief that Merlin would return just as Shadoe had clung to the hope that sharing Merlin's last hours had been a mere dream. What he wouldn't give to see his da. To hear his fatherly lectures, the feel of his reassuring grip on Shadoe's shoulder. To see those white hawkish brows mesh in frustration at him. Frustration well merited.

Through a wash of tears, Shadoe stared out the cavern's gaping hole and concentrated on the light vaulting across the ashen sky. His shoulders quaked. He'd never allowed himself to mourn his father's passing.

Rayn's emotional openness set him off. He must regain control. It was crucial. After crushing his tears, Shadoe turned about and said in a confident baritone, "He died peacefully and was swept up to the gates of heaven."

Rayn sniffled then wiped her tears and nose with the back of her hand. "On a whirlwind of fire?"

"Aye!" Shadoe's breath hitched in bewilderment. "How did you know?"

Her ruby lips curved upward, and she leaned toward the fire's warmth. "During our last weeks together, Mer confided that God had revealed to him the last moments of his life. He would spend it with you, and moments after he died, a spewing fire would carry the vessel of his soul away."

"It did."

"I was selfish, Shadoe." She picked up a twig and poked at the fire's embers. "I wanted Mer, and refused to bend to God's will, to accept that Yahweh allowed me to know how Merlin would pass into his kingdom. Now that I've heard it did indeed happen, I'm relieved. I'm at peace."

"You aren't serious?" Shadoe gawked.

"Aye, I am. God is sovereign," she stated confidently as a yawn broke from her lips.

Shadoe didn't answer for he was still digesting their exchange. He leaned against the cold wall and drew his shaking legs up to his chest. He felt ill. He wondered if he had acquired Rayn's cold. "What did the Merdyn say before he left you?"

"That he had to find you before Yahweh called him home. He needed to pass on his legacy and give you his blessing."

"And so he did."

"Aye?" She tilted her head at his whisper.

"May I be so bold as to ask your age?"

Fighting another yawn, she nodded. "Seventeen come autumn."

Blood rushed to Shadoe's temples. She'd just confirmed Perceval's statement. "And your full name is Rose Rayn du Lac," he stated matter-of-factly, hoping, even praying, he was right.

"My friends address me as Rayn, they do. My Christian name is Emerald Rose Rayn du Lac."

"Emerald?" His voice cracked. *Demon's fire! Guenevere requested I protect her Emerald Rose, not the blasted talisman!*

"Aye. Da says it's because my eyes are as green as the emerald tors of Caledonia and as bright as the emerald talisman King Arthur once wore." She shrugged. "I've rarely seen my eyes. Are they really that color?" She scooted uncomfortably close.

Shadoe stared into her verdant gaze.

His senses spiraled.

His stomach pitched.

"Nay." He pulled back abruptly.

Her mouth pouted with confusion.

"I mean, they are an unusual green . . . I guess."

Rayn lifted a soft auburn brow. "Thank you. I think." As if wounded by his apathy, she rocked back on her heels and gazed at the fire pit. The firelight cast a soft glow on her features. Despite being ill, her full lips reminded him of lush wild berries, and her button nose was cute enough to kiss. *Curse the del! What am I thinking?* His heated gaze drifted to her layered clothing that could not conceal the fullness of her bosom. *Enough!* He grabbled for his cloak and tossed it at her. "Here, wrap this about you. It will get colder, and you need to get well."

"What about you?" She accepted the cloak, her expression wary.

"I'll be fine. I've slept in harsher conditions." He drew a ram's skin from his satchel and spread it on the ground.

Rayn settled in on the opposite end of the fire.

"You'd be better off here." He indicated the smoother floor and half of the ram's wool on which he stretched out.

"Whist, I'm sure." She rolled her eyes.

"Don't flatter yourself, lad." A grunt of annoyance burned his lips.

She snorted like a lad.

"When the draft changes, you'll wish you'd accepted my offer."

"Where's Echo?" Rayn changed direction.

"Eating." He padded a rock with his satchel.

"You mean she's killing, she is?"

"We do it to eat." He chuckled.

"Aye." She swept debris from the spot she'd chosen. "But the savageness."

"Humph!" Shadoe tipped his head sideways but held his tongue.

"What?" She sent him a testy look.

"Humanity never ceases to amaze me, Lady Rayn."

Her eyes lifted uncomfortably at his formal address. "Why?"

"We who are set apart from the rest of God's creation slaughter our own with little conscience yet are intolerant when a wild creature does what's instinctive to its survival."

∽

The wisdom behind Shadoe's words seemed unsuited to his cynical nature. Merlin would have spoken such candid truth, and had it come from him, Rayn would have humbly answered, "You're right, Sire."

"What?" He smirked.

She grit her teeth. *Demon's dung, I spoke out loud.*

Trying to dismiss her admission, she noticed the thick muscles of his upper arms and became fascinated when he turned his back to her and pulled his damp tunic over his head. To distract herself from his bare back, she settled into her makeshift bed. When the firelight flickered across Shadoe's upper torso, Rayn chewed her lower lip in fascination. Disfiguring scars that she'd seen on abused slaves marred Shadoe's shoulders and broad back. She closed the gap between them and knelt to stare at his seasoned injuries. Not one inch of his deeply tanned skin seemed to have escaped the whip's talons. Even worse was the deep discoloration, evidence of fire branding. Curious, she reached out and touched a jagged scar.

Searing pain tore through her fingertips, up her arm, and transferred to her back. Rayn opened her mouth to scream. Her voice froze in agony. Horrible visions invaded her mind's eye. She experienced the torture of a branding iron and the stench of scorched flesh.

Her flesh.

Her heart raced from the pain.

She wheezed, struggling against her torturer.

Death pressed upon her, held her prisoner.

A strong hand gripped her wrist. Tossed onto her back, Rayn's wrists were pinned to her sides. The burning vanished. When she opened her eyes, Shadoe un Hollo Tors, his face contorted in rage, straddled her hips with his muscular thighs. She couldn't move, let alone breathe.

"As you value your life, do not ever touch me like that again!" he growled.

Frightened by his violent behavior and her strange phenomenon, Rayn struggled to force the words past her lips. "I'm sorry, I . . ."

Unconscious of his strength, he squeezed her wrists tighter and glared into her eyes. "What did you see, feel?" he demanded.

She fought against his restraining clasp. "I don't know. Never before . . ." She dropped her eyes to her throbbing wrists. "Let go!" she hissed.

Shadoe's eyes cleared suddenly as if coming out of a trance. But without apology, he rolled off Rayn yet continued to glower at her.

Rubbing her wrists, then her neck, she sent him a dubious look. "You seem to know that I encountered something very strange and frightening. You tell me what it was, Enchanter."

"I've no time for this," he snapped, running splayed fingers through his tousled hair. His hands shook.

"We've all night," she challenged. "I want an explanation now!" Rayn's train of thought got diverted by something she'd not seen in two years. The Emerald Rose of Avalon swung from his neck, and she stared in awe. "I remember now, I do. I saw a jail cell, fire, and branding irons. Smelled burning flesh. Felt pain that was mine yet wasn't."

"With whom else have you shared this experience?" he demanded.

Confused, she shook her head. "No one . . . ever." Her voice steeled with resolve as she realized he'd noticed her gaze locked on the amulet. "And I never want to again. 'Twas horrid, it was!" She looked into Shadoe's hawkish eyes and realized the truth. "It was you. I was there. I saw and felt what you felt. Oh, Shadoe, I'm sorry."

His rigid features softened. "It's not always an unpleasant experience, or so I've heard it said."

She gawked. "Being tortured?"

"No . . . sharing another's familiarity."

"You mean you've been through this before?"

Shadoe inhaled a breath and breathed it out. "Nay, but the Merdyn told me it was long known among the inhabitants of Ayris that some people possessed special aptitudes known as the sleeping senses."

"Sleeping senses?" Rayn crinkled her nose, and then sneezed.

"Aye. Senses that Adam and Eve possessed until the fall. Although God's Word doesn't address it, we believe he put these gifts to sleep so that mankind could not use them for evil."

"Then these are gifts of the Spirit?"

Shadoe shook his head. "Nay. These are special attributes of our minds. 'Tis said that clan Ayris possessed them, but in the latter days, they abused their abilities and served the Adversary instead."

"So the Adversary controlled them?"

"In time. Remember, the Adversary is the great deceiver. Even today he seduces those who hunger for love or recognition. He comes as the prince of light, convincing them he is Yahweh, even rescuing them from demons. The Adversary gives them powers in exchange for their eternal souls. Some do not realize what they have sacrificed. Others know exactly what they lost and rejoice serving the fallen angel."

Fascinated, Rayn's eyes widened at his disclosure.

"Many Ayrisians became false prophets, soothsayers, deceivers with words. They manipulated the innocent with promises of speaking to those who'd died. In truth, these liars spoke to demons. They also foresaw future events and catastrophic changes in this earth. Worse was the dependence they engendered for minor issues of daily life—what color clothes to stitch, what foods to eat, whom to marry. All this was contrary to God's divine purpose to communicate through visions the issues of great relevance. Aye, they poisoned people's minds with signs from the stars, nature, and the casting of stones and bones."

"They sound like sorcerers," Rayn commented.

"Aye. They have many names, but they are not of God. Yet the greatest deceit was giving God the glory for their abilities. Thus they tricked most humans, and still do. Yahweh's wrath came upon these liars, those who served them. He ripped away the gifts. There was a handful of clan Ayris who remained faithful to God and retained the inborn gifts of Adam and Eve. Thus, what we just encountered is but a wisp of Eden's breath, another gift is that of speaking without words."

"With one's thoughts?"

"Aye, but that only happens between . . ."

"Between who . . . what?" She sat up astutely and dusted herself off.

He pulled a heavier tunic over his head. "It just rarely occurs, is all. I doubt it will happen again." His tone was steely and final, as if he hoped to stop further discussion of the matter.

"You wear the Rose." She yawned deeper, wrapping herself in the warmth of his cloak.

"Aye. And I'd prefer you didn't announce it to the world," he said with a tone of further annoyance.

"I'm sorry it's such a burden, I am." She watched for a reaction. She got one. Even in the firelight, she could see the muscle of his left cheek pulse and his dark brow arch. His nostrils, unless she was mistaken, flared with anger. Like before, he recovered quickly.

"'Tis in the best interest of all concerned that Mordred not know I am back, let alone possess this. For as a gold crown in Rome symbolizes Caesar, so does this talisman represent the high chieftain of this Isle of Might. Were Mordred to acquire it, he would gain control of the tribes."

Her eyes lighted with revelation. "Heaven's wings! With Merlin gone, you are high steward."

"Lady Rayn, it means nothing. There is no longer a realm called Camelot or a high chieftain. Therefore there is no high steward," Shadoe snorted.

"Then why did you return when it's evident you didn't want to?"

"My issues are with Sir Lancelot, not you."

"You needn't get testy," she groused. Rayn cupped her hands beneath her head and concentrated on the shadows cast by the fire. She sneezed again.

"Here." Shadoe shuffled over to her side.

Propping on her elbows, Rayn looked at the crushed dried herbs he offered her. "What are they?" She suspiciously squinted as to identify them.

"Something to cure your ailment and help you sleep."

"You mean to knock me out, don't you?"

"If that was my desire, it'd be easier to hit you over the head, brat." He smirked.

Rayn met his hawkish dark eyes. The crooked lift of his full mouth set her at ease. Accepting the herbs, she chewed, tasting a distinct licorice and mint flavor.

"Wash it down." He handed over the goatskin.

She drank deeply of the sweet wine.

"Now sleep." He took the skin and turned away.

Curling up, Rayn glared at Shadoe's back as he went down on a knee and fed the fire. Over the past two days, she'd spent most of her time engaged in verbal combat with this confounded man. She was literally exhausted in mind and body. She sneezed again. Worse, she'd hardly spoken to God or asked him for guidance, let alone patience.

Wine-induced sleep washed over her, warming every fiber of her being, lulling her to sleep. Still Rayn struggled to pray.

Abba Father, please forgive my indignant tongue and thoughts of dislike toward Shadoe un Hollo Tors. Perceval insists Shadoe received you into his heart as a child. Yet I see no sign of that eternal relationship. Indeed, I know not whether Shadoe is your child.

Shadoe's hard heart gives him pause for being rude, self-involved, arrogant, and, most of all, disrespectful to you. But I, on the other hand, bear no excuse, for your Spirit abides within me, and I know that my ill behavior does not please you, Lord.

So please use me as a witness to your merciful love. From this moment forward I shall resign myself to letting Shadoe see you in me—aye, e'en if it kills me."

Chapter Sixteen

SOMEWHERE WITHIN THE predawn hours, the wind shifted. The updraft ceased. Awakened by Rayn's coughing, Shadoe wondered how soon before she crept closer to the cave's mouth where he slept. Not long. Cracking open an eye, he watched Rayn creep around and slide her bedding in front of him. Later, Echo padded in, shook off the rain, and to Shadoe's dismay, settled not between them but at Rayn's side. She draped an arm over the wolf and nuzzled close, speaking softly to the wild creature that chose to share her warmth with Rayn instead of him.

Shadoe made lethal eye contact with Echo, but his disfavor did not affect the wolf. Turning his back to them, Shadoe tried to sleep and failed. His heart pounded. His palms sweat. The muscles of his body were taut. Many reasons contributed to this stress, the main one a few feet away: Emerald Rose Rayn. "Glory, why her?" he muttered. He realized he was talking to God, but for the moment it mattered not.

And why didn't I know it sooner? Keep your wits, man. Don't get involved. You returned for one purpose and found it. Arthur's progeny. That fact had been determined by the soul sharing we experienced. Of course, that's if one believes only a person whose veins flow with Ayris blood can share the Eden's breath.

Shadoe was of Merlin's loins and Niamh's womb. Rayn, on the other hand, was definitely of Guenevere's womb. Shadoe reluctantly concluded she was also of Arthur's seed. It seemed the only logical answer for what had happened. This meant the case for Arthur's throne was stronger than ever. In Ayris, a princess, even the youngest, had equal claim to the throne as a prince.

Shadoe flipped over to find Rayn facing him. Although her left arm concealed her features, her cap had slid off to reveal a halo of hair that glistened with the hues of autumn leaves and was secured with streamers of blue fabric.

Shadoe shut his eyes and groused, *She can paint her face with blue lime, but she cannot fool me. Blue eyes? Green eyes? Does it matter what I thought to have seen and what is obviously real? Rayn's protective eagle, her auburn hair, and that intoxicating sweet laugh mean one thing. This long-legged, headstrong brat rescued me from the belly of Loch Lady. By all that's sacred, Rayn du Lac is the enchantress I vowed to find and claim for myself. God is indeed a vengeful God!*

∽◌∽

Rayn awoke well past dawn with a smile on her face and ailments improved, save for a few sniffles. Robins and larks chirped. The air was fresh and cool from the night rain. Wisps of smoke from the dying embers drifted over her and out the cavern's door. Perching upright and stretching, she realized she was within feet of the cave's throat. Curses! She had intended to return to the other side before Shadoe awakened none the wiser.

Behaving as if she had no problem being found out, she turned to where he sat cross-legged. An expression of contemplation played upon his lips as he toyed with a faded blue ribbon. Rayn patted her head, relieved to find her hair tucked securely beneath her tan cap—too securely. Her angst-ridden gaze returned to the ribbon, and she forced down the knob in her throat. *He knows! And how much?* She blushed, recalling the sheer shift she had worn that fateful day. Da would have her flogged if he knew she'd bathed without her escort and companion, Iona.

"Umm, where's your pet wolf?" she asked hoarsely, trying to divert attention from the obvious.

"Where's your pet eagle?" he countered.

"Mer's not a pet."

Shadoe's brows slanted at the familiar name she'd given the predator bird. "Nor is Echo."

"Glad we've got that settled." She pulled her legs up and rested her chin on her knees, engaging his stare down. Meanwhile she became keenly aware of her physical discomforts. Her dry mouth and teeth needed cleansing. Her bladder was overfull.

Several moments of annoying silence passed before Shadoe cleared his throat and dangled the bloodstained blue ribbon like fish bait. "I'll keep your secret if you keep mine, Enchantress." He waggled his brows.

"And what's your secret, aye?" She blushed at the suggestive nature of his address.

"I can't swim. Now yours?"

Rayn struggled to keep her promise to God. She failed the first try. "I havna' the faintest idea what you're talking about, Apprentice Enchanter." She tossed his cloak at him, and then prayed silently, *Oh, merciful Jesu, forgive my lying tongue.*

"Mayhap I should refresh your memory?" He reached over and tugged the cap off her head. Her heavy tresses tumbled down her shoulders, covering her face.

She parted her hair and glared back.

"Ah yes, you were bathing in a cliff pool off Loch Lady Falls and wearing—"

"I saved your miserable life, I did!" she injected before he could say more than she wanted to hear. "And it's a miracle we survived, considering you were out to steal the sword of King Arthur, you were."

"I was?" He gawked at her.

Rayn shot to her knees and closed the space between them, wearing an indignant glower.

"Of course." She grasped his right hand and jabbed his palm that still bore scabs. "I pried your hands off the cursed blade, I did." She examined his callused palm and the fading scar. When their gazes locked, she let go and crawled back, then chaffed her hands against her breeches as if she'd soiled them.

"I confess I am forever in your debt, Enchantress."

"Then you admit you were seeking Excalibur?"

"Exactly what do you want?" He pushed up and crept toward the cave's entrance and the sunshine that awaited him.

"The truth I be wanting," she called after him.

Shadoe turned and shook his head. "The truth is not always pleasant, brat, and not necessarily what we want to hear."

"I want to hear you weren't trying to steal Excalibur," she spouted in frustration, realizing what she truly wished was for him to be noble like Merlin.

"You want honesty?"

With her hands on her slender hips, knees braced, and her shoulders squared, she nodded.

"I've been a thief, a hired sword, and a gambler most of my life." He looked candidly back at her.

"That's your answer?"

"What does your heart tell you?"

Her shoulders slumped. His honesty took her totally by surprise.

"I mean," Shadoe continued, "I'm pretty tarnished around the edges, Princess."

"We're all tarnished. That's why God sent us his only Scion to die on the cross and—"

"Enchantress." His tone was thick as he leaned against the cavern wall with his back to her.

"What?"

"I know exactly what Jesu did. What you don't understand is that I no longer care nor want him in my life."

Her heart thudded with spiritual upheaval. "Then sorry I am. You believe he deserted and hurt you deeply."

An uncomfortable pause passed. "I'll be back."

"I need relief myself, I do."

He looked over, surprised at her bluntness. Her face colored.

Rayn glanced away. "Well, I do, and parched as a stone, too, I am."

"After I catch our meal and we breakfast, I'll get water," he said in a clipped tone. "Restart the fire so we can eat, if it's not too much trouble." He gestured to the pile of wood he'd stacked outside. "And don't go anywhere until I return."

She made a rude face at his exiting back. "Only if I can go alone," she said, mimicking his condescending tone. What happened to the mysterious gentleman he'd been the night before? What had happened to her vow to be like Jesu? Shadoe was no closer to Jesu than before he dropped into Loch Lady. *Really, Lord, 'tis a difficult soul you've assigned me to rescue. At least he admitted to being so.*

Startled, her thoughts swept back to Merlin's prophecy: *In regard to your godsend, well, I do not recall stating his armor gleamed. You must remember his sinful humanity. In all honesty his leathers are weather worn, and his armor is tarnished around the edges.*

Rayn plopped onto her bottom. Nay, not Shadoe! Mayhap, she'd heard wrong. No doubt it was merely a coincidence that Shadoe saw himself that way. What other explanation was there? Yet Merlin knew her godsend well, knew his strengths and weaknesses. She shut her eyes and revisited her last conversation with Merlin.

⁓

"*Your godsend will come when the full bloom of womanhood is upon you. But I doubt you'll recognize him; in truth, you will probably dislike him and he you.*"

"*Nay, Mer. I'll know him, and we will be friends first off!*" She squeezed her eyes shut and expelled a dramatic sigh. "*For he will fall headfirst in love with me, he will.*"

Merlin groaned and rolled his weary eyes. "Oh, I've no doubt he will fall headfirst for you—quite literally I suspect."

∽⧜

Shadoe had leapt—fallen—over Loch Lady Falls!

Rayn shot to her feet and slammed her head against the granite ceiling. Pain shot through her head. "Ow!" she wailed then cursed.

Echo stuck her head in the cave's mouth and cocked her gray ears at Rayn.

"Whist, what are you looking at, aye?"

The wolf whimpered and backed out.

"Go ahead, run off to your rusted master." Rayn rubbed her aching skull, then lifted her frustrations heavenward. "'Tis said you have plans for me, Jesu. If Shadoe un Hollo Tors is my godsend, I seek a patient, compassionate, and respectful heart toward him. Above all, grant me a visible sign that you intend us to be one . . . because I still don't like the man!"

It took fifteen minutes to fire up the damp twigs beneath the dry wood. Ten more minutes, and thirst outranked hunger. Shaking the empty goatskin, Rayn groaned. Shadoe was still gone. By the time he returned, she'd have died from thirst—and discomfort. Stepping onto the ledge, she gazed about but saw no signs of fresh water except for the mud pools from last night's deluge. Craning her neck, she looked up to find the rock face too smooth to climb freehand, but she suspected there might be fresh water as the western slope was grassy.

Rayn went back into the cave, laced up her sandals, and then considered the darkness of the innermost cavern. If there was a bear's den on the other side—which she highly doubted—there could be another exit. Stringing the goatskin over her shoulder, she hunkered down and moved into the shadows. When she came to a dead end, she slid her hands along the stone surface until she felt a small opening. Prying out loose rocks, she smiled at the distant dim light only to gasp at the potent scent of animal dung and something wild.

With the taste of dust in her throat, Rayn ignored her instincts and pulled enough stones free to shimmy through the elevated breach that spanned about six feet. Landing on solid ground, Rayn gagged from the stench of fresh animal droppings. Heading for the light, she found a gaping hole of earth large enough for a brown bear to crawl through. With winter but a few months past, the bears still utilized the den. Once outside, she scrambled into the thick bush and trees and moments later emerged feeling the better for it. Within five minutes of tramping and thirstier than ever, she fixed her gaze on a watering hole.

Rayn smirked. Too easy. She'd be back before Shadoe returned. She approached the pool, opening the goatskin in the process. She'd just filled the hide and tied it off when water splashed across from her. Springing to her feet, she spotted two cubs on the opposite bank, tussling. Rayn froze, and then relaxed. They were adorable, oblivious to her presence.

The air filled with the flapping of wings as birds suddenly took to the air. From her near right, Rayn heard rustling, and then pine needles crunched behind her. Turning, she spotted Shadoe hunkered down by a tree about thirty feet away, his features taut, his eyes narrowed and sparked with anger.

"I've got water," she proclaimed and tossed the filled skin over her shoulder.

"You've got trouble," he hissed, gesturing behind her.

Rayn glanced back to see a large brown bear moving ponderously out from the pines, its ears perked and wide black nose testing the air. Rayn started. The blood rushed to her limbs as the mother bear set its sights on her. The bear lifted up on its hind haunches and growled. Every instinct told Rayn to run, but Shadoe signaled her to stay still.

Straining her eyes, she barely discerned Shadoe with his sword drawn, crawling through the brush toward the mother bear. The she-bear was still occupied with Rayn, who stood between her and her cubs. Shadoe advanced, putting himself between Rayn and the irate bear.

Great! Now the bear will have a main course and dessert. The sound of the cubs splashing and wrestling in the water made the dangerous situation seem absurd.

Can't the mother see her cubs are not in danger? And what of my gift with animals? Surely the bear senses my inbred bonds with nature?

"Hey, bear!" she called out, striking the water with her staff and heading in the direction of the cubs. "Over here. Let's talk."

Releasing a fierce snarl, the bear dropped down on all fours and lumbered toward her; of course, it had to go through Shadoe first. Rayn now realized that this bear was not up to negotiating.

The next growl she heard came from Shadoe, who motioned Rayn to drop. If she dropped, she would land in the water. That made no sense. She preferred to run and did—not away from the bear but toward it. Rayn shrieked a loud war cry that took the bear off guard, causing it to halt and stare as she came alongside Shadoe. Shadoe sent Rayn an exasperated look before grabbing her arm and dragging her away from the pond.

"Run, confound it!" he ordered.

A ferocious roar exploded from the bear as brush and twigs snapped from its weight. Shadoe led Rayn on a zigzag trail as they raced hard, trying to lose the irate mother. Suddenly, the ground ahead disappeared. Shadoe jerked Rayn into his arms, and they peered over the green precipice. A steep hillside dropped away from them. The bottom looked far away. Behind them, the bear was closing in.

"Jump!"

"Are you mad?" She panted and gestured at the steep incline and the thorn bushes that occupied the bottom half.

"No," he hissed. "She won't come after us. But if we stay, she'll attack."

"Use your sword," Rayn argued, trying to keep steady.

"Now who's mad?" He pointed as the bear rose up on its hind feet and advanced.

"I will *not* jump!" Rayn dug her sandals into the ground.

"Then I will." Shadoe gripped her shoulders, swept her feet out from under her, and leaped, pulling her with him.

Rayn screamed!

The world whirled past and the wind was firmly and repeatedly knocked out of her body. Her ribs hit the stump of a fire bush, and she landed beneath the prickly plant with Shadoe astride her.

Spread-eagled on her back, she waited for her head to clear before she opened her eyes. When she did, she found that Shadoe faced the cliff and was propped with his forearms on either side of her as he rested on top of her. Although she couldn't crane her neck far enough to see what he was looking at, she assumed it was the bear. The air was silent except for bees buzzing overhead.

"Is it there?" she asked, wiggling to be free of his weight.

"Aye," he whispered, "stay still!"

Shadoe's tone was threatening, and she complied. She had only a side view of his deeply tanned face. She was so close, she could smell the essence of him, and it made her feel delightfully strange. Scents of leather, linseed oil, and a fragrance similar to autumn leaves clung to him. His dark, nape-length hair caressed her chin, and she could almost imagine the rough texture of his day-old beard against her chin. When her eyes settled on the fullness of his mouth, Rayn shut them. Her body felt as if every muscle was bruised and every bone broken, but she was starting to respond to the comfortable weight of him, although her lungs felt as if they would explode.

∽⃝

Shadoe watched the bear stalk back and forth as if it were pondering whether or not to slide down the steep incline. He hoped the beast didn't think they were worth the bother and the danger of leaving her cubs.

Beneath him, Rayn's breathing had become irregular. She'd started wiggling again. Even propped off her chest, he could feel the gentle swell and curves of her body and realized how much she'd managed to conceal by her layered clothing. And her attempt to bind her bosom proved unsuccessful in this position. Most distracting was the sweet fragrance of her that invaded his senses and disarmed him so that he lost track of the bear. When he looked up again, he couldn't see it.

Rayn managed to crane her neck far enough to see the knoll was barren. "It's long gone, it is!" she huffed, sliding her left arm between them and jabbing Shadoe's chest. "Let go of me," she groused, trying to jerk her leg free.

"I'm not holding you." He pushed to his knees, raising his hands in defense.

Rayn looked down to see the leggings of her left leg was snagged by a fire bush, as was her right arm. "I'm hung up on the thorns," she said more kindly and winced as she tried to pull free.

"Hold on." He hunched over her and began freeing her leg from the talons of the bush.

Using her free hand, Rayn tugged on her sleeve and then flinched in pain. Her efforts only made matters worse.

∽◠

"Cease squirming!" He released the last strand of material from the branch, and then turned his attention to her sleeve, which was snagged at her forearm. As he pressed near, Rayn felt the heat of his breath on her cheek, saw the concentration on his blue-shadowed face. His masculinity overwhelmed her. When a lock of his dark hair trailed her brow, she thought she would swoon. Did he hear her swift-beating heart, she wondered, sense her turmoil, or notice the color staining her cheeks? No one but Da, Percy, and Tristam—and of course Iona— had ever been this near.

∽◠

Shadoe was having similar problems keeping his mind on his task, but the sweet essence of her was intoxicating. Her hair had fallen out from beneath her cap. He knew how her tresses shimmered like crimson flames. Feeling clumsy, he broke off the thorns and pried them from her sleeve.

"There," he said, knowing her face was turned to his, her lips slightly parted, her sweet breath fanning his face. Then his eyes met hers. Green orbs with wisps of blue, the purest emerald jewels he'd ever gazed upon. Those emeralds beckoned and held him captive as no earthly jewels ever had.

How and when the kiss began was debatable, but the current surging between them was so intense that they clung to one another as if their next breath depended upon it.

∞

Rayn became enveloped in feelings so powerful that she thought she was fantasizing. Never in her dreams had a kiss felt like this. Then again she'd never been kissed . . . until now. She felt giddy, dizzy, and strangely nauseous. The reality of their passionate embrace hit Rayn full force. *This was wrong! Sinful!* With a desperate strength she sought to break free, but Shadoe's powerful weight held her prisoner.

No doubt the sharp contact of her head banging his was not what he expected. "What the . . . ?"

"Get off!" She panicked, writhing under him.

"Wait a moment," he snapped and jerked his arm from beneath her, causing her head to smack the ground. At the same time, the edge of a sword bit his upper spine.

"You heard the lady," another voice dictated from behind him. "Get off from her now!"

"With pleasure." Shadoe untangled himself from her slender limbs and pushed to his feet, keeping his hands raised, his back turned.

Expelling a gleeful yelp, Rayn leaped up and smiled at the stranger, who held a sword on Shadoe. "God's merciful angels," she exclaimed and rushed toward the man, whose face was concealed by his hooded cloak.

"Are you all right, dear heart?"

"Aye, my knight in shining armor," she sighed. "You've rescued me again, you have."

"Rescued!" Shadoe mocked, peering suspiciously over his shoulder at the outlander who'd slipped a possessive arm about Rayn's waist. "I'm the one who needs rescuing." He rubbed his stinging forehead and attempted to turn.

The stranger jabbed his weapon between Shadoe's shoulder blades. "I'm not prone to slaying defenseless men, Sir, but one more move and I will."

The ring of familiarity in the man's voice caused Shadoe to tilt his head and prompt, "You aren't still mad about that wench in Naples are you?"

"She emptied my purse!"

"But she was worth it, aye?"

"Shadoe?"

"Galahad, you old boar!"

"Don't you bore me," Galahad growled, and both men broke into laughter over his pun.

"I try not to." Shadoe chuckled and turned about.

Rayn rolled her eyes in disgust.

Galahad lowered his blade but held Shadoe at bay. "You'd best have an explanation for being on top of my sister and kissing her no less!"

"I do. First, this brat nearly got me killed when she came between a bear and her cubs. It chased us through the trees and over that ridge." He gestured at the eighty-foot slope. "Then after we stopped tumbling her royal highness was snagged on a thorn bush, and after I'd freed her, she kissed me!"

"I did not!" Rayn sputtered with a pleading look to Galahad, who calmly assessed her.

"Okay, wee sister, did you anger a bear, get chased down a hill, and get caught up on a thorn bush?" he asked with a suspicious glimmer.

"I didn't kiss him!" She crossed her arms and glared at Shadoe.

"'Tis a matter of opinion," Shadoe muttered, knowing that whoever kissed whom, he'd enjoyed it a lot. Now he felt light-headed. Maybe that was a good sign. Kissing Rayn made him ill. Kissing a woman had never made him nauseous before.

"You weren't exactly fighting him, Rose Rayn," Galahad commented coolly.

"How long were you watching?" She fumed.

"Long enough to see your arm about his neck." The knight set his hands on his slim hips.

Shadoe chuckled and took pleasure watching her squirm.

Rayn huffed. "Whose side are you on, brother?"

"God's," he retorted. "And I know you well enough to know that everything Shadoe said is no doubt truth. Glory!" He ruled over her with the authority of an older sibling. "You are forever getting yourself in snags, Emerald Rose Rayn!"

Despite the ire in his voice and eyes, Rayn did not flinch. Shadoe was no longer pleased. If Galahad could not make her squirm, odds were no one ever would.

"What am I to do with you?" Galahad snarled with a penetrating gaze.

"Could I make a suggestion?" Shadoe offered.

"No!" they answered in unison.

"Fine." Shadoe stomped off to where Destrier grazed some distance away.

"Where are you going?" Galahad shouted.

"Wherever you two aren't." He kept walking.

"Fine!" Rayn called out.

Galahad stalked after him.

"Just why did you return?" Galahad caught up and snared Shadoe's right shoulder. Shadoe halted, turned, and looked into the younger man's demanding expression. He glanced at Rayn, who still mulishly stood, scowling at them. "God only knows!"

"Apparently," Galahad said in a low threatening tone. "But hear me well, Shadoe un Hollo Tors. If you've any propriety left in you, the scene I just witnessed will never happen again! My sister is young and innocent, and I intend she remain that way until marriage."

Shadoe had never been one to make excuses for his actions, nor did he now. But he'd seen Rayn's passionate reaction to Galahad's arrival. If that wasn't love, Shadoe had learned nothing of the subject during his travels. Striding by Galahad's golden stallion, Shadoe whistled for Destrier and Echo and headed for the cliff to retrieve his belongings.

"She's all yours, Galahad."

"What's that supposed to mean?" The younger man kept up with him.

Shadoe snorted and picked up his pace. "Look, she's no more your sister than she is mine."

Galahad stepped into Shadoe's path. "How much do you know?" He glanced back to see Rayn leading his horse in their direction.

"Where do you want me to start?" Shadoe held up five fingers and counted off. "One, Merlin came to me and begged my forgiveness for abandoning me; two, he had the audacity to die in my arms; three, he underhandedly assigned me to find and protect Arthur and Guenevere's progeny; four . . ." He lifted the Emerald Rose of Avalon from beneath his tunic. ". . . he gave me this blasted talisman."

"That was a mistake." Galahad rolled his eyes.

"You are right!"

"That's not what I meant," Galahad defended.

"Aye, it was." He glanced at Rayn, who was coming upon them. Shadoe hissed to Galahad, "I want nothing to do with your political agenda. Lance, Percy, Tristam, and no doubt you as well are intent on avenging Arthur's and Guenevere's deaths."

"So you've foreseen all that after being home only this short time?" Galahad scoffed.

"One doesn't need to be an august enchanter to see the obvious. I know who and what Rayn is, friend, and it's not fair."

"To whom. You? Afraid you might have to actually stand on principle and follow through?"

Shadoe felt the honest bite of Galahad's assessment.

"This isn't about me, Galahad. It's about her." He rolled a shoulder in Rayn's direction. "You're right. She's a naive girl. And your father intends to pit her against Mordred and Morgause. The brat hasn't a chance!"

"First off, Rayn is a woman, something you apparently just discovered. Secondly, she's an accomplished warrior, and thirdly, she is not alone in this. That's what we're here for."

"Leave me out of your self-righteous war, Galahad, and for pity's sake, leave Rayn as she is, believing she's Lancelot's child, believing she's common like everyone else. You should worry more about destroying her with your self-serving cause than about who instigated her first kiss."

Galahad glowered.

"Enough, both of you!" Rayn was upon them. "'Tis worried I am about Da and Perceval and how Tristam and the villagers fair. We must get home." She motioned to ride Galahad's stallion, and he hastened to her side, mounted the horse, and then swung her up onto his lap.

Noting Galahad's gallantry, Shadoe made eye contact with Rayn, expecting to see gloating on her face. To his surprise, she dipped her head and looked away. He could only wonder what that was about, but then decided not to. Rayn's knight in shining armor had returned, and that was just fine with him.

Chapter Seventeen

ASTRIDE DESTRIER, Shadoe held back, observing the couple gallop-ing ahead of him. Obviously, Rayn enjoyed Galahad's company as he filled her in on his adventures during his absence. She rode sidesaddle, nestled in the crook of his left arm, her green gaze fixed on his classic Romano-Briton features. Even in other men's eyes, Galahad was quite comely. His wavy blond hair and prominent cheekbones were like a Greek sculpture, or so it had been said, though never by Shadoe.

Although his stature was three inches shorter than Shadoe's, Galahad's stocky build had transformed into solid muscle from years of military discipline. Any man who dared challenge him would be wise to think twice. Galahad had never lost a match, excluding the stalemate with Shadoe two years prior. The irony of the matter was they'd argued over a woman, a Roman beauty she'd been. Galahad had known the vixen for what she was, an opportunist, and he had warned Shadoe.

Assuming Galahad intended to take the beauty for himself, Shadoe challenged him to a duel and, in a jealous rage, Shadoe has almost killed him. Their friendship ruined, Galahad left Shadoe to his own devices. Only when the noblewoman nearly dragged him into the pits of poverty and depravity did Shadoe realize Galahad had been right. And because of that deceitful woman, Galahad and Shadoe had not spoken until today's meeting. It seemed ironic their reunion would be due to a woman.

Well, a female anyway.

When a smile split Galahad's handsome face and he broke into laughter, Shadoe groaned despite himself. Rayn had Galahad's undivided attention. He was completely enamored with her. Knowing the truth of her birthright, Galahad no doubt had set his sights on Rayn long ago. Surely that was why he'd yet to marry. It could also explain Merlin's statement about Galahad's destiny. No doubt it included Rayn.

Shadoe felt foul. Why had he given the less-than-ladylike female any concern, let alone kissed her? What had he been thinking? Surely his actions had been incited by his keeping the pledge of celibacy to Merlin sixteen months ago. Blazes, he'd resorted to kissing an unruly brat who fought like a man and dressed like one besides.

Yet knowing Rayn was the beautiful enchantress of the loch haunted him. For the last two weeks he had been unable to shake her image or his burning desire. Then again, there'd been such distance between them at the falls. Mayhap he imagined her sensuous form and long silky legs. Aye, he looked across at her and rationalized he'd only seen what he'd wanted to see. The loch had cast its spell upon him. Rayn was no raving beauty, especially with her hair tucked tight beneath the Phrygian felt cap, and her oval, freckled face grubby with dirt and grass stains from their tumble down the knoll. Besides tattered, baggy leggings and breeches, she wore two tunics and bindings to conceal her breasts.

The most delicate aspects he could see were her sandal-clad feet, which were pleasingly small for her height. Save for the wealth of glistening reddish brown hair she kept hidden, Rayn was ordinary. Yet each time her voice rose in velvety laughter, the blood in his veins heated and his pulse quickened. Something about this lawless spitfire with large green eyes intrigued him, and he wished the stars it didn't.

∞

Rayn snuggled within the secure hold of her older brother. Galahad was home! Joy over his return should have been her central focus. It wasn't. A ways behind them, Shadoe rode upon his black steed, his features stolid, expressionless. No doubt he hated her. After all, she'd accused him of initiating their kiss. Trouble was she didn't know who had kissed whom first. Worse, she'd enjoyed his kiss ever so much.

Abba Father, what have I done? True, I asked you for a physical sign that Shadoe is my godsend, but we are not spiritually yoked. At every opportunity he denies you. So how can our being together be your will? Please, Lord, forgive my inappropriate behavior. Extinguish the delightful feelings Shadoe ignited within me. Help me understand your will. And above all, impress him to receive you into his heart. Amen.

Rayn peered over Galahad's shoulder, and for the span of several heartbeats, she met and held Shadoe's walnut brown gaze. What she saw and felt made her jolt against Galahad. Had Shadoe spoken in her ear, his feelings could not have been clearer. He was as bewildered by their kiss as was she.

❧

Within three hours of returning to Ayr, Shadoe heard the cheers of the villagers as Lancelot and Perceval galloped into the city's square.

That night after Rayn had gone to sleep, the men met in council. Shadoe's fears were confirmed. Lancelot and his comrades intended to strike against Mordred and drive the Saxons back to the sea. Moreover, they intended to proclaim through the land that Rayn, the rightful heir to Arthur's throne, was to reclaim the demesne of Camelot, and make Caledonia a land to be reckoned with.

After arguing each point and outlining the flaws of their plan, Shadoe retired to his quarters, intent on leaving the next day. One thing held him back: Emerald Rose Rayn.

❧

With Iona at her side, Rayn stood before the sealed gate of Camelot. It was barely visible beneath the overgrown vines and bushes. "Whoa! We're actually going to do it, we are!"

"So wondrous it is!" Iona exclaimed.

"Pure madness, it is," Shadoe groused, staring at the sixty-foot entrance to the Roman-style fortress.

"And most likely improbable. It will take years to restore," Lancelot muttered.

"Nothing is impossible with God." Winking at Iona, Rayn glanced over to see the ambivalence on her father's face.

"Oh, ye of little faith." Shadoe gave him a chastising grin.

"I thought you were the one without faith?" Galahad addressed Shadoe.

"It's not wrong to rebuild a fortress, especially one as fortified as Camelot. Nor wrong to defend yourselves against Mordred and the Saxons. It's resurrecting what can never again be that troubles me."

"In reference to what?" Lancelot's brows shifted in suspicion.

"Just what I told your daughter: the lost splendor of Arthur Pendragon cannot be restored," Shadoe said.

"It is God's will," Lancelot defended.

"Or yours?" Shadoe drew his sword and, aided by a tight-lipped Galahad, slashed at the thick vines and saplings that blocked the way.

"So where did Perceval and Tristam go off to?" asked Galahad as the three remaining men cleared a narrow but manageable path to the gate.

"They'll be about shortly, they will." Rayn delighted in their curiosity and returned her attention to the now accessible gate of iron and black oak. Only she and Iona knew Perceval and Tristam's whereabouts, and she wished they'd hurry.

Rayn cast a side-glance at Shadoe, and her heart tripped. Seeing him standing with the men in her life, she could not help but make comparisons. Lancelot was the tallest, strongest man she'd ever known. Shadoe was taller than any man present and, from what she'd seen of him, stronger as well. Despite his outward prowess, however, the intensity of his personality impressed and annoyed her most. He was stubborn, a quality that was readily evident. He remained aloof to her and hadn't exchanged a word with her in days. Although he acted as if their kiss never happened, she thought of nothing else. Right now he looked anything but pleased with the reopening of Caer Camelot. If she didn't know better, she'd think he believed the caer was cursed.

The unexpected creaking of wood and metal on metal caused the group to step back. Seconds later, the great entrance to Caer Camelot slowly swung open. Rayn unconsciously gripped Shadoe's forearm. Realizing her action, she let go, but not before glimpsing his bowled-over expression and the nerve twitching in his jaw—the same twitch she'd witnessed before they'd kissed.

"Here we are," Perceval announced from overhead, standing on the sixty-foot-high walkway. "Welcome to Lost Splendor, welcome to Caer Camelot!"

"I ne'er thought to see this day!" Iona broke into tears, and Rayn hugged her tight.

On the other side, Tristam stepped clear and beckoned like a proud doorman. "Percy and I have kept the gears oiled. We rebuilt the outer and inner baileys. And we couldn't have done it without Rayn's and Iona's help."

The astonishment on Lancelot's face made Shadoe observe, "I assumed you knew."

"Nay, I rarely come here. When I do, I enter through the caverns and use the quarters in the rear of the caer." He wandered farther onto the gravel-smoothed premises and rubbed his jaw. "I had no idea."

"Then you are pleased, Da?" Rayn smiled hopefully.

"Aye, more than you know." He embraced her.

"Well?" She looked to Galahad, trying to read his stoic expression.

He smirked. "What can I say except it's amazing." He gestured about, and then met Shadoe's grim expression. "Her dedication is unmatched, is it not, Shadoe?"

He shrugged.

Rayn flinched.

"Now mind you," Perceval announced as he descended the stairs, "the outer walls need work, and the stable's roof wants mending; the barracks and grain bins are gone since the fires. But with help from the citizens of Ayr, Caer Camelot will soon be a stronghold to contend with, even for the likes of the Saxons."

"You've done your homework," Shadoe replied, avoiding Rayn's confident gaze.

"That they have." Lancelot sighed as he walked arm in arm with Rayn toward the inner keep's walls. There, the second gate stood open with invitation. He hesitated.

Rayn stretched on her toes and kissed his beard-roughened cheek, then whispered, "'Tis all right, Da, we'll do this together, we will." She nodded to Galahad, who came alongside and engaged her other arm.

Meeting his son's smile, Lancelot nodded, and they strolled into the inner bailey, across the grounds, then up the stone steps and into the inner sanctum of Camelot. Behind them, Tristam, Perceval, and Iona followed.

Shadoe hung back, but Rayn was too caught up in her father to care.

She glanced at Lancelot as they approached the eighty-foot row of towering marble pillars. They passed through them and onto the fresh-scrubbed granite floor, then to the great hall. Sunlight poured down from the overhead portals and across a vast interior. Tristam had previously ignited the wall torches, floor lamps, and incense Iona had prepared to renew the musty air. Rayn heard Lancelot's sharp intake of breath and glanced up to see tears in his eyes.

"When did you do this?" he inquired with a husky voice.

"As you said, you don't come often. We did it with help from supporters in Ayr and the remaining clansmen of Camelot. But Tristam, Percy, and Iona have maintained it for years."

"Of their own will?" Galahad turned and curiously surveyed the two older men.

"Not entirely," Tristam admitted. "One could say the Merdyn prompted us a mite."

"Aye," Perceval agreed with a sheepish smile as he glanced back at Shadoe. "He believed the past should not be forgotten or neglected. Besides, he was adamant that Camelot would once again shine and that God had a special plan for each of us who'd survived those horrific days so long ago."

∽◎∾

Shadoe's heart filled with confusion and ire. Apparently, his father had remained connected to everyone but him. Forcing his thoughts back to the caer, he looked about. It appeared smaller than when he was a youth, yet he was still moved by the forty-foot vaulted ceiling and the six-foot-diameter marble pillars supporting the roof. Romano-Briton architecture dominated the structure and even more so the Ayris influence.

Strange, but not until Shadoe had visited the southern portion of Britannia did he realize the sparseness of Rome's influence north of Hadrian's Wall. Most structures here were still stick and wattle. The fortresses of the Picts, Celts, and Saxons could not match the tons of stone and massive timbers that supported Caer Camelot, or the many unique aspects of Ayris architecture. The iron gate-covers of Caer Camelot stood an unparalleled advancement in fortress design that even Rome could not duplicate.

The fortress seemed to stand defiant to all who would have seen its conquest or ruin. Shadoe suspected it had angered Mordred to desert this massive caer. The torch marks on the stone blocks and pillars were evidence that he'd tried to burn Camelot, but because of the stone construction, the caer had survived with only minor damage. Crossing to one of the walls, Shadoe traced a finger along a burn line where a timber had fallen.

"All the timbers that burned have been replaced," Tristam explained.

"The main support beams weren't singed. She'll withstand a siege of warriors just as she did twenty years ago."

Shadoe met Tristam's twinkling eyes. Just like Rayn and Perceval, the former knight was elated. Although Shadoe felt moved by the effort they'd put into restoring the keep, he could not dismiss the strong sense of foreboding that had been with him since the first time he'd entered Caer Camelot with Rayn.

This was not meant to be.

∽∾

Oil lamp in hand, Rayn took the upward winding staircase with trepidation. She had no reason to leave the main floor of the keep. As there was but the handful of them, Lancelot insisted they reside on the first level of the caer until confident its upper structure was indeed stable for habitation. Rayn had no problem with that; in fact, she was more comfortable sleeping in a stable than in the grand bedchambers of this keep. Still, she could not deny the urge to further explore this spectacular home of Arthur Pendragon, just as she had as a child with Merlin.

Standing before a chamber door at the end of the main passageway, she lifted the rusty latch and pushed the heavy door ajar. Midday light trickled through the broken roof tiles and the heavy curtained parapet that jutted out from the room's exterior wall overlooking the sea.

The sparse furnishings of a double cot, table, and two chairs were arranged around the centralized fire pit designed with a chimney that became lost in the high rafters of the ceiling. The room was not large, but well suited for a husband and wife, for lovers. Rayn's gaze widened with awe at the simple eloquent room, Arthur and Guenevere's bedchamber.

The room's stone-block walls were blackened from years of neglect. Upon further examination and a little spit and polish with her tunic sleeve, Rayn found what she knew to be hidden there. Just as in the great hall, bright, bold murals of everyday life in Caledonia peeked out at her. Rayn's heart and mind flooded with fond memories. The last time she stood inside this chamber, she'd been with Merlin.

Leaning against the wall, Rayn pressed her eyelids shut and strove to recapture that day. She could smell the scent of his black ram's wool cloak: a blend of salt air, cedar, and smoke. His tender, loving eyes peered down at her from beneath wisdom-whitened brows, and his deep calming brogue came as a familiar echo on the wind. In her mind's eye, she once again walked with him, expectantly listening as he told her how Caer Camelot came to be.

"There are many legends surrounding this caer, Princess. There is one truth. The caer, along with Wind's Haven Isle, is under an enchantment."

"You mean a druid spell, Mer?" she excitedly asked.

"Nay! Least not like the pagans believe. Camelot is under God's protection. He has a purpose for this caer that even I do not know. Long before Ayris vanished, my people sailed to these western shores. The first land they called home was Wind's Haven, a mountain of an island jutting out into the icy Atlantic Sea. It was upon this tor that they erected an altar to Yahweh."

He drew her to the balcony and waved his staff toward the harbor. "Seizing the opportunity for trade and commerce, they built a causeway from the mainland to this rocky shore and constructed the very port you see today."

"I thought the bay was formed by nature. Men built it?" she asked incredulously.

"Aye. My ancestors were great engineers. And being peacekeepers, they had no plan to fight the fierce Picts that dwelt here. Thus, they built a fortress that would provide an impregnable haven against nature and man. They carved it from the heart of this very tor and called it Camelot, which means God's footrest. Because of its awesome structure, Camelot was held in reverence by the pagans, and all the while that clan Ayris dwelled here, peace existed among the tribes."

"Not like now," she sadly commented.

"Nay, not like now. Even a century after clan Ayris left, Caer Camelot remained. Then King Uther came, and I with him. Here Uther acquired lands and wealth and created clan Pendragon, to which thousands of men and women pledged their allegiance. Uther realized he needed to name his demesne and chose what seemed most appropriate: Camelot. The lands and caer were passed on to Arthur. Someday Camelot will be yours, Princess."

"Mine? But I'm not the Pendragon!"

"Title has nothing to do with God's plans, lass." Leaning heavily on his staff, he knelt in front of her. *"Camelot is your legacy, Emerald Rose Rayn. Camelot is a symbol of hope for what will one day come: peace everlasting among the dwellers of this Isle of Might. For even when God's hand crumbles these granite walls and vanishes Wind's Haven, Camelot shall remain here . . ."* He gently nudged her chest. *"In your heart."*

Rayn jolted awake to find herself inclined on the dusty bed. She'd not thought of that discussion for years or of its significance until now. *My legacy! More than a caer or a holding? Oh, Mer, once again you left me with a riddle. I still don't know what you meant. For this place is of stone, and Wind's Haven has yet to vanish.*

With a yawn and stretch, Rayn realized she'd been asleep but minutes yet felt sluggish and disoriented. As Merlin's words faded, she knew she was not alone. The temperate room chilled. Her heart thudded in her chest, yet when she turned toward the source of the chill, she smiled at the familiar man and woman standing before the cold fire pit.

"Look, husband, she has returned to us." Guenevere smiled warmly at Rayn and put out her arms.

Arthur Pendragon stepped confidently toward Rayn. "I knew you would come back."

Nodding, she stood and curtsied. "My Lord . . . My Lady . . . I am honored by your presence."

"And we by yours, fair daughter of Lancelot. It has been far too long since we've communed."

Rayn chafed her upper arms.

"Oh, my sweet child, you are chilled," Guenevere said in that motherly tone that warmed Rayn's heart.

"Come sit here by the hearth," Arthur gently invited her. She approached them, and a chair magically moved across the stone floor and came to sit beside the fire pit. A blaze instantly kindled.

The king and queen settled on the stone slab that edged the circular hearth and turned their attention to the young woman before them.

"Now," Arthur said with a paternal smile, "tell us all that has happened to you of late."

"Aye," Guenevere encouraged, "there are others with you, and we sense they have come to stay."

"Actually, we have. We intend to make Caer Camelot our home. That is if you don't mind?"

"Mind?" Arthur quipped. "Never. Why, we've been alone far too long. But there is one we are curious about."

Rayn crinkled her nose in confusion.

Guenevere went on in her gentle tone. "We sense a great friction between you and this stranger."

"Oh, you mean Shadoe." She shrugged. "No doubt he's quite annoying at times, he is."

"We could haunt him for you, dear. You know, scare him off if you like?" Arthur suggested with a mischievous wink.

Rayn grinned at the thought. "I appreciate your offer, Sire, but I prefer to get rid of him myself."

"As you wish," they said in unison.

"His name is Shadoe?" Guenevere inquired.

"Aye, Shadoe un Hollo Tors, Merlin's scion. Remember? But when you last saw him, he was but a youth. Da told me that you, my sweet queen, died in Shadoe's arms."

The king and queen looked strangely at each other, then at Rayn. The air chilled. Arthur and Guenevere vanished. Rayn bolted from her chair and looked around the chamber, wondering why they had left so abruptly. Mayhap, she surmised, Lady Guenevere did not wish to re-live the last moments of her life.

Drawing a breath of disappointment, Rayn quietly left the chamber, intending next time they met to apologize for her rudeness. Then she'd ask Guenevere why she'd not told Rayn the truth, not confessed that she was Rayn's mother.

Chapter Eighteen

RAYN STROLLED THE grounds of Camelot and took mental notes of improvements to be made. Afterward, she walked along the craggy coastline. The rocky cliffs of Wind's Haven meant that excursions to the shore were treacherous but also kept the island fortified against attacks by sea. This left one of two choices: crossing the causeway then walking the shores of the mainland, or taking one of the underground passageways to the western side of the island's rugged, beautiful seaside. Rayn chose the latter because she wanted to visit the tide pools where she and Merlin had spent many an afternoon studying ocean life.

Exiting the cavern, she was greeted with the thunderous spray of swells cresting the breakwater. Overhead, Mer glided against a canvas of azure skies and aqua seas. She watched the predator swoop and snatch a fish from the sea, then fly off to enjoy his meal. The thought of fresh edible fish made her mouth water. She wished she'd brought a line along. Nearly mid-afternoon, it was too late to return for one now.

Rayn laughed at the seagulls soaring and diving about her. Glancing up, she noted a larger bird's shadow. She thought it to be Mer, but the long black wings belonged to a vulture. Rayn cupped her hands over her eyes and watched the mysterious bird soar over her. This was not the first time she'd seen a vulture. Yet when it landed on a nearby boulder and stared at her through beady golden orbs, fear spiraled the length of her spine. It seemed the bird was inspecting her with keen, almost human interest. Before she could reflect on the bird's threatening attitude, Mer swooped down with talons bared. The vulture screeched and took off.

After laughing at the vulture's cowardly retreat, Rayn made the tedious trek across the slippery boulders. She leaped onto the sandy loam and tramped across the beach with her staff. About a quarter mile down the shore, she came across the lagoon where the waters of the loch and the sea met. Beside the lagoon, tide pools teemed with fish trapped by low tide. Recalling how Mer had captured its prey, Rayn pondered utilizing her stinger to accomplish the same feat. In a small shallow, she held her knife over the water and waited. After six strikes that resulted in the fish swimming free and Rayn getting wet, she conceded defeat.

Rayn approached the largest pool but stopped mid-step. In the two-foot deep pond, wearing only breeches rolled to his knees, stood Shadoe. Rayn crouched behind a sand dune topped by swaying sea grass. A few feet away, Echo slept on her back, but lifted her eyes warily at Rayn's arrival. When Echo recognized Rayn, she drifted back to sleep. Rayn's gaze returned to Shadoe.

With the sun shining down on him, his bronzed body was unlike that of any man she'd ever seen. Rayn's breath quickened. Her mouth dried. Even marked by whip and iron, he made her pulse pound, and warmth crept across her cheeks. The sensation vanished as she studied the patchwork of scars that crisscrossed his broad, muscular back. She relived Shadoe's agony as a youth being brutalized and flogged by Mordred's whips and chains. She'd never encountered anything like this sharing of memories between them, and even the idea of questioning the how or why frightened her. Rayn shuddered, and emotion clogged her throat, causing her eyes to tear. She wanted to hold that frightened boy, comfort him and—

With the speed of a raptor, Shadoe snatched something out of the pool, and tossed it onto the sandbar a few feet away. Rayn gasped at the fat sea bass flapping on the sandy shale. Still in the water, Shadoe leaned over the quiet pool and extended his hands as if to pray. Less than a minute later, he flipped another fish onto shore.

Rayn was impressed.

"What are you doing?" She sauntered into view.

∽∾

Shadoe stood upright and shielded his eyes from the sun, squinting at her approach. She disregarded the familiar scowl. Setting down her staff, she slipped off her sandals and rolled her breeches and leggings up to her calves.

"You'd best not come alone," he said with annoyance.

"Mer was with me until he caught a fish, but you're here now, you are."

"I was afraid you'd say that." Shadoe's gaze slanted when he saw she wore little more than a loose-fitting tunic. Eyeing her attractive bare calves, he silently cursed. No doubt with the rising heat, she was more comfortable, but this was not a good situation. Realizing he was not properly dressed, he exited the pool, caught up his tunic, and drew it over his head.

With my lack of fortune, Galahad's watching from some vantage point, waiting to pounce and devour me.

Echo groaned and stretched as if the human's conversation was disrupting her nap.

Rayn gestured at the various-sized fish he'd dropped into a goatskin sack. "Is this your meal?"

"I told Iona I'd catch enough for everyone." He put his back to her, tucking his tunic into his breeches.

"Well," she said, wading into the tide pool. "We'll need more than three. Tristam can eat two by himself, he can. I'll catch more."

"It's not as simple as it looks." Shadoe searched for his sandals as he sheathed his stabbing sword at his waist.

"If you can do it, it can't be difficult."

Her retort made him grunt, and he perched atop a low boulder. "Don't let me stop you, Princess."

Rayn met his sarcastic smile, planted her feet on the sandy silt base of the pool, and mimicked his stance. Pulling up her sleeves, Rayn extended her arms and watched the plump fish, as well as the other creatures of the tide pool. She held her position for a few minutes. Shadoe was slightly impressed. A bass swam toward her, and she lunged for it. Rayn toppled to her knees, splashing water over her head and scattering the fish.

Shadoe exploded with laughter. He hadn't been so easily amused in years.

Rayn crawled back onto her feet, shaking the salt water from her clothes.

"That was neither fair nor droll, it wasn't." She glowered at him.

He lifted his hands. "Aye, you're right. Try again, and I promise I won't distract you."

Rayn eyed him warily and got back into position.

"Might I make a suggestion?"

She glared.

"Didn't think so." He shrugged, leaned against the rock, and observed passing clouds. When he looked back at Rayn, another bass came into view.

As Rayn made her move, so did the fish. Water spouted everywhere, but the only thing she caught was a handful of seaweed and a starfish. Frustrated, she glanced at Shadoe's stone-faced expression.

But he couldn't keep the mirth from his eyes.

Wiping the water off her face, she grudgingly conceded, "Okay, show me . . . please?"

"Put your feet farther apart, bend your knees, and lean over so your hands . . ."

He slid off the outcrop, approached the water's edge, and cupped his hands.

Rayn obeyed but was unable to reach the same position while maintaining her balance.

"Nay. At this pace, we won't eat until the twelfth hour." He entered the pool and stood behind her. "Stand like a knight but at ease so the fish can swim between your legs."

"Like this?" She bowed her knees and leaned forward, her buttocks thrust firmly against his muscular thighs.

Shadoe gave a sharp intake of breath. *Mercy!* Rayn glanced back at him but appeared unaware of the cause of his reaction.

Leaning over her arched back, he grasped her wrists and turned her hands inward over the pool's surface. "When the fish swims by, scoop from beneath, grab hold, and toss it on shore."

"Aye." She sighed against his cheek and tipped her head to look at him.

Shadoe swallowed. Their eyes met and fused like wildfire. "Watch the fish, Rayn."

⤳⟋⟍

She trained her eyes on the water and the fish but was keenly aware of Shadoe's masculine scent, the natural way their bodies molded to each other. She could feel his beating heart and her own seemed to slam against her ribs.

Two fish darted toward her. A bass went around her, behind Shadoe, and then swam back toward her. Rayn prepared to strike. "Now?" she asked softly and squirmed against him with excitement.

"Aye," his guttural tone scorched her earlobe. He let go abruptly and sent her off balance. The fish scooted off. Shadoe marched past her, muttering unholy words. Adding, "Need a long, cold swim," he charged into the shallow lagoon.

"Where are you going?" she called in confusion.

Shadoe swam through the waters until he was out of sight. Rayn scratched the tip of her nose, rolled back her wet sleeves, and took her stance in the pool again.

Men. I'll never understand them.

⤳⟋⟍

Iona brought a trencher of fish to the low table and set it beside hot, flat cakes of bread. Before anyone touched the meal, they held hands and broke fast, giving thanks for the bountiful food.

Afterward, Lancelot proudly announced, "Rayn caught these fish free-handed."

Sharing a trencher with Iona, Rayn confessed, "Well, I had some help from Mer and—"

"That old buzzard needs a mate," Galahad interrupted. "'Tis not natural for a predator to spend so much time with humans."

Tristam and Perceval disagreed and defended the eagle, then commented on Shadoe's wolf.

"As I was saying . . ." Rayn tried again.

"Odd," Iona's voice was loud enough to gain attention as she broke bread and passed the flat loaf to Perceval. "Shadoe said he was hungry for fish, but he's not here. Who saw him last?"

Her mouth full, Rayn raised her hand, but no one noticed.

"I haven't seen him since the dawn," said Lancelot.

"I—" Rayn tried to swallow her food.

"I saw him early afternoon. He was brooding. Mayhap, he's left for good," Galahad broke in.

Rayn rolled her eyes.

"I doubt that." Tristam took a drink.

Perceval shrugged and looked at Rayn. Chewing a moist piece of fish, she swallowed fast and wiped her mouth with the back of her hand. "I've been trying to tell you . . . he was at the tide pool with me three hours back. I got wet and—"

"Wet?" Iona asked incredulously.

Rayn nodded and took another bite. "Uh-huh, I fell in. But it felt good it did, being so warm today."

"And Shadoe was there?" Perceval picked out fish bones.

"Aye. He caught the first three bass, then drenched me, he did." She giggled.

"Oh my." Iona fanned her flushed cheeks.

Rayn frowned at Iona's strange behavior, and then engaged her father's heedful gaze. "Whist, one minute he was teaching me how to catch fish and—"

"Exactly how was he teaching you?" Galahad urged with a snarl.

"Well, I stood in the water. He reached from behind me and showed me how to move." She gestured with her arms and hands.

"I bet he did," Galahad muttered, setting his food back on the trencher that he was sharing with his father. Rayn thought Galahad looked ill.

Iona stared bug-eyed at her.

"And did it take long?" Tristam inquired casually.

Rayn noted her father's complexion had darkened and wondered if he was ill, too. Odd, the fish were fresh and tasted delicious. She turned back to Tristam. "Aye, we stood that way several minutes. But just when a fish swam within reach, Shadoe almost knocked me over and bolted. He acted as if Satan himself was at his back."

"No doubt he was." Perceval guffawed.

"Where did he go?" Iona asked in a puckered voice.

Rayn sipped water from a bowl. "That was indeed the strangest thing of it. You know how the lagoon joins with the loch and the sea?"

They all nodded.

"Well, he walked into the lagoon and swam away."

"Did he say anything?" Perceval tried to control a mischievous grin.

She nodded absently, and then frowned at her empty portion of the trencher. "Aye, something about needing a cold swim."

Lancelot coughed.

Iona shook with half-restrained mirth and a flushed face.

Perceval and Tristam failed to restrain ripples of mirth.

Galahad shot up from the table, cursing beneath his breath. Rayn eyed her brother's retreat and looked across at the trencher that father and son had been sharing. "Da, are you going to eat Galahad's portion?"

Lancelot shook his head no and breathed out a heavy sigh. "I've no appetite."

Rayn glanced at the other knights, who also declined. With a greedy grin, she snatched up the unclaimed food. "Then I will. I'm famished, I am."

∞

Strolling arm and arm with her father through the outer bailey, Rayn sensed he was distracted. "Da, what troubles you?"

Guiding her to a stone bench, Lancelot smiled down at her. "Aye, you know me well, child."

"I try." She hugged his arm and nuzzled her head against his shoulder.

Lancelot embraced her and pressed his lips against the widow's peak of her auburn head. "Rayn, you are a woman in full bloom. I've done my best to father you, but there are some areas in which I've miserably failed."

He fidgets like a cat.

"And one of those areas is the matter of men and women."

She sought to put him at ease. "Da, Iny and I had that discussion long ago."

"I fear she left out a few things."

"Such as?"

He plunged ahead. "In most men's eyes, you are a comely woman. You are beautiful, Rayn."

With her braided hair tucked beneath her cap and her figure cloaked in manly apparel, Rayn snorted. She'd never thought herself beautiful or even eye-pleasing, at least not compared to one like Iona. Her father was being kind. "I don't care about most men, Da, as long as I am beautiful in your eyes."

"Of course you are, my Emerald Rose." He reached down and, slipping the cap off her head, released her braids. "More than anything I want your happiness, daughter. Thus, I will select a husband for you."

She untangled her arm from his and gawked as if he'd struck her. "Da, we've spoken of this before. As your daughter, I honor and respect your desires for my happiness, but there is no man who will have me as I am."

"Rayn! This is foolish talk."

"Is it?" She stood and jabbed her finger to her chest. "Look at me, Da. This is what I am, and proud of it, I am. I wish I were a man! But Yahweh does not always give us what we want. I will live with what he's given me, a woman's body and a woman's heart. Yet this woman prefers riding, hunting, fighting men's wars, and using my head. Most women do not get that opportunity, although I do not blame God."

Pacing before him, she talked with her hands as she always did when riled. "Did you know that when I was thirteen and of age to marry, I asked Galahad why none of the men I took a fancy to ever returned my affections? Painfully honest, he was. 'Because you are strong-willed, physically skilled, and independent. You, Emerald Rose Rayn, frighten them.'

"Of course, he was quick to mention he'd also threatened each of them and they were not good enough for his wee sister. While I cherish his brotherly intervention, I suspect there is truth to their being intimidated."

"But—" Lancelot raised his hand.

"And why have you not attempted to marry me off before this?"

"Because I've found no man good enough for you."

"Whist! Because Galahad's right about whom I am, Da. You can dress me in silks and perfumes, but it will not change the person inside whom God created. What husband can you find who will love who I am and not change me to suit his needs, to make a lady out of me?"

"The truth is I want you to wed someone who doesn't plan to change you, Rayn, for I am somewhat responsible for who you have become. I desired you to be capable and independent, and I am proud you possess these qualities."

He stood and placed his hands on her shoulders, then met her defiant gaze. "Jesu does have a godsend for you. And I assure you this mystery man will love you for your strengths as well as your astounding beauty. He will pray for your weaknesses as he does his own. He'll love your stubbornness and your warrior and equestrian skills, as well as your devotion to help the less fortunate. Above all, he will love your relentless faith in Yahweh."

Fighting back tears, Rayn reached up and kissed Lancelot's whiskered chin. "So what has any of this to do with the stir because Shadoe taught me to fish? And why did Galahad charge off like an angry bull over it?"

"I didn't think you noticed." Lancelot lifted a brow.

"I was hungry, Da, not blind."

"Well, I can't speak for Galahad, but for me 'tis simple. It's no longer acceptable for you to be alone with any young man . . . including Sir Shadoe."

She balked, and then laughed. "Oh, Da, Shadoe's older than Galahad."

"Aye, he's twelve years your senior, but in my old eyes he is young. He is also experienced in the ways of men and women."

Remembering their kiss, Rayn glanced up at the gossamer sky and was thankful the ebbing light concealed the heat that warmed her cheeks. Still, she was up to the challenge. "I'm confused, Da. 'Twas acceptable for Shadoe to escort me to Wind's Haven only minutes after we'd first met . . . and to spend an entire night in a cave with me. But suddenly it is wrong for us to fish together?"

She smiled innocently as her da tried to frame an answer to this cool logic.

"This isn't about fishing or Shadoe. Nor were those other incidents controllable. It is about preparing you for a suitable husband and about shaping the perceptions of others. I expect Shadoe to be proper with you at all times. But I prefer not to worry on the matter. Thus from here on, you will not go anywhere unescorted. Iona is to be your companion."

Rayn balked. "'Tis unfair! I can care for myself, I can. Why is it the moment we move into Camelot you put me under lock and key? We may abide in the caer of a king and be organizing an army, but you are not a king, nor I a princess. Why, we aren't even a clan! So, whose perceptions are you concerned about?" She crossed her arms over her breasts and waited for his answer. "Moreover, what exactly are you with-holding from me?"

Lancelot opened his mouth to answer, but Iona was upon them. "Lance? Rayn? Here you are. I need help with the bedding, Rayn."

Rayn noticed the relief on her father's face, gave him a suspicious look, and turned to join her friend. "Of course, I'll help, Iny."

She looked back over her shoulder to Lancelot.

"We will talk later, Da."

Sighing, Lancelot failed to answer her.

Chapter Nineteen

RAYN MANAGED TO extract a reluctant promise from Galahad that he'd not disclose to Lancelot—or to anyone else—the kiss with Shadoe. Late that evening, she went in search of Shadoe to speak her mind. Even at the beach, he'd acted as if the kiss had never happened. She couldn't forget it. That kiss had rocked her world and confused her more than ever about men, especially Shadoe un Hollo Tors.

Dismissing her father's order, Rayn explored every chamber of the caer, and then headed to the first place she should have gone, Merlin's chambers deep within Caer Camelot's natural limestone foundation. Only she and Lancelot knew of the chambers or how to reach them. Rayn concluded that if Shadoe were indeed Merlin's scion, finding him there would disperse any doubts she had about his birthright.

In the past, she'd entered from beneath the falls of Loch Lady, but from inside the caer it was logical to use the stairs. After Lancelot retired, she left the main floor. Igniting a torch, she descended the spiral spine of carved stone that led into the underground sewers. The crumbling deposits of cement revealed the sewers' deteriorating condition.

Hunkering down, she came to a dead end. Running her hand along the wall, she counted blocks, then stopped on the seventh, counted three blocks over, down two, and pushed. The door of stone could now be pushed to the left along a track. It moved with little noise. It's iron gears and counterweights had evidently been given a recent coat of grease. She stepped across the threshold and into the constant cool temperature of the mountain.

Wall torches had been lit along the ancient passageway called the Dragon's Back. Clearly, Shadoe was not fond of dark places. Extinguishing her torch, she left it at the entrance and followed the natural, twisting passage down past a maze of doorways. Many led nowhere; others led to death. Stumbling over a skull and arm bone, Rayn's respect for the dangers of the Dragon's Back kept her alert.

It was almost ten minutes before she stood on the landing of a cavernous high grotto. Two other chambers jutted off in the distance. From here, Rayn could perceive a dim, shimmering light that did not originate from her own torch. Over two years had passed since she'd seen the Crystal Chamber from this vantage point.

She now put her plan to discern Shadoe's true feelings into action. She removed her felt cap, tucked it into her belt, and released her braid, shaking her hair and running her fingers through it to clear the tangles and let it flow free down her back. Although she still wore a tunic, breeches, and hose, she made an effort to look as feminine as possible. Rayn pinched her cheeks and bit her lips to raise as much color to her face as would be possible to discern by torchlight.

Merlin had taken residence in a part of the ridge where moisture had seeped freely through the stone to form extraordinarily beautiful, delicate columns that extended from roof to floor. The formations had earned this cavern its name, the Crystal Chamber, giving it a magical quality in which one could imagine the presence of stone companions. Obviously there were real people in the chamber now, for she could hear voices. In fact, she seemed to be coming upon a bitter argument. One voice was audible, Shadoe's. *Who is he talking to?* Rayn entered, then halted at the astounding sight.

Within one of the large crystal rocks stood Merlin looking far younger than the last time she'd seen him. She closed her eyes and opened them. Merlin was still there, and Shadoe seemed to be arguing with him. Merlin was talking, even gesturing at Shadoe! *Merlin's dead! Isn't he?*

Was this a dream or something else? Sorcery! Magic! No matter, she was certain it was not of Yahweh. She would retreat before being found out. Stones crunched beneath her sandals. Shadoe waved his hand over the lower half of the crystal and Merlin vanished.

She heard Shadoe's groan; he turned and scowled at her. Rayn moved to leave, but he was upon her. "What are you doing here?" His mouth drew tight and thin, and his eyes narrowed with provocation.

She glanced nervously about and answered truthfully, "Looking for you."

"So you've found me." His dark brows arched to a high angle over his hawkish brown eyes.

Curious she glanced toward the crystal monolith where Merlin's likeness had vanished. It shimmered brighter than the rest. "Talking to Mer, aye?"

"If talking to the reflection of a dead man accomplishes anything. Merlin taught you about crystal imagery and speech?"

She didn't want to lie, but she wanted to understand what she'd just seen and heard. Merlin's likeness and voice were somehow imprinted on or within that crystal stone. More important, Rayn needed to gain Shadoe's trust. "Merlin taught me many things I never knew existed, especially about Ayris." She gestured to the spellbinding chamber of crystal monoliths. The chamber seemed to possess a light of its own. "Though I admit I never expected to see Merlin's image in one of them." *Is that a lie?*

Shadoe frowned. She doubted he believed her.

"Nor I." He scrubbed his chin, looked her straight on. "At least not after all these years."

Despite the tension, Rayn ambled about the chamber. "Did he share the secrets of Ayris with you?"

"Hardly. I only know what he did entrust is to be kept secret, that not even Arthur knew the extent of the accomplishments of Ayris."

Rayn nodded, feeling more comfortable with their conversation. "I, too, took a vow," she confessed. "Merlin said that Ayris had been greatly blessed and God revealed to that people much of what mankind would one day achieve. Clan Ayris were the first to see the wonders of God's universe, they were."

"They also abused that knowledge," Shadoe said grimly, "and this is all that's left." He waved a hand at the crystal monoliths. "Meaningless information that is beyond present mankind's comprehension."

"That's not true."

"And why is that?"

"I don't think man is any less intelligent than when God created him."

"Really?" Shadoe scoffed.

"Sin is the problem. Sin interferes with our ability to use that intelligence to better this world or give Yahweh the glory for who we are and who we can be through him. No doubt the awesome power these strange pillars possess is from a source so minuscule our human minds cannot comprehend it, let alone see it, at least not this generation."

She felt the full weight of Shadoe's attention and blushed. Was it possible she'd impressed him?

"I don't suppose you know what Merlin called the unseen source within the crystals?"

"Atoms." She softly giggled. "I think he named them after Adam."

"Indeed." Shadoe pressed his lips together, accepting that his father had confided much in Rayn and that she continued to intrigue him. "However a casual pupil you were, you learned something at his feet. The Greeks named these tiniest pieces of the world, not Merlin. They thought not of our first father, since they lived in ignorance of him. Merlin said the Greek view of atoms was poorly founded, for it was based in pagan beliefs. Yet they had unsuspectingly touched on the truth."

"Aye, you were the wiser apprentice. More often than not, when he instructed of such serious matters, I was wishing to soar above God's creation, not take it apart to its atoms." She whirled about at the memory of those days with his father.

⬦

Shadoe tried to be unmoved by Rayn's free spirit and the freedom of her tresses of burnt crimson as they whished about her during her childlike dance. But his heart thundered. The flickering torchlight made her hair appear on fire. He'd tried to convince himself she was neither pretty nor that he was attracted to her. He'd lied. She was exquisite. His roguish gaze concluded that her freckled, oval face was flawless, her lips ruby red, and her large green eyes so luminous as to match the emerald of the talisman when it caught the sun's brilliance. Odd, he would make such a comparison, but it seemed significant knowing she was the true Emerald Rose of the Isle of Might.

Her boyish dress aside, he tried to rationalize how he'd ever mistaken her for a boy or even a young girl. Of course, she disguised herself with every intention of looking young and masculine. Even as his gaze drifted to her mannish apparel, he found himself pondering what she concealed beneath the oversized tunic. White fire fueled his veins, and he forced his gaze away from her, struggling against the desire she kindled within him. As she sauntered closer, his eyes settled on the gentle swing of her hips and the defined feminine motion that no layers of clothing could conceal.

Shadoe had known many beautiful women. Rayn was not a classic beauty. Her features were too delicate, too innocent, too childlike, to match the sophisticated sirens of Rome or of Gaul's ports. But that innocence disguised the passionate heart he had seen when the Saxons endangered the children of Ayr. He had tasted that passion on her lips and felt it in her arms days earlier. He was glad he'd not tucked in his tunic. Glory help him, he must keep space between them.

Crossing his arms, he asked, "Does Galahad know you're here?"

"Why should he, now?" She crinkled her cute nose.

"Because I'm not out to gain more enemies than I already have."

"I understand my brother takes his responsibilities for my protection beyond what seems necessary. Truly, I do not want to cause strife between you. But I needed to see you alone, to talk about the other morning with the bears." She failed to meet his attentive gaze. "I realize what happened was not intended by either of us."

"Got that right." He half smiled. "The next time you incite a mother bear, leave me well out of it."

"I was talking about our . . . embrace and . . . kiss, I was." She riveted her gaze on her sandal-clad feet and shifted her stance.

"Oh," he mouthed. "Sure . . . that should not have happened either. And the next time you decide to kiss someone—"

"Excuse me!" Her head snapped up. "Not only were you on top of me, you most certainly kissed me, Shadoe un Hollo Tors."

"I assume your conviction is based on firsthand knowledge. You have been kissed before?"

"I—of course." She flushed from the tip of her chin to her hairline. "Many times, I was." She avoided his gaze.

"Really?" He took a step forward. Rayn took a step back. "Then why are you flustered over something so trite as kissing me?" He reached out and fingered a lock of her hair.

Rayn bolted like a hunted deer.

Shadoe enjoyed seeing her squirm. *Kissed many times? Never! And if others had kissed her, he didn't like it.* He expelled a roguish laugh and noted the pulse of that delicate vertical vein between her auburn brows. "As I am more experienced in the art of making love, I am willing to take responsibility for whatever repercussions might result from my unfortunate lack of propriety in handling the situation."

"Whist! I never said I laid with a man." Rayn turned on him. Ire infused her green eyes. Her freckles were an extension of her rose-tinged complexion.

"I assumed if you'd kissed that many men then—"

"I never!"

"Never what? Been kissed or laid with a man?"

He saw her tears well. He'd not meant to make her cry. He tried to touch her. She pulled away.

"I've never been kissed or have been with a man."

"Then why say you had done either?" His frustration escalated.

She blushed deeper. "Because most women my age have families. Until we kissed, I'd only imagined . . ." She toyed with a crimson curl.

Shadoe was speechless. The lass was pure as rain, and he'd—

"Did you like kissing me?" She glanced up.

"Aye, I did." *Fool, why not announce it to the world?*

"So did I."

This lass is not only honest but bold!

When she crinkled her nose, she totally disarmed him. "Does that mean we sinned?"

Shadoe rubbed his jaw and avoided eye contact. "Let's just make certain it doesn't happen again."

Rayn released a sigh and nodded. "I explained to Galahad that I'd prefer Da and the others not know about the incident. He's agreed. I assume you're amenable to that arrangement?"

Although the idea of how Galahad would use this tidbit didn't set well with him, Shadoe shrugged. Offering his back, he exited the crystal chamber into the antechamber. Merlin had occupied it when he wished to be away from the outside world. The chamber was a living quarter with tables, benches, terra-cotta oil lamps, and a centralized fire pit. When fueled, the fire was vented through openings high in the cavern's ceiling. Shadoe lit a lamp to make it apparent he was staying awhile. More important, he couldn't handle being alone with Rayn much longer. His vow to Merlin taunted him. "You should go now."

"Now that you've found my da, I assume you'll be leaving?"

The uncertainty in her voice caused Shadoe to face her. "Eventually."

"What does that mean, aye? It's obvious you don't want to be here. You disagree with Lancelot's strategy to force the Saxons out of Caledonia and Britannia."

"The Saxons aren't going anywhere, Rayn. They're here to stay—at least in Britannia."

"That's not true."

"Believe what you will." He sorted through the scrolls on Merlin's table, looking for one in particular.

"Then you have the gift of foresight?"

Shadoe chuckled darkly. "I have no gifts, Emerald Rose Rayn."

"But what you said about the Saxons."

"You really have been in your own wee world," he scoffed.

"I know what the pilgrims tell me," she defended.

"Then they tell you the Anglo-Saxons control most of the eastern coastline and as far west as Glastonbury, and that the Jutes and several other Germanic tribes have also invaded. The reason the pilgrims are moving north is to escape their iron hand."

Rayn stiffly shook her head no, then yes. "Many come to Caledonia because they would rather deal with the Picts than with the Saxons, but I didn't know 'twas that bad."

"Well, it is. The Saxons continue to arrive by swarms, thanks to Hengist, Mordred, and others like them." He brushed layers of dust off the granite tabletop, and then strolled to the west wall that had been carved with niches. Large compartments held stacks of parchment scrolls or rolled, oiled hides. After years of neglect they remained intact in the dryness and steady, cool temperature of this inner wall. Shadoe chose a particular hide and opened it on the table. "Here, I'll show you."

Rayn came beside him, and Shadoe felt her appraising gaze. "What?"

She rolled a slender shoulder. "You really are Mer's scion."

"Last I checked, aye."

She smiled back. "I'm glad." She leaned forward and innocently brushed his arm as she looked down upon the detailed outline of the Isle of Might.

Rayn's touch ignited Shadoe's fervor. He couldn't breathe. His fingers itched to caress her, to . . . *feel Galahad's blade slitting his throat!* Reality cooled his blood. Shadoe trailed a finger northwest from the lower east coast of Britannia, until the width of his hand covered more than half of Britannia.

"The Saxons have conquered all this. Most Britons and Celts have sur-

rendered to their new conquerors. I don't know how far north of Hadrian's
Wall they will push, and I doubt they will pursue the highlands of the
Picts. But if they seek to control the west shores, we are in their path. Ayr
was once a vital shipping and fishing haven, and 'twill prove profitable to
revive the harbor. The Saxons know this; so do the Scotti."

⁓

"Dark skies! Now you have the Scotti invading us?" She threw her
slender hands heavenward in mockery.

His mouth flattened. "The Scotti have been raiding south and north
of here for years, Rayn. They aren't as organized as the Saxons, but
they will be in time. That attack we survived last week was just a practice run."

"So we are in harm's way?" She skimmed her hand over the map.
"Yet you have not the courage to stay and fight these interlopers."

"I am no coward, Emerald Rose Rayn!"

Rayn's head went up at the ferocious voice issuing from the enchanter.
She wanted to understand his purpose. "Then why?" she challenged.

"This is not my war."

She scoffed. "These people were your family, your clan. Why, then,
did you return?"

Shadoe glared, and the muscle along his jaw pulsed. "For a specific
reason. Furthermore, I don't dislike you or anyone else."

"But you're unhappy about being home, you are."

"I have no home. This place, Caer Camelot, is only the structure
that once housed my family." He rolled up the map, returned it to the
nook in the wall, and kept his back to her. "I learned long ago that all
that shimmers is fleeting. I'm glad Camelot has become your home,
but I don't believe in second chances with places . . . or with people.
We have one chance to be happy, and if we don't succeed, well, from
then on, life is plain hopeless."

The pain behind those words softened Rayn's heart. So far, the only emotions she'd seen from this man were ire, annoyance, and one ardent moment when he'd kissed her. Now she sensed utter despair. "I don't believe that, Sir. Yahweh doesn't want you to fail, and he doesn't want your life to be miserable. Jesu is the God of second chances. Seek him out and experience his unconditional love."

Shadoe turned and met her smile of encouragement with a stone countenance. "I didn't ask for your council, brat, nor do I seek it. Understand?"

No, she didn't, but the black look on his face warned her not to pursue the matter.

"I suggest you go." He glared her down.

"But—"

"Nah ah!" he bellowed and stalked toward her, waving his hand toward the exit.

She wasn't afraid of him. Then again, she didn't have her staff. Either way, she would have the last word. Planting her hands on her hips, she stood her ground. "I'll leave when I'm ready—"

Shadoe harangued her, spewing Celtic curses. Disgusted, Rayn vacated the chamber, shouting, "Well, I may be a brat. But I am not now nor ever shall be a princess! And you are not a knight!"

Shadoe glumly watched the glow of the torch retreat through the passage. "What I would give that you were not a princess, Emerald Rose Rayn Pendragon and that I was your knight. Oh . . . what I would give."

Chapter Twenty

NIGHT BY NIGHT, odd noises of hammering disturbed Rayn's slumber. The sounds emanated from Camelot's main hall, directly below Rayn's chamber. She assumed it to be craftsmen remodeling damaged stonework. Tonight, only minutes after it began, the clamor ceased. Now awake, however, Rayn let her curiosity get the best of her.

Slipping by sleeping servants and dozing guards, Rayn held a clay oil lamp and stood before the makeshift drapes that separated the king's high seat from the rest of the great hall. The throne had not been occupied since Mordred's hasty departure years prior. Tentatively, she parted the dust-soiled tapestry. Behind the tapestry two enormous pillars crafted by the original builders flagged the elevated royal dais.

Even in the recessed shadows, she could distinguish the extraordinary architecture that surpassed anything Rome or Greece had ever constructed. Here the echoes of a great, lost empire remained hidden from the world. No wonder Mordred coveted this fortress; nowhere else was the imprint of Ayris more evident than at Caer Camelot.

Rayn tiptoed across the carpet rushes to the brightly painted mural of the Isle of Might. It occupied more than a third of the solid granite flooring before the dais and thrones. Thanks to the original craftsmen who'd designed the atlas to Arthur's specifications, it had been restored. The map accurately depicted Caledonia and Britannia's physical relationship to Gaul and the Roman Empire, including outlying islands that the Irish Scotti identified as Eire.

Respectfully, she approached the dais and granite throne from which Kings Uther and Arthur once ruled their peaceful kingdom. As she took the three steps up the dais, stone chips crunched beneath her bare feet. To her surprise, a chisel and mallet occupied the throne's seat.

Rayn's heart thumped with ire and remorse. Bad enough Mordred had disfigured the throne's Pendragon emblem before he left. Now someone dared to further defile Arthur's seat! If she caught the insect in the act, he would regret it. Her eyes brimmed with tears. She'd never seen the Pendragon insignia but knew it had been of a dragon in flight, bearing the blessings of God upon the Pendragon lineage.

The waning lamp oil caused the flame to sputter, yet she would not be deterred. Rayn brushed her palm across the chair's high stone back, feeling the fresh deep grooves of a stone carver's blade. As she passed the lamplight across the backrest, she beheld a wondrous sight. The damaged emblem had been restored to the image of a fierce dragon. An amulet hung from the creature's neck. One claw held a sword, the other claw held a fish and crucifix, and its hind claws clutched a long-stemmed rose.

Rayn stared in awe at the ferocious dragon, and then touched the sword. "Excalibur." Her fingers trailed to the crucifix and fish. "Jesu, the almighty Fisher of Men." She caressed the amulet. "The Emerald Rose of Avalon." It was a representation of the talisman Shadoe wore.

Her thoughts spiraled with a stunning acknowledgment as her hand lowered to the blooming rose. Rayn's breath hitched. Her heart thudded against her ribs.

"The rose represents the Pendragon women. They are said to possess both the inner beauty and godly nature of a rose and the tenacity of thorns. I assume you know that."

Rayn had not known and turned to face the source of this fascinating revelation. Shadoe emerged from the darkness. His muscles flexed beneath his leather jerkin, and the blue shadow of a day's growth of beard made him appear more roguish than ever. She wondered how long he'd been there. Becoming cognizant of her indiscreet garb, she hastily secured her palla over her shift.

"As for the dragon, the Ayrisians were one of the few tribes who did not believe the creature represents evil. 'Tis rumored dragons could swim and fly and some survived the great flood. Which is why the Merdyn insisted they still exist. Did he ever tell you there's a dragon right here on Wind's Haven?"

Rayn nodded absently. Dragons had always been one of her favorite topics. Right now, however, those mythical creatures were far from her priority. *No doubt, I look indecent.* She wondered how to leave with some measure of dignity.

Shadoe picked up the chisel. "I confess I'm no stone carver, but I tried my best to recall the original from memory. Your father, Tristam, and Perceval were most helpful."

"Surely you did not carve this?"

"You doubt my ability?" he charged with a crooked smile and then waggled his brows.

"Nay." She turned her gaze to the high seat to conceal how impressed she was. "'Tis just . . . you are a man of much propensity—high-dives off waterfalls, rescuing children, eluding mad bears."

"I prefer to think of them as attributes . . . or as you would say, *blessings.*"

"So you bless yourself, do you now?" She gritted her teeth. *Rats' breath! Why do I blatantly provoke this man?* Rayn rolled back her shoulders and pondered the odds of reaching the drapes before he did. Shadoe appeared to be smiling. *Then again, the devil smiles, too.* "Milord, I didn't mean it that way, I didn't." She tried to step around him.

"Aye, you did." Shadoe moved in as if for the kill.

Rayn stood her ground, even as a fine stone shard wedged its way into the soft arch of her right foot. She winced.

He stood near her, hovering over her, his breath caressing her cheeks. "Someone has to bless me. Everyone knows I receive naught but curses from you, Princess. Then again, ladies of nobility do not curse." He rubbed his jaw in mock wonder.

She held her tongue, biting it to do so. *He's testing me, he is, but I will pass inspection. Heavenly Father, restrain my sinful desire to cudgel this arrogant soul with a tongue-lashing he'll ne'er forget.*

"The princess has nothing to say? Feeling poorly?" He frowned, and then with the back of his hand, he touched her forehead with feigned concern. "Odd, you aren't fevered, yet you appear distressed."

God release me! Rayn felt her sinful temper tearing free. Simultaneously the oil in her lamp went dry. The chamber was cloaked in darkness. Panic struck, Rayn took a step back, jamming the sliver deeper into her foot. She stumbled against Shadoe.

"Oh!" She gasped as he swept her to him, lifting her off her feet. In the midnight light of the chamber, Rayn became conscious of Shadoe's masculine, earthy scent and of the lightning that charged her veins in the boldest manner. "Let go," she rasped, frightened not of him but herself.

"I intend to, once I am certain you will not fall upon your face once more," he hissed huskily as he tramped away from the dais and throne. "Be assured this floor is harder than Perceval's lap or any mud puddle."

∽

In the shield of darkness, Shadoe grinned, while the spunky lass clung to him as loosely as possible. The sweetness of pressed honeysuckle petals scented her silky hair, and he was severely aware of the soft body that filled his arms. No layers of undergarments or tightly bound chest bandages to conceal her femininity. Mighty seas, but the enchantress would yet disarm him. Mayhap that was her intent. Bathed in soft lamplight, wearing the sheer blue palla over a calf length under-shift, her waist-long auburn tresses barely concealed her sensual attributes.

Surely, she knew he'd been refinishing the marble throne backrest? He'd not kept it a secret. How long had she stood waiting his arrival? His ire shifted to himself as he realized how long he'd stood behind the pilaster watching her. She deserved no anger, but he had again found himself coveting what could not be his. Shadoe stepped to the other side of the curtain, strode past the sleeping guards to the centralized fire pit, and placed her on the elevated hearthstone.

Rayn stared up at him, searching his rigid features. "I . . . thought you intended to drop me," she softly confessed.

"I'd never drop a wounded creature, not even a tenacious one like yourself."

∽◯

Despite the openness of the great hall and the dozen or more sleeping servants, Rayn felt secluded. She gazed at the slouched guards, willing them to awaken yet hoping they would not. Whatever was amiss with her that she could not think rationally with him so near? Shadoe lifted her foot to examine it in the glow of the embers, and Rayn clutched the hem of her shift. She wished she'd worn her floor-length palla.

His face was tense with concentration as he used his tunic sleeve to brush the blood aside from her foot. There was barely illumination as he worked the sharp point of his stinger gently around the stone. There was nothing soft about his sun-weathered features. The crinkles beneath his hawkish eyes were not from laughter, she concluded, for he rarely laughed. The deep scar that engraved the center of his cleft chin and disappeared beneath his beard stubble gave him animal magnetism. His full lips pursed in concentration as—

She flinched as he dislodged the shard. He tossed it into the fire.

"Merlin trained you in herb lore. Have you a cleansing infusion of febrifugia?"

"I've used most of my dried herbs after our encounters with Mordred's raids this spring. Nor have I ever heard of febrifugia."

"I suppose not," he acknowledged. "'Tis mainly found in the Mediterranean. Although Merlin had a patch in his herb garden at one time."

Rayn grimaced and looked toward the fire pit. "No doubt he did. I fear I am not the best caretaker. The garden has fallen under neglect. I prefer to collect my herbs fresh from the woodlands and moors, I do."

It disturbed her that Shadoe was conversant with the healing ways, yet as Merlin's scion, he should be. She realized that she saw Shadoe as her rival for Merlin's affections. *But my beloved Mer is dead.*

Reaching for a discarded bowl of mead left on the stone steps, Shadoe turned Rayn's foot sideways and poured the aged rye brew over the cut.

"Ow!" she protested as the liquor made contact with her wound.

He smirked at the foul glower she turned on him. "It is the next best thing to an herb plaster." He dabbed away the blood. "Keep it clean and—"

"I'll do my own healing, I will." She jerked her foot from the heat of his strong hands and proceeded to stand unsteadily, trying to keep the cut free from the rush-strewn floor.

"As you wish, Princess." With no sign of injury for her lack of gratitude, he picked up a small torch from the edge of the fire pit, held it in the coals until ignited, then ambled back toward his task.

Her eyes widened at his respectable behavior. Why didn't he argue with her, why didn't he try to . . . "Kiss me?" *Glory! Did I say that out loud?*

Shadoe halted mid-step, scratched his head, and turned around. "'Tis an invitation I hear, or wind in the rafters?"

He mocks me—and with good cause. She tossed her head back and attempted to be glib. "'Tis merely a test, Sir." *Now I'm lying! What next?* He closed the distance between them and shoved the burning head of the torch into the ashes of the pit. Rayn wished to hide, but the only available cover were the occasional whiffs of smoke from the fire pit.

"Tread softly, vixen. It is not wise to test me."

She swallowed but said nothing as he slid the palla off her head, then draped her waist-length hair over her left shoulder. His fingers caressed the tresses. Drawing the hair to his face, he inhaled the heady honeysuckle. "I do not think this is a test; I think you want me to kiss you, aye?" His heavy-lidded eyes lured her closer.

Rayn shook her head in what even she knew was feeble denial. Yes, she wanted to kiss him, wanted to feel his passion embrace her, and by the ardent look in his eyes, he had every intention to follow through.

With his long, eloquent fingers, Shadoe gently cradled her face and tipped her head so he could look into her intrepid gaze. Their eyes locked and something beyond words passed between them. Shadoe's lips brushed her chin and then cheek, his intimate caress burning a path toward her mouth. When he ceased she gazed up into his smoldering dark eyes. No man had ever looked at her this way before. Rayn coveted it, wanted his kisses and so much more.

Shadoe traced a fingertip along the widow's peak of her hairline, then curled his fingers into a fist and dropped his hands to his side. She saw his concentration, then something she didn't comprehend. It was as if he saw her for the first time. "You are much like your mother, Princess." His whisper was layered with emotion. "And best I remember that." He cleared his throat and put space between them.

"And what is that supposed to mean, Sir?" Her skin tingled from his touch.

Shadoe cleared his throat.

She tipped her head, curious of his words.

"Do you know what a kiss between a man and woman signifies, Rayn?"

"That they are attracted to each other," she suggested hopefully.

"Aye, but the simplicity of a kiss should be more than physical attraction. It should mean the beginning of love and commitment. I'd rather disappoint you than hurt you, Lady. Therefore, I suggest you return to your quarters before Lance finds you not only improperly attired but unescorted as well."

Rayn was unimpressed and insulted. "So you feel nothing for me, not even physical attraction?"

"Nah ah." His hands directed traffic. "I never said I wasn't attracted to you, Rose Rayn. But I made a vow to the Merdyn—"

"To refrain from lying with women?" Color tinged her cheeks. It was forbidden for men and women to discuss this subject openly, yet she was doing just that, and even worse with a man to whom she was attracted.

"Aye, that is part of it."

"Vows of celibacy until marriage are common among followers of the Christ, Sir, for I, too, honor the vow of chastity until I wed my godsend."

"Well, my vow of celibacy has naught to do with God or marriage."

"Oh." Sitting on the hearthstone, she crossed her legs so her injured foot was clear of the floor. "Then why ever would you make a pact with Mer if 'twas to no purpose?" Her question was one of true puzzlement and curiosity.

He frowned and drew a breath of obvious desperation. "It is no concern to you, Princess. Now the hour is late. I intend to retire and advise you do likewise." He turned toward the throne room.

"Just like that, you dismiss me?" she huffed, her curiosity frustrated.

"Aye," he said gruffly.

She shot to her feet and stared at his stolid back, watching the muscles ripple beneath the taut fabric of his blue tunic. "I do believe you fear me, Apprentice."

She heard him snort. Another insult tossed in her face.

"I suggest *you* should fear me, brat."

"But I don't." She hobbled up behind him, daring him to turn and look at her.

Shadoe turned and laid a hand of restraint on her shoulder. She cupped his hand with her own. In the instant they touched, Rayn toppled backward in time. Her eyes became those of a small child peering through the cracks in a door. In the next room an angry exchange ensued between her father and Iona.

"Leave us, Iona, and ne'er come back! Had I known of your affair with that seed of the Adversary, I'd never have entrusted my Emerald Rose to you."

"True I bear his child, but my feelings for him have nothing to do with my allegiance to you or my devotion to Rayn. I loved Guen, and I'd never allow harm to come to her child."

"That might be, but I cannot take the chance Mordred won't seek you out or that you won't lead him to us. I've arranged a ship with guards to escort you to the Isle of Erie and the high courts of Dal Riada."

"Dal Riada? 'Tis far away."

"Aye. I'm extracting a good turn from an old friend. Present this to King Eric." He handed her a missive. "He will attend your safety and the needs of the bairn. If you truly don't mean for Morgause or Mordred to know about the child you carry, then you'll go where they'd least expect."

She nodded grimly.

"You will go now, Iona, before I change my mind and—"

"And put a stinger to my throat?" she challenged with tears in her eyes.

"We are all expendable, Iona, myself included. By all that's sacred, I'll do whatever I must to protect the Rose. Depart now, and I'll not let the others know of your deceit or the babe you carry. I will tell them you left to tend your lands in Gaul. Leave before reason changes my mind!"

"Can I see her first?"

"Nay! She's but a child and will forget you in time."

"Forget me! Whose breasts she has suckled all these years, who rocked her to sleep at night, who nursed her through the fever, who—"

"Enough!" Lancelot's voice raged defiance. "Go to Eire or to Mordred, but if you choose the latter, I will know and will hunt you down."

"Nay, Iny!" Crying, Rayn scrambled to her feet and tried to grasp the door's latch, but it was just out of her reach. Tears racked her body as she pounded on the door, but when at last it opened, Lancelot stood in her path and scooped her into his restraining arms. Rayn struggled against him, beating at his face and chest, but to no avail. Looking over his shoulders, Rayn saw the teary-eyed Iona on the threshold watch her tantrum, then turn and quietly leave.

❧

"Rayn!" Shadoe tried to restrain her fists hammering his face and chest. He had to disengage from her. It had happened again, but this time the roles were reversed; he'd been propelled into Rayn's past.

Her screams aroused the guards, and they were upon Shadoe in an instant.

"I did nothing," he explained as Rayn proceeded to brutalize him and a guard. Another guard caught hold of her arms and pulled them behind her back, but she jammed her foot into his shin, and he released her.

Shadoe caught her and spoke softly, stroking her hair. After a few moments, she relaxed and opened her eyes. Exhausted and confused, she looked around the great hall and the bodies that gathered to gawk at her. At last, she looked at Shadoe as if to comprehend what had happened. "I don't understand. . . ."

"It has passed now. Are you all right?"

"Aye." She nodded. "But so weary. I want to go to my quarters, I do."

He signaled a guard and a female servant. "See her to her apartment."

They obeyed, and Rayn went quietly. Glancing back, she held Shadoe's concerned gaze, then turned and walked away.

Shadoe glared at the audience until they returned to their stations. Settling on the hearthstone, he touched the welts on his face from Rayn's nails. He'd been there with her, and for a few moments, he was that wee child witnessing her beloved companion being threatened by Lancelot, being sent away. He wondered if Rayn realized the significance of that exchange thirteen years ago or what she'd seen through the eyes of a child.

He comprehended what he'd viewed in that agonizing scene. Iona had conceived Mordred's bairn. This meant Iona had been with Mordred long after he'd seized Camelot. Shadoe would have done the same had he been in Lancelot's sandals. Iona was back, and he wondered why Lancelot had let her return to Rayn's life, especially now.

A shiver tracked the length of Shadoe's spine; his attention inadvertently drawn to the west corner of the chamber. Sound traveled in the great hall—even the scurry of a mouse could be detected. This was different. He'd sensed it earlier, and his inner eyes and ears alerted that he'd not been alone in the throne room, then or now. Neither was it the sleepy servants returning to their straw mats that he sensed but pure evil. Evil had watched and listened to the exchanges between him and Rayn, and evil watched him at this moment.

Gazing up into the rafters, he glimpsed a large bird's silhouette, felt its beady yellow eyes boring into him as if it could see his soul. Shadoe stared until he heard the beating of wings. The creature vanished. He knew he should have confronted the entity, knew it was harmful to Rayn. He also knew he was not prepared for the encounter . . . not yet.

Chapter Twenty-One

IONA SAT LOW IN her saddle, huddled beneath the band of ancient, gnarled willows southeast of Caer Camelot. Her mare prancing in place beneath her, Iona glimpsed skyward and wondered how long she'd been waiting, and then distracted herself with other thoughts. A new moon dodged the incoming clouds. Rain hung heavy in the muggy air.

How much longer should I wait? Should I even have come? Their meeting was bound to jeopardize everything she'd regained during the past eight years: Lancelot's trust, Rayn's love. Still, she had come.

She reached into the folds of her palla and removed the crumpled scroll to scan the familiar Latin signature of Mordred Pendragon. He'd requested to see her, begged her to come, said he'd never stopped loving her. It took days before she'd acknowledged his note. Tonight she'd ridden unescorted to their former trysting place, but she needed to return to Camelot before dawn, before anyone discovered her indiscretion.

She knew Mordred had committed inhuman atrocities, even tried to kill Shadoe and Rayn. *I still love the man, but I love Rayn more.* She would hear Mordred out, and then she would do what she'd never had the will or opportunity to do so long ago. She would bid him farewell and leave him in peace—she hoped.

It seemed befitting that Iona's thoughts wandered to Rayn and her amazing faith in Yahweh. Iona had yet to make a commitment to the Christian Lord that the others had made. She had experienced enough of his authority against the likes of Morgause to acknowledge his presence, but her druid heritage remained a constant contradiction to this Savior. Still, she was a good person. Surely he knew that. Surely that was enough.

She knew what Rayn would say. *"The world is filled with good people doing good things. But our works cannot save us, for Jesu completed the work when he died on the cross. We must only believe and trust in him alone."*

Yes, they'd had plenty of conversations over the years, often resulting in arguments. Iona realized it had been months since Rayn had engaged her in a religious discussion. What were the last words Rayn had offered? *"I've said what I can, Iona. The opportunity is yours now. You know the truth. I must let the Spirit of God guide you to receive him into your heart. Please do not tarry, for he could return at any time. If you want to talk, I'm here. I will always love you, Iona, and pray."*

Pray. That one thing Iona knew Rayn would always do for her. Of all the gods to pray to, Iona concluded that Christ was the strongest contender. But if Iona prayed for anyone, it would be for Mordred.

Dismounting, Iona walked to the tallest willow. Even in the dark she found the scarred bark where, twenty years prior, Mordred had carved their names in Latin. Fourteen years old she'd been, barely a woman, yet never had she loved anyone as intensely as she had loved Mordred Pendragon. Tears welled and threatened, but she restrained them. Mordred was not the innocent lover of her youth. He was ambitious and ruthless. Lancelot believed he possessed neither heart nor soul. Whether or not he was under the witch's spell, he was as treacherous as Morgause.

Horse hooves thundered against the rain-thirsty earth. Riders were advancing. Tugging the reins, Iona urged her horse further into the dense copse. As they came upon her, she discerned at least eight soldiers flanking a single rider.

"My beloved Iona?" Mordred's husky voice inquired.

Despite the years, Iona knew his voice like her own. Her heart beat so fast that she could barely breathe, and she led her horse out into the open. "I'm here."

"Please show yourself."

Lowering the veil of her palla, she turned toward the rider who advanced from the others. The clouds dispersed, and moon glow revealed Iona's face to the riders. The dark-cloaked figure came within a few feet of her and dropped the mantle off his head. Iona's breath hitched in her throat.

"The years have been generous to you, Lady Iona," Morgause said in a taunting feline voice.

"I—"

"You are surprised to see me, Lady du Maur?"

"Morgause le Fey!" she managed.

"Aye. I've come in my scion's place. He's occupied with more pertinent matters than keeping a tryst with his childhood lover."

A shudder of alarm traveled the length of Iona's spine, but she tried to sound confident. "Then you can relate to your scion that I, too, have pressing concerns." She gestured to mount her steed. "Since Mordred summoned me and failed to appear, he can come to me. I will take my leave now."

Morgause signaled her soldiers, and they surrounded Iona. "I think not. Oh, you will see Mordred. But we have been in need of a woman-to-woman discussion for far too long, don't you think? I'm so longing to hear about my grandscion and where you have hidden him away."

Iona gasped.

Morgause cackled like a crow.

Her warriors brandished swords and aimed them at Iona while a man jerked the reins from her hand and sent her stumbling to the ground. Fear seized her. Iona attempted to swallow, but her mouth was dry as stone. She'd been led by her heart instead of common sense and would now endure the penalty.

Iona made it back to Camelot unnoticed. Still atremble from her encounter with Morgause, she hurried to the safe seclusion of her chambers and curled up on her straw mat. With a shudder of dreadful realization, she bolted to her feet. In order to protect those she loved, Iona had done something she had vowed never to do. She had made a pact with a daughter of Satan. And by all that was sacred, she hoped she'd never regret it.

∽

Word of clan Pendragon's resurrection reached the citizens of Ayr and the surrounding countryside. By week's end, droves of villeins, craftsmen, and curiosity seekers had pitched camp, some outside the caer and some within the outer bailey walls. Previous farm tenants returned to Wind's Haven and had Lancelot's blessing to take up residence, while along the island's coastline, fishing communities set up residence and built piers. The excitement became contagious.

With the revival of Wind's Haven and Camelot, Lancelot set out to select an army to defend west Caledonia. The timber walls of Ayr's fortress were being rebuilt as well as the bridge that had once connected Ayr to Wind's Haven's causeway. Once in place, the walls would encompass Ayr and make Camelot only accessible through the city itself. Even the damaged channel underwent repair. Merlin had designed it to divert the sea from the causeway. Moreover, the dark memories that had once shrouded Wind's Haven and Camelot dissipated.

By the second week, folks of trade offered their services, and in their wake came gypsies, acrobats, jugglers, and minstrels, along with the usual riffraff and thieves who occupied thriving communities. During the day, the din was that of a busy marketplace; by night, the music and laughter of an alehouse. Now in the mid-morning sun, folks from opposing clans mingled peacefully in the outer courtyard. From a south turret's guard walk, Shadoe scrutinized the crowd, spotting the colorful, blue-painted bodies of some Picts who'd dropped in.

Lancelot had armed guards placed at strategic locations not only in Ayr and Caer Camelot but also over the entire Isle of Wind's Haven. The knights wondered how long before Saxon spies arrived. Shadoe's senses told him they were already here. The more important question was, how long before Mordred appeared to inspect their efforts? His gaze settled on two burly, red-bearded men, who attempted to blend into the crowd. Shadoe motioned a sentry and gestured toward the strangers. "I believe we have guests."

The young guard nodded. "Who are they, Sir?"

"If I'm not mistaken, they're Scotti."

The man's pimpled complexion went stark white. "Scotti!"

"Quiet," Shadoe ordered calmly. "We don't want to alert them, and I expect they're just here to look us over. Please inform Sir Tristam. He will deal diplomatically with the matter."

With a salute, the sentry hurried off.

Redirecting his attention to the circus below, Shadoe felt as if time had stood still for Caer Camelot. "'Tis astounding," he commented.

"Not really."

Shadoe turned to find Rayn sauntering up behind him, smearing her hands against her knee-length tunic and black braes. Her hair was bound and tucked beneath her Phrygian cap, but auburn wisps caressed her flour-dusted cheeks, evidence of time spent in the summer kitchen. Since their last encounter, they'd avoided each other, and he'd hoped it would stay that way. Wrong.

Odd, he'd always been drawn to petite, full-figured women with dark features. Yet now he found himself intrigued by fiery hair, alabaster freckled skin, and luminous green eyes enhanced by long dark lashes. Rayn was above average height and slender as a reed—or most of her was.

His gaze lingered on her bosom, once again bound tight and giving the impression she had none. Shadoe knew differently and he became painfully aware that he was staring and not in a polite way. Still talking, Rayn didn't seem to notice his indiscretion. He just wished he knew what she'd been blathering about.

"And they need something to believe in, don't you agree?" She came alongside him and glanced over the wall's battlement. Setting her back to the busy scene below, she leaned against the mortared wall and folded her arms over her breasts . . . chest. *Glory!*

"By restoring Wind's Haven?" he guessed and then glanced away to regain his composure and adjust himself.

"Aye. Gives them purpose, it does. Many of them were Arthur's tenants or servants and not one of them a slave. Any man who swore allegiance to Arthur was made a freeman."

"And they raised up a golden calf."

"For one who has lost the faith, you seem troubled with what others believe."

Arching a brow, Shadoe indicated the multitude below. "Few if any are Christians, Rayn. Pagans, druids, the Romano-Britons who bow to Roman gods—and they outnumber you. They expect several things, and I doubt much of it is motivated by belief in Yahweh."

"Well, Apprentice, just what do you foresee of their expectations?" There was an edge to her voice, a challenge.

"One does not have to be a seer to know they want the return of Arthur Pendragon."

She crinkled her nose. "And just how did you come to that absurd conclusion?"

Shadoe leaned forward, his mouth but inches from hers. "I asked." He stared into her bewildered expression before stepping back from her tempting moist lips.

"But why would they ever think . . . ?" Her complexion heightened with color, and she turned, gazing down upon the hundreds of eager faces.

With a smug look, Shadoe crossed his arms and assessed her.

"I've said nothing, Sir!"

"Didn't say you did. But all this . . ." He gestured about them. "You think no one noticed your quiet little efforts these past years? You don't think Mordred hasn't been spying on your clan? I wouldn't be surprised if he's preparing an attack as we speak. You've done everything but hang the Pendragon banner over the gates. Our quarrel is not against the Saxon tribe but Mordred. And the Saxons will side with Arthur. According to your da, King Hengist has yet to give Mordred his complete support. Seems Hengist also awaits Arthur's resurrection."

Rayn snorted. "Insane!"

"Not to pagans. The soothsayers insist Arthur sleeps beneath within the hollowed tors, and the moment he awakes—"

"Whist! That's as bad as the belief that Arthur spawned a scion with Guenevere when everyone knows my father and she . . ." Her lashes shielded her eyes from his direct, attentive look. "Well, everyone knows I'm Guenevere's child."

Shadoe felt a definite knot in his throat and swallowed, wondering if he'd heard her correctly. His silence caused her to look up. Shadoe failed to hide his reaction.

"You didn't know?"

"I . . . didn't know you knew." He straightened his tunic.

"It's the worst-kept secret in Caledonia and Britannia." She smiled, setting him at ease. "Da has never straight-out told me. Ashamed, I suppose, but I'm not. I don't condone their sin, but because of it, I live. So I've forgiven them as God has also done."

Shadoe felt astonished by her merciful nature. Then again, she was a constant contradiction. "You're not at all resentful?"

"Only in not knowing her alive." She sighed longingly. Her eyes misted. "But being here, I am close to her always, I am." Rayn smirked as if she knew something he didn't.

Shadoe studied her. Her hair color and eyes were Arthur's, but the splash of freckles against ivory skin, her full lips, and refined nostrils reminded him all too well of Guenevere. The cap tucked low on her head concealed her widow's peak, but the delicate vertical vein on her forehead was evident. He recalled how that vein flared when Rayn became provoked. Like mother, like daughter, he mused. "Your mother was a godly woman who loved you more than life. She died keeping your identity from Mordred."

Rayn nodded, and her smile faded. "I know. Merlin said you were with her."

Shadoe offered a regretful nod. "Aye." He'd not been ready for this and hoped she'd probe no further.

"She died bravely, did she?" Her keen green eyes searched his face.

"Aye." His voice clotted. "She stood up to Mordred."

"And what of you, Shadoe un Hollo Tors?"

He looked at her blankly.

"Did you also stand against Mordred, defend my mother?"

"I was just a boy."

She crossed the distance between them and definitely stated, "I killed my first Saxon at fourteen years defending family and friends."

"I'd done the same by twelve fighting at Arthur's side."

"And did you defend my mother in her hour of peril?"

"I tried, Rayn, but I was outnumbered, overpowered."

"So you lived, and she died?" she accused.

Shame swamped him hard and deep. Although 'twas not the first time he'd been confronted with the events of that horrible night, it was the first time he'd felt the need to explain. Ugly pride rose to silence him. His voice deepened. "Don't judge what you don't know, Princess. You weren't there." He turned away to end to their morbid conversation.

Rayn was not put off easily, and softened her approach. "I'm not judging, Shadoe. I just want to understand." She clutched the cuff of his sleeve.

Shadoe lowered his hot gaze to where her fingers had captured him. He stated in a bitter tone, "I suggest you discuss the matter with your father . . . because I don't want to understand. I want to forget."

"I don't believe that."

Shadoe's hand covered her small hand and removed it. She didn't back down, not even at his lethal glare that intimidated most men.

"If you wanted to forget, you wouldn't have come back here." She lifted her chin.

"I returned to find your father and did. I will be gone on the morrow."

"So you're going to run again?"

"If you're smart, you won't pursue this," Shadoe said in deadly low tones.

A winged shadow fell across them. Mer swooped low, and perched on a nearby tower as if to observe their fierce exchange, which was escalating in intensity.

Shadoe looked up at the great bird, and although he didn't sense immediate threat, he knew the winged predator guarded its mistress. He wondered how the eagle managed to appear whenever he and Rayn were at odds. It unnerved him almost as much as Rayn did now.

Her ire surged, and the slender blue vein in the center of her fore-head became more pronounced. "I thought you different, Enchanter!" She twisted from his hold and rubbed her wrist. "I hoped you not only possessed the Merdyn's strengths but your own as well."

"Cease comparing me to Merlin. I am neither apprentice nor en-chanter. I am my own man!" He spun on a leather heel and stalked off.

He heard Rayn tramping after him. "Whist, you indeed are a bone-headed, selfish blackheart, Shadoe un Hollo Tors. You're nothing like the prophecies foretold you to be."

He halted, and then faced her, his wrath and exasperation with her at full tide. "That's because I'm not a part of your cursed prophecies! I'm not the conjured hero of some disillusioned brat who expects to be fawned over like a lady . . . but doesn't know how to behave or dress like one!"

Rayn froze mid-step. Shock drained the rose from her flour-kissed cheeks, and her lips quivered before she turned and fled in the oppo-site direction.

"Wait!" He moved to intercept her, but a powerful hand clamped onto his upper arm and slammed him against the wall. Hitting the stone blocks with his right shoulder, Shadoe peered into the livid, red-faced features of Galahad, whose other forearm pressed against Shadoe's neck.

"I wondered whether you were still a tactless donkey, Shadoe. You are!"

"You're right," he conceded against the chokehold, "but I've learned to apologize." He shoved against the stocky knight but met stony resistance. Shadoe could have broken the man's forceful grip but refused to fight his friend, especially over Rayn. "Let go!" he gasped.

"So you can hurt her more, aye?" Galahad's viselike grip tightened, and he pressed Shadoe into the wall but lessened the pressure on his windpipe.

"That was ne'er my intention, though it seems continually to be hers," he ground out, watching her scurry down a ladder.

"Wrong!" Galahad snarled into his face. "Rayn has never done you harm, although she's managed what no one else has—making you confront your black heart and lack of commitment to anything worthy . . . least of all to any person."

Galahad's accurate scrutiny caused Shadoe's belly to knot. "Still eavesdropping, old friend?"

"Still watching out for my own." He gestured in the direction Rayn had fled. "I've been patient with you because your annoying presence here is to be brief. Let's face it, *old friend,* you didn't return with a willing heart, and whatever your duty is, I hope it's nearly complete."

"It is!" Shadoe didn't divert his hardened gaze from Galahad's.

"Good." The knight released him.

"Do you love her?" Shadoe asked straight out, flexing his bruised shoulder.

Galahad snorted. "Of course. Always have." He stalked to the ladder. "I would die for her, Apprentice." He turned and met Shadoe's stolid expression. "Would you?"

A soldier stepped onto the guard walk and acknowledged the men as he passed them to take his post.

Shadoe didn't answer.

"Stay clear of Emerald Rose Rayn," warned Galahad.

"I'm trying."

"You don't deserve that godly woman."

"I know. And you've no need for concern." Shadoe tried to sound as candid as he felt.

Galahad clambered onto the ladder, stopped midway, and looked to where Shadoe stood above him. "Aye, I do have need for concern. She's gone and fallen in love with you, she has. And you are indeed a bigger fool than I imagined if you don't see it."

∽

Tears streaking her cheeks, Rayn fled to the inner banks of Loch Lady, stripped off her clothes, and dove in. Overhead, she heard the squeal of a predator bird, but it was not Mer. A fierce dark vulture soared toward the water. That was odd, for such scavengers did not fish, nor did they dive like a predator. Awkwardly but steadily the bird headed straight for her. Rayn dunked just before its talons could wound her. Coming up for air, she found the predator gone. Was it the same vulture she'd seen at the beach? With strong powerful strokes, Rayn swam to shore and reached through the straw grass for her clothes. Instead, dry linen and a fur cloak dropped before her. Rayn looked up to find the Lady of the Loch a few feet away.

"Please come out of the water, Lady Rayn. Dry yourself before you are chilled."

Rayn took the white cloth and quickly rubbed down. Then draping the warm cloak over her shoulders, she wrapped her hair in the linen. With an anxious heart, she faced the beautiful woman, whose shimmering, chestnut hair billowed about her flowing azure gown. Her brilliant blue eyes smiled at Rayn from behind a white silk veil. Rayn's eyes were red from crying, and fresh tears threatened to spill forth. She felt ugly in the presence of the ever-beautiful high priestess of Avalon, who according to ancient beliefs was the Enchantress of Loch Lady or the Lady of the Loch.

"He's hurt you again," stated the lady over the thunder of the falls.

Rayn nodded and worried her quivering lower lip with her teeth.

"Men are stupid creatures sometimes." She gestured Rayn to follow her.

"Most times," Rayn corrected, and then announced, "my clothes?"
She indicated the heap of tunic, breeches, and undergarments as she
retrieved her sandals.

"Forget them. I've something better." The lady proceeded to stroll in
graceful steps through the straw grass and then into the shadows of
the pines away from the falls. Rayn faltered, but when the Lady did not
glance back once, Rayn followed. She was hurt, angry, cold, and now
curious. She'd not ventured into the coolness of these pines for a long
time, mayhap because she'd been frightened about the tales of woodland spirits. Needless to say, stories of the Lady of the Loch disturbed
her, too. Over the last two years, however, she'd had several encounters
with the mysterious woman, and never once had Rayn felt frightened
or the least imperiled.

Barefoot, she hastened across the carpet of pine needles to find the
lady at the door of a thatched-roof hut surrounded by beautiful wild-
flowers and songbirds. She also found Echo stretched out a few feet
away, snoring softly. Ah, so this was where the absent she-wolf lived
since Camelot had been invaded. A recognizable screech alerted Rayn
to Mer's presence as he gave his greeting. Rayn smiled. If Echo and
Mer thought the lady safe, that was good enough for Rayn. Entering
the modest, comfortable quarters, Rayn adjusted to the soft lighting.
Besides a cold hearth, the hut's scant furnishings included a bench,
low table, cot, and trunk. When she discerned the lady standing by the
opposite wall, Rayn walked toward her.

"It is unwise to come closer, child, but please, open this." The lady
indicated a trunk in the midst of the rush-carpeted dirt floor.

Rayn paused, then dropped to one knee and lifted the lid. Her gaze
settled on flowing gowns of scarlet reds, misty greens, sky blues, and
snowy whites. A quick examination revealed undergarments as well as
gold-threaded, embroidered girdles and belts and shimmering orna-
ments of gold and silver with precious jewels. Stunned, Rayn looked
across at the lady. "I don't know what to say."

"Then don't. They are yours, Rayn." She smiled through the veil.

Rayn lifted a red gown and held it against her. A flush of surprise spread across her cheeks. She'd not expected the petite woman's clothes to fit her. This made no sense. Her puzzled expression engaged the lady's.

"They were your mother's, Rayn, and now are yours."

"But how did you . . . ?"

"'Tis not important. What matters is it is time for you to become a lady of nobility." She glided closer yet maintained distance.

Rayn frowned and set the gown back in the trunk. "One must first be a woman."

The lady went to the east wall, and then ordered Rayn, "Remove the linen and cloak and come here."

Rayn hedged, but for reasons she could not fathom, she unbound her wet hair, dropped the wrap, and clothed her breasts with her waist-long locks. With tentative steps, she closed the gap between her and the lady, who stood near a large metal object that shimmered brightly in the sunlight. Rayn found herself staring into a five-foot-high plate of polished silver.

The lady stood behind the mirror and supported its frame. "This is a looking plate."

"I . . . I know, My Lady," thinking of the polished sword blades from which she'd often tried to see herself. "I've just never seen one so large." She gasped at her reflection and took a few steps back.

"You have nothing to be ashamed of, child. You are created in the image of Yahweh. You are lovely . . . more beautiful than your mother. Now come and look closely."

"For what?" She timidly approached the mirror.

"For the woman you seek."

"She's inside the looking plate, My Lady?" Rayn naively peered at the face of a young woman she'd never before seen.

"Nay, Rayn, she is you." The lady laughed softly.

"Why do you help me?" Rayn glanced over the mirror's frame and met the lady's smiling eyes.

"Please, call me Niamh."

She nodded.

"Because I love you, Emerald Rose Rayn."

She drew the robe up to her neck to cover her breasts. "You despised my mother, you did."

"I was a different person then. Contrary to what the fishwives say, although I hated many people, your mother was never one of them. She remained kind to me. The Spirit of God filled her heart, and her faith in Yahweh touched me when nothing else could."

Sensing the Spirit's presence between them, Rayn smiled back. She believed the lady.

∽∞

Niamh leaned the mirror against the wall and stepped behind Rayn where the sunlight spilled about the young woman's slender form. Niamh's gaze rested upon what appeared to be an imperfection on Rayn's left shoulder blade. She took a step forward, her trembling shrouded fingertips almost grazing the tender flesh. A slight breath escaped Niamh, and she pulled back in time.

"What is it?" Rayn turned, peering into the clear blue eyes of her hostess.

Niamh smiled beneath her veils. "Something wonderful, Rayn, truly wonderful."

Rayn's delicate brows arched with wonder, but before she could ask more, Niamh gestured about them. "This is our secret place, Rayn. Tell no one of it, or of our visits. Stay as long as you like. The looking plate is yours, as are these garments. I will teach you the craft of being a lady of royal blood. For now, you must become comfortable being a woman. No more binding your breasts, no more manly clothes, no more concealing your glorious sun-kissed tresses."

"But he will know!" Rayn fretted, catching up her robe to keep warm. "He'll think I did this because of him."

Niamh tipped her head and smirked beneath her veils. "Of course, my dear, men always think it's about them. Now tell me the real reason."

Rolling back her slim shoulders, Rayn candidly declared, "Because I am an Eve, and I want to be the woman God created me to be."

With a nod of approval, Niamh turned and stepped out into the sunlight streaming through the canopy of pines. Gazing off toward Camelot, tears of remorse streamed down her cheeks. Niamh whispered, "Oh my dearest scion, Shadoe, she loves you for who you are, right here, right now. I pray you are more like your father than like me. Do not make the dreadful mistake of not recognizing your godsend. Learn to love her well."

Chapter Twenty-Two

"WHERE IS SHE?" Lancelot barked orders as he crossed the inner bailey's hard earth. The centurions paled at their commander's rage.

One man spoke up. "Sire, we've searched the island, even Ayr, and questioned the villeins . . . but there has been no sight of her."

Tristam came to Lancelot's side. "I spoke with Galahad. He and some soldiers are searching the bogs and will—"

"It's my fault!" Lancelot dragged his hand through his thick silver hair. "I should never have opened the caer's outer gates. Now every thief and mercenary has found his or her way inside. Glory, she could be abducted, dead even."

Shadoe trotted up on Destrier with Echo following and then cantered over to where Tristam directed search parties. He leaned across Destrier's muscular neck and long, sweeping mane. "What's amiss?"

"As if you don't know! Galahad told me about your rude outburst with Rayn this morn. Now she's run off . . . gone for hours. 'Twill be nightfall." He waved a thick-muscled arm toward the setting sun.

His features tightening into a scowl, Shadoe ordered, "Tell Lance I will be back with her."

"So you know her better than the rest of us, aye?" Tristam charged. "We've searched the loch, falls, everywhere, and still no sign of her."

Shadoe didn't know the why, but he knew where to find her. Motioning Tristam to step aside, he turned Destrier about and galloped out of the courtyard.

❦

Rayn had left Niamh hours ago. With a fresh outlook on life and a bundle of feminine accessories including gowns, she'd headed back toward the caer but decided to take the less obvious route. She'd needed to think, not just about Shadoe but also about Camelot and the battle that would inevitably transpire between Lancelot's troops and Mordred's. She was all for being prepared to defend oneself, but she'd overheard enough to know that Lancelot planned to strike first. She'd never seen her father this aggressive, but she concluded he'd not acquired the reputation of the Silver Lion by being passive.

With many thoughts to sort out, she ventured to the craggy shores of Wind's Haven and sat on a prominent ledge. There, she watched the sun's fireball drown in the gilded blue sea, while a ring-shaped moon bathed the night world in a milky glow. Perched on the boulder, with the staff balanced between her knees, she closed her eyes, savoring the spicy sea air, the thunder of crashing surf, and the salty mist on her face. Long ago, Rayn had realized that this windy isle, this enchanted place called Camelot, was the only home she'd ever desire.

Now mid-June, a tempered zephyr ruffled the tendrils about her face and raised gooseflesh on her skin. In a few weeks it would be high summer and balmy enough to swim the cold Atlantic waters. That didn't mean she couldn't play in the surf now.

Slipping off the boulder, she leapt the course of wet stones to the shore, pulled off her felt cap, and then dressed down to her chemise. With arms outspread, she charged into the surf, leaping as the waves crashed against the beach and past her knees.

❦

He observed her for some time. He'd been so long without a woman's caress that he'd almost forgotten the pleasure of those physical sensations. Watching the enchantress, he battled the desires of his flesh as well as his heart. He'd made a promise to his father, yet his willpower felt miserably weak. How could any man walk away from such temptation?

Yahweh, help me, he groaned beneath his breath. *Turn my eyes and thoughts elsewhere.* He snorted when he realized he was calling upon God. *I'd best not to do that again. I don't need God; I only need to rely upon myself as I've been doing all these years.*

Shadoe forced his gaze from Rayn, but seconds later the velvety peal of her laughter ascended over the banking waves. From his vantage, the moon's light revealed her lithe figure and flowing tresses. Illuminated in the last glimpses of twilight, she was innocently beguiling and dangerously alluring.

Shadoe grasped something else. How alike they were. In many respects, she, too, was a loner, strong willed, self-sufficient, not fitting into or conforming to society's expectations. Those admirable characteristics were about to be tested. Lancelot had almost a hundred soldiers searching her out. Instead, she was running free with the sea, oblivious to the repercussions of her actions.

∽✺∼

Rayn basked in the bliss of no worries, commitments, nothing except being one with her Creator as she chased in and out of his briny seas and barely eluded getting drenched. Only when her feet and calves became chilled did she start back up the beach, and even then, she twirled about until giddy and lightheaded. Thus her collision with the wall of solid muscles ripped the air from her lungs in a loud gasp. Startled, she stumbled but was rescued by firm, warm hands. Fearful and breathless, she looked into the man's face.

"Hey now," he gruffly decreed drawing her wet body close.

"How in thunder did you—"

"Magique," he mocked and held her at arm's length.

Rayn felt further vexed that he seemed to read her mind. Barely dressed, she felt affronted as his dark eyes evaluated her with indifference, never dipping below her face. *Is he made of stone? Am I so unsightly?* Her skin burned from where his fingers clutched her bare forearms.

The knife-edged look she pinned him with would have made a sane man flee or at the least release her. Shadoe did neither. "Most of Camelot is in pursuit of you, brat," he growled, dragging her up the steep incline of sand and shale to where Destrier waited.

"Unhand me!" she squealed, twisting in his firm grip.

"Not until you're in your father's care."

She pointed to her bundle of clothes. "At least let me dress!"

He eyed the distance to the clothes and shrugged but walked her over to them. "Then dress!"

"Turn about," she snipped.

Echo bounded over to them.

"Watch her," Shadoe ordered the wolf before he faced the sea.

Rayn glared at his broad back and tugged on her breeches. "What's all the bother over, anyway? It seems I can't inhale of late without permission."

"That's between you and Lancelot. Since the reason for your departure was my doing, I will escort you home."

Rayn smiled. Although he hadn't offered an apology, it was good to know he felt some discomfort about their quarrel. Then again, she didn't want him to think she'd been brooding over his insults. "Do not credit yourself for my absence, Sir. I often tramp off on my own, I do."

Shadoe glanced back just as she tucked her tunic into her breeches and secured her waist with a leather sash. "Then you are more self-centered than I imagined. Not a single person knew of your leave or whereabouts."

"I'm not self-centered." She wound her damp hair and tucked it under her cap. "I admit my words were brief, but I told Iny I was going to the loch to swim, I did."

Shadoe faced her with his jaw set rigid. "Really. Well, this isn't the loch, is it?" he countered. "And that was how many hours ago?"

Rayn knelt and patted Echo's head, scratching behind the wolf's dark, furred ears. Her voice softened, and she looked up at Shadoe. "I made a mistake, and sorry, I am." She picked up her precious bundle and, hugging it to her chest, looked at him. The moon's glow was bright enough to reveal the stupefied expression on his face. "'Tis an apology, but then you don't know how to be contrite, do you now?" She walked toward Destrier, while Echo loped alongside, nudging Rayn's hand with her wet muzzle.

Shadoe followed in silence.

The Arab trotted over and snorted. Rayn caressed the wide smooth spot between the horse's keen brown eyes.

Shadoe set his leather-clad foot in the stirrup and swung onto the saddle. "Climb up," he extended his gloved hand.

"I'll walk, I will." She tramped off.

"I'm sorry, Lady," he muttered above the ocean's voice.

"What?"

"Sorry." He steered Destrier to her side.

"A wee louder, please?" She looked up into his face, seeing the pain such humility caused him.

"Satan's fangs! I beg pardon for the spiteful way I treated you this morn."

"And you are forgiven." She engaged his hawkish golden eyes, and with a winsome smile, she tossed him the cloth package. He caught the fat bundle, and then after she offered her hand, he swung her up and onto the saddle behind him.

To her surprise, he handed over her staff. She blushed, for she'd left it back in the sand.

"By taking better care of that, you'll take better care of yourself."

"Are you implying I'm in danger?"

"For one who poses as a warrior, you've become lax and should never be unarmed."

He is a constant contradiction.

"So where were you?" he pressed.

"About," she offered, engaging his lean waist with as loose a grip as possible.

Shadoe gave Destrier a slackened rein, and they cantered away from the beach. "You were with Lady of the Loch."

Rayn flattened her spine and feigned confusion. "I don't know what you mean."

"Aye, you do. Nor would I add untruths to your transgressions for this day."

Rayn faltered. "How do you know such things?"

"Just do." He shrugged.

Silence hung between them.

"Are you not even curious?" Rayn prodded.

"Of what?"

"Of how your mother fares?"

She felt his back muscles stiffen. "I know she's ill."

"Dying, she is."

When he didn't respond, she pressed on. "She has the plague of leprosy."

He reined Destrier hard and twisted in his saddle. "Then it's no rumor?"

Regretful, she shook her head. "Nay. Although by God's grace, she appears normal for short periods of time and—"

He cut her off. "You had physical contact with her!"

"Nay, we didna touch," she protested.

Shadoe leaned into her, his eyes ablaze with rage. "That makes no difference. No one knows how it is passed. I've seen the horror of leprosy. How it lingers and slowly devours the body. Why it may not affect you for years, or be upon you in days. Do you know what risk you've put yourself in? Lancelot will be furious and rightfully so—"

"Enough I tell you!" she ranted. "My destiny is in God's hands. Niamh is your mother and near death. She loves and cares most desperately for you. She wants to see you. So what are you to do, aye?"

Offering his back, Shadoe put his heels to Destrier's haunches, and as the Arab trotted off, he snapped over his shoulder, "Nothing, Princess. Absolutely nothing!"

Angry beyond words, Rayn was about to retort when a projectile whistled between them. Shadoe swept his arm behind instantly, hard enough to knock her off the horse. He threw himself off to join her in the same fluid motion. Unprepared, Rayn hit the ground hard, and her skull slammed into a stone, making her head spin. She had no time to clear her mind as Shadoe dragged her against a high boulder and looked her over.

"Are you hurt?" he whispered with concern.

She shook her head, although the throbbing of her head said differently. "What hap—"

The sound of an arrow slicing through the air could be heard and its thud in the darkness nearby. He pressed his palm to her lips. Rayn tasted the salty essence of his hand. She glanced about the sand dune. The Arab was not to be seen. The moonlight revealed Shadoe's deep concentration. Prying off his fingers, she motioned she would be quiet.

Sweat trickled down her ribs. Her heart pounded, and she concentrated on the Lord, praying for his protection. When she felt his presence, her heart calmed.

Overhead, darkness melded with the soot colored clouds. Rayn hunched beside Shadoe and leaned into him, waiting. The hammering surf was so intense she couldn't hear anything else, but she felt Shadoe's hot, brisk breaths on the nape of her neck. She shivered. His muscled left arm remained about her waist while his right hand grasped the hilt of his sword. A sticky, wet warmth dripped onto her bare forearm.

"You're hurt!" She twisted about and touched his left forearm.

"Just winged," he insisted.

Before she could examine him, a screech from the heavens caused them to look up. Mer circled, his vast wingspan casting shadows on the beach. Rayn smiled. While most eagles nested for the night, Mer remained the exception. This made her ponder Echo. She hoped the wolf was all right. She caught another shadow in the heavens and wondered if it was the vulture. No matter. Mer considered it a threat and gave it chase.

"Stay put!" Shadoe let go and scrambled to the nearest dune. The sound of another arrow burned the night air but missed him.

Rayn scanned the face of the tree-dressed rocks from whence the arrow had been fired. The shooter was familiar with the lay of the land. She reached into her tunic to find her stinger missing. At least she had her staff. Mer screamed again, and another arrow struck the sand a foot from where she crouched. The shooter was getting closer and would most likely not miss the next time.

A horseman galloped across the beach. Shadoe glanced at Rayn, judging the likelihood of making the trees before the enemy was upon them; the odds were not in their favor. Just south of Rayn, he recognized the mouth of a cavern, an underground entrance into Camelot. He gestured, and she glanced back, spotting the opening.

He called to her, "When I stand, run for cover, understood?"

She nodded.

∽◦

Seconds later, the rider came within view, and Shadoe leaped in front of the horse, eluding its deadly hooves. The steed reared up and dismounted its rider. Before the downed horseman could react, Shadoe pressed his sword to the stranger's throat, aware he was now in the open, a target for the bowman. He hoped Rayn had used the commotion well. When the clouds cleared the moon, the man's face was revealed.

"Galahad?" Shadoe declared and retreated with his sword.

The knight cursed and came to his feet. "Hell's fire!" Galahad swung a clenched fist at Shadoe.

Shadoe ducked. "Quick, take cover. I thought you were Mordred!"

Galahad followed Shadoe behind a boulder but kept an eye on him. "Why would you think that? And what are you doing here?"

"Escorting Lady Rayn home. Someone attacked us. I thought you were a bowman." He looked past Galahad and noted a dozen foot soldiers with torches.

Galahad confidently glanced back, and then snarled at Shadoe, "Skilled archers in Caledonia are rare. Now you expect me to believe that you knew Rayn would be on the farthest reach of Wind's Haven and that an archer shot at you?" his voice dripped with cynicism.

"'Tis true, brother!" Rayn declared as she tramped up the beach and wedged herself between them, then slapped a broken arrow into Galahad's hand.

Galahad stared at the splintered shaft, then at Rayn. With a huff, he noted, "So why are we not under attack now?"

"No doubt it's getting a bit crowded," Shadoe scoffed and tipped his head to Camelot's approaching warriors.

Shale rained from overhead. The howl of a wolf followed by growls ricocheted from the upper ridge.

"It's Echo!" Rayn motioned to go after the wolf, but Shadoe snatched her arm and pulled her back.

"Echo's self-sufficient, Princess. 'Tis her opponent I'd fear for."

Galahad ordered his men, "Search the timberline and those cliffs. I want the assailant alive!" He turned to Rayn. "As for you, sister, you have explaining to do." He put his hands on her shoulders and guided her toward his horse.

"I was riding with Shadoe," she insisted.

"Aye, and he nearly got you killed had I not come along." He fixed his gaze on Shadoe, challenging him to dispute his accusation.

"Shadoe saved my life, he did." She dug her sandals into the sand, bringing them to an abrupt halt.

"I doubt the arrow was meant for you, sweet sister. He has many enemies." The knight indicated Shadoe.

Barely conscious of their contentions, Shadoe riveted his interest on the lone band of trees from where they'd first been attacked.

"What is it?" Galahad asked.

"Take her home—now," he said forcefully.

"It's not safe for you to stay here," Rayn said as she turned and tried to make eye contact with him.

Shadoe ignored her. He whistled, and Destrier trotted out of the woods. Removing her bundle, he tossed it to Rayn and met her troubled expression. "I can take care of myself, Princess."

"Aye, that he can." Galahad hoisted her onto his horse.

"Watch out for the vulture," she cautioned.

Their gazes held for a moment. Shadoe arched a brow before nodding.

With Rayn astride, Galahad mounted, and they galloped off.

Knowing the abrasion on his arm was not from an arrow, Shadoe trekked to the remnants of a dead tree tangled in tall shore grass. He eyed the stinger that was buried deep in the spongy wood. Placing a firm grip on the gold handle of the stinger, he tugged it free. The moonlight was bright enough to examine the delicate, deadly weapon. Shadoe's heart thudded with recognition. He never thought to see this stinger again. This meant that the last person he saw in possession of it was most likely the one who had just tried to kill him . . . and Rayn.

Mordred!

Chapter Twenty-Three

SHADOE DIDN'T LEAVE.

Rayn didn't ask why.

It infuriated her that she was glad he remained, but she didn't have the faintest idea why she felt that way. For the most part, she kept clear of him, and he did the same with her. And yet there remained a constant sense of security having him there. Often when their gazes locked, a mutual understanding transferred between them. Shadoe had stayed because of her.

Meanwhile, Rayn's transformation into womanhood was subtle, so gradual that she began to wonder if anyone noticed, especially Shadoe. She rarely wore breeches. She arranged her hair in long braids with head coverings of variously colored pallas that matched her gowns. She wore perfumed oils and bathed regularly.

Iona was exuberant with Rayn's alteration and did not question her charge's sudden turnaround. Rayn was thankful, for she'd no intention to betray Niamh.

Still, not carrying her sword proved the hardest transition. Rayn felt naked without it. Outside the caer, she had her trusty fighting staff, and she always wore a sheathed stinger hitched to a gold-threaded belt or necklace.

Although Rayn had changed her outward appearance, Iona and Niamh quickly pointed out that she needed to carry herself like a lady and especially watch what came out of her mouth. When Rayn eagerly sought Iona's guidance, the regal woman nearly swooned. Since her return, Iona had desperately attempted to soften Rayn's appearance and behavior. Rayn had always defied her. Now between Iona and Niamh's private council, Rayn learned the art of being a woman and a lady. Much to her surprise, she liked it.

In the midst of her transformation, Rayn directed traffic at Caer Camelot with a firm, attentive hand. Although Rayn, Perceval, and Tristam had worked hard to spiff up the outer courtyard and the great hall, the rest of the enormous keep and outer buildings had nearly twenty years of neglect to be dealt with. Even with the arrival of willing servants, the maintenance seemed endless. Most often, Rayn was in the thick of things, just as soiled and bone-weary as her staff. She willingly undertook any chore, no matter how demeaning, and that included repairing the elaborate indoor Roman plumbing. The sewer often plugged at a specific junction and, with the castle's being occupied, had become a serious problem.

Despite their daily toil, the residents of Camelot made time to relax. Evenings included sitting about the great hall's centralized hearth, sharing stories and oftentimes making music. Much to Rayn's amazement, Shadoe was gifted in the art of storytelling and playing the lyre, and he possessed a beautiful balladeer's voice. Within a week's time, it became the custom prior to bedtime that he amused the orphaned children with fables and song. Not only did the children enjoy his nonsense tales of dragons and flying horses, he seemed to like the children. Glimpsing this sensitive side of Shadoe only wore down her defenses, so Rayn tried not to be present.

The children were as much Iona's mission as Rayn's. The women aimed to find Christian families to take in these waifs. Although others gave the children attention, Lady Iona seemed pleased by how much time Shadoe devoted to them. She raved about Shadoe's soft heart and often commented on what a good father he would be.

Rayn began to wonder if her companion had designs on Shadoe. A few years older than Shadoe, Iona was pretty with the classic Roman features of dark flowing hair and a flawless olive complexion. Rayn often wondered why Iona had never married and just where she'd gone when she left so long ago. Wagging tongues proclaimed that six months after Rayn's birth, Iona had delivered Mordred's stillborn child. Three years later, Iona had carried the second of Mordred's bairns. That time she fled Caer Tintagel to Dal Riada on the Isle of Eire where she hid the child for fear Morgause would cast a demon into the innocent babe, just as she had done to Mordred.

Upon her return six years later, Iona insisted that she had gone to her family estate to salvage what the Saxons had not stolen or destroyed. Rayn suspected there were missing pieces to Iona's story, but she respected the woman's privacy. Now, though, as she heard Iona laughing and talking with Shadoe, Rayn began to imagine the noblewoman worldlier than she portrayed.

Rayn knew that Iona didn't walk with God, and she suspected that lack of faith created a bond between her friend and Shadoe. Moreover, the attention Shadoe showered on Iona became most upsetting. Rayn told herself Shadoe could pursue whomever he desired. Certainly a single kiss shared months ago did not bind him to her.

For the most part, Rayn kept busy and was thus less likely to think about Shadoe. For his part, Shadoe, along with Lancelot and Galahad, was occupied with transforming the villeins and tenants into an army of Caledonia's finest foot soldiers. Many of the families were displaced Britons who had fled Britannia to escape the Saxons. Now with the enemy encroaching on their new homeland, they were more than willing to fight.

While Lancelot possessed years of experience on the battlefield, Shadoe and Galahad had firsthand knowledge of the newest tactics and weapons from Rome and beyond. Although Shadoe and Galahad seemed to work as equals, Rayn noticed what others were acknowledging. Shadoe personified a confidence and leadership that went unchallenged by the former knights of the Round Table, and to date, an additional twenty warriors had been knighted.

One thing troubled Rayn. Galahad possessed a carefree attitude and could be a leader when needed, but he did not possess the drive to lead, as did their father. Since Shadoe's arrival, it appeared Lancelot was gracefully and willingly standing down to Shadoe. Rayn didn't like it one bit.

Moreover, she had yet to soften her resistance to Shadoe's adamant opinion that she, a woman, had no business fighting the battles of men. No doubt he still burned because she'd saved his life at Loch Lady. For that reason she did not visit the exercise field as she would have in the past. But every dawn from her bedchamber, she peered out over the exercise field while Shadoe trained the soldiers. She rehearsed the new maneuvers until she collapsed, exhausted. Therein presented a problem. Her snooping on Shadoe led to ardent thoughts that in turn brought her to her knees, begging God to give her the fortitude to deny the conflicting passions Shadoe evoked within her.

On such a morning Rayn had begun to earnestly pray when a bang on her bedchamber door made her scramble to her feet. "Come in," she commanded, smoothing her rough woolen vestment.

Iona entered, her cheeks flushed from the exertion of climbing the stairs. "Rayn, it's happened again! Hurry!"

∽∾

Torch in hand, Rayn ventured into the dank darkness of the sewers until she could not only smell but also see the leaking refuse from the blocked tiles thirty feet away. She suspected the blockage was in the elbow curve of tiles just like the last time. Perceval said he recalled experiencing the same problem when Arthur occupied the keep. But at that time the keep had been teaming with menservants who'd been assigned various duties, one being the upkeep of the sewage tiles. No one still living knew those skills, thus Rayn became apprentice plumber.

Bracing herself, she stepped ankle deep into the fowl sewage and banged her fist against the overhead tiles, hoping to dislodge whatever clogged it. Three days earlier, two dead rats had blocked the drain. This time, she expected a cat or dog to fall out. Another blow with her staff. Still nothing broke free.

"Blast!" She stretched, catching the edge of the tile and yanking. Disgusted and with barely room to maneuver, she pushed aside the loose tile and reached inside, her arm disappearing in the wet slime. The tips of her fingers touched something solid but mushy. Cringing, she pushed up on her toes and caught hold. Timing was everything. Pull and run had become her motto.

She yanked.

The gush of rushing water vibrated the tiles.

Too late to retreat!

∽◦◦

Shadoe stood in the garderobe, emptying a fourth bucket of water into the carved stone hole. He grinned when the plugged reserve flushed clean. "There, Iona, good as ever. All Rayn had to do was—"

"Aaahhhgh!" A scream reverberated up through the tiles.

"What . . . ?" Shadoe dropped the bucket.

Iona gasped. "I tried to tell you she went below to open the drain!"

Shadoe cursed and took the steps two at a time. Torch in hand, he crept into the caverns and trudged through the shallow underground stream. It drained into the centralized cistern supplying the entire keep. Passing the cistern, he hunkered down into the low, manmade sewer ditch and held his breath. *Glory, this reeks!* It had been years since he'd clambered around a sewer—not something one did willingly. Yet even Shadoe remained amazed at the Roman ingenuity that had built the freshwater ductwork below and the outflowing sewage tiles erected overhead. He turned left and headed uphill, wondering if he'd taken the correct tunnel. A few gulps for air later, he spotted a moving silhouette on the wall. The being came into view. Shadoe grimaced at the creature dragging a dead torch in one hand and staff in the other.

Most women would have been wailing. Not Rayn. Her irate Pict muttering sufficed. *Were I smart, I'd retreat.* He bluffed instead. "So what are you doing down here, Princess?" He tried not to inhale.

Her expression was priceless. "Some skull-head used the garderobe after I gave specific orders not to!" She wiped her wet sleeve across her face.

"So is that a new fragrance you're wearing?"

"It is called dung, Sir. No doubt you think it suits me, you do."

"Nay," he injected sincerely, "but then most noble ladies don't clean sewers."

"I'm neither a lady nor noble! I'm trying to repair a neglected caer and failing miserably at it, I am." She slumped dejectedly against the wall.

Shadoe set his torch in a wall mount and came beside her. Dismissing her rancid smell, he dropped to one knee and swept her wet tangled hair off her face.

∽

The warmth of his callused hand on Rayn's chin made her shiver. He was being compassionate; something he didn't do often, and thus didn't know how to do well. *Of all the people to find me in this disgusting condition, it would be Shadoe. I stink like a dung heap, yet he acts as if I'm a fresh rose. What's wrong with this man?*

"You're quite the woman, Rose Rayn."

Woman! Her heart soared. "And you must have an iron-clad belly, Sir Shadoe."

"Oh, I assure you if we remain in these tight quarters much longer, I shall prove you wrong." He chuckled, stood, and then extended his hand.

Accepting, she stumbled into his embrace. Rayn righted herself, but Shadoe didn't let go. He smiled down at her, and she wondered if he wanted to kiss her. Absurd, was it not?

Rayn braced her hands against him as if that would quell the desires he lit within her. Instead she felt the muscular hardness of his chest and the swift thud of his heart. She glanced up to find Shadoe guardedly searching her face . . . for what? Acceptance? Denial? *Oh, if he'd just give me a sign. Anything?* Then she felt it—the slightest pressure of his hand against the small of her back.

"I . . . I must bathe, Sir," she said in a wispy voice.

"Aye." The heat of his breath flushed her cheek. He drew her closer, and her resistance melted. Her arms went limp to her sides.

She closed her eyes in anticipation. Shadoe cradled her chin and tilted his head until their lips brushed. He nibbled her lower lip and her arms instinctively circled his neck as her body molded to his lean solidity. A pleasurable sensation similar to heat lightning surged between them. His kiss was delicious and intoxicating, his hands caressing her ribs and upward. Rayn's lips parted at the teasing flicker of his tongue. Lightning struck! And then—

"Lady Rayn?" Iona's voice echoed down the tunnel as she emerged with four guards and Lancelot. "Are you safe?"

"I'm fine, Iona!" Rayn put distance between herself and Shadoe.

Lancelot's torch flickered across the couple's expressions, and he fixed a glare on Shadoe. "That is a matter of opinion, daughter." Stifling a gag, he growled. "You are to be chaperoned, yet here you are—"

"Covered with muck and in the secure company of Sir Shadoe," she said haughtily. Fetching up her staff and holding her head high, Rayn dared not look at Shadoe, who had turned to retrieve his torch.

Engaging the arm of a gagging Iona, Rayn snapped at Lancelot, "If you are so concerned about my well being, Da, I suggest you appoint someone else keeper of the sewers."

Lancelot blustered as she stalked away. Motioning the guards to accompany her, he turned on Shadoe. "Why do I feel there's more than just a foul stench about?"

"Don't weary your ailing heart, friend," Shadoe said, lightly tapping Lancelot's chest. "The future sovereign of Camelot is as pure as the waters of Avalon, except for her scent. A hot bath will cure that."

"Such a washing would benefit you as well," the knight snorted.

Shadoe laughed, but the parental concern on Lancelot's countenance revealed he'd not been sidetracked.

"Hear me out, Shadoe un Hollo Tors. I did not keep my ward locked in a tower. She has the mind of a scholar and a warrior's skills to defend herself and her clan—talents that saved your life, I might add."

"For which I am eternally grateful. And your point, Lance?"

"That despite her independent nature, her heart is naive. She has been shielded from men like you." He thumped Shadoe's chest with a strong, blunt finger.

"Men like myself?" Affronted, Shadoe waggled a brow at his friend's accusatory tone.

"Aye . . . rascals and rogues. You are older and too worldly for Rayn. More importantly, you are a contradiction to what I've reared her to respect."

"And you are not?" he disputed.

"I've changed my ways. But only because God changed me," Lancelot stated with fervor.

"I'm glad for you, friend. Rayn has done well by your parenting. So I will put your mind to rest. I've no designs on your daughter. She does not attract me in the sense that you fear."

"Then in what do you find the attraction?" He looked unconvinced.

"Her convictions," Shadoe deduced, realizing the candor of his reply.

"Anything else?" Lancelot remained leery.

"She has grit, Sir, more than most men, and she possesses great potential."

"And?"

"'Tis time she learned to be a lady . . . at all times," Shadoe stated as they exited the sewers and its stench.

"Asking for a miracle, are we?" Lancelot cracked a grim smile.

"You don't sound hopeful."

"Have you paid her any heed of late, Shadoe?"

More than you know, he mused uncomfortably.

"Well, if you did, you'd notice that she wears her hair in braids with a palla and dons a dress; she has done so for several weeks."

Shadoe nodded. "Well, that's a start, Sir. Anyone can drape a pauper in gold-threaded robes. Yet a robe can't transform a beggar into a king."

Lancelot frowned. "Argument taken. I know that lass better than anyone. In all honesty, she's more at home in these sewers than wearing fine linens."

"Guenevere did both."

"Guenevere was the daughter of a king."

"So is Emerald Rose Rayn."

Halting at the stairs that led from the sewers to the upper level, Lancelot looked at Shadoe's firm, set features. "You accept her birthright?"

"There is something special about her." He swept splayed fingers through his hair.

"Then you see it?"

"What?" Shadoe arched a brow.

"Arthur's blood and inherent gifts?"

"Possibly." He looked away.

"If these old eyes sense her uniqueness, then you, Steward Apprentice, should be able to fully see her uniqueness," Lancelot huffed.

Uncomfortable with their exchange, Shadoe shrugged. "It's not what I sense that matters, friend. With Rayn as Arthur's legitimate heir, and if we can convince the neighboring tribes to unite and stand against Mordred, he might back down."

"I appreciate your help, Shadoe un Hollo Tors." He slapped the younger man's upper back.

"It's going to take a lot of work." Shadoe revealed his skepticism.

"Aye, we've less than a month."

"That's insane!"

"I call it faith." Lancelot chuckled. They took more stairs, and his breathing became labored. "I sent messengers to the clan leaders for an assembly in three weeks."

Shadoe paled. "It is too soon!"

"Not soon enough. Within three weeks, your duty will be done . . . and you can do what you've craved since the day you arrived . . . return to Gaul, Italy, or wherever it is you call home."

"What do you know about my duty?"

"Everything. As scion of the High Steward of Caledonia, your duty is to signify the rightful heir to Arthur's throne with the Emerald Rose of Avalon you wear over your heart."

Shadoe's hand went protectively to his chest, and his cheeks heated with surprise.

Lancelot guffawed. "You think I didn't know you hold it? To whom else would the Merdyn have entrusted the crest of the Pendragon?"

"You would have preferred he'd given it to Rayn himself," Shadoe noted.

"Aye. But he didn't, did he?"

Shadoe mused. "I'm sure he was tempted, but it would have been foolish to place such a burden upon a child."

"And it wouldn't have been by the pandect of our ancestors. Merlin always was one to follow law." He arched a slate gray brow at Shadoe. "You know you could have left the day you found me."

"Aye."

"But you didn't, and for that I am thankful."

Shadoe grew ill at ease with the direction of their conversation. He started to climb again. Lancelot came alongside and snagged his arm. Shadoe halted mid-step. Lancelot's stern expression meant one thing, a lecture.

"Shadoe, I have never been a man of words, much less of compliments. I believe that if a man does his best, he doesn't need praise from others to confirm what he already knows to be true. However, there have been occasions when I've bent that rule and this is one such time."

Here it comes! Shadoe braced for the storm.

"You, Shadoe un Hollo Tors, are as reluctant a High Steward as there's ever been. But whether you realize it or not, you have filled your father's empty sandals with such ease I often have to force myself to remember you are not the Merdyn. Your leadership qualities are exemplary. You have the perfected skills of a seasoned warrior, and whether you earned them rightfully or wrongfully is no longer of consequence. Furthermore, your comprehension of battlefield strategy is unmatched. Your political knowledge and, might I add, your moral conduct is above reproach." Lancelot took a deep breath. "There, I believe I've covered everything that comes to mind. But also be humble enough to realize there is always room for improvement, and never settle for less!"

Shadoe was absorbing the idea that Lancelot du Lac had complimented him. The moral conduct issue disturbed him most. "I'm unworthy of such tribute, Sir." He looked at a flickering wall sconce.

"I know," Lancelot harshly ground out, and they continued their ascent.

Shadoe glanced over to find the knight grinning and he managed to smile, too. "But your time frame is far too short. Forgive my bluntness, Lance, but I think you're touched." He pointed to his head.

Pausing to catch his breath, Lancelot leaned on Shadoe. "Nay, I'm not witless. But I am dying, friend."

Shadoe started to protest, but Lancelot raised his hand. "And with the Scion of God as my witness, I'll not leave this world without attempting to free my homeland of Mordred's tyranny."

"What of Rayn?"

"I will tell her."

"Everything?"

"Aye," Lancelot sighed, "and it will be the most difficult thing I've ever done . . . telling her I am not her da."

Shadoe nodded soberly and assisted him up the remaining stairs.

Reaching the main floor, Lancelot ventured, "You don't approve?"

He sidled a scowl at the ailing man. "I think Rayn has a right to her heritage, but this is not her war. Everyone seems to expect a miracle because she is Arthur's daughter."

"By all that is sacred, she is of Arthur's loins!"

Shadoe sobered. "And I realize the ramifications of that pronouncement, but I fear you do not. The very lie that has kept her safe all these years, you willingly discard and, in so doing, will seal her fate. Furthermore, if you convince Mordred she is Arthur's daughter, he'll want Rayn as his queen—demand it, I'd expect. I spent almost two years in the keeping of that monster. I know something you don't."

"That Mordred is not Arthur's scion?"

Shadoe's eye's widened. "Aye."

"Merlin told me."

"So if Rayn denies him, you can be certain he'll put a sword to her belly just as he did to Guenevere!"

"And like her mother, she'll submit to neither." Lancelot nodded smugly.

Shadoe glowered at his longtime friend. "Then you have sentenced her to death, Sir, and if not death, marriage to a pagan chieftain. For if you introduce Rayn as a queen without a king, every eligible chieftain will be challenging for her marriage bed. I pray that you've elected a righteous husband for her."

"I have. Galahad."

"An honorable choice." Lowering his gaze, Shadoe's jaw worked as he digested what he'd long suspected. He felt Lancelot's scrutinizing look. He felt ill.

"Not necessarily what you'd prefer, aye? It would appear that stone you call a heart has sprung to life . . . at least where Rayn is concerned."

"Best look at your own heart, Lance. You claim to love her, but that you are willing to sacrifice her for personal revenge says otherwise."

"You insult me! I'd never place Rayn in harm's way. Have you forgotten Mordred killed Guenevere in cold blood?"

"Don't patronize me. I was there! The horrors of her death plague me always. If anyone wants revenge against that offspring of Lucifer, 'tis me. But I also pledged to my dying queen I'd not avenge her death, that I'd allow God to judge Mordred."

"And I promised Arthur to free his people and restore Camelot to its former splendor."

"What has that promise to do with Rayn?"

"Everything! Camelot is her inheritance and home."

Shadoe pressed the palm of his hand against the familiar stone wall. "This was my home once, but home is not a tower of cold stones, it is family and—"

"God," Lancelot said with finality in his voice.

"Aye. Tell me, Sire, have you sought God's council about this vow to Arthur?"

Appearing astonished, Lancelot stared at the candor in the younger man's face. "I have."

"And what was his answer?"

Hesitating, he glanced away. "He has yet to speak to my heart."

Entering the great hall, Shadoe looked at the ailing knight and confidently replied, "Mayhap the answer is in his silence."

Lancelot opened his mouth to reply, but no words came. Shadoe turned and left.

∞

Rayn scrubbed her skin until it burned, and all the while she scrubbed, she thought of Shadoe. The man had truly gotten under her skin, and, unfortunately, everyone seemed to know. Her ears still rung from not only Iona's reprimand, but her father's as well.

She had yet to understand Sir Lancelot. Truth was, despite an occasional dispute between the two men, she assumed Lancelot was fond of Shadoe. But the words her father had spewed at her moments ago still rattled her.

"Shadoe is here for one reason, daughter, and 'tis not to woo you!"

Rayn was her usual defiant self. "I need no one to tell me whom I can love, but I assure you I am not in love with Shadoe."

"Bah!" Lancelot bellowed. "Love is not part of Shadoe un Hollo Tors' vocabulary. I do not want you disgraced or heartbroken. Please, lass, see matters for what they are."

"Nothing happened, Sir!" *Oh, yes it had!* "The man loathes me, and I him." She put a comb to her wet hair and turned her back to her father's oration.

"Sometimes that is how it begins." He slumped onto the bench, grumbling.

Rayn's eyes widened, and she faced him. "How what begins, Da?"

Weariness slackened his features. He waved his hand in dismissal. "You honestly don't like Shadoe?"

Rayn gauged her reply, "He annoys me immensely, Da. I try not to give him a second thought, and I suspect the feeling is mutual. Shadoe has no designs for a woman who fights like a man." She crinkled her nose. "Let alone tramps about in stinking sewage."

Lancelot ran his palm down his bearded jaw, and going to Rayn, he embraced her. "God has great plans for you, Emerald Rose Rayn, so please do not let the desires of your heart get in his way."

Pondering his words, Rayn looked up at her father. "But I don't know God's plans."

He hugged his daughter again and spoke softly against her brow. "I do, and very soon I will tell you."

Before Rayn could answer, Lancelot planted a kiss on her wet head and left her to wonder of God's plans.

Chapter Twenty-Four

THE CHARCOAL CLOUDS were drenched with God's tears.

His voice echoed in the thunder.

His eyes flashed bolts of lightning across the midday sky.

It was raining.

Again!

A torrential downpour, the third day of storms with periodic hail. Rayn worried over her garden, worried over the fields of grain the new tenants had planted. Most of all, she worried about the waifs confined to the great hall who were wearing on everyone's nerves, including hers.

For a moment of solitude, she stood beneath the archway of the caer's rear doorway, watching two goslings squabble over a puddle. "You silly birds, there are more than enough puddles, and yet you fight over one, you do."

"Such is the way of man." Shadoe came alongside her and looked out onto the bleak, wet day.

He had not privately graced her company since their encounter in the sewers, but the rain had confined everyone, including Camelot's budding army. She struggled for conversation as his arm brushed hers and sent a tremor through her limbs. "Your words of wisdom, aye?"

"Arthur's." He turned sideways, dipped his head beneath the low stone arch, and gazed into the yard. A comfortable silence hung between them. When he turned his attention back to her, his black brows arched to a high angle over even darker eyes, as if he saw her for the first time.

She gulped and hoped he'd not heard her swallow, nor could hear the swift patter of her heart. *Heavens, he is so tall and broad of shoulder that he fills the doorway.* She clasped her hands behind her and leaned against the damp stones, trying to maintain a proper distance. "Da tells me new recruits arrive daily, and soon we will have a thousand strong, we will."

"Aye, but we need three in order to do battle."

"Three more men?"

He snorted. "Nay, three cohorts."

She caught the hint of a smile on his lips.

"But then you knew that." He winked.

"Did I?" she taunted. "Surely not. For I am a mere woman, who has no right in the war room, let alone on the battleground. Thus I should think my stupid question would amuse if not please you, it would."

"I contend I like my women beautiful and charming. But I never said they should have stones for brains."

"Whist, you could have fooled me." She looked back at the geese to find they had come to a truce and made the puddle big enough to share. "But you believe women should not engage in the wars of men, or discuss political matters, or . . . heaven forbid . . . express an opinion?"

His mouth turned down at its corners, and then his deep chuckle rumbled like distant thunder. "This warrior knows when he is being lured into a trap, formidable lady."

Rayn's eyes narrowed in warning. "'Tis the way of my Pict heritage for women to participate in battle and politics, as 'tis the way of your Celt lineage, yet you deny such tradition."

"Name one woman who did all of the above and was a success," he challenged, crossing his arms over his broad chest.

"Cleopatra."

"She was no battle maiden. But if you consider suicide success . . ." His lips twitched.

"I believe any life without Christ Jesu not a success, but then we were discussing the roles of men and maidens, not salvation." ·

"That we were."

"I want to be included in the Round Table discussions, I do." She stood tall and looked him straight on.

Shadoe shrugged. "Take up that issue with your father."

"Then you don't object if I am present during your conferences?"

"Nay. Guenevere was always privy to the political agendas and combat strategies. Arthur not only respected but encouraged her wisdom."

"Really? Then you don't object if I participate on the practice field with the other warriors?"

∽

Shadoe drew a pointed breath. The spitfire had a devious way of manipulating him. That he more often than not took her bait was not only unnerving, it made him desire her more. "Again, I think you should discuss this matter with your da."

"Are you saying you are not the one enforcing the restrictions that have been placed upon me since your arrival?"

"Aye." He nodded smugly at his own honesty.

"Whist, I'll be." She gazed out into the yard at the playful geese.

When she turned back, he held her beguiling, obstinate expression and barely managed to not kiss her. Rayn trailed the tip of her tongue across her lips. By all that was sacred, she was the enchantress. Shadoe stared into her liquid green gaze and became lost. Here within his grasp stood the sole reason for his sleepless nights these last few months. Dare he admit he'd sought her out just now, that he had to feel the warmth of her smile, inhale the sweet intoxicating scent of her? Aye.

And yet I've but one duty. Being in these tight confines with her is not part of the bargain. So I should return to my quarters . . . anywhere but here with her, alone. And yet, I cannot.

"Has your father talked with you yet?"

"In reference to what? For it appears he and I need discuss many things, aye?"

Shadoe hesitated. It was not his place to inform her of her birthright. He looked for a way out of this sensitive discussion. A damp breeze swept into the doorway, and Rayn hugged her bare arms.

"You're chilled." He caressed the gooseflesh of her forearm.

"Aye." She placed her hand over his, and he drew her near.

"Rayn," he breathed out her name and lowered his head, never breaking their fervent gaze. The green embers of invitation in her eyes fueled the fire within him.

"Rayn! Shadoe!"

Breaking apart, their heads turned to meet Galahad's fierce countenance as he approached them.

"'Tis not how it looks," Rayn tried to explain before her brother yanked her out of the doorway and placed her behind him.

"It never is!" Galahad snarled, not taking his glower off Shadoe. "Rayn, Da wants to speak to you. Now."

"But I—"

Shadoe strolled back into the keep. "Obey your brother, Rayn. We'll talk later."

She nodded but clenched Galahad's arm. "Nothing happened."

"And with God as my witness, nothing will." Galahad growled at Shadoe as he escorted her off.

Shadoe drew a weary breath and shut his eyes, reprimanding himself. What was happening to him? Why on earth couldn't he keep his hands off the wench? Surely it was a test, but whose? He had to deny her and the desires she roused within him. If Galahad challenged him to combat over the maiden, he would be better to look the coward than confess she'd gotten into his blood. He had plans, places to go, people to meet. There was nothing to stay here for, not even Rayn. If she was indeed Arthur's progeny, she could never be his. Rayn was destined to rule this Isle of Might. And he, Shadoe un Hollo Tors, remained unworthy of this wee woman who measured up to any man he'd ever admired.

Shadoe dozed over the maps and battle strategies strewn atop the Round Table of the war room. Standing, he stretched his sleeping limbs and chastised himself for even looking at the battle plan. Yahweh willing, there wouldn't be an engagement, and he would be away from Camelot within the week.

Dusk had set in. He extinguished the oil lamp and then turned toward the open doorway that led to the great hall. Here servants, soldiers, and even Perceval and Tristam chose to sleep. After making do with earthen beds most of his life, Shadoe had taken up residence in one of the second-floor bedchambers. It was also where Galahad, Lancelot, and Rayn resided, and Shadoe felt obligated to accept the room offered him. Obligation had never been a word in Shadoe's vocabulary, but lately it seemed to have become a part of his life, and as much as he'd disliked it two months ago, he accepted it now.

He was actually dealing with the most important aspect of his life, his spirituality. If he could blame anyone for making him consider confronting his issues with God, it would be Rayn. Her joy in God seemed forever present. He sensed the peace that her faith brought to Caer Camelot. For most all who came in contact with her, no matter their beliefs, commented on her loving, nurturing nature, which she openly credited to the Lord Jesu Christ.

Often, he'd hear her lovely voice lifted in praise to God. And even a man as hardened as Shadoe could not help but be moved by her vocal worship. Although he'd not admit it to anyone, he envied what she had: a close relationship with God. Shadoe had once known a lad who had such faith and a powerful bond with the Christ; he wondered what became of that lad and if it was possible to find him again.

Shadoe's thoughts returned to Rayn. Even though the soggy week had worn on everyone's nerves, she seemed unscathed. Instead of dwelling on the negative, she looked at the positive, making use of the forced confinement to ensure that Caer Camelot get as comprehensive a cleansing on the inside as it was getting on the outside. Besides these extra chores, many days had been spent repairing leaks in the main keep as well as in the outer structures.

It had been three days since the last storm, and the occupants of Camelot had fallen back into routine. Hopefully by tomorrow, the exercise field would be dry enough that Shadoe could train the infantry. Glory knew they needed an outlet for their youthful energy. He and Lancelot had broken up four brawls to date, each one bloodier than the last.

Today was the Sabbath, and most folks chose to retire early in order to rise at dawn and return to the normal daily routine. Still, laughter and the strums of a lyre emanated from the great hall. For a moment he thought to join them. He'd not eaten and had missed his hour with the orphans, but then he'd been doing that a lot of late and intentionally. He'd never intended to become attached to them, but he had, making it harder to maintain his longtime assertion that he didn't desire an emotional bond. While Lady Iona did not understand his decision, Rayn never mentioned it. Then again, she didn't appear interested in his relationship with the orphans.

Thinking of Rayn, he decided to check on her whereabouts before he made his rounds of the courtyard and then retire for the night. He couldn't explain why, but he had an even greater sense of foreboding about her welfare.

About to amble out of the war room, Shadoe felt the chill of death ripple through his limbs. It was the exact sensation he'd experienced the first time he'd entered this room with Rayn months ago. The flesh at the base of his skull prickled. He was not alone. Evil permeated the air. He looked back into the large room, seeing nothing but shades of darkness. Not willing to deal with the ominous presence, Shadoe hastened into the hall to join the activities. As he rounded the corner, he heard Rayn's airy laughter and concluded Iona had the night's duty of supervising the children for bed.

Because of the warm, humid air of summer, only a modest glow emanated from the scarlet cinders of the centralized hearthstone. Over-head, the roof's stone panels had been pushed ajar for fresh air. Rayn's meticulous housekeeping had returned the great chamber to its former splendor. The wall torches illuminated the brightly painted mosaic walls and their peaceful scenes of Caledonia. Had such a time once existed? Might such a world be again?

Rayn sat at the crowded table where Lancelot, Tristam, Perceval, and several of the newly appointed centurions were eating the evening meal. Although his stomach growled from hunger, Shadoe's attention fixed on Rayn as she laughed at some witticism Galahad shared with her. Knowing Galahad's lame sense of humor, Shadoe wondered what the knight could possibly say to bring such mirth to Rayn's brilliant green eyes and add cherry luminescence to her cheeks. The sight of them face to face, holding hands, caused Shadoe's jaw to clench. Pivoting, he took the stairs two steps at a clip.

Wall torches were spaced every ten paces on the inside wall and pro-vided adequate illumination from the serpentine staircase onto the high arched passageway. A trickle of fading light issued from a high portal at the far end of the passageway. Inexplicably, the light trans-formed into a transparent blue orb that stopped and hovered in front of Rayn's quarters.

Shadoe assumed his eyes were tricked by the play of natural light and torchlight. He walked forward. The blue sphere grew larger and began to gyrate.

"Who goes there?" he called out.

No answer. The illumination brightened. The air turned frosty. Shadoe saw his breath and felt the prickling at the base of his skull. He knew this to be a warning from his soul. He'd experienced it as a child when Merlin had cast demons from a villein woman. He wanted noth-ing to do with this malevolent creature. The sphere of light split in half. Two entities! Shadoe prepared to stand his ground. He gripped the hilt of his sword yet knew such weapons were useless against this enemy.

Taunting him, the lights danced around him in a circle of pulsing shadows. "What do you want?" he demanded. The bright orbs spun faster and faster.

"Depart, Shadoe un Hollo Tors. Depart Camelot!" a demonic male voice ordered.

"I will not go, nor do I fear you."

"Then you will die," the voices, one male and one female, said in unison.

"In the name of Almighty Yahweh, I command you to be gone!"

The dark blue lights merged again and mocked him. "Almighty Yahweh? You have no god but yourself, scion of Merlin. You have no faith. You rejected the Christ the day you fled Belizar. You are nothing but demon's dung to your God. But we promise you riches beyond your imagination! Beautiful women. Oh, but you prefer Rayn. We can arrange that. Give us your fealty."

Sweat beaded Shadoe's upper lip. He trembled and turned from them. "Lying spawn of the Adversary, get behind me!"

The entities hovered inches from his face. "You have no authority over us! There is no Merlin or angels to save you. Alas, no one cares about you, least of all your miserable soul, which is already ours. You just don't know it."

"Shadoe?" Rayn called out as she stepped onto the landing.

Before he could speak, the spheres of lights vanished, as did the frigid cold. Immobilized with fear, Shadoe could not answer her.

Rayn rushed over to him. "Whom are you yelling at? And why don't you answer me? Why is it so cold? Glory, you're freezing, you are!"

"Go back," he managed to say, ignoring her concern as she touched his tremulous shoulder.

"Glory, what's all the fracas about?" Galahad cleared the stairs, wielding his sword.

"Nothing!" Shadoe jerked free of Rayn's hold and sent her off balance. Without looking back, he charged down the rear staircase and into the courtyard.

Leaning against the wall, Rayn watched his swift departure. He'd been terrified and had lied to her. She intended to find out why.

"What was that about?" Galahad slipped his short sword into its leather sheath.

"I don't know." She shrugged and gestured to return to the hall.

"Before you retire, Father wishes to speak with you."

"Aye, I know." She smiled as he turned toward his chambers. "Are you retiring for the night?" She hoped she didn't sound too nosy.

"Nay, I want to spend time in prayer. I will see you before you go to sleep." He bent over and kissed her brow. Then, putting a finger beneath her chin, he tipped her head upward and gazed into her eyes.

Rayn smiled back, wondering what he was about to say, but as had been his nature of late, he just smirked. "Have I told you what a beautiful woman you've become, Emerald Rose Rayn, and how very proud I am of you?"

Rayn nodded and kissed the back of his hand. "Aye. You tell me daily, and I am proud to be your wee sister. I love you, I do."

"And I love you." They walked to his chamber's door, and Rayn sauntered toward the staircase, realizing Galahad was waiting until she'd cleared the main landing. She waved and hurried toward the great hall. Rayn grinned. No doubt Galahad had waited because he suspected she'd follow Shadoe into the courtyard. He was right.

Chapter Twenty-Five

A MOMENT LATER, Rayn quietly entered her room, donned her tunic, breeches, and braes, then braided her burnished tresses into a plait and bided her time. Rayn's belly growled with hunger, but when she emerged, the servants had already cleaned the last scraps off the great hall's table. Most ladies would have lost their temper over such an indignity. Not Rayn, as she'd spent most of her life serving others and eating when she found time. Entering the summer kitchen, she caught up a chunk of flat bread and cheese and headed for the courtyard and fresh air.

The thunderstorms had rinsed the stone-laid yard clean. Rayn smiled at the sweet fragrance of honeysuckle in bloom. Looking up, she saw the sun nestling behind the tors; night was just minutes away.

The lifestyle of Caer Camelot had changed drastically from weeks back when it seemed all of Britannia had descended upon them. The dust had literally settled, and those who remained at the great fortress were servants, tenants, and the recruits for Camelot's army. The air was now nearly silent, save for laughter from the thatched huts that had been raised as barracks by the walls. The lilt of a flute drifted across the outer bailey walls from one of them. Overhead, sentries stood watch from the portcullis. Several guards walked the grounds, and a servant passed, bowing in respect. Rayn had not gotten used to folk displaying such respect toward her, which led her to wonder what had become of the honorable Shadoe un Hollo Tors.

No more had she thought his name than she spotted his tall form moving along the east wall. Since he'd taken over Merlin's apartment, Shadoe had also donned the enchanter's black ram's cloak. Rayn speculated it was Shadoe's way of connecting with his deceased father. *The cloak suits him well,* she thought as he slipped beyond the stables and out of sight.

Curious, she munched on her cheese and followed. When she spotted Shadoe again, she held back. He disappeared almost every night after the evening meal and wasn't seen again until dawn. Rayn assumed he went off to Merlin's crystal caverns. Regardless, she had to speak with him. She wanted to know what had happened in the passageway, and she wanted to know his intentions toward her.

Rayn kept her distance while he strolled across the walled acres of the courtyard, checking the eighty-foot high embankment walls and the recent repairs. In due course, he strode across the exercise field and into the stand of ancient oaks near the far end of the north wall.

With the frequent rains had come hatching of mosquitoes. Rayn swatted at a swarm that escorted her across the field, wondering if her snooping was worth the nasty bites. The night teemed with life. Crickets chirped and fireflies flitted about, while overhead bats swooped, sampling the banquet of mosquitoes.

Outside the copse, Rayn hesitated, no longer noticing the pesky insects. For years, legends of phantoms and evils spirits had prevented her venturing farther. The druids revered this wood and called it the Sacred Oaks. Rayn's breath sharpened. Was it possible Shadoe had reverted to the pagan ways of his ancestors? Was he druid, as Merlin had once been? *Dear God, let it not be so.*

She needed to know. Stealing into the dense wood, she found the overgrown path used by both her people and the druids. When a prickly bush scratched her arm, she muttered a curse, deciding that she'd ask Lancelot to cut these pagan trees for firewood.

Rayn heard a voice from the circular clearing ahead. She stopped, hearing but not understanding the melodic chant. Shadoe's song was mystically inviting, but she feared it to be demonic as it lured her deeper into the wooded grove.

The veil of night slipped over the sun, while overhead one lone star sparkled like a rare jewel in the velvet sky. Rayn came to the rim of a clearing, where in the midst crumbled remnants of staggered pillars comprised the ruins of a stone building. Shadoe knelt at a granite altar.

Rayn recalled the history of this ruin. Here over an ancient druid altar, King Arthur had erected a Christian chapel where he and Guenevere were wed and, so few years later, were buried. After taking Camelot, Morgause defiled the sanctuary. The walls of stone were toppled; the altar was desecrated with animal sacrifices; and if rumor were true, bairns were sacrificed as well. Evil dwelt here, yet something else made its presence felt—peace.

Shadoe stopped chanting and lay prone on the earthen floor until the most wretched cry ripped from his chest.

Rayn jolted and covered her mouth to hold back the gasp burning her lips.

Shadoe's clenched fists slammed the earth in a series of blows.

Fear seized her. Rayn winced and then gripped her hands. Her nails bit into her palms. She felt each painful blow as if her own fists pummeled the ground. She shouldn't be spying on him. Yet what in glory's name could cause such agony? The cries of anguish that poured out of him drew tears from her eyes as she fought the urge to console him. Fear prevailed.

Turning on her heels, she fled, not stopping until she had entered the safe haven of Camelot. Breathless, Rayn leaned against the bailey wall and sought the only source that could give her comfort. *Lord! Don't let what I witnessed be what I fear most: that Shadoe has conceded to the Adversary. I beg you, Abba Father, draw him back to your embrace.*

Before Rayn had time to think, an armed sentry approached her. "Mistress, Sir Lancelot wishes your presence in his quarters."

Drawing a sigh of resolve, she nodded and went to her father.

⤳◦◦

"Sit down, Emerald Rose Rayn," Lancelot commanded.

Rayn did as told but not without argument. "Really, Da, this is madness. Shadoe has behaved honorably he has. Why I haven't seen him since . . ."

Lancelot didn't seem aware of her hesitation. "I didn't call you here to discuss Shadoe's indiscretions, daughter, or is there something else you wish to tell me?" He stared sternly into her eyes.

Rayn blushed and lowered her gaze to her clenched fists, noting the white of her knuckles and feeling the bruised sides of her hands. "Umm . . . no, Da."

"You left again with neither an escort nor a guard. Not only have you disobeyed my will, but also Iona is at her wit's end because of your lack of courtesy. She is protective of you, Rayn, and each time you tramp off without her. . . . You should know she considers herself unwanted. She might very well leave."

Rayn exhaled with surprise. "I had no idea—"

Lancelot waved a commanding hand. "Although the Saxons and Jutes long ago plundered her estates, Lady Iona is of noble blood, Rayn. Yet you treat her like a commoner, like a servant, not worthy of your favor."

Rayn balked. Never to her knowledge had she abused or slighted Iona. Although of late, she spent more time with Niamh. Realizing her error, she awaited Lancelot's rightful lecture. Moments passed. When at last she looked up, she found him at the window, staring off into the night sky, his hands clasped behind him.

Rayn went to him, and he turned to face her. He looked gaunt. Rayn suspected her inconsiderateness to be the cause. "I'm sorry, Da. I didn't mean to anger you or hurt Iny's feelings. I love her like an aunt, I do. I will go to her and apologize, I will."

Lancelot reached out and embraced her. "That would be the right thing to do, child. And I'm sorry that I've put you under lock and key . . . but I've my reasons."

She nodded against his chest and promised she'd never disobey him again. Glancing up, she noted how Lancelot no longer seemed larger than life to her. Oh, he was still tall and imposing, but somehow different. Rayn could remember when Lancelot du Lac was the handsomest man she ever knew. And in her eyes, he still was—with the exception of Shadoe. Lancelot had significantly aged since coming to Camelot. The laugh lines beneath his eyes were more pronounced, and his redish blonde hair was now mostly grayed. Most noticeable to her was his failing stamina. His breathing seemed labored, and it was often an effort for him to walk or ride any distance.

She wondered, had Mordred tortured him at Belizar? This seemed the only explanation she could accept for the swift deterioration in her father. Lancelot never did anything small or slow; as long as she could recall, he had walked fast, ridden fast, and fought hard. He was the only man she knew who could exist on a few hours of sleep. Even that had changed. Most often Rayn and the household were up before him. Whenever she inquired about his health, he dodged the matter.

"Da," she began, but he cut her off as he stepped back and gazed tenderly into her face.

"I told you that we needed to discuss the future, Rayn, but first you must know about the past." He led her to a bench and, sitting beside her, gently took her hands in his large, callused ones and faced her. "This is not easy for me."

Rayn smiled encouragingly. "Nothing you say will divide us."

Lancelot breathed a troubled sigh. "I pray you remember your words, lass, for what I'm about to tell you is the hardest thing I will ever do. Please know that I love you more than my own life. You are the greatest blessing God ever bestowed upon me." He caressed her cheek, and when she kissed the back of his hand, he sighed. "You would make any father proud."

Lancelot's words seemed to snag in his throat, and Rayn had to quell the trepidation surfacing within her. Lancelot had always been conservative in his feelings. Rayn knew he loved her, and that was sufficient.

"Tell me," she urged and caressed his whiskered jaw.

Gripping her fingers, he met her trusting eyes. "It's your birthright."

"Then let me spare you, Da. I know my mother Lady Katherine was not killed by Saxons after my birth. Indeed, she was a fictitious character you created to pacify me. I know of your love affair with Queen Guenevere. She was my mother, she was."

Lancelot lowered his head. "Aye, in my heart I've suspected you've known for some time, but as long as you did not ask, it allowed me to believe you unaware."

"How could I not know? Everyone else does! Are you that ashamed of her, ashamed of me?"

"Ashamed? Never! I meant to protect you."

She stood and crossed her arms. Although she knew the truth, she needed to hear it from Lancelot's lips. "My mother did not die during my birth, did she now?"

"Nay," he answered and searched her eyes. "She died a few weeks later. She chose death over revealing you to Mordred and Morgause. She loved you, and she died so you might live."

The silence between them was deafening.

Rayn spoke first. "Then the rumormongers didn't lie about you and Lady Guenevere's affair?"

"Aye, Guenevere was your mother. Nay, I did not sire you . . . although I selfishly wished I had."

Rayn nearly collapsed, save for Lancelot's quick embrace of her. Looking up into his troubled gaze, her eyes welled with tears. "But you and she . . . were lovers."

Lancelot shook his head. "Never! In my heart I sinned against God and my loyal companion Arthur Pendragon. For I desired the beautiful Guenevere as I never desired Galahad's loving mother, Elaine. My adulterous betrayal broke Elaine's fragile heart and took her life. Long ago, I accepted the blame for that, and only through God's grace have I received Galahad's absolution. Now I seek your forgiveness, Rayn."

Too stunned to think of anything, how could she forgive the only man she'd believed to love her? Rayn could not. Not only had he lied about her mother, Rayn was not of his loins. Nor were she and Galahad siblings. She had no one! Pulling free of Lancelot, she glared coldly at him.

He relinquished her and continued with a diffident tone, "Rayn, I swear with God's angels as my witness that although Guenevere was flattered by my attention, her faith redeemed her. She refused my advances."

"Are you saying she was not in love with you?" Rayn added cynically, "Look, Da, I grew up hearing the rumors that you bedded her. Be honest with me."

"Your mother was more in love with your father than she could ever be with me, and for that you should be eternally grateful."

"My father?" Rayn asked in disgust. "How many men did she seduce?"

Lancelot snatched her arms and drew her roughly to him. "There was but one man she ever seduced, let alone ever loved: your father, Arthur Pendragon."

Trembling, Rayn collapsed into his arms and looked up. His eyes were wet with tears of truth. "King Arthur?" she asked softly.

Lancelot nodded and, gently cupping her chin, redirected her gaze to his. "Aye. The mighty Pendragon's blood burns hot in your veins along with Guenevere's. Why, it's a miracle I survived rearing you." He mustered a grin.

Rayn managed a feeble smile and sniffed back tears. "Does Shadoe know?"

"Aye, but like most, he assumed Arthur sired a scion."

"Tristam and Percy?"

"Aye, always. They took a vow, as did I, to protect you. Your father placed his wife and his unborn child in our protection before he died. Four months after his death, you were born here in Camelot. And you were just weeks old when Guenevere, fearing for your welfare, asked me to spirit you away to safety and, if necessary, raise you as my own—to do whatever was needed to keep you from Morgause's claws."

Rayn slipped out of his arms and looked anxiously about, raising her voice toward the walls. "But if this is true, I would have known." *They would have told me!*

He shook his head. "I couldn't risk telling you. The fewer who knew your identity, the safer you remained. But the time is at hand and—"

Rayn stalked the chamber, looking about.

"Father? Mother, why didn't you tell me I was your daughter?" she screamed out. "Why?"

"Rayn, what are you talking about? I just explained it was for your welfare." Lancelot reached for her, but she recoiled.

"Answer me!" she shouted to the room. Without a backward look, Rayn fled Lancelot's chambers and ran out into the passageway.

∽

Although bone-weary, Shadoe could not sleep. By now Rayn had learned the truth of her birthright. He wondered how well she'd received the news. It wasn't every day that one learned one was a princess. From now on, Rayn would never be the same. And as of tonight, Shadoe would never be the same, either. For in the ruins of the chapel, he'd sought God's forgiveness and made peace with Christ. Shadoe experienced God's unconditional love for the first time since his youth. He realized that all this time the Holy Spirit had dwelt within his heart and continued to pursue him. God had never left him. Shadoe had left God. As soon as the opportunity arose, he would tell Rayn the good news. Meanwhile, he asked God for one thing: to reveal what if any future he and Rayn had together.

A knock on his door brought Shadoe to his feet. Opening it, he met the distraught eyes of a short-winded Lancelot. "Is Rayn with you?"

Shadoe stepped aside, revealing his empty quarters to the panicked father. "Nay. She was with Galahad a few hours back."

Sleepy-eyed and securing his sword to his belt, Galahad charged up behind his father and glared accursedly at Shadoe. "What has this blackguard done now?"

"Nothing," Lancelot explained. "I told Rayn the truth and thought her to be receptive. Then she started talking to the walls, blaming someone I couldn't see. Perhaps she is angry at God, but she fled before I could stop her."

"Blaming someone for what?" Shadoe asked.

"For not telling her that they were her parents."

Shadoe's pulse quickened. "God forgive me! Since my first visit to Camelot I've sensed an evil presence. Then tonight I experienced something unearthly near the war room. But I refused to believe it. I didn't want to confront what I feared most. The fishwives claim the spirits of Arthur and Guenevere haunt Camelot."

"Spirits!" Galahad sneered. "There is none but the Holy Spirit of Yahweh in this blessed keep, least of all the walking dead!"

"Nor do I believe the spirits of the dead walk these halls, Sir. Nay, something far more dangerous. We must find Rayn!" Catching up his cloak, Shadoe accompanied Lancelot into the hall where Tristam and Percy sat with servants, drinking and joking.

"Have you seen the Lady Rayn?" Shadoe called to them while Lancelot stopped to catch his breath.

The knights shot to their feet and looked to the servants, who all shrugged. Iona entered with her stitching in hand. "Aye, she passed me by the king's bedchamber, but I doubt she'd go there alone."

Shadoe vaulted up the stairs past Galahad. The four knights and Iona struggled to keep pace with him.

Near the door to the king's chamber, Shadoe pulled them to a stop. "We must not all rush in. We need council—and prayer."

"And since when do you pray, Shadoe?" Galahad scoffed.

"Since I recommitted myself to our Lord Jesu," he stated assertively.

"I'll be!" The younger knight eyed up Shadoe and then nodded his acceptance.

"I am glad you are back within the fold, scion of Merlin." Perceval slapped a firm hand across Shadoe's shoulders.

"As am I," Tristam added, then nodded to Galahad.

"Well, I don't understand," Lancelot huffed dismissing their exchange. "Guenevere died here, but I've never seen or heard anything frightening or even odd within these walls."

Perceval and Tristam muttered similar sentiments.

"That's because none of you was an impressionable child wandering the enchanted ruins of Camelot," Shadoe explained.

Lancelot admonished himself. "This is my fault. She was barely six years old, babbling about Arthur and Guenevere as if she knew them intimately. I should have suspected something was amiss."

Galahad spoke up. "Aye, she grew up hearing truth and legend of the splendor of Camelot. But above all, Mordred, Morgause, and Niamh lived here. No doubt the demons accompanied them and decided to stay."

Shadoe motioned for their silence and spoke in a lower voice.

"Merlin taught me a bit about these fallen angels. Like the Adversary, demons can only act upon the knowledge their victim provides them. The Adversary doesn't know a person's future but can learn a person's past," Shadoe explained. "That same overconfident angel who tempted Jesu in the desert assumes he can steal a true believer's soul."

"But Rayn belongs to God," Tristam injected.

Shadoe nodded. "Aye, she does. And Satan's minion can only thrive among us if they are fed. They remain at Camelot because of Rayn's heart desires."

"The Merdyn taught you well, Enchanter," Tristam complimented.

Lancelot gripped Shadoe's forearm. "Are you saying my Rayn, a handmaiden of God, is possessed by demons?"

Shadoe shook his head. "No, as a child of God, she cannot be possessed. But these spirits have used her longing for family and connection to the old Camelot for their own ends. They exist in our earthly realm because of her and will do anything to keep it that way. This I know full well."

Wringing her hands, Iona asked, "Do not demons tempt Christians daily?"

"Aye." Shadoe lit a wall torch. "But even those who walk in the light of the Scion fail to recognize the Adversary's angels. I believe he has taken advantage of Rayn's childhood fantasies."

"But to what end?" Perceval inquired.

"To take her eyes off Jesu Christ. Any distraction from God is a victory for the Adversary, and I speak first hand, good Sirs." Shadoe instructed the others, "Wait here and cry out to Jesu until I call."

Lancelot unsheathed his sword. "My love for Rayn has not wavered, Shadoe. If there are demons to fight, you'll not go alone." The other knights presented their swords and made similar declarations.

Shadoe put his hand on Lancelot's wrist and directed the sword earthward. "Swords will not win this battle, old friend. Faith in God is our only defense—and Rayn's. I ask that you bend a knee and pray. It is the only way. Through our faith, God will unmask the true faces of her apparitions and show them for who they are—disciples of Satan."

"I saw Merlin cast demons out of a boy," Tristam injected and shuddered. "It wasn't a pretty sight, and the stench . . . disgusting."

Shadoe glanced at his companions and solemnly nodded. "I don't expect this to be pleasant."

"Do you know what you're doing, Shadoe?" Iona put a trembling hand on his shoulder.

"No. But God will lead me." He pressed a kiss to her brow.

Iona's eyes brightened. "I'm glad to see your God has returned to you, Shadoe."

Shadoe released a humble sigh. "He never left me. I left him, and he pursued me. Like the Shepherd's lamb, I was lost, and now I am found."

The knights locked gazes, appearing skeptical of Shadoe's godly confidence. "Well, I do not know what happened between you and Yahweh, but you seem to be renewed in Christ Jesu." Lancelot slapped Shadoe between his shoulder blades.

"Very new." Shadoe's lips pressed into a strained smile as he met Galahad's guarded expression. He didn't blame the suspicious man.

"Please believe me, friend. This very night, I sought God's forgiveness and favor and have received it. I am committed to Yahweh."

Galahad nailed Shadoe with a look of discernment. "I know God's Spirit never left your heart, Shadoe. What was a flickering ember now glows hot and bright for all to see, and his words speak through your lips."

With joint agreement, the men embraced Shadoe, while Iona looked away. He'd hoped his good news would convict her. It apparently had not.

Shadoe turned to the knights. "It is imperative each of you pray with fervency."

They dropped to their knees.

Shadoe bent a knee, bowed his head, and openly prayed, "Merciful Da, secure these humble servants with the armor and shield of your powerful Spirit. Let the sword of your truth strike the enemy with fear. Do what you will with us, Lord. But we implore thee protect Rayn. Open her eyes to the deceit of these demons. Lastly, show your infinite power! Hurl this evil back to where it came: the fiery bowels of Hades. In Thy Scion's holy name, we pray. Amen."

Taking up a lit torch, Shadoe entered the chamber, which shimmered with a misty blue light. The frigid air stank like a soured washrag.

"Rayn?" He took a few cautious steps forward.

A lone figure sat cross-legged on the bed.

"Go away," she hissed, without glancing at him. "You are not welcome here."

"We must talk."

"About your deceit with Lancelot and the others?"

Shadoe walked over and stood before her. "Is that what *they* told you?"

"Aye, among other things. You, Shadoe, scion of the Merdyn, would drive them away . . . out of my life. I won't let you. They are my parents, and they want me!" She glared into his torch's light with frigid, cat-like eyes.

The defiance in Rayn's voice warned him the demons had gained a strong foothold. Then again, they'd had years to manipulate her. "If they are your parents, why didn't they tell you the truth? Why didn't you know before Lancelot told you?"

"Because they vowed not to interfere with Lancelot's fostering me."

Shadoe shook his head. "No, Rayn. It's because they didn't know the truth of your heritage; they could only act upon things you revealed to them—"

"Absurd! You act as if they are wicked. They are good. Unlike you, they love me for who I am."

I do love you! Yet to talk of my heart will mean nothing to you now. "Rayn, listen to me—"

"Nay!" She bolted off the bed and challenged him directly. "Nothing you can say will change my mind." Her auburn head swerved to the right. "Yes, Da, I know. Don't worry."

"Are they talking to you?"

"Aye." She sent him a smug look. "If you see angels, would you not see and hear all spirits? It would seem you are not as powerful as the Merdyn."

"And did Merlin also converse with them?"

"Nay, he sent them away. They didn't return until he left. His powers were great. . . ." Her voice trailed off.

"The Merdyn's gifts were not his own, Rayn. They were of the Holy Spirit, and it is the Holy Spirit who resides in your heart and has sealed your salvation from these charlatans."

"So that is why I see them and you don't," she taunted. "Arthur and Guenevere said that means you, Shadoe un Hollo Tors, aren't redeemed by the Christ, who rescued you from Hell's Gate and let all those innocent men die in your place!"

Doubt crept into Shadoe's heart. *What if they are right? What if I'm not redeemed, not a child of God? What if God has forsaken me?*

Falling to his knees, Shadoe confessed, "Oh, God, I am unworthy of you, but this handmaiden has a saint's heart and has sought to serve you always. Grant her grace, Lord. Deliver her from her enemies. Command your angels to guard her from these slaves of perverse deceit who would devour her like hungry lions. Help us stand against the Adversary."

Tremendous peace and confidence sluiced over Shadoe. God was with him! Opening his eyes, he met Rayn's astonished expression and tears. Her eyes were beginning to open.

She walked to the bench and addressed the demons. "Why did you want me to say those terrible things to Shadoe? I can speak for myself, I can."

Shadoe came alongside her. "Rayn . . ." he said, with an authority that redirected her attention to him. "Be still and know he is God! Know he will never hurt you or leave you in your hour of trial."

She seemed to yield. "Be still, and know that I am God," she acknowledged softly. "Merlin said that was my mother's favorite Scripture. That in knowing God we know he is sufficient for all of our needs. He is sovereign."

"Aye. So why do these two lead you toward fear? Rayn . . . King Arthur and Lady Guenevere had no reason to fear Merlin or me. Arthur was like my brother and Guenevere a sister to me. Thus, their open distrust is hurtful and causes me concern."

"Because they fear you will send them away."

"Where would I send them?"

Rayn brushed a stray curl from her face and looked back at the dais, listening to their answer. She argued. "Shadoe would never send you there. He loves you."

Shadoe didn't have to hear their remark to know they spoke of Hades. He arched a brow at the invisible beings, whose oppressive hostility made it difficult to breathe. Still, he spoke loud and assertively. "Why would you not want to be with our heavenly Father? God assures us that all who believe in him shall have eternal life. I know Arthur and Guenevere trusted in Jesu Christ, the Scion of the true living God. They put him above all others."

"Lancelot told me many a time of their unwavering faith," Rayn nodded her head.

"Why would God deny your parents access to heaven and make them prisoners of these lonely cold walls?"

"For me," she replied adamantly.

Shadoe placed a finger to her lips, and then spoke for her ears alone. "Is Jesu not enough?"

She hesitated, looked at the dais, then back at Shadoe. "Of course, but—"

"And did he not sacrifice his life that you might live?"

She nodded, smeared a fresh tear, and then drew his hand to her cold cheeks. Shadoe felt the wall between them crumble. "Remember the thief on the cross beside Jesu?"

Rayn dropped his hand and stepped back. "What of him?" Shadoe sensed the demons struggling to undermine him. He realized the faster he spoke the truth, the harder it was for them to influence Rayn.

"The moment the thief came to faith, our Lord Jesu said to him, 'Today, you will be with me in paradise!' Rayn, your mother and father reign with Jesu in heaven. These beasts are charlatans, a diabolical conjuring of Morgause. They are sent by Lucifer to deceive you, to turn you from God and those who love you."

"Morgause le Fey?" Rayn's eyes seemed more alert now, and they widened at the possibility.

"And when you arrived, they seduced your innocence and indulged your childhood fancy about Arthur and Guenevere. Even though Merlin called upon God's Spirit and drove them out of the caer, they returned after Merlin's final departure from Camelot. Didn't you ever wonder why?"

"Now I remember. After Merlin left I became lonely. I asked them to come back. They did." She smiled at the dais.

Shadoe realized he must keep eye contact. "Rayn?"

Hesitant, she looked back at him.

"Is not everything we do to be done to God's glory?"

"Of course."

"Then if God allowed your parents to return, I assume they'd have praised him in your presence and given the glory of this reunion to Jesu Christ?"

The muscle along Rayn's delicate jaw tightened; her green eyes shifted from Shadoe to the beings and then back to him. "Nay . . . they've said nothing of Yahweh." She looked at the dais and incredulously asked, "Mother? Da?"

Blood red lightning illuminated the loft. Thunder crashed. Furniture and debris flew about like flying gnats. Iona cried out.

Shadoe managed to crane his neck toward the open doorway. Swords drawn, Lancelot and the other knights attempted to rise, then collapsed and began praying against a screaming wind. The powerful storm slammed Shadoe to the stone floor and pinned him there.

Against the fury, he refocused on Rayn. She remained standing and unharmed but yelled at the invisible couple. "Leave him be! Shadoe is right. My parents would not fear him. They would not harm him. Above all, they would give Jesu the glory! Now tell me then. Who are you?"

An angry guttural growl emitted from the dais as two giants in the likeness of King Arthur and Queen Guenevere materialized before them. Sprawled on the floor, feeling like a war-horse had kicked him, Shadoe focused on the apparitions.

Guenevere extended a beckoning hand to Rayn. "We are your parents! En route to heaven we asked God to let us remain with you, to guide you on your journey through life. He denied us. But the Prince of the Air came to our aid. That is why we are here."

Shadoe balked. His heart thumped painfully against his ribs. The demon sounded like Guenevere. Then he recalled Merlin writing that demons were capable of altering their shapes. Shadoe and the others were hearing and seeing what they expected to see, Arthur and Guenevere.

"Aye, we love you more than anything, more than God, daughter, and could not bear the thought of being apart from you. Thus, we forfeited our souls to the angel Lucifer. What greater love is there than for a father to lose his soul for his only begotten child?"

Shadoe glared as they blasphemed Holy Scriptures for their demonic gain.

"Please, Rayn, come to us. Be with us forever." Arthur stepped toward her.

She glanced back. Lancelot and the others were held prone on the floor, too. Lancelot gazed up at Rayn pleadingly. She looked down at Shadoe, as if weighing him and all she believed against the pleas of her parents.

Shadoe felt Rayn's doubt dent the demons' powers. He scrambled to his feet. "Rayn, Yahweh will never deceive you. Furthermore, you are God's child, and they cannot have what he has claimed as his own. Your happiness does not rest in anyone dead." He looked the handsome couple straight on. "No godly parents would want their child to suffer for their sins. Get behind me, servants of the Adversary, slaves of eternal fire!"

"He lies!" Arthur and Guenevere roared in unison, their voices exploding with demonic hatred.

"Nay," Rayn shrieked in rebuttal. "You lie! My parents reside in paradise with my Lord and Savior, Jesu Christ."

"Deny us and suffer!" Arthur bellowed. The power of his voice picked Rayn off the floor and tossed her against Shadoe.

Shadoe caught Rayn and, turning her about, looked into her terrified gaze. "Don't fear them. They cannot harm us."

"Watch us! We will never leave Camelot, nor will any of you leave alive!" hissed the one called Guenevere.

❧

The chamber door slammed shut. A stench worse than the sewers permeated the thick, humid air. Despite Shadoe's confidence, Rayn shook. Her heart felt ready to explode. She'd actually believed these vile creatures to be her parents.

The demons ignored Rayn and directed their rage at Shadoe. Brimstone pummeled from the ceiling. Shadoe and Rayn clung to one another, but she remained unscathed. The hell stones slashed Shadoe's skin and face; shredded his clothes. Crimson blood flowed from the deep cuts, and angry blisters erupted from the burns. Shadoe winced and groaned but stood still, sheltering Rayn.

She pushed against him to break free. "Let go! It's me they want."

Shadoe clenched her shoulders and stared intently into her eyes. "They want to divide us, Rayn. We can't let that happen. If God is for us, who can be against us?"

Rayn met his indomitable gaze. Something seemed different. He didn't run from this conflict. If anything he seemed determined to fight. This affected her so powerfully that Rayn glared over at the demons. "I stand with this man. I stand with God."

Arthur glowered back. "So be it!"

The jagged hot pellets struck her full force, searing her scalp, cutting her face. Yet the physical pain did not match the pain of her heart. Shadoe pulled her closer, sheltering her.

He called out, "For God will give his angels charge to protect us!"

"We see no angels," they taunted.

Her back and shoulders bruising from the flaying stones, Rayn prayed for help.

His lips close to her ear, Shadoe said, "Keep your eyes upon Jesu."

She nodded against his heaving chest.

"Be still and know he is God!" Shadoe's voice surged above the uproar.

For one eternal moment, silence reigned. Although wind and rain blew, the hailstorm ceased. Rayn felt Shadoe's arms drop away. She opened her eyes. Shadoe stood with his arms and face lifted heavenward. The demons' swaggering smiles waned; their features contorted with dread. Even in human form, they were ugly, atrocious creatures! A compelling power made it difficult to look away. Resisting them, Rayn shut her eyes and concentrated on God's awesome faithfulness.

"No!" the dark angels screamed at her.

"Be still and know he is God!" Shadoe's voice resounded.

Rayn lifted her arms and joined him in praise. "Be still and know he is God!"

A luminous white light descended upon the chamber. As the shimmering light encompassed the room, the evil storm strove to rise against it. Shadoe lowered his arms and drew Rayn into his embrace. Her head burrowed beneath his protective arm, she squinted at the light and experienced an overwhelming sense of serene security.

Two gigantic beings adorned with bronze armor plates and gilded swords of fire emerged from the light to stand between the demons and Shadoe and Rayn. Rayn gasped. They were at least fifteen feet tall. Their features were indistinguishable for the white light they radiated was blinding. She glanced at Shadoe. He also saw them.

The light about the beings dimmed, and Rayn beheld the most beautiful faces she had ever seen. They were neither male nor female yet possessed both attributes. One entity smiled upon her with a love so intense, Rayn wept with joy. Shadoe addressed the taller form.

"Tomas?"

"You may release the Lady Pendragon now, for she is no longer in harm's way."

Shadoe dropped his arms from Rayn, but clasped her hand within his as they faced Tomas.

The angel acknowledged them but spoke to her. "This day, Pendragon, Yahweh has delivered you from the Adversary. Now look upon the true faces of the creatures that feasted upon the desires of your heart."

The demons no longer seemed concerned about Rayn or Shadoe. Their attention was riveted on the guardian angels. The female demon transformed into a hideous, two-headed serpent with fangs and spoke in a language Rayn had never heard. Tomas responded in the same dialect, but his voice sounded like thunder. They spoke the tongue of the spiritual realm. The serpent lunged at the second angel, but the angel's lightning-swift sword sliced through the monster. Its ugly heads toppled to the floor and exploded into ashes while the demon's body burst into flames.

Seeing its companion vanquished, the lone demon roared in fury and became enveloped in icy flames that reeked of burning flesh and sulfur. Rayn and Shadoe gagged and struggled for air.

Matching the angel's height, the demon summoned an enormous black sword into its hand. It proceeded to take on many forms, each one more hideous than the last. The closer the angels advanced, the more disgusting the creature's form became. It cursed in Gaelic. The dark angel shot flames at the guardian angels, who passed through the fire unharmed.

Even as she tasted bile, Rayn did not believe the angels would be harmed, for they wore the armor of God. The second angel wielded a sword and sliced off the demon's arm that held its weapon. Another sword materialized in the demon's left hand.

The creature snickered and bellowed in a human voice that echoed through the caer, "You've not won the battle, Tomas!"

The Archangel advanced. "Hear me, dark one. The war was won five hundred years ago on the cross! And so is this battle!" Tomas rammed his sword through the demon's belly until it protruded from its back.

The demon's hideous features contorted with pain and shock. The angel jerked the sword free. A shaft of light erupted from the wound, rippled through the demon, and consumed it. With an ear-piercing scream, the demon burst into a fireball and vanished.

Rayn was not prone to fainting, but the moment the demon vanished, colors swept in front of her, and she toppled forward.

Breaking her fall, Shadoe drew her into his arms and fell to his knees. Tomas stretched out his hand toward them. A white light shot from his fingertips, washing over the couple. Their cuts and burns disappeared. Tears bathed Shadoe's face. He lifted his head and cried out, "All glory and honor to our Lord Jesu Christ!"

∽◠

Morgause le Fey doubled over. Her belly knotted in excruciating pain. Bloody black vomit spewed from her mouth. Writhing in agony, she cried out, "What have I done? How have I wronged thee?"

The answer came as the death rattle of his demons resounded in her ears. "Nooo!" she wailed and dragged herself to her reflecting glass. There, she beheld two images: the repulsive lines of age loosening her firm tight flesh and the man God had used to destroy her demons, Shadoe un Hollo Tors. "I curse you, scion of Merlin, and your descendants. By the pit, I shall see you dead and soon!"

Chapter Twenty-Six

SHADOE HAD COVERED every measure of Wind's Haven without one trace of Rayn. Since the night of the deliverance five days ago, she had honored everyone with her company but him. God had indeed filled the God-shaped hole within his heart since then. But another emptiness remained and only Emerald Rose Rayn could fill it. Shadoe ached for the smallest courtesy of her smile, her sparkling green eyes, and her small freckled nose wiggling in laughter at one of his jokes. When had his need for her approval and friendship become the priority of his life? When had he fallen in love with her? Were he still a betting man, the first day he'd spotted her at Loch Lady Falls.

Rats breath!

He was a love sick fool!

She was the air he breathed. The fervor that heated his veins. The essence that filled the void in his lonely existence. Rayn had become his lifeline and he was going mad not knowing why she wanted nothing to do with him.

Now as he crossed the fast-flowing burn at the top of the falls, he spotted her gathering herbs. Shadoe halted, then bent to scratch behind Echo's right ear. "Thanks, lass. Next time I'll just follow you or that blasted eagle."

Basket in hand, Rayn turned at the sound of his voice. "Go away, Enchanter." She picked up her staff and sprinted further into the dense woodland. Shadoe remained undaunted. In a few steps he snatched her arm and swung her about to face him.

"Unhand me." She glared at where his hand held her wrist.

"Not until you explain why you're avoiding me. Are you angry at me?"

She pulled back and looked away from him. "I am not angry with you, Sir. I'm ashamed, I am."

"Of me?"

"Nay, of myself."

"For glory's sake, why?" He scrubbed a hand over his face and into his hair.

"You mean that the august enchanter, Shadoe un Hollo Tors, scion of the Merdyn, doesn't know the answer?"

"Nay, Rayn. I am just a simple man of God."

"No longer, Sir. News has spread of your encounter with the demons, of how you drove them out of Camelot and back to hell. The pagans call you Enchanter. The Christians call you Prophet. Now you tell me, aye, just who or what are you, pagan or believer?"

"I thought the demise of those demons answered that question. 'Twas God's hand alone that sent them to their demise."

"My memory is clouded. I know God is responsible for destroying the demons. But before that, I saw you in the chapel ruins wailing to heaven—or was it hell?" She stared him straight on.

"Spying on me again, aye?" Shadoe rubbed his jaw.

She flinched but did not back down. "Not spying. I'd followed to ask you what had upset you in the passageway. Later, Da told me you'd encountered the demons there."

He nodded. "I did. That meeting became a spiritual awakening for me. I realized that I needed God."

Gently clutching her shoulders, Shadoe said with an emotion-sated voice, "For years my heart was barren, my soul wandering the desert of iniquity. Yet despite my ire with Yahweh and my willful desertion from his righteous path, he never abandoned me. Despite my protests, he brought me back to this blessed isle, to those who were . . . and still are . . . my family. More importantly God used you, Emerald Rose Rayn, to show me how much I desired to be with him. For that, Rayn, I am forever grateful."

"And what I'd witnessed in the oaks that night?" She wrung her hands and looked hopefully into his eyes.

"Was a broken, contrite man pleading with his Lord Jesu for forgiveness," he answered unashamed. "I recommitted myself to Yahweh, Rayn."

"To God be the glory! Oh, I've prayed that it would be so, fervently in truth, Milord Shadoe." Tears of joy glistened on her freckled complexion. "But at times, I even doubted you'd ever known him. That's why I thought you'd accepted the pagan gods."

He smiled, revealing his gratitude. "Aye, I know. And I despised your conviction and witnessing to me, so I let you believe I was not God's child."

"And I was unceasingly hard on you." She swatted tears from her face.

"Aye and rightfully so. You are faithful to Yahweh, and in turn, you have shown your faith in me, Lady Rayn. The other night, I did nothing more than you did. I believed in God and asked for your deliverance. It was God's Holy Spirit and his angels who cast those demons back to hell. 'Twas your faith that rescued us."

"Your faith, your angels," she said sadly. "It would seem the only angels I see are Lucifer's. I should not have been deceived. I believe in our Lord Jesu. I pray and confess my sins. I seek to do his will. Yet I could not see the evil consuming me because I'd put my desire to know my parents above all else, above God. My faith is nothing compared to yours, Shadoe, nothing." She fell to her knees and wept.

Shadoe drew her up into his arms. He inhaled the sweet fragrance that was Rayn's alone, felt the softness of her molded to him, and thanked God. Shadoe spoke huskily against her brow, "Hear me, Emerald Rose Rayn Pendragon. Your faith rescued me from an abyss of misery, revealed to me the beauty of life that I'd long forgotten. True, you fell prey to Satan's trappings, but remember, that happened when you were a child. Children have vivid imaginations and are able to believe the impossible without a reason. Sometimes Satan takes advantage of that innocence, just as he did with you."

"But I failed God."

"Did you? What's most important? How the problem came about or how it was resolved?"

"I suppose the outcome matters most to Yahweh." She dried her tears on his shoulder.

"Aye." He set her at arm's length so he could look upon her. "He is pleased with you, Rayn. Your faith revealed the demons' true identities."

Accepting Shadoe's reassurance, she forced a smile that caused his heart to quicken. "Then you believe God has forgiven my lack of trust in him?"

"Do you?"

"Aye, forgiven, I am." She reached up and laid her hand across his. "Now I need to thank you for coming to me in my time of need, for not leaving me to die."

"Leave you?" Shadoe squeezed her hand, wanting desperately to be done with this conversation so that he could kiss her. "That I would never have done, fairest lady."

❧

Rayn blushed and glanced down at her manly attire, clothes she still felt the most comfortable wearing. It continued to delight her when he called her lady, and that he thought of her that way. Feeling his hooded eyes upon her, she prayed God to give her the fortitude to resist her desires. Letting go, she put a few more feet between them. "Sire, although I'm certain that you are weary of this subject, I need to understand something."

"Aye?" He strode forward, and she found herself backed against a tree. She glanced about for a means of retreat. Shadoe leaned over her, his hands braced on either side of the tree. She was trapped. *Blast!* She breathed in the familiar scent of him. *'Tis not fair.* Her mind reeled as she sought to keep the conversation flowing. "The . . . the demons. According to Da, you said ghosts don't exist . . . I mean spirits of the dead roaming the earth. You said that ghosts are demons who take on the identity of the person who died."

He nodded. "The Merdyn had more opportunity to study the holy writings, and he put much effort into this study, in Father Jerome's Latin text, but even in the Greek and Hebrew. Yet he admitted that only a little is revealed about the realm in which Tomas and the demons, and even Yahweh, dwells. The Merdyn believed that sometimes imprints of the past are visible to the eyes of the present, but when we die, we go directly to one of two places: heaven or hell. Thus, my conclusion is that the demons preyed upon your desires."

"But I don't recall walking through Camelot, hoping to meet my parents or Arthur and Guenevere."

"The demons were already here." He brushed a wispy curl from her cheek, and she trembled from his touch. "Remember, Mordred deserted the keep less than three months after his arrival."

"Aye . . . claimed it was haunted, he did." She nibbled her lower lip.

His gaze on her mouth, Shadoe cleared his throat. "I imagine Morgause summoned the demons, but they became unmanageable. No doubt she still has a connection to them. Morgause and my mother served the lord of the flies, Lucifer. And after this incident, I fear that is still the case."

"Niamh is no longer under Satan's hold, Shadoe. Do you know how much joy it will give her to know of your encounter with Satan's cadre and that you walk in the light of God like Merlin? Whether you believe me or not, she, too, walks with God."

His tone took on a bitter harshness. "I suspect that is what she wants us to believe." He shut his eyes, his jaw tightened, ending the discussion.

Rayn sensed this was not the time to discuss Niamh. "You acknowledged one of the angels as Tomas."

"Aye, Yahweh sent him to free me from Belizar." He opened his eyes.

"Not everyone sees angels or knows of things to come."

"I am no prophet. I do know the future."

"I beg to differ, Sir. 'Your scions and daughters will prophesy, your young men will see visions.' So says God's sacred Word. You foresee the Anglo-Saxons ruling Britannia, you do."

"And one day far from now, a tribe known as Normans will rule the Saxons, not to mention the Scotti, who will . . ." He stopped and rubbed his brow in wonder, then met Rayn's astonished gaze.

"You know the future, Shadoe! Who are these Normans?"

"That I don't know. The words just formed on my tongue. I can't control what I prophesy. It comes from Yahweh."

"Then you truly are a prophet. The druids would call you an enchanter. Just like Merlin, you are blessed with the gift of prophecy. Tell me, sweet enchanter, what of my future? What of yours?"

Shadoe stepped back and trailed his hand through his thick black locks. His rugged features shaded. "'Tis not always a blessing, Rayn." He glanced at her and started toward the falls. She caught up her basket and staff and hurried after him.

"What does that mean? What do you see?" She snatched his forearm and made him stop.

"If I am gifted with the foresight as was my da, then I will never know my own future, Rayn, any more than Merlin knew his."

"But Mer foresaw his own death, he did."

"Only because it related to me. You think I am always seeing things, knowing things. It doesn't work that way. God only reveals what he deems needful for me to know. Please, Rayn. It is imperative you understand that God's ways are not always ours."

"Maybe if you ask?" She looked into his eyes with hopeful expectation.

"I did. And we need to accept what he reveals."

"I don't like your tone, I don't."

He didn't reply.

Rayn tried another strategy. "You said before that you'd no idea upon our first meeting that I was Arthur's daughter, yet you called me princess. 'Tis proof enough that you suspected I might be your godsend, it is."

He chuckled. "I maybe suspected it subconsciously, but believe me, Rayn, the reason I called you princess then, and still do, has naught to do with you being my godsend or with your birthright."

"Then you mean it as an endearment?" She recalled Merlin had also called her princess.

"I suppose . . . sometimes." He rubbed his jaw as if in thought and winced.

"Sometimes? And the rest of the time you mocked me, you did." She huffed.

"Well, you do possess a superior air. Thus, it seemed natural to address you as princess." He winked. "But there is an inborn reason for your demeanor. You are of royal blood, Emerald Rose Rayn, and Ayrisian heritage. So I no longer have a choice in how I address you. You are indeed a princess and a most lovely one at that."

"I don't like it." She crossed her arms and stared belligerently into his smug gaze. "I'd rather you call me princess in mocking than from protocol. Why, I'd rather you called me brat."

"That I can no longer do."

"Whist! Furthermore, I don't feel like royalty, nor do I want to. I only want to be yours, Shadoe. Is that so much to ask of God? I . . . love you, Shadoe un Hollo Tors." There. She'd said it! Her heart felt like a melon ready to burst, as if she'd die if he didn't feel the same and want the same.

Shadoe brushed a curl from her cheek, and his callused fingers trailed from her temple to the hollow of her neck, flaming her blood with sensations she'd only dreamed about. He leaned closer, his eyes searching hers. She saw his desire, saw his love.

Rayn toyed with the salt-tinted locks of his temples, noting the stark contrast as they blended with his darker hair. *You are so handsome, my knight, so beautiful.*

"Rayn, I want . . ." He towered over her and skimmed her brow with his lips. Locking her hands about his muscular neck, Rayn sighed and tilted her head, wanting his lips on hers, wanting to feel the masculine coarseness of his beard stubble against her cheek. And this time without the stink of the sewers between them.

She kissed him!

Rayn feared having shocked him, but the fierceness with which his arms drew her into his embrace, the hungry heat of his mouth on hers took her breath away. They were meshed as one, their hands exploring each other as if uncharted territory. Pleasurable, masculine groans and feminine sighs were captured within their lovers kiss. So this was love, this was—

"Wrong!" Shadoe growled against her wet open lips and pulled away.

"Huh?"

Shadoe's eyes flashed fire. His brow knit low and tight, and a flush stained his sun-kissed complexion. With a guttural groan, he broke their embrace and stepped back.

"Whist! What's wrong?" Her mind reeled with desire and confusion at his rejection.

"Please, Rayn. Don't pursue this," his strained voice held desperation. He turned a moment, adjusting himself before facing her again.

"I thought," she blushed. "Did my kiss not please you, aye?"

"Please me . . . you have no idea!" He dragged a hand through his hair and shook his head in frustration. As if to distract her, he reached within his tunic to remove an object wrapped in a swatch of tanned leather. Shadoe handed it to her. "This is for you."

Tentatively, she folded back the swatch and found a gold-hilted stinger with a slender curved blade. Her fingers curled about the delicate hilt. It seemed to mold rightly to her hand.

"This stinger belonged to your mother."

She brightened. "Aye, Lancelot told me that Arthur himself crafted the blade as her birthday present. But it had been lost, it had. How did you find it?"

"That's of no importance. What does matter is Guenevere would have wanted you to have it."

She slipped the treasured stinger into her belt. When she looked up, she met his bittersweet gaze. "You had another vision, didn't you? Tell me!" She tried to engage his attention but failed.

Silently, he led her through the woods and up to the highest point above the thundering falls. Neither tried to speak for one had to yell to hear. Rayn simply followed until Shadoe directed her up a boulder outcropping, halting before the highest rock. Turning to her, he spanned her slender waist with his hands and set her upon it. He stood one boulder below at her right side. Rayn smiled lovingly at him, curious about what he was trying to tell her.

"Look about you!" he shouted above the roar of the waterfall.

Nodding, Rayn obeyed. The view was breathtaking. From here she could see the entire island of Wind's Haven including Camelot. When she looked eastward, she saw the rugged mainland of Caledonia, while to the west sat the smaller outer islands and the unending aqua sea.

"Is this what you saw?" she yelled to him.

With a solemn nod, Shadoe swept his arm across the vista. The roar of the falls vanished, and when he spoke, it was with an authoritative tone that captivated her. "All you see and even beyond is yours, Princess Emerald Rose Rayn Pendragon, and shall be passed on to your children's children, for God Almighty has shown me."

Looking back on the spectacular view, Rayn corrected him. "You mean our children." The falls' thunder returned. She looked back to smile at Shadoe. He was gone. Confused, she climbed off the boulder and scurried down the outcropping, calling out to him.

Rayn failed to find Shadoe. On her homeward trek, however, she found Galahad in a quiet glen near Loch Lady. Like Shadoe whenever possible, Galahad spent time away from the caer. Now barefoot, wearing a worn green tunic and faded tan breeches, he did not look like a knight of the Round Table. Lying prone, his face pressed into the earth, Galahad's form reminded her of the cross. He was deep in meditation, and she didn't intend to interrupt him.

Amazingly, birds, squirrels, and chipmunks went about their business as if Galahad was part of the landscape. He'd obviously been in this position for some time. So this was where her brother came to escape the flurry of Camelot's court. Rayn attempted to slip away unnoticed when a twig snapped beneath her sandals. Birds fluttered from the open glen.

"Don't go, sister."

Sighing at her clumsiness, Rayn stepped out of the brush and rolled her shoulders. "I'm sorry."

"Don't be. I was about to head back." He stood and walked toward her.

"You knew I was here?" Rayn cocked her head in surprise.

"Aye." He swept a hand through his tousled blond hair. "You've grown clumsy this last while."

"You noticed, aye?" She blushed and watched a flight of grasshoppers spooked by Galahad's approach. She hoped he'd not blame Shadoe for her lack of grace.

He nodded. "Not that we've had that much time together, mind you."

Her emotions still jumbled from her encounter with Shadoe, Rayn realized she'd neglected Galahad this last while. "What has happened between us, brother?"

"Nothing, I hope." He grinned and laced his sandals to his feet, secured a worn leather belt about his lean waist, and then slipped his sword into its sheath.

Rayn shrugged. "We're not the same anymore."

"Nay. It would indeed be boring if we were, my Rose." He bent over and kissed her cheek, then tweaked it with his thumb and forefinger.

Catching his hand, Rayn brought it to her lips. Without hesitation, Galahad swept her into his arms and swung her about as he had when she was a child. Rayn squealed with joy. It had been so long since she'd laughed with him. Around and around she went until Galahad began to teeter from dizziness. Breathless, they tumbled to the ground and hugged.

Glancing at her handsome brother, Rayn decided to raise a matter she'd meant to broach before. "There was a time when you had a lady for each arm, brother. Since your return, many pretty faces have sought you out, but you've not courted a one of them. Why would that be, aye?"

Galahad stood, then drew Rayn to her feet and brushed the dead grass and autumn leaves from his clothes. "It amazes me that a princess with so much to do would manage to keep accounts on my love life."

Rayn flinched. Although his tone wasn't harsh, his sharp wit made its mark. "I only meant that—"

"I know what you meant, sister."

"We aren't brother and sister, Galahad." She blushed as that reality settled in her heart.

"I don't need that defined either." Galahad cupped her chin and gently directed her gaze to his bright eyes. "But no matter what the world says, we will forever be family, aye?"

"Aye," she agreed and kissed his rough cheek. He returned the kiss and for a moment they held each other tight, Rayn nuzzling her face to his chest, recalling all the times she'd taken comfort in her brother's embrace. She would miss him. Rayn abruptly sensed a change in Galahad. Did he expect her to read his mind? *'Tis like talking to Shadoe!*

She stepped back from him. "You are very vigilant in your prayers," she observed, gesturing at the flattened grasses.

"I want to be with God more than with anyone else, Rayn." He looked down at her. "Do you understand that burning desire?"

"Aye, I can't wait for his return."

"Nor I. You know that all I've wanted was to be a warrior and knight of the Round Table."

"And an honorable noble knight you are, Galahad. Your name is spoken with favor in every household."

Color stained his cheeks. "I'm ashamed to admit I've not always been noble or honorable."

"We are all flawed, brother."

"Aye, and this past year I've come to realize just how much. I've also grown discontent and restless in my chosen profession." He started strolling across the glen toward Camelot.

Rayn followed on his heels. "What are you saying, brother?"

He shrugged. "I'm not sure yet. But I need my life to be more than it is. I need to account for more than how many Saxons and Jutes I've slain. Or how many fair maidens I've rescued or wooed."

Rayn giggled.

"You find this amusing, wee sister?"

"Aye . . . and nay. Mayhap it's just a matter that you have grown up." She winked at him. "Or that you need to listen to the voice of the One within your heart."

He smiled. "That is what I seek to do."

"Then in his time you will know what he wants of you, aye?"

Galahad halted a moment and stared at her as if seeing her for the first time. "Have I mentioned you possess the wisdom of Ayris?"

"Nay, but now is as good a time as ever." She winked, and he winked back.

Linking her arm with his, she allowed Galahad to escort her along the arbored pathway he'd worn down during his visits to the glen. Rayn glanced up and, for the first time in years, beheld a peace in Galahad she'd never before seen. She suspected her words had given him comfort, but she knew there was but one person to thank. God.

∽

The clouds of dusk hung still against the apricot sky. Birds had ceased their singing. No zephyrs rustled the autumn leaves. Time remained painfully frozen for Shadoe. Only the seductive song of Loch Lady Falls touched his senses. His heart felt as if it had been ripped from his chest, for from the vantage of the falls' peak, he had watched their playful banter, embraces, and kisses. Jealousy, betrayal, hurt, and anguish assaulted his soul and threatened to conquer his godly spirit. Whatever shards of hope Shadoe had been cleaving to vanished. The evidence had been set before him. Yahweh had spoken. Galahad was Rayn's godsend.

From then on, Shadoe discussed nothing but business and showed the utmost propriety in Rayn's presence. He made certain, too, that they were never alone. The chasm between them broadened.

∽◯

Rayn feared she'd made a dreadful mistake, assuming that Shadoe cared for her, let alone loved her. Her doubts had increased, too, when Galahad impressed upon her that, despite Shadoe's recommitment to Jesu, the attraction Shadoe felt for Rayn was purely physical. Rayn's heartache and frustration transformed into outbursts of defiance, most often directed at Shadoe. Yet he responded to her tantrums with a tolerance no one else showed. Eventually, she realized her self-indulgent eruptions were unproductive, especially to the future of Camelot. Although the tension between her and Shadoe never dissolved, Rayn sought God's council. God gave her peace, and she became cooperative, especially when Shadoe advised her.

Chapter Twenty-Seven

"ARE YOU READY?" Lancelot gripped Rayn's shoulders so tightly, she winced.

She gently pried his right hand from her shoulder. "Aye, Da. I swim like a fish, I do."

"This is different and dangerous. More than a hundred men have drowned." His white brows meshed, and he grimaced with concern.

Rayn's heart pounded with her own anxiety and fear, but she'd not let Lance see it. She reassuringly touched his bristled jaw. "I know, Da. I will be careful. As agreed, if I've not surfaced by the count of two hundred and fifty, send a diver after me."

"I wish there was another way." He sighed deeply.

"There isn't. In two days I will be seventeen full cycles old. If I am the true Pendragon, the Celtic stone will release Excalibur. If not . . ." She glanced to where her brother knights and Galahad stood looking just as restless as Lancelot. She'd wished Iona had come, but the lady had chosen to stay at the caer.

Lancelot drew her into his arms, and Rayn rested her head on his shoulder. For the moment, she drew strength from him and took in God's creation. All around the cove, whiffs of campfire smoke made pockets in the air. The cobalt sky was laden with soot-quilted clouds. The spray of the waterfall chilled the midmorning air, while a northwest zephyr ruffled the treetops, sending copper-painted leaves sailing above the mist-draped loch. Autumn loomed. So did Rayn's seventeenth birthday—the same age Arthur had been when he'd drawn the sword from the stone. Another course of prophecy had intersected her life.

Rayn forced her anxious thoughts elsewhere, and her soul felt the threat before she saw it. Her gaze swept the familiar terrain. Less than forty feet away on an oak branch perched the vulture; its eyes, pinned on Rayn, glowed fiery red. Rayn swallowed. She'd never feared vultures, but this one she knew to be evil.

"What is it?" Lancelot noted her distraught expression.

"The vulture in that oak. It's always about of late."

"What vulture?" Lancelot scratched his beard as his gaze swept the trees.

Rayn's mouth dropped open. The predator had vanished without a trace.

"You're just nervous, lass." Lancelot hugged her tighter.

Rayn was about to argue when Echo cleared the bushes near the oak tree. No doubt the wolf had frightened off the raptor. She hoped so. Overhead, Mer glided on an air stream. Rayn's attention turned to her right, where near the ceiling of the falls, Shadoe stood at the edge of a stone pool. He'd not explained why he watched from such distance; neither had she asked.

Stepping back from Lancelot, Rayn scanned the audience. Everyone from villeins to chieftains had gathered to witness her success or failure in recovering Arthur's sword, Excalibur. A few acres away across the moorlands, Picts perched on their horses. More than enough reliable men would witness either failure or victory. She felt certain Mordred's moles were among the gathered. Shadoe had several hundred men patrolling the cove and banks of the large loch, for there remained the chance that if Rayn salvaged the sword, someone would try to steal it.

A silence of unease saturated the glen. Even the rumble of the falls seemed hushed. But within Rayn's heart raged a turbulent storm. The Adversary taunted her faith with fear and doubt. Her rock-based faith stood against the gale. *In the name of Jesu, I command you viper of iniquity to depart from me!*

Peace embraced her. The Adversary had fled.

Thy will be done, Abba Father! There was nothing else to ask. God knew her heart. From that confidence, a wave of spiritual warmth enveloped her, and she smiled with joy. When she looked up, Rayn scanned the cove one last time, hoping to see . . .

Yes! Her keen gaze spotted the flowing blue veils and white palla on the opposite shore of the cove among the pines. Niamh! Hunched over, she appeared to be limping. Rayn feared for Niamh's life if others discerned the leper's presence. Still, the brave woman had kept her promise to encourage Rayn. Cupping her hand over her eyes, Rayn looked up at Shadoe. She couldn't discern his features, but he faced the pines. Rayn's heart lurched. *Oh, Lord, please let them reunite and have Shadoe forgive her before—*

"Rayn?" Galahad stepped forward and rested a hand of encouragement on her arm.

"Aye." She smiled bravely at him, and then scrambled up the highest boulder. Drawing a deep breath, she dove into the loch.

∽◦∽

Shadoe counted 180, 181. Rayn was a strong swimmer, but he could not contain the gut-tearing sensation of foreboding. His mind replayed the pivotal event four months ago: his hand frozen to the sword's jeweled hilt until Rayn gently clasped his wrist. The sword not only budged but also had slid within its prison of stone.

What if their roles were now reversed? *God, show me!* A heavenly revelation washed over him, and as he reached 210, Shadoe dove off the protuberance and into the loch.

∽◦∽

Rayn tugged and prayed for release from the cold steel that bound her hands. Upon her touch, the sword had slipped from the Celtic stone, then seized up midway. The exposed part of the silvery blade refracted a sliver of sunlight that breached the dark, churning waters. Rayn didn't understand what held Excalibur in place. She couldn't grasp why God had allowed this wee triumph and then changed his mind. Her outer extremities were numb from the frigid water, and the strong current pummeled her back and limbs. She could not hold her breath much longer. Rayn looked down upon the current-washed bones of her predecessors, but her prayer did not waver. *Thy will be done!*

Feeling sleepy, Rayn shut her eyes. A strong, warm hand caressed the length of her forearm, then her immobile hands. She opened her eyes and met Shadoe's buoyant smile. *God be praised! He's come!*

Shadoe pinched her nostrils shut, then, kissing her, he breathed into her mouth. Rayn drew the precious air into her lungs. Pulling back, Shadoe's grip tightened. *Pull with me, Rayn!* His voice rang in her mind as if he had spoken out loud. With a nod, she obeyed. Excalibur slipped like hot grease from the Celtic stone, as did the air from Rayn's lungs.

She surrendered. A beckoning white light seduced her, but as she soared toward that source of unconditional love, a physical embrace restrained her.

Rayn, don't you dare leave me!

She attempted to respond to Shadoe's desperate call, but her desire was set upon the hypnotic light, upon God!

☙❧

"Rayn!" The masculine mandate jolted Rayn awake.

She coughed, and then sputtered. Water shot from her mouth and nose. Pushing up on unsteady elbows, Rayn gagged as water continued to drain from her lungs. Voices of joy rallied her. Lancelot, Galahad, and Shadoe knelt at her side. Amazingly, she didn't feel too cold, for she'd been wrapped in two woolen cloaks.

With smiles of relief, Galahad and Lancelot hugged her. Beyond them, she saw Shadoe's anxious smile and mustered her own in return. His waterlogged leather jerkin clung to his lean muscular frame, and his wet hair was slicked back from his head. A drop of water trickled from the cleft of his strong jaw, and his lips were blue from the cold. Before she could address his condition, Perceval rushed up and draped the black ram's cloak over Shadoe's shoulders. Shadoe hugged the cloak around him, then looked back at her.

"Excalibur?" she asked, glancing around.

"Here." Lancelot laid the sword at her side.

"Why, it's so big!" Her astounded words broke the silence, and men chuckled at her remark.

"Aye. Your father was a large man," Tristam exclaimed.

Sitting up, she traced a shaky, cold finger along the shimmering blade and met Shadoe's vigilant gaze. *It took us both to free it, Shadoe!*

No one must know. He leaned into her and touched her cheek, then rocked back on his heels, a strange light flickering in his eyes.

"Aye," she replied and shook her wet head as the reality settled in her. *We speak without words!*

That too must remain our secret. His chestnut gaze locked with hers in a conspirators bond.

The breath of Eden? She tipped her head in amazement.

He simply smiled in reply.

"But you cannot swim!" Confusion laced her hoarse voice.

He rolled a broad shoulder. "I've been practicing."

"And forever thankful, I am."

"I guess we're even then." He smoothed the wet tendrils of hair back from her face, and his hand lingered.

"Aye." She hoped, nay prayed, this moment could last forever.

Grunting, Galahad shattered that possibility. "Come, sister. You must return to Camelot to show the world that you are the true Pendragon!"

Before she could argue, Lancelot tugged her to her feet. As her damp cloaks fell off, Lancelot placed a warm sheepskin about her shoulders. Galahad hoisted Rayn onto her mare. Shadoe stepped forward and presented her the sword of Ayris. As their cold fingers brushed, his strong jaw trembled. Tears rimmed his amber eyes, and for a single heartbeat, she saw the gangly youth who had finally fulfilled his vow to his king, Arthur Pendragon. In that moment, Rayn knew she would love this knight in tarnished armor forever.

$$\infty$$

More than a hundred delegates gathered two days later, representing Celts, Britons, and Picts along with an Irish Scotti king whose arrival further agitated the charged atmosphere. Shadoe moved restlessly about the great hall, evaluating the motley crowd. Men of every age, some accompanied by their wives, were present. Only the high chieftains were allowed weapons. The rest of the guests had been relieved of their swords at the front gate, but that didn't mean there wouldn't be trouble.

Compared to the Roman Senate, there was nothing remotely formal about this political assembly. But most of the chieftains knew nothing about political protocol and probably never would, as their drunken voices confirmed. He wished they'd also excluded wine and mead at the gate.

Despite the tight security, Shadoe felt a strong sense of unrest. Word had reached Mordred and Morgause of the gathering, but that was the plan—at least Lancelot's. So far, Shadoe had not seen anyone who remotely resembled his aunt or half brother. Yet he could not shake off the foreboding; Mordred was present.

Taking his place beside Tristam and Galahad below the dais and thrones, Shadoe muttered to Tristam, "The demon's spawn is about."

"You've seen him?" Tristam's square jaw flexed.

"Nay, but I feel his presence."

"We can't act until he shows himself."

"By then it will be too late." Shadoe glanced up to the landing and the drawn draperies, behind which Rayn prepared for her introduction.

"She's safe." Galahad nudged Shadoe's ribs.

"She is a lamb. Mordred's a vulture. The only way she'll ever be safe is when he and his whoring mother are dead!"

Galahad shifted from one foot to the other and gripped the haft of his sheathed sword. "Well, I do wish we'd get on with this formality. I want nothing less than to drive my sword through that infidel's heart."

"Patience," Tristam insisted. "Some things are worth the wait."

"This is a bad idea!" Shadoe ground out. "We don't even know which chiefs are loyal to our cause or which ones stand with Mordred. Why, they will devour her and never think twice about it."

"One would think you have no faith in your counseling skills, Steward, or in Rayn's ability as an astute student of the political arena. And," Galahad snickered, "you are familiar with her honed skills of self-defense."

"If I were high steward, which I'm not, I would be insulted. Likewise, I do not make light of Rayn's ability to retain pertinent information. But her tenacity, intelligence, charismatic nature, and warrior expertise do not mean she can command an audience, let alone a kingdom."

"Humph! She has more qualifications than most of our guests," Tristam gruffly assessed.

"And that we shall soon see, aye?" Galahad smiled with confidence.

"Shouldn't your place be at Rayn's side?" Tristam met Shadoe's unsettled gaze.

"She must do this on her own."

"But you are high steward," Galahad reinforced. "You should escort and introduce her in accordance to the statutes of—"

"My post is transitory! I agreed to publicly legitimize her birthright. Nothing more. You should be pleased by my decision," he snapped, his restraint unraveling.

"What I think doesn't matter, Shadoe. Like it or not, your duty is not just to Rayn but to this demesne."

"Is it really? I highly suggest you worry less about my duties and concentrate on your own responsibilities to Rayn and Camelot. You've a full platter, you have."

Galahad's burnish brows bristled with confusion, then insolence.

The muscle along Shadoe's mouth throbbed so fiercely that pain shot through his jaw. For an intense moment, the two men glared at one another. Shadoe looked away.

He pondered Rayn's state of mind. Shadoe had intentionally set an emotional boundary between them, although spending eight to twelve hours a day together had made it difficult. Were it not for his rededication to Yahweh, Shadoe would have wedded and bedded her by now and not necessarily in that order. He did everything possible to discourage her attraction toward him, including encouraging her to spend more time with Galahad. Rayn did not seem to mind, and although the sight of them together hurt, Shadoe accepted it. Unlike Lancelot with Guenevere, Shadoe had not the fortitude to be in the presence of a woman he could never have. He would not tempt Rayn or himself. He would not challenge God's will.

From the opposite side of the hall, Perceval's voice boomed in proclamation. "Silence all! Make way for the firstborn of King Arthur and Queen Guenevere Pendragon, Princess Emerald Rose Rayn Pendragon."

Shadoe glanced back at the chieftains, who to his surprise, respectfully obeyed and created a wide path down the center of the hall. All heads lifted and turned. A servant opened the portiere of the upper landing, and sunlight spilled through, illuminating the woman at the threshold.

Shadoe stared at the enchantress poised upon the mezzanine. Rayn turned and gracefully descended the stairs. Most men would only notice her natural beauty, but Shadoe absorbed every facet of her. Rayn's naturally crimped hair was drawn back from her forehead to emphasize her distinct widow's peak. The floor-length silk palla of deep green attached to her circlet headpiece draped her left arm. From the gold circlet of inlaid pearls, her curls of coppery red cascaded to her small waist and slender hips.

Shadoe's attention shifted. The simple, flowing lines of the long-sleeved Byzantine dress were offset by the fabric's elaborate pattern, a predominant motif of red roses with thorny green stems against white silk, bordered in gold palmettos. Her waist was cinched with a narrow belt of gold and pearls. Gold slippers adorned her feet. Rayn had said he'd be pleased at the symbolic attire of her mother's gown. He was.

Although she looked regal and confident, beneath Rayn's calm exterior Shadoe sensed fear and anxiety. Engaging her nervous gaze, he held it steadfast with a reassuring smile.

At the edge of his view, Shadoe noted that Galahad's expression held more than brotherly admiration. The rugged young knight met Shadoe's scowl, and the wall between them thickened.

Silence enveloped the hall. Rayn's graceful descent was met with wide eyes and gaping mouths of lustful appreciation. But Shadoe wondered how many of these clansmen were canny enough to take on the strength of this wench.

∽

Rayn's mouth felt dry as sand. At the bottom of the steps, Lancelot and Iona came forward to escort her through the tightly pressed bodies and stretched necks.

Resting her hand on Lancelot's extended arm, Rayn trembled.

Lancelot patted her hand and smiled. "You're doing grand," he encouraged softly.

Iona offered a supportive smile and a wink.

Rayn had long concluded she wanted to faint, expected to faint, but keeping eye contact with Shadoe, she found the fortitude to proceed.

"All bend a knee and bow your heads!" Perceval commanded from behind them.

Once again a majority of the gathering obeyed, though here and there a man stood in sullen hauteur.

As Rayn approached the dais she thought her heart would burst, but her anxiety was lessened by Shadoe's failure to bow, so intently was he studying the crowd's reaction.

"Bow!" Galahad snatched Shadoe's sleeve cuff and yanked him to the floor. Shadoe acquiesced, but Rayn still felt his attentive gaze. At the dais she turned and faced her audience but fastened her eyes on Shadoe. He said he'd be her anchor during the coronation. He was true to his word. Without pretense, her lips yielded a smile for him alone. He returned his own, and her heart soared.

"My Lady," he said respectfully. "It is an honor to serve you."

"Rise." She beckoned him to her side. "And the rest of you stand," she commanded in fluent Greek, Celt, and then Pict.

A gruff cough broke from Lancelot, who stood a rung below her. "My Lady, it is proper protocol for your subjects to bow before you."

"I am not God!" she protested. "Nor are they my subjects."

"It is a sign of respect," Iona sternly whispered behind her.

"'Tis one of servitude," she groused. "Up everyone! I am not your sovereign."

Muttering their confusion, they conceded.

"I don't understand," a Briton chieftain bellyached. "'Twas rumored there was a child, but he was slaughtered with Guenevere." A hundred pairs of eyes gaped at the man who fumbled with his words. "I mean she's no prince. She's a cursed maiden . . . a girl!"

"We Picts acknowledge the woman as chieftain, as queen of her clan. It is our way!" the Pict chieftain blasted the Briton.

Laughter erupted only to be replaced by voices of discord.

Lancelot stepped forward and raised a hand. "My lady and lords, there has been hearsay, but I swear upon my life that Emerald Rose Rayn is the legitimate heir to the demesne of Camelot. And as her father before her, Princess Pendragon will reunite the clans of Britannia and Caledonia. Before Arthur's death, I, along with the remaining knights of the realm, swore an oath to my king. A vow I made to care for the child of his seed and Guenevere's womb until she was of age to take her rightful place as Pendragon. By all that's sacred, I have kept that promise. This very day she is seventeen full cycles. The Merdyn's prophecy is fulfilled."

More voices raised and lowered.

Galahad addressed Rayn but spoke for all ears. "I was raised believing that you were of my father's loins and Guenevere's womb. Four years ago, my father told me the truth of your birthright. I, too, have upheld that pledge of silence and promised to protect you from those who'd see an end to the Pendragon legacy." Galahad swept a bow to Rayn and loudly pronounced, "Indeed she is Arthur Pendragon's bairn." He smiled at Rayn, who stretched out her hand to him. They embraced.

"Rubbish!" A voice boomed from the chieftains. Caithest Uais, high chieftain of the Celts south of Hadrian's Wall, gave Rayn a critical look and spoke in his native tongue. "And just how are we to know you speak truth, Galahad? She looks like a fair-skinned Guenevere, but that is no proof she is of Arthur's seed. Like Arthur's, Lancelot's locks were sun-red in his youth. Mordred willna believe her a threat unless he knows beyond doubt she's Pendragon."

"Lord Caithest?" Rayn released Galahad's hand and walked to within a hand's span of the bulky chieftain, who had more hair than face. "You fought alongside Arthur Pendragon, did you not?"

"Aye," he bragged. "Four battles or more we done." He grinned toothlessly.

"Then you knew him well, knew the scars on his battle-worn flesh, you did?"

"If you mean had I seen him stripped down after war, aye, I did." He patted his braided white beard.

"And did not the king bear a birthmark on the back of his left shoulder blade?"

"Aye, a strange mark said to be the brand of the gods. The Rose of Avalon, the druid priests called it."

Five of the eldest chieftains nodded agreement with Caithest's explanation.

"And did not the druids foretell that Arthur's progeny would bear this brand upon birth?"

"Aye, but I do not know if Mordred bears the seal."

Rayn stepped into the chieftains' midst and released the palla from her shoulders.

"Lady Rayn, no!" Perceval moved to block her from the men's view. Before he could intervene, Rayn turned and dropped the left sleeve of her palla, revealing a delicate, distinctive ruby birthmark on her shoulder blade in the shape of an open rose.

"Blessed Avalon!" Caithest burst out. "It's the mark of the rose. She is the Emerald Rose Pendragon!" The others accompanied him with shouts of awe as Rayn moved among them.

"Blessed Rose of Sharon," Lancelot said with a believer's pride.

Just as Rayn was about to pull her palla in place, a tall, distinguished man came forward. Garbed in a felt cap and cloak of scarlet linen, he approached to look at her shoulder. After allowing him the view, Rayn turned her head and met his stoic expression, then rearranged her gown before facing the gathering. King Caithest knelt before her, and every man, including the distinguished stranger, dropped to his knees. This time, Rayn did not discourage them.

"'Tis my greatest hope to bring peace to our troubled shores, Sires, and to do so we must unite. We must become one to defeat Mordred," Rayn announced confidently.

Caithest's voice boomed through the hall. "I've heard it said that Mordred's army is twice the size of yours."

"Indeed." She acknowledged him. "But if our tribes unite, we will overrun the Saxons three to one."

"And if King Hengist joins forces with Mordred," a gruff looking Pict spoke in broken Greek, "their number will more than double ours."

"There must be a declaration of war before there can be defeat," declared the kneeling outlander. "I've neither seen nor heard any threats from Mordred, yet you cower like pups before a prowling beast with no claws."

Caithest countered, "Oh, Mordred is not without claws! That beast abducts our young men and women, burns our fields, slaughters our livestock, and then demands taxes! If ever I have the chance to slit his throat, I will!"

"Well, Caithest Uais, here I am!" The man came to his feet.

Baring their weapons, Shadoe and the knights surrounded Rayn. Lancelot signaled his officers, and armed men blocked the hall, leaving no means of escape.

The guests staggered to their feet and separated. The men put themselves between their women and the imminent danger. Caithest unsheathed his blade and advanced. It took seven of his comrades to overpower the large Celt and pull him back into the crowd.

"I meant not to frighten anyone, least of all you, fairest maiden." The scarlet-cloaked outlander swept a practiced bow. Removing his cap and tossing his cloak over his right shoulder, he revealed a head of reddish blond hair. His features were flawless save for a few age lines below his eyes. His blue eyes flashed confidence. The nostrils of his Romano-Briton nose flared with each breath, and his muscular frame projected an image from the past.

Chapter Twenty-Eight

FEVERED HATRED SURGED through Shadoe's veins. Mordred! The devil incarnate had the audacity to set foot in Camelot, surrounded by his enemies. Or was he? Shadoe scanned the multitude, noting a handful of chieftains, whether conscious or not of their actions, standing behind Mordred. The rest had migrated to the far right where Rayn stood protected by armed guards of Camelot.

Mordred appeared unmoved by the effect his presence had on the assembly, or the hateful glares riveted upon him. Looking about the grand architecture, he commented, "Ah, Splendor Lost, sweet Camelot, it is indeed a pleasure to be home."

"You've no right here, Mordred!" Galahad stalked forward, his drawn sword level with Mordred's chest.

Mordred raised his arms. He was defenseless, his missing left hand replaced by a leather gauntlet. "Am I not Pendragon, am I not Arthur's firstborn?"

"You are his bastard," jeered a Briton. Others joined in unison.

"And am I the only bastard within these walls?" he challenged his accusers, who grew silent with fault. Still Galahad did not lower his sword. The adversaries glared at one another.

From the ominous quiet, Rayn calmly announced, "On the contrary, he has every right to be here. He is my brother."

Heads turned, including Shadoe's, as Rayn ordered from her realm of security, "Let me pass!"

Lancelot blocked her. "Rayn? You know he's not of Arthur's loins, nor is this the time or place—"

"I beg to differ, Da." She put her hand to his cheek, smiled, and whispered, "Let me be Pendragon and speak with my false brother." Stepfather and stepdaughter stared at each other, but before he agreed, Lancelot looked to Shadoe, who nodded. With obvious reluctance, the knight stepped aside and motioned his men to do likewise.

Rayn followed Lancelot's gaze to Shadoe's stolid features. Only when his hawkish eyes met hers did she realize he felt as uncertain as she did about the outcome of this encounter. Strangely, it gave her strength. His presence always did. He knew her legs felt like willow branches and that her heart threatened to burst from her chest with fear. He also knew she would not let any chieftain or warrior see her insecurities. She was Pendragon.

She stepped gracefully through the assemblage and touched Galahad's arm, meeting his stubborn expression. "Dear Galahad, sheathe your sword."

He obeyed and stepped beside her, but his warrior gaze never left Mordred.

Rayn turned back to Mordred, who observed her with peculiar respect. He was not what she had expected. Then again, minutes ago he could have rammed a dagger into her ribs, but he hadn't. Why? For an intense moment, they looked each other over. Rayn had heard much about Mordred's impiety. She'd imagined him to be repulsive, but he was indeed striking. His eyes were the brightest blue she'd ever seen; one could become lost in those eyes—

"*Rayn!*"

She jolted and swore Shadoe had shouted at her, but when she glanced back, she realized he'd not spoken out loud. This Eden's breath was most unnerving. Rayn looked at Mordred, wondering what spell he sought to cast upon her. After all, this man had slain her father on the battlefield and then butchered her mother in cold blood. She must not forget the capacity of evil that resided in him. At the same time, one of Rayn's officers approached Lancelot and whispered into his ear. The immediate pallor on Lancelot's face warned her of bad news.

Rayn pressed her attention on Mordred. "I assume you have come to challenge my birthright, *brother?*"

He arched a burnished brow at her accuracy. "I came for several reasons, wee *sister.* Might I add that your lack of courtesy in not inviting me to this monumental occasion cuts deep to my soul."

"I was told you had no soul," she countered with a curt smile.

He snorted as he scrutinized the faces of the attendants, acknowledging six high chieftains who flanked the other delegates. "My, but it appears most of Britannia and even the painted beasts of Caledonia have come to acknowledge your monarchy." He sneered at the Picts. One of them lunged forward, but Perceval blocked him. Speaking the Pictish tongue, he calmed the furious man.

A young Briton stepped forward and introduced himself. "I am Laxton, scion of Can un Scye. My da fought beside Arthur in battles against the Saxons, Scotti, and the likes of you, Mordred. My father's health is waning, thus I've come in his place."

Laxton addressed Rayn. "If you are Arthur's true progeny, then I pledge you my support against this vermin." He glowered at Mordred.

His proclamation well received made it apparent where much of the clans' loyalties rested. Still almost half of them kept silent, which unsettled most, Rayn included.

Mordred shrugged. "Like the rest of you, I saw the mark of the Pendragon, but it could be a tattoo like their body markings." He gestured to the Picts.

Once again, quarreling voices buzzed.

Before Rayn, Mordred smirked. Although surrounded by his enemies, he displayed no evidence of fear. For the moment, Rayn couldn't help but compare him to his half brother, Shadoe. She glanced at Lancelot and the other Round Table knights, who scoffed at Mordred's suggestion. When she looked at Shadoe, he motioned her to stay calm.

She tried.

Mordred proceeded to stroll about the great hall as if he owned it. "For centuries before this land was claimed by Arthur, specific mandates of his Ayrisian forefathers had to be fulfilled before one could rightfully be proclaimed regent. Thus, one needs more than a birthmark, Lady Emerald Rose Rayn, to maintain the Pendragon seat of power." He strode confidently to the dais, and taking note of Arthur's restored throne, he turned and forcefully addressed her. "One needs the Emerald Rose of Avalon! One needs a high steward! One needs Excalibur! From where I stand, you have nothing but a possibly forged birthmark."

"And what have you?" she challenged.

"My birthright as Pendragon that not even this sorrowful band of kings can deny!"

Her head high, Rayn glided toward him. "No one has ever denied your lineage, Mordred, until now." She caught the flicker of a nerve at his jaw. *He knows! He might use this to his advantage. It could also backfire for all these years he's lied to the world. How will the truth be received? Surely, he fears the worst, or he'd proclaim the truth, would he not?*

"That aside," she continued, "your lack of conscience and humanity makes even the most barbaric of these men better than you or your mother could ever be!"

"This isn't about my mother." He eyed her with a tensed brow.

"Bah! You don't breathe without Morgause's permission." Lancelot grunted.

Mordred's fair features transformed to a lethal hue of scarlet. "My mother is senile and dying. She has no influence over my decisions or actions."

Lancelot stalked forward, his patience obviously dissipated. "Hardly. With magique she retains the disguise of youthful beauty. But I saw her true face. She is hideous to look upon. Her heart is both cold and dead; her soul long forfeited to the Adversary. And you are nothing more than her puppet, and when she's used you up, she will spit you out like rotten meat. You control nothing and have no will of your own, Mordred. You are a pitiful, impotent creature!" Lancelot lunged forward, but Perceval, Tristam, and Galahad seized him and pulled him back.

Mordred maintained an unnerving air of calm. "Well, this pitiful, impotent creature has two thousand legionaries surrounding Ayr. If I have not safely joined them before the sun reaches its height, they will descend upon Ayr and this caer with a vengeance that will make my last siege of Camelot look like child's play."

Fear froze most men in place.

"Now I suggest you present better evidence that this Lady Pendragon imposter is indeed who she claims." Mordred boldly lounged on the arm of the throne.

The man's arrogance overwhelmed Rayn; insecurity tightened her heart.

Galahad charged forward, but Tristam and Perceval restrained him. Mordred yawned as if bored with the entire affair.

Rayn held her ground. "Would all three of your mandates suffice?" she countered with a devious smile as Lancelot came to her side and put an arm of security about her.

"By all means, let the circus begin." Mordred acknowledged her defiant expression.

"Mordred! It's been a long while." A voice split the tension.

All heads turned.

"My Lady Pendragon." Shadoe stepped forward and swept a bow to Rayn.

She smiled.

Mordred squinted at the dark-robed stranger, then bounded off the dais.

Shadoe turned from Mordred and addressed the curious guests. "For those who do not know me, I am Shadoe un Hollo Tors, scion of Merlin, High Steward to King Arthur Pendragon."

Although there were grumbles and accusations of Merlin's betrayal, Rayn noted that most of the chieftains seemed wonderstruck.

Shadoe removed his mantle of black ram's wool. "I also made a vow, good sirs. A promise to find the Emerald Rose Pendragon . . . and I did." He turned to Lancelot. "You are all acquainted with the sword Excalibur?"

Nods and verbal acknowledgments echoed back.

Shadoe proceeded. "On the eve following Arthur's death, Excalibur was returned to Loch Lady from whence it came. There, an angel of God Almighty prophesied only the true Pendragon could free the sword from the Celtic stone. More than a hundred men have died trying." He glared at Mordred.

"Two days ago, in the presence of high chieftains from every tribe and the knights of the Round Table, Lady Rayn dove into the loch and freed Excalibur from the Celtic stone."

"Aye, 'twas quite the drama. They saw her bring a sword from the loch. It could be forged like her tattoo. That proves nothing," Mordred accused.

"Perhaps this will." Shadoe signaled a guard. Six large men emerged from behind the scarlet drape, pushing a heavy, planked platform across the dais. Stationed in the middle of the platform was the Celtic stone, the golden hilt of Excalibur protruding.

Mordred balked with recognition. "But the stone. How did it—?"

"It appeared here shortly after Lady Rayn pulled the sword free." Iona walked forward and stared Mordred straight on. "I saw it happen. Or do you doubt my word, Lord Mordred?"

The color of Mordred's handsome features waned, and then softened as he gazed upon the beautiful woman from his past. For one moment, Iona let down her noble guard. Rayn saw the pain of heartache etched in her friend's face. When Rayn glanced at Mordred, she glimpsed an emotion that conflicted with his vile reputation. *Regret*. With a shake of her head, Iona's stern expression returned. After Mordred neither disputed Iona's claim nor gave her chase, the woman stepped back into the crowd.

A moment later, Shadoe challenged every man and woman to try and free the sword from the stone. Some scoffed. Some recoiled in fear, recalling those who'd died.

"I assure you all. No one will die, because it has already been released by the Pendragon," he insisted.

When no one came forth, Perceval and Tristam tugged the hilt to show it was safely locked within the stone. King Caithest and a Pict chieftain also tried to free it. The sword failed to budge, it's shimmering light dimmed, causing the crowd to step back and murmur among themselves.

Shadoe looked at Mordred. "Well, Pendragon, if you are the rightful heir to Arthur's throne, I'd think you'd be eager to prove it. At least you will not drown as did the men you forced to go in your place."

Rayn saw fear in Mordred's eyes. She pitied him.

"It is a trick." Mordred accused.

"Prove it." Shadoe challenged.

Sweat beaded his brow and upper lip, but Mordred approached the rock. "I've but one hand," he defended.

"It only takes one," Caithest stated.

Placing his right hand on the jeweled hilt, Mordred pulled twice, thrice. What happened next was unexpected even to Rayn and Shadoe. The sword turned to rust; the jewels held no light.

Stunned by the sword's transformation, the onlookers backed further away. The hall went silent with fear.

Mordred let go of the hilt and retreated into the crowd.

Shadoe stepped forward and announced, "The Lord God Almighty has revealed the heart of this man and possibly that of others. You, Mordred, do not place your entire faith in Jesu Christ. Thus you are unworthy to possess the sword of Pendragon or even release it!"

Mordred shot a lethal look at Shadoe.

Dismissing his half brother's hostility, Shadoe offered his arm to Rayn and escorted her up the dais.

Nervous, she whispered in his ear, "But we both must—"

"Hush," he said softly.

The hall grew quiet. Rayn's chest ached from the force of her beating heart. His right hand covering both of hers, Shadoe guided her trembling hands to Excalibur. The moment their hands touched the hilt, the sword returned to its former luster. Pulsing warmth surged through their fingers, and the sword began to slip free. Shadoe let go and stepped back. Rayn released the heavy metal blade from the stone. Holding it high, she faced her peers. Mordred's threats fled her thoughts.

High chieftains, lords, knights, and warriors hooted their approval. Ladies cried out in astonishment; some swooned.

Confident pride sluiced over Rayn. She had proven herself! She was Pendragon. Anxiously, she searched the crowd and found Lancelot. Unabashed tears stained his bristled cheeks. The rest of her family hugged and congratulated each other. Finally, she turned to Shadoe. She saw tears in his eyes, but the moment their gazes locked, he seemed to withhold himself and simply gave her a solemn nod of approval. She wanted him to take her in his arms and kiss her, but his reserved composure told her it would not happen.

Rayn's arms ached from the weight of the sword, and as she lowered it, she wove off balance. Shadoe caught her and the sword. When his fingers gripped the hilt, the sword's blade flashed with white light. Rayn didn't know who else saw it, but she certainly had. Her anxious gaze shot to Mordred, whose hardened expression revealed he'd witnessed it as well. Rayn swallowed and looked at Shadoe. He nodded.

Handing the sword to Galahad, Shadoe unclasped the chain around his neck. When the sparkling jewels of the amulet came into view, the chieftains murmured among themselves.

"I assume the elder chieftains recognize this talisman?" Shadoe engaged Mordred's pale countenance before he set his sights upon Rayn.

"Glory . . . 'tis the Emerald Rose of Avalon!" one called out.

A succession of *ayes* echoed through the great hall.

Mordred no longer looked pompous.

"Or do you suppose this is also fake, Mordred?" Shadoe suggested.

When Mordred held his tongue, Rayn glanced from the dazzling jeweled amulet to Shadoe's intense countenance. For a moment, she swore Merlin stood before her.

"In accordance with the law of Ayris, it is my honor to present Arthur's rightful progeny with the Emerald Rose of Avalon, given by the Merdyn to High King Uther Pendragon and later to Uther's scion, Arthur. Only a sovereign who walks in righteousness with the One is to wear the blessed jewel first worn by Joseph, High Steward to the Egyptian pharaoh. This signet of high steward made the exodus with Moses' people from the land of the pharaohs to the Promised Land of Canaan. Over time, great rulers, including King David, have worn this talisman as an outward sign of their covenant with the living God, Yahweh."

Shadoe stepped behind Rayn and slipped the amulet around her neck. As he did this, he whispered to her, "Wear this with honor, My Princess, as did your father, Arthur, and his ancestors before him. Remain loyal to this land and to its people. Always place Yahweh above all."

Tears welled in Rayn's eyes, and she clutched his hand at the back of her neck. His strong fingers gently tightened on hers and then let go.

Applause and cheers erupted around her.

"Princess Emerald Rose Rayn," Mordred's acknowledgment dripped with sarcasm as he stared with covetous eyes upon the jeweled amulet resting over her breasts.

Rayn held his callous blue gaze.

"You are in need of a husband, a high king to rule at your side," Mordred gloated.

Here it comes. Rayn glanced to where Shadoe and Galahad stood attentive to the exchange. The voices in the room lowered to a simmer of anticipation.

"First let us discuss the truth of your lineage, shall we?" Rayn countered loudly.

"I'm surprised you'd want to," he smirked.

"I don't fear you, Mordred."

"'Tis not my desire that you do. Quite the opposite in fact."

His suggestive leer left nothing to her imagination. Chagrin heated her cheeks.

"But, just what do you imply about my lineage, Lady?" Mordred's tone had hardened in defense.

"That Arthur did not sire you."

Silence swallowed up the hall.

Rayn's confidence soared, and she spoke for all to hear. "Your mother, Morgause, shared the bed of Merlin un Hollo Tors, and then finding herself with child, she seduced Arthur and deceived him into believing the child to be his. When Merlin determined the child was his own, Morgause threatened him so greatly that he vowed to keep silent."

"Bah!" Mordred countered. "What threat could she make that would keep Merlin from telling Arthur the truth?"

Lancelot stepped forward. "That she would sacrifice you to her pagan gods and eat your heart at a banquet table."

"Nay! My mother would never do that!" Mordred balked.

"Aye, nephew, my sister, Morgause, would have indeed slain you." A terse feminine voice lifted as a hag in filthy rags limped forward, dragging one leg behind her.

Heads turned. Shrieks of disdain and shock rallied through the hall.

Rayn knew that voice. The Lady of the Loch! Rayn sidled a glance at Shadoe's ashen features. As surely as if Rayn had touched him, she felt his shock and pain. This was not how Rayn intended them to meet. Niamh had planned differently.

"It's the leper!" a Briton lady screamed and bolted into the crowd.

"Aye, the Enchantress Niamh!" announced another.

Many fled toward the closed doors but were restrained by guards.

"Do not fear me," Niamh beseeched. "I mean no harm. I follow the Fisher of Men, and I have come so that you may know the truth. My lover, Merlin, spawned Mordred. I do not excuse his indiscretion with Morgause, except to say that, like Arthur, Merlin was seduced with magique. I vow that Merlin and I loved each other, but Morgause could not stomach that fact. She turned us against each other, tore my scion Shadoe from my bosom, and tried to slay him. When I challenged her, she condemned me to this."

She straightened and released her veils. Rayn was as shocked as the others. Until now God had allowed her to see Niamh as the beautiful woman she'd once been. Niamh's black hair hung in stringy clumps separated by bald patches. An ear was missing, and an ugly cavity replaced her nose. Gray, scaled blotches scarred her lips and cheeks. Only her beautiful blue eyes, lids, and lashes remained unscathed.

Mordred looked as if he were ill and backed away.

Niamh held Rayn's tearful gaze before she looked at Shadoe. "I'm sorry we had to met this way, my scion."

Rayn's heart leaped with joy when Shadoe extended his hand to Niamh. His mother recoiled. Shadoe pulled her into his embrace. The moment, however brief, brought unity to the assembly with a collective gasp.

Niamh forced herself from Shadoe's arms. "I had to see Rayn's birthright sanctioned," she declared, "and his denied," she said, looking at Mordred. But her blue eyes held no condemnation, only pity.

"Who would you believe, this . . . *vile* being or me?" Mordred desperately shouted.

"I do!" King Caithest Uais lumbered forward. "I knew this woman before her beauty was cursed. She is Niamh le Fey! I also believe Morgause seduced the Merdyn and King Arthur . . . just as she did others. I'm certain there is more than one man here who shared her bed in their youth, yet unlike us, Morgause has not aged a day. There's but one source for that type of magique—" He shuddered with revulsion. "Morgause sleeps with the Adversary, and her scion is no better!"

Jeers attacked Mordred. The man paled. Clearly, he'd not expected Niamh's arrival or this response to her testimony. When he advanced on Niamh, Shadoe planted himself between Mordred and his mother and drew his sword. The leper hobbled off; the crowd allowed her adequate clearance.

"Mother!" Shadoe called out.

The woman, having replaced her veils, halted and met his distraught gaze.

No words were exchanged, but those blue eyes shimmered with tears of love before she turned and left the great hall. Rayn looked at Shadoe, seeing his pain. *Why doesn't he go after her?*

Instead, Shadoe turned his attention to Mordred. Rayn wondered what Mordred would do next, but Galahad pointed her toward her guests, who inundated her with questions. *Politics!* Rayn groaned inwardly, wishing her high steward would return to her, yet intrinsically knowing he would not.

Chapter Twenty-Nine

"I SUGGEST YOU LEAVE while you can." Shadoe glared Mordred down.

Mordred had recovered his poise. "I never thought I'd see you alive."

"I feel the same, brother," Shadoe said with more civility than he felt, and escorted Mordred to the courtyard with six armed knights. With security high, few people occupied the grounds, save for a servant leading a sickly ox toward the gate, no doubt, Shadoe assumed, to slaughter the poor creature.

Less than thirty feet away, Mordred's men awaited his command. As if to display his poise in this hostile environment, he dismissed them with a wave.

"Your resemblance to Merlin is uncanny, Shadoe." Mordred looked him over.

"While you, brother, are your mother's scion."

"My mother keeps nothing from me. I assumed it was that hideous creature who withheld the news from you."

Before reason could stop him, Shadoe clenched Mordred's throat in a stranglehold. Mordred wheezed, and his complexion deepened to crimson. His guards ran toward him.

"That creature happens to be my mother," Shadoe growled. "*Your* mother is responsible for Niamh's illness! I swear by all that is sacred, Morgause will pay for her transgressions."

Camelot's sentries and Mordred's men merged on the scene of the struggle. Shadoe summoned his emotional reserves, and released Mordred, motioning the soldiers back.

Rubbing his neck, Mordred reclaimed his dignity. "I'm fine!" he insisted hoarsely, halting his Saxons in their tracks.

Shadoe's gaze drifted to the leather gauntlet that bound Mordred's missing hand.

"You can be assured that I think about you every day." Mordred raised his stump.

"No doubt. And hundreds of childless parents think about you as well."

"I weary of being blamed for the sins of my mother," Mordred grumbled and turned on his heel, stepping onto a secluded alley path.

When Mordred had advanced a few paces, Shadoe said, "Do you really?" His tone was not taunting but doubtful. He held Mordred's gaze with firm conviction. Shadoe pitied his half brother, and he prayed silently, *Lord, if there's a chance for Mordred, please give me a sign.*

Inexplicably, a shroud of regret slipped over Mordred's callous countenance. The imposter prince suddenly staggered and drooped against the caer's wall like a puppet without strings. His eyes looked lost, forsaken. Tortured. "Aye, my brother," he said, as if from far away. "There are many things I regret. I am doomed, you know. I will never know the peace of your Christian faith." In a voice filled with desperation, Mordred cried out, "Merciful God, if you exist, free me!"

Tears tracked his cheeks, as he slumped down the wall and curled into a fetal position. To Shadoe's shock, this soulless man began to whimper like a babe.

Shadoe went down on one knee and cautiously lifted Mordred's limp head. Mordred's features appeared lifeless, yet he wept. This could be a trap. Alone and out of the view of others, Mordred could pull a knife on him or have an assassin in the shadows.

An iridescent blue light flickered in Mordred's dark eyes, and his face contorted in a way not humanly possible. Shadoe shuddered. The memory of Rayn's demons still vivid, he acknowledged the obvious. "Depart from this man, dark angels!"

"Who are you to mock us?" resounded an unnatural voice from Mordred's lips. "We obey Morgause le Fey! Our numbers are many. Best flee, Christian!"

The Holy Spirit surged through every fiber of Shadoe's being. He gripped Mordred's shoulders and supported him against the wall. "Mordred? You called upon God. He alone can deliver you, but you must want to be free of these demons."

The demons hissed vulgarities.

Mordred raised his head, and Shadoe saw the battle waging within his half brother.

"Please?" Mordred begged and wept.

Shadoe nodded. "Hear me, tools of Satan. In the name of my Lord Jesu Christ, I command all of you to depart from this man!"

Mordred's body went cold, and he shook so hard Shadoe could barely contain him. Shadoe recalled Merlin mentioning that often demons could grow so comfortable in their hosts that they were unprepared for exorcism. Hoping that was the case, Shadoe prayed fervently.

"Nooo!" the demons' voices escalated to a crescendo. "Don't send us back. Our master will devour us. Send us somewhere else."

Shadoe realized they'd not leave willingly if he returned them to hell. Offering up a prayer, he sidled a glance at the sickly, stumbling ox. "In the name of Jesu, enter the ox, you murderous demons!"

A stench similar to rotting flesh expelled from Mordred's mouth and body. Shadoe swore he heard a thousand tortured cries. He looked about, but no one, not even the guard thirty feet away, seemed to notice. Mordred drooped against the wall. Across the yard, the ox went berserk. Bellowing like a rabid animal, it tore free from the servant's rope and ran for the gate. Missing the opening, the ox rammed headfirst into the stone wall and buckled. Guards and the servant raced to the ox, which had sprawled on all fours. A guard lifted the creature's limp head and declared it had broken its neck.

Shadoe offered up a prayer of thanks, then looked at his half brother.

Mordred pushed away. He appeared disoriented as he staggered to his feet. But his arrogance rebounded.

"What's this?" Mordred smeared the tears from his face, then spit out a mouthful of grayish green slime. "So did you try and poison me as well?" He looked accusingly at Shadoe and wiped his mouth clean.

Speechless, Shadoe shook his head. Should he explain? Was Mordred's strange recovery an act? Shadoe wanted to probe further. "Mordred, I—"

Lancelot cleared the corner and looked about suspiciously. "I believe your time is up, Mordred, unless you want to wage war against these kings. I can assure you that were it not for Princess Rayn, they would have torn you limb from limb."

Mordred scoffed.

"Mordred?" Shadoe politely injected. "Other than six minor kings not worth mentioning, the other clans have pledged their loyalty to the Pendragon. The remainders of the warriors are in transit as we speak."

Mordred's lips thinned, his brow tensed as he seemed to calculate the numbers. "I'm not worried. They are mostly barbarians with no battle strategy or experience."

"Then you highly underestimate the power of Yahweh, brother."

"And the intelligence of our high steward." Lancelot smacked Shadoe across the shoulders so hard that he staggered.

"High Steward! I didn't think you possessed the discipline, or the guts, to take on such a task," Mordred chuckled.

"I will serve her as best I can," Shadoe asserted. He hoped he sounded credible.

"Then with your permission, I would speak with her before I go."

"I think not," Shadoe countered and blocked his way into the hall.

"I have as much right to court her as they do."

"No one woos my daughter," Lancelot injected hotly.

"Do not weary yourself convincing me differently, Lance," Mordred sneered. "Every one of those drooling fools knows that as a princess soon to be queen, she needs a king. What they don't know is the prophecies foretold that the Pendragon would join with the endmost of Ayris. I am that elect. No doubt when she learns the truth, she'll pick me over a savage." He challenged Lancelot and Shadoe's glares.

"Don't be so sure," Lancelot muttered.

"Oh, but I am. Lady Emerald Rose Rayn will be my bride, and the chieftains will pay me homage before the first highland snow blows. In truth, I suspect they will demand our marriage, for they are not about to sacrifice the lives of their clans for a woman." With that said, he made his grand exit.

∽

After Mordred left Camelot, Rayn saw Shadoe with Iona. Their discussion seemed emotionally heated. When Rayn looked back, Shadoe was gone. Rayn politely freed herself from a Pict chieftain and threaded her way through the crowd.

She tugged Galahad's sleeve. "Where is he?"

"Who?"

"Shadoe."

"Gone," Iona offered. "Toward the stables, I assume."

"Do you think he went after Niamh?" Rayn looked her companion straight on.

Iona shook her head. "Nay. He—"

"What?" Rayn gripped her friend's arms and forced her to look up.

"He's leaving. No doubt my fault." Iona looked as if she'd cry.

"What do you mean?" Rayn commanded.

"Shadoe said he sensed I still loved Mordred, asked if I am in league with him. I'm not! I loved him once, no more! You must believe me, Rayn. I'd die for you before I'd return to Mordred."

"I believe you, dearest. But I doubt that you are the reason Shadoe left, it was only an excuse." Rayn touched Iona's tear-marked cheek and turned to leave.

Galahad snatched her wrist. "Where are you going?"

"After Shadoe," she asserted.

"Do you think that's wise?"

She looked into her foster-brother's handsome face. She saw concern and something else. "I don't know what you have against Shadoe, but it best have nothing to do with his departure."

"I'd like to take the credit, but if he's gone, it was not my doing."

Rayn lifted her skirts and fled the hall.

When Galahad rushed after her, Tristam stopped him. "Let her be."

"But she's going to Shadoe."

"Then let her. Shortly you will have her for the rest of your life," Perceval injected.

Galahad halted and stared at his friends. "Whatever are you blathering about?"

"There was a second vow Lancelot made to Arthur. If Arthur's child was a lass, she was to wed you," Tristam explained.

"You aren't serious!" Galahad felt the blood drain from his face.

Taking him by the arm, the knights escorted Galahad back to the war room. "Oh, but we are."

∓

Entering the stables, Rayn's chest burned from her sprint. Shadoe's ram's cloak draped the open gate of Destrier's empty stall. Taking his cloak, Rayn mounted her mare bareback and galloped past the guards toward the causeway. Ahead in the midday sun, Shadoe escorted Destrier on foot. Echo loped beside him.

"Shadoe!" she called when he slipped his foot into the stirrup. "Why are you doing this; why are you leaving?"

"I've fulfilled my vows to Merlin, Arthur, and Guenevere." He settled into the saddle and began to canter.

"Nay," she sought to restrain the tears that singed her heart as she rode abreast of him. "It has just begun, it has."

"Don't pursue this, Princess," he threatened, keeping his eyes on the road.

"Then you are glad to depart?" she challenged.

"Ecstatic! At last I can return to civilization." He bridled Destrier to a walk. The rigid line of his jaw revealed his mindset.

"You'll be alone again."

"And I intend to keep it that way this time."

"What of your mother?"

"What of her?" His stone-chiseled features revealed nothing.

"I saw how you held her. You called her Mother. Surely you care."

"It was an impulsive act. No doubt I'll soon become a leper. Ironic justice, don't you think?"

He sounded like the old, self-centered Shadoe. What had happened in the last hour? Why was he so cruel, so pagan? When Echo playfully nipped Rayn's ankles, she leaped off her mare. Nearly tripping on her hem, she came beside Shadoe and grabbed his stirrup-secured leg.

"Go back before Galahad sends an army after you." He dismounted Destrier and turned on her.

"You . . . you forgot this." Rayn shoved his ram's cloak at him. With a grunt of disgust, Shadoe tossed it onto his saddle.

"What has Galahad to do with us?" Her voice quivered with confusion.

"Everything." Shadoe gritted his teeth.

∽◯∽

How chillingly simple it is to convert to that vulgar man of my past. Yet seeing her windblown curls and moist green eyes nearly breaks me. I can't reveal my heart. Far too much is at stake. "There is nothing between us, Princess!"

"Cease the formalities. What of the embraces and kisses we shared, your personal endearments?"

"Kisses and words, nothing more. Do you think you are the only wench I've flirted with?" Shadoe tossed his head back in mockery.

"And is that how you flirt? With sensual kisses and intimate caresses?" Rayn retorted with hurtful fury.

Shadoe pinned her chin with his rough fingers. "Sometimes with much more. Why, I could have had you in my bed the first time we kissed. Ah, it is easy when the wench is love struck like yourself." When he saw the pain his words brought her, Shadoe steeled his emotions.

"I am no love-struck fool, Sir." The delicate vein between her brow throbbed in her forehead, and she pulled away. "'Tis a woman, I am!" she said with a tremulous voice.

"Aye, that you are." He ogled her with a rakish gleam.

"You foul, piggish cur!" She arched her hand to slap him, but he caught it mid-flight and pressed it to his moist lips, savoring what he'd never again taste. Rayn.

"I thought you cared about me!" She yanked free and rubbed her palm against her palla as if to erase his kiss.

"I cared about bedding you is all!" At last he'd drawn blood.

"Why are you so brutal?"

"It is my nature, brat. Always has been."

"Nay!" she argued. "I've seen your gentle nature. I've seen the man of God you've become. A poor liar you are, Shadoe un Hollo Tors. May the Holy Spirit convict you!"

"Best you start praying, Princess," he jeered.

"I don't understand." Her long eyelashes glistened with tears. Her bosom heaved.

"Cease your insufferable whining, brat!"

"Is that all I am to you, High Steward?" Rayn balked.

"Aye! So you'd best start behaving like a queen." He looked away from her, away from Camelot. If he didn't leave now, he never would.

"Have you no heart, Shadoe? No dignity?" Her voice trembled, and Shadoe heard what he needed to hear: a hint of disgust for him.

"Dignity is my last concern. If I had dignity, I'd stay and take my father's station. But I am not Merlin. Nor do I meet the expectations of anyone at Camelot . . . not even my mother. As for a heart . . . well, there are some things not even God can change."

Yahweh, forgive my irreverence. He forced himself to look at her and donned a cold facade.

"Forgive me. I regret that I compared you to Merlin or expected you to be like him. You're not the Merdyn. I like you for who you are. I always have. Please stay? We need you. I need you to help me be a good queen, I do." Rayn gripped her hands so tightly he saw the whites of her delicate knuckles.

This isn't working! She's too quick to forgive. "Look, just because I'm recommitted to Christ Jesu doesn't mean I'm happy with all this." He swept a hand toward the caer. "I've a wanderlust heart, always have. I resent being here . . . resent you."

Swabbing her eyes with the back of her hand, Rayn's cold response burned with hostility. "Well, it's no secret that you've been miserable here, High Steward. Forgive me. I meant Apprentice. I must indeed be foolish, for I imagined you and I were each other's godsend. What about the breath of Eden we share?"

Lord God, you're not making this easy! "If experiencing each other's pain and speaking without words means we're Ayrisian godsends, I want nothing of it. Camelot's your destiny, not mine. Your loyalty is to God. Obedience to God doesn't guarantee happiness. Best you realize that, Princess!"

"Then I will obey God and do what is best for my people. Unlike you, I care more about others than about myself." She straightened her slender back and shoulders.

Her words were like a sword to his heart. When Shadoe glared into her steadfast expression, he saw her conviction. It gave him the strength to do what he must. He caught up Destrier's reins, put his foot in the stirrup, and swung himself onto his saddle. Horse's hooves thundered on the road behind him. He looked over his shoulder and spied Galahad leading six other riders.

"Where will you go?" Rayn's desperate voice tugged at his bleeding heart as she managed to run alongside him and match Destrier's gait.

Bursting into a gallop, Shadoe left her in his wake.

∽

Emotionally bruised and betrayed, Rayn stumbled and then fell, scraping her knees. Closing her eyes, she swallowed the nauseous bile that soured her throat. When a warm wet tongue slobbered her face, Rayn opened her eyes to find Echo planted in front of her. Rayn hugged the wolf tight, then hoarsely ordered, "Go with him."

As if refusing, the wolf whimpered and nuzzled closer.

"I guess you have free will, too." Releasing the wolf, Rayn stood, cringing from the pain in her bruised knees. Her silken gown was soiled and tattered, but she cared not.

Echo wagged her tail and dropped her ears and head in submission to Rayn. However small the joy, Rayn appreciated the wolf's turncoat loyalty. Head high, she walked toward the approaching riders. *I will not cry! I am Princess Emerald Rose Rayn, daughter of Arthur, the Pendragon.* But when she stole a glance back and saw Shadoe's retreating form, her heart and soul wept. *My God, why has his heart turned from me?*

∽

Bruised and bleeding, Shadoe stood rope-bound before the Round Table.

"Release me!" he demanded, glaring at Lancelot.

"As he says," Lancelot instructed the guards, then dismissed them.

Rubbing his wrists, Shadoe charged forward and slammed his fists against the table. "I thought we were brothers." He scanned the stolid faces of Tristam and Perceval, who sat on either side of Lancelot.

Perceval huffed. "As did we. But a true brother does not desert his kin in their time of need."

Shadoe swiveled. He glared at the older knight. "My work is finished. You wanted me gone."

"Our wants are not important," Tristam explained. "And if it's of any interest, Rayn isn't pleased that we brought you back . . . forcibly."

"So this is not her doing?" Shadoe flinched as he dabbed blood from his cheekbone.

"O' course not." Lancelot scratched his bearded jaw. "I take responsibility for your condition. You have my apology."

"What good's an apology if you hold me against my will?" Shadoe growled.

Lancelot pushed to his feet, his stance clearly unsteady. Shadoe saw the lassitude in his friend's demeanor and pallid complexion, realized Lancelot had told the truth. He was dying.

"It's not my wish to hold you prisoner. Princess Rayn needs an ambassador, someone with diplomatic experience. You spent time in Rome and know the ways of the senate. Since we no longer have Rome's guidance in matters of war, you are the most qualified. Sit." Lancelot indicated Shadoe's former seat to the right of Arthur's chair.

"I'll stand." He would be anything but cooperative. He sensed Lancelot was about to broach a topic he'd rather avoid.

"You're not going to make this easy, are you?" Lancelot arched a white brow at Shadoe's stubborn countenance.

"Would you if our stations were reversed?" Shadoe touched his bruised left eye and winced.

"Nay. Then I will be candid." A smile lifted beneath Lancelot's beard. "You know Rayn's in immediate need of a husband."

"Aye, I understand that she and Galahad will—"

"Nay, Galahad will not marry Rayn," Lancelot stated.

"She refused him?" he incredulously asked, glancing at the other knights' bland expressions.

"Rayn doesn't know I'd intended their union."

"And she won't." Galahad strolled into the oval chamber and closed the door. "I've pledged myself into God's service."

"But you're in love with her. You must marry her or she'll be thrown upon the mercies of the clans!" Shadoe snarled at this man who would break Rayn's heart.

"Oh, I indeed love Rayn. But I am not in love with her, nor is she in love with me."

"But I saw you together in the glen."

"Spying were you?" Galahad accused.

"Nay! I just happened along." His ire elevated. "The two of you were embracing—"

"Like a brother and sister," Galahad asserted. "The next day I told Rayn my intentions to share the eternal gift of salvation with the world."

"The world? Bah! This is about Camelot and Caledonia. Would you have her marry Mordred?" Shadoe glared from one man to another.

"Of course not!" Lancelot snarled.

"One can marry and still be a priest," Shadoe argued as he stalked within inches of Galahad.

"Correct. Nor do I rule out ever to marry. For now it is my choice to remain celibate. Furthermore, being a good husband doesn't mean I'd be a good king. I know my strengths and weaknesses. Political leadership is not my strong point. Rayn needs someone who is her equal, someone she will trust exclusively when it comes to the final decision. I am not that man."

"And just who is?"

His breath short and ragged, Lancelot struggled to stand between the sparring men. "Rayn has agreed to do whatever is necessary to secure the Pendragon throne."

"She has, aye?" Shadoe snorted.

"And as high steward of Camelot, it is your duty to advise her on such decisions."

Shadoe grimaced. He regretted having taken on that transitory duty. "You need someone who has the other tribes' recognition."

"Had you stayed awhile, you'd have heard the decision of the clans' tribunal. They will only support Princess Rayn's war against Mordred if you agree to be her husband."

A nervous grin tugged at Shadoe's lips. "I do not appreciate your sense of humor, friends."

"It is humorless to us as well, Shadoe. Rayn needs a husband, a trustworthy one," Galahad stated.

"Well, that leaves me out!" Shadoe rolled his eyes.

Galahad guffawed, as did the other men. Shadoe joined them until Galahad stopped laughing. "I confess it has been a long time since I've trusted you, Shadoe. Still, with God's help, you have changed for the better. You can handle Rayn's temperament. Obviously you care about her. Da has convinced me you are up to the challenge of not only making her queen but an obedient wife. I agree. You are the only man we'd trust with Rayn's life and her heart."

Shadoe felt ill. His logical mind and wanderlust heart were far from agreeable on the matter. He could have what he wanted, Rayn, but at what expense? Slumping into his chair, he shook his head. "Mercy, if you're out to insure I stay on as high steward, you needn't concoct such extreme measures."

"I'll admit it did cross my mind," Lancelot confessed. "But I must indemnify Rayn's welfare. Despite what you think about my need to avenge Arthur, I will not force her into a marriage with a barbaric Saxon like Hengist or with Mordred, who as the present high chieftain of Caledonia has the right to her."

"He's an imposter and dares to suggest he is the endmost of Ayris!" Galahad growled.

"He is. Firstborn to be exact," Shadoe acknowledged bluntly.

Lancelot snorted. "For someone with the gift of foresight, you, Sir Shadoe, are a buffoon!"

"Excuse me?" He glared at the senior knight.

"God spoke to me today through Mordred. We know the prophecy of the union between the last descendants of Ayris. It was foretold long before Merlin was born. To our knowledge, there are three full blooded Ayrisians left: you, Mordred, and Rayn Pendragon.

"Since none of us, including Rayn, want her wed to Mordred, that leaves you, Shadoe, to join with the Pendragon. For you are the endmost of Ayris, the last-born male." Lancelot looked at him, as did everyone else.

The clarity of Lancelot's words shocked Shadoe's soul. He had not interpreted the prophecy that way, but it did make sense. *Endmost— last, not firstborn!* "You're mad if you think she loves me or would want me after what I last said to her. Ask her!"

"I did." Lancelot circled Shadoe like a bird of prey.

"And?" Shadoe held the man's determined gaze.

"She called you a crude, overbearing, annoying, pompous—"

"Mule's behind, among other vulgarities that neither a lady nor a princess should utter." Tristam smirked. "Most impressed I was."

"Aye, we will have to work on that." Perceval chuckled.

"Would you like to hear my opinion of her?" Shadoe's eyes narrowed. His jaw tensed.

"We're quite aware of your opinion about Rayn. And you know she's in love with you, Shadoe. That's why you left." Galahad smirked. "Which says a lot about your maturing character."

Lord Jesu, don't let them ask if I'm in love with her. "Excuse me, but she doesn't sound or act like a woman in love." *Nay, he'd not forgotten her vow of love at the waterfall, but was that real love or youthful infatuation? Doubt plagued him.*

"Of course not. Her nature is not conducive to admitting to herself or to you of how she truly feels," Lancelot asserted.

"Well, my nature is, and I refuse to marry the brat."

"I don't think so. You, the endmost of Ayris, will marry my daughter, and it will happen this very hour." Lancelot strode forward and glared at him with a severity that Shadoe feared.

"I am high steward of Camelot. Never in the history of Camelot or Ayris has a high steward and nobility wed one another."

"Mayhap, but I do not recall there being a law that denied such union. Secondly, you have been personal with her. That gives me cause to demand one of two things: your life or marriage." Lancelot halted within a hand's span of where Shadoe sat.

Shadoe shot to his feet and looked to the other knights. Each nodded with Lancelot.

"This is blackmail! I don't deny I kissed her." He glared at Galahad. "You saw it happen, and I accepted responsibility for that poor judgment on my part, did I not?"

"Aye," Galahad confirmed.

"And the other times?" Lancelot prodded. "I'm certain they involved more than a shared kiss, no doubt caresses of an intimate nature."

Chagrin warmed his features as Shadoe realized the evidence against him. Months ago, he'd have lied his way out of this; now, as a recommitted child of God, he would not. "I, too, am liable for those indiscretions."

"That makes you accountable to do the honorable thing. Wed her," Galahad charged.

"Aye!" Tristam and Perceval chimed in.

A block in the wall slid open, and Rayn advanced from the hidden passageway. "Cease!"

The five men turned to face her, surprised by her arrival.

"How dare you spy on us!" Lancelot made a lame attempt to grasp the moral high ground.

Striding into the room, Rayn waved him off. "And how dare you scheme an arranged marriage behind my back, Da?"

"'Tis done all the time, little sister." Galahad tried to be glib.

Rayn was not sidetracked and marched to Shadoe's side. It took all her resolve to temper her shock over his battered face, especially the bloodshot hue of his swollen eye. "He is not to blame. I initiated the embraces. I forced myself upon him—"

"Rayn! I'll not have you lie on my account." Shadoe's eyes glinted with suppressed fury.

"I lie on no one's account. We each have our version, our belief of what happened, we do." She put herself between him and her family. "Besides, you made it clear you don't want this marriage any more than I. Now what do we intend to do about it, aye?"

Before Shadoe could speak, Galahad asserted, "You must choose which scion of Merlin you will marry, and might I advise you to pick the lesser of two evils." He nodded in Shadoe's direction.

"But I wish to marry neither. I will not marry a man who wants me for political gain, nor will I marry someone not in love with me, whom you had to beat into submission." She pinned Shadoe with a wintry glare.

"Well, I don't know about the submission part." Perceval rubbed his bruised jaw.

Shadoe glowered at his friend's paltry humor.

Lancelot took Rayn's hands and gently encouraged her. "I ask that you do what any queen would do. Do what's right for Camelot and, above all, right by Yahweh!"

Galahad walked over and, cupping Rayn's chin, he engaged her stubborn gaze. "Listen to me, wee sister. I want the best for you and, above all, your happiness . . . but Da is right. You are very possibly the answer to our people's salvation. It's been less than a year since I was in Rome."

"Aye?" she asked.

"All these years after his death, Arthur Pendragon's name is revered and respected among the kingdoms, including the Anglos, Jutes, and Saxons. Moreover, the name of Merlin un Hollo Tors is powerful in the political arena. Thus the union of these two influential names will be noticed. This marriage could reunite the tribes of Caledonia and Britannia." He looked back at Shadoe. "And as high steward, you know this to be true."

"Aye, I acknowledge your observation, friend." He looked to Rayn, then properly addressed Lancelot. "Might I have a private word with Rayn?"

Lancelot nodded permission.

"Princess Rayn?" He gestured to the doorway.

Every fiber in Rayn told her to say no, for his voice was anything but inviting. Still, she complied. She expected him to stop outside the war room, but he directed her to the doors of the Pendragon bedchamber.

At the threshold, she paused. Shadoe looked back and met her intrepid gaze.

"I want to talk, Rayn. Nothing more."

"And I wanted to talk earlier, but you denied me the courtesy. Why now?"

"Issues have changed. Would you rather I beg?"

Feeling her sore knees, she snorted. "It might help."

"Please, Princess Rayn, allow me a few minutes?"

With a reluctant nod, she eased by him and strolled to the center of the chamber. Shadoe went to the veranda. He unlatched the veranda doors and flung them ajar, then gestured her to his side. Straightening her spine, Rayn closed the distance and stepped out onto the balcony, which barely allowed them room to stand.

"I have considered your father's request, Rayn. Have you?"

Drawing a deep breath of the salty breeze, she turned and looked up at him. "It is no request, Sir. He demands we marry, he does."

"Request or demand, it is all the same to me. 'Tis a marriage of convenience meant to salvage this." He swept his left arm before them, and Rayn gazed upon the sweeping panorama of autumn-kissed tors, glens, and vales. "You see the enchanted isle of Wind's Haven and the demesne of Camelot extends beyond this little island, Rayn."

"I know," she mulishly countered.

"And there is more at stake than Camelot . . . there's your beloved Caledonia and Britannia, the Isle of Might, the very soil your father and mother fought and died to protect."

Shadoe set his hands on her shoulders and turned her to face him. "You are the Emerald Rose Pendragon, Rayn. Your parents perished so that you might live and reclaim your lineage. If our marriage will provide the safe harbor that ensures the opportunity to reunite the tribes against Mordred and the Saxons, then I support Lancelot's command that we marry." He looked deeply into her tentative gaze. "But it would be a marriage in name alone."

"What are you saying?" Rayn's breath broke sharply.

"There will be no consummation. When the time is appropriate, I will leave."

Rayn gaped. "You expect me to believe after all we've—" She blushed and looked away.

He turned her toward him. "There is no doubt we desire each other, Rayn. But I suspect you have confused passion with love. Even you don't want to be married, at least to the likes of me," he said with such confidence that she found herself nodding. "We'd make each other miserable."

Rayn struggled with her heart and lost. "You're right, Shadoe, I don't wish to marry," she lied, then turned to look upon the artwork of God—Caledonia. "Nor would you be my first choice." She smiled to herself, recalling her childhood infatuation with Merlin. "But if we are to wed and not validate the marriage, how do you propose we convince my father and everyone else? It is tradition the bed linen is displayed to the court, is it not?"

He scowled. "Aye, we will worry about that detail later. For now, we must convince your father that we want this marriage."

She stiffened. "And just how do we do that?"

"Convince them we are in love," he whispered huskily, as he raised her off the veranda. With a passion that sent her thoughts reeling and her limbs trembling, he kissed her.

Despite what her mind told her not to do, Rayn responded to the tingling heat of his mouth on hers. Instinctively, her body yielded to the muscular leanness of his manly build, and she knew that resisting him would be the hardest test of her life. His body was hard and yet his touch was soft and seductive as he urged her lips to part for him.

In the midst of their shared fervor, she heard the thunder of applause. Twisting in Shadoe's arms, she found her father and Galahad inside the bedchamber along with Perceval, Tristam, and Iona. In the doorway, several servants and soldiers clapped approval.

Her cheeks abloom, Rayn wiggled to be free of Shadoe. Although he set her on her feet, he held her possessively to his side. When she looked up, his crooked smile confirmed she'd responded just as he'd expected. Shadoe had known they were being watched.

"That wasn't difficult," he murmured.

Feigning a smile for their audience, Rayn pinched his waist and got the reaction she desired. A strong wince of pain.

❦

Less than an hour later, the wedding got underway. The chieftains seemed quite pleased that Shadoe, instead of Galahad, stood at Rayn's side—even more pleased that is wasn't Mordred.

Despite her discontent with Lancelot's manipulation of the matter, Rayn secretly felt thrilled. She was about to marry Shadoe. That didn't mean she'd forgotten their hostile exchanges. Rayn's faith in God inspired her. She knew that Shadoe had meant to deflect her affection for him, for he'd been doing so since the day after her deliverance from the demons. In her heart she believed he loved her, and she desperately wanted to know why he refused to admit it. Thus, she spent her brief preparation time seeking God's sanction of their union. Although she would not tell Shadoe, Rayn had every intention to make their marriage a success.

When Rayn insisted that Niamh be present, Shadoe didn't argue. To their surprise, Lancelot informed them that Niamh had never left Caer Camelot. Instead, she had collapsed just outside the hall. When even the servants had refused to touch Niamh, Perceval and Tristam took her to a private room. Upon hearing this news, Shadoe went to his mother, giving Rayn hope that he would reconcile with her. Twenty minutes later, Shadoe guided Niamh to an acceptable distance, just out of sight from the guests.

Although memorable, their wedding ceremony was not exactly what Rayn had envisioned. There were plenty of witnesses. Come the morrow, Mordred and Morgause would know of the marriage, and trouble would ensue.

During the ceremony, Shadoe and Rayn didn't exchange a glance. Galahad performed the Christian sacrament, which included the joining of hands, vows of faithfulness, and a blessing from God. Five minutes later it was over. Rayn had wed her godsend—or had she?

Chapter Thirty

SHADOE TURNED TO his bride. He wondered which of them felt more miserable. He felt manipulated, and she no doubt felt betrayed. He'd spoken cruel words to her. Words of a desperate man doing what he thought to be right, thought to be God's will. Yet the moment Galahad had pronounced them husband and wife, Shadoe felt God's hand on their union, however short that union might be.

How can I explain to Rayn what I foresaw just after I spoke with Niamh? How do I tell my beloved wife I don't see myself living beyond the next three sunrises—and that I will die in battle? How could I do this to the woman I love?

Shadoe's morbid thoughts were displaced when Rayn turned to Lancelot, who held Excalibur. The knight handed the large sword to her. With its silvery blade pointed earthward, Rayn pressed her lips to the jeweled hilt and then presented it to Shadoe.

"As the righteous High Queen of Camelot, I hereby offer Excalibur to my righteous High King, Shadoe un Hollo Tors Pendragon!"

Astonished by her generous tribute, Shadoe went slack-jawed.

Rayn's shoulders sagged, and she muttered, "Please, Milord, or my arms will break, they will!"

Shadoe grinned and, accepting the sword, he leaned into her. "I suppose you want your staff, aye?"

They faced their guests. "I already have it," she murmured back.

With a smirk, Shadoe offered Rayn his arm, and she held on. Around them the tribal chieftains cheered and applauded. At his side, Rayn looked regal and poised, but she trembled against him. When he escorted her down the dais, she buckled. Shadoe swept her limp body into his arms. Rayn had fainted.

∾

Rayn awoke in the royal bedchamber to the murmur of voices. Iona's pinched features loomed above her.

"Where . . . where is Shadoe?" Feeling disoriented, Rayn sat up and arranged her dress and palla. No doubt she looked a fright.

"He's been called away," Iona explained and brushed Rayn's messed curls with her fingers.

"Oh." Rayn's heart lurched with suspicion.

Lancelot stepped forward and caressed Rayn's troubled brow. "It's Niamh. She collapsed on the mezzanine above the hall. Shadoe is with her. She refuses to stay in the bedchamber we gave her."

Guilt assaulted Rayn. "Then I must go to her."

"Nay, you're exhausted, lass. Rest a while," Iona crooned.

"I'm better now," she said as she pushed to her feet. Searching her father's anxious expression, she smiled. "Don't worry, Da. God will protect me from her illness." Then she did what she did so well—disobeyed. On her way to the door, she heard Lancelot's sigh of resignation. Looking back, she blew him a kiss. He shook his head and chuckled.

Rayn left her chamber but not without an escort of two guards and Iona, who seemed distracted. Rayn halted and turned to her friend. "What's wrong?"

The dark beauty appeared weary of heart and soul, but she replied quite the opposite. "I'm just glad you married Shadoe."

Rayn gawked. "But you love him, Iny."

Iona's flawless complexion blotted crimson, and her eyes gleamed with mirth. "Me in love with Puwee? Surely you jest! He's a boy! Of course, grown now, but I've never fancied myself in love with the apprentice. Why, I've known for years that you and Shadoe would one day fall in love. The Merdyn said so. And to witness that divination come true—why I couldn't be happier for either of you!"

Tears rimmed Rayn's eyes, and she clenched her friend's arm. "Oh, Iny, all this time I feared you hated me."

"Hate you! Never." She glanced to where Shadoe sat with Niamh on a fur-draped stone bench that overlooked the hall below them. "I've loved but once in my life, Rayn. I even had a child for a few days until I . . ."

"Please, tell me, Iny."

"I named him Honor, but I left him in Dal Riada." Her shoulders trembling, she looked away.

"Oh, Iny!" Rayn pulled Iona to her breast. "Why?"

"To protect him from Morgause. But he's safe now and—"

"Honor is Mordred's scion?"

"Aye." She nodded. "Shadoe's nephew."

"Do Mordred or Morgause know?" Rayn ventured.

Iona looked away. "Aye, Morgause does. She tricked me into meeting her and threatened my scion's life unless . . ."

"What?" Rayn felt the bile churning in her belly.

"I never pursue Mordred or tell him about his scion."

"She is that threatened by you, aye?"

"Would seem so. But she doesn't realize her blackmail is no longer a sacrifice. I lost Mordred years ago." Iona grasped Rayn's shoulders with the fierce passion of a mother. "Thus far Morgause doesn't know Honor is in Dal Riada of Eire . . . and Mordred must never know."

Rayn solemnly nodded. "I vow to protect your scion's identity and location at all costs."

Iona released Rayn and stiffened her spine with clear resolve. "Thank you, Princess. Now I've no more regrets. The gods gave me first you to love and then the orphans. I'm forever thankful we've found them all families, but if more orphans come, you will care for them?"

Hugging her best friend, Rayn crinkled her nose in confusion. "But surely, you're not going anywhere, Iny. You and I will grow old together, we will."

Iona embraced her. "Of course we will, my sweet Rayn." Her voice was melancholy. "Now learn from one who made a horrible mistake in her youth. I left the man I loved because I feared the Adversary more than I trusted your Jesu."

Rayn pulled back and looked into her friend's tearful gaze. "There's still time, Iona. If you'd only open your heart to him—"

"Hush. We can talk later about your God. Now do be patient with Shadoe. Love him for better and worse. And when you confront Morgause, don't believe anything she says. She's unable to tell the truth." Iona's voice strangled with emotion. Lifting her skirts, she fled to her room.

Rayn turned to pursue her. Lancelot emerged from Rayn's bedchamber, dismissed her guards, and addressed her. "Let Iona go, Rayn. She needs time."

"Time is fleeting, Da. I fear for her soul."

"And rightly so. Iona has a good, decent heart, but that will not save her. Iona has heard God's voice, and his Spirit knocks at her heart's door. But she alone must open her heart to receive his gift of eternal salvation. All we can do is pray. Alas, I fear Iona chooses the love of a man over God."

"Heaven's light. Iona really does love Mordred!"

"Aye. Iona was the greatest obstacle ever put between Morgause and Mordred. The witch could not stand the influence of Iona's goodness on Mordred. Morgause knew that if they married, she'd forfeit control of her scion. Iona was with child when you were born. Morgause cursed Iona and the child, and Iona grew so frightened, she lost the bairn before birth."

"Why didn't Mordred stop Iny from leaving him?"

"You really don't understand the capacity for evil Morgause possesses. She filled Mordred's mind with lies . . . she even said the children were mine."

"Then you know about Honor?"

Lancelot scowled. "Aye, despite everything, Iona could not stay away from Mordred."

"I remember the day she left us, Da. Why did you send her from me?"

Lancelot's features paled. "I . . . I had no choice. After Camelot fell, we fled to Tintagel. There, life was peaceful. Iona loved you and nursed you like her own. But here at Camelot, Mordred grew despondent and depressed. The fishwives said Mordred had been possessed by demons Morgause had summoned to control him.

"Yet according to hearsay, he regretted slaying Arthur, Guenevere, and those poor innocent babes. He went to the chapel and called out to God. That's when Morgause demolished Arthur and Guenevere's crypts, and the chapel became a druid shrine. Mordred still threatened to leave Camelot. Apparently, Morgause thought if she persuaded Iona to return, Morgause would recover control of her scion . . . and no doubt gain control over Iona. When I heard of the tryst, I feared for your life, especially when Iona confessed she was with child again. I knew if she returned to Mordred, the child would become another pawn and—"

"You forced her to leave?"

"Aye. If she hadn't, I would have slain her. It was years before I realized she would never have betrayed us. That is when she returned."

Rayn recalled Mordred's expression when he'd seen Iona in the hall earlier. "Is it possible he still loves her?"

"That fiend's incapable of love!" Lancelot snarled.

"You once said that about Shadoe." Rayn reminded him as she tipped her head to where Shadoe sat with his mother on the second-floor mezzanine.

"I guess all things are possible with God." Lancelot gently tweaked his daughter's cheek.

She leaned into his touch. "Aye. All things are possible, Da, and mayhap one day . . ." She sighed.

"I hope this marriage between you and Shadoe wasn't a mistake. What we saw on the balcony was real?" A frown furrowed his brow.

Before Rayn could answer, Tristam called Lancelot to join him in the hall. Lancelot pressed a kiss to her brow and excused himself. When Shadoe walked toward her, perspiration beaded and trickled down her back. What now? What would she do? She wished Iona had not left. Shadoe stopped with ample breathing space between them. Rayn experienced relief at his considerate stance. His eyes shimmered with moisture. Shadoe never cried, did he?

"Niamh wishes to speak with you," his voice sounded hollow and distant. The muscle at his jaw flinched with tension.

"She should sleep, Shadoe." Rayn glanced over to where the Lady rested her head against the bench's backrest.

"She refuses. Go to her." His voice held no leeway. "Please, Rayn?"

Rayn searched his face, saw his desolation, and nodded.

"I must rejoin our guests and speak with Caithest." He took the stairs to the hall below.

Rayn walked over and settled on the bench alongside Niamh. The Lady's eyes were closed, and her breath came in short, shallow jerks. Rayn's gaze noted the blue tinge of the woman's fingernails. She knew the signs of impending death. However selfish, Rayn bowed her head and asked God to either cure Niamh or free her from her agonizing existence.

"Don't grieve for me, child. I am content."

Rayn jolted. She had thought the Lady asleep. "How can you be?"

"Because God himself is sufficient for me. And today, he gave me back my scion. He also gave me you, sweet Rayn. Ah, to witness your holy union of marriage was my last request." She put her hand to her bosom and sighed. "Jesu has blessed this weary soul more than I ever deserved. God willing, I will soon join him and my beloved Merlin in paradise. But I regret that you are not as happy as I."

Rayn looked away from those knowing eyes. "I don't understand."

"This should be the happiest day of your life, but it's not."

"How can I be happy when he is not?" She glanced to where Shadoe discreetly watched them from the floor of the hall below while Caithest jawed his ear.

Niamh lifted her head, and her blue eyes glistened. "Oh, dearest child, don't be fooled by his aloofness. Shadoe's still in transition with his renewed faith. Thus, he is still foolishly insecure, proud, and confused . . . but don't ever believe he doesn't love you."

"He told you as much, did he?"

"Aye, he talked only of you." Niamh nodded.

"But he left me!"

"Aye, because he felt he had no choice. Shadoe came to Camelot out of a sense of guilt and duty . . . but he stayed because of you. Like this arranged marriage, he's had no choice in these matters except the one to leave." A wretched cough shook the woman's fragile body.

Rayn gestured Niamh to rest, but the Lady waved her off. "Please, my time is short. Now listen to me, Princess!"

The woman had never been so assertive. Rayn found it refreshing. "As you wish, My Lady Niamh."

Niamh appeared to smile beneath her veils. "Matters being what they were, my scion assumed you would wed Galahad. He even assumed you and Galahad to be in love with each other . . . but that your feelings for my son were mere infatuation. Shadoe believed a marriage between you and Galahad was God's will, and despite his consuming love for you, he left. He had resigned himself to living without you rather than disobeying Jesu. But then he was forced to return and marry you. Don't you see, Rayn? For his entire life, Shadoe has been struggling against God's prophecies and other people's expectations. So now . . . instead of being honest with you and turning to God, he's done what he does best . . . he's rebelled."

"Oh, Niamh, I'd no idea."

"Really?" The lady wheezed. "So much alike you two are."

Rayn caught the twinkle in Niamh's clouded eyes. "I guess we are in some ways."

"Some?" She scoffed. "I've yet to determine who is more stubborn. As your husband, he is head of the household. So, in love, I suggest you learn to obey him."

"Obey?" Rayn gulped.

"Aye, to respectfully honor your husband, Rayn. Trust his final decisions in all matters. I assure you that whatever you give to your husband in love, he will return it twofold." The Lady of the Loch set her deep blue gaze upon Rayn. "Shadoe loves you so desperately he was willing to leave Camelot and never return. He'd die for you, Rayn."

Rayn twisted on the bench and looked at Shadoe. Her heart thudded against her ribs. Had her prayers been answered? Did Shadoe really love her as desperately as Niamh said?

While Shadoe seemed to be listening to Caithest, he stared up into the rafters. His handsome countenance turned dour.

"So what am I to do, My Lady?" Rayn asked Niamh.

"Tell him you love him and—" Niamh's head swerved to the rafters. Pushing to her feet, her voice trembled. "Spirit of God, guard this place! The hag is amongst us!"

Rayn looked to the high, dark ceiling. A ripple of pale sunlight illuminated the vulture's beady eyes. Rayn shuddered. From an open winnock opposite, Mer dove into the hall and soared past her, squawking his arrival. The golden eagle's entrance caught the crowd's attention. Claws outstretched, Mer flew toward the rafters, but the vulture eluded the eagle and swooped toward Rayn and Niamh. The Lady of the Loch stepped in front of Rayn.

Niamh called out, "Almighty God, reveal this worshiper of the Adversary!"

The vulture hovered over the mezzanine. A gray mist enveloped the large bird, and feathers drifted to the gathering below. Morgause materialized before Rayn and Niamh. Rayn had heard of Morgause's shapeshifting ability, but she'd never believed it true. Iona was right. Morgause was evil personified. She was also beautiful!

Onlookers cried out at this mystical transformation. Stunned, Rayn glimpsed Shadoe and Galahad tearing up the steps with their weapons drawn. Morgause seemed oblivious to the panic she'd caused or the approaching knights.

"How dare you!" Morgause accused Niamh.

"I did nothing. God did." Niamh limped confidently toward her beautiful sister.

"Then hear me, especially you, Princess, or is it Queen? Of course, your title doesn't matter." Morgause glared at Rayn with an animosity that made Rayn shudder.

"I am Pendragon!" Rayn found her voice.

She felt Morgause's covetous gaze dip to the Emerald Rose of Avalon that hung over Rayn's bosom. "Well, Pendragon, you've stolen everything, but even now Mordred's legions trample your fields and slaughter every man, woman, and child in their path!"

"No!" Rayn stepped forward. Niamh blocked her.

"You dying, old leper," Morgause snorted. "Will you defend this Pendragon?"

"Aye, with my life." Niamh demonstrated a courage that could come only from God.

"As will I!" At the top step, but several feet from the mezzanine, Shadoe drew Excalibur.

The witch turned and snarled at him. "Shadoe, you foolish enchanter, you think you can kill me?"

"That I don't know, witch. But Jesu Christ drove the demons out of Mordred today, so I would not be so certain that he is slaughtering anyone."

Morgause's complexion blanched. "You lie!"

"That I no longer do," he said with conviction as he took another step.

"He is high steward," voices boomed from below them.

"And now he is high king!" declared Lancelot.

"And you, Morgause, are dead!" Iona shrieked and emerged from the shadows with a dagger in her hand. "You'll never hurt anyone again, especially Mordred."

Morgause was forced to take a step back, poised on the edge of the mezzanine. Still, she appeared confident. "He's mine, Iona. Always has been. You were but a distraction to him."

"Nay. He loved me, still does. But you destroyed his soul." Iona took another step closer. "Everyone listen! This harridan tricked me and sought my alliance!"

"Nay! Lies, all lies!" Morgause defended.

Niamh also advanced and dropped her veils to reveal her diseased, rotting flesh. Morgause cringed at Niamh's approach. Rayn realized Morgause truly feared her sister's leprosy. Rayn glanced at Shadoe, who like the others stood transfixed upon the unfolding, dark drama.

Never taking her blue eyes off Morgause, Niamh announced to everyone, "Lady du Maur speaks the truth. My sister has long been dead to our world. This vile creature is of Satan and has defiled the splendor of Camelot. Everyone, heed my warning. Flee Wind's Haven before God's judgment returns. Prepare for battle. Mordred's army is coming!"

Morgause's demonic laugh echoed through the hall. Rayn glimpsed an exchange of glances between Niamh and Iona. Before anyone could intervene, they lunged at Morgause.

"No!" Rayn yelled out. Too late, Shadoe leaped the last step to the mezzanine.

Morgause screamed.

The women wrestled.

Iona's dagger was knocked from her hand, and she went for Morgause's throat.

Morgause clutched Niamh's head and brutally twisted. Rayn swore she head the Lady's neck snap. A breath later, the three women plunged off the mezzanine, crashing onto the granite floor thirty feet below.

Screams of shock echoed through the hall. Then all went silent. Three bodies lay crumpled in an eerie embrace with Morgause on top. Shadoe held Rayn as she looked down to where the guests slowly walked toward the lifeless bodies. Scarlet blood seeped from Iona's crushed skull. Niamh's neck was unnaturally bowed.

A succession of screams followed. Morgause's body transformed into a gray, swirling mist that shape-shifted into the vulture and flew up toward the winnock. Perched on a rafter, Mer dove after Morgause.

Rayn had no time to act.

Two archers shot at the escaping vulture.

They missed.

Mer cried out. An arrow pierced his chest. Mer flapped his expansive wings, struggling to stay in the air.

"Please, God! No!" Rayn stumbled blindly down the stairs with Shadoe on her heels. The eagle fell beside Iona and Niamh's bodies.

Rayn knew before she reached the floor that her beloved friends and Mer were dead. Falling on her knees, her heart thundering fiercely within her chest, she thought she herself would die. *Oh, God, I so want to die.* With a trembling hand, Rayn reached out to the dearest woman she'd ever known, Iona. Rayn was barely aware of Tristam and Perceval separating the bodies . . . of Shadoe's grief-stricken countenance as he replaced the veils over Niamh's face, then lifted his mother into his arms and carried her away. . . .

. . . of voices escalated and lowered.

Orders shouted.

Armed men running to and fro.

Rayn drew into herself and her loss. *Oh, God! Iny! Why didn't I see your broken heart sooner? Sweet, Iny, forgive me?*

Picking up Mer, Rayn hugged the large raptor, her tears wetting the feathers still warm to her touch. This wild creature of God, this golden eagle, had died for her. Rayn felt Lancelot's unsteady hands draw her to her feet. Gently, Perceval pried Mer from her grasp. Rayn looked back to see Galahad and Tristam take up Iona's body.

Lancelot turned her to him. "We haven't time for proper burials, perhaps after—"

"The war?" Her eyes glistened with the indignation of denying Niamh and Iona the memorials they deserved.

"Aye. My daughter, we've just received word from our outposts.

Niamh was right. Mordred has crossed Hadrian's Wall. You must give the call to arms before it's too late."

"We'll do it together, wife." Shadoe presented his outstretched hand to her.

Wife? His tender address took her unaware, and Rayn found strength in his strong, warm purchase. Before leading her to the dais, he led her behind a pillar into a secret passageway. The low, block door was open. Rayn sent an anxious glance at Lancelot, who urged her to go with Shadoe.

Inside the dank passage, the iridescent glow of a wall sconce framed Shadoe's face. A small frown between his brows revealed his deep thought. Ambivalent, she looked up into his gold-flecked eyes. A tear tracked his cheek. Rayn reached up and touched his moist pain. A tremor shook Shadoe's frame, and as he captured her hand, he kissed it, then folded her in his arms. They wept. In that moment, something beautiful transpired between them. *Eden's breath.* But this time there were no bad memories, no pain. They felt only peaceful oneness. They were creating their own memories. They were one.

"Together in Christ, Rayn," Shadoe said softly against her brow.

Rayn jolted from their connection and met his tender gaze. "I love you, husband."

His eyes glistened, and his mouth tugged into that lopsided grin she'd come to covet. "I know."

She smiled amorously back. She wanted to kiss him, wanted to hear—

"I love you, Emerald Rose Rayn."

The world stopped.

So did Rayn's heart.

She couldn't speak.

"Well," he raised an eyebrow, "had I known that's all it took to silence you, I'd have said it months ago." His callused fingers tenderly captured her face.

"You weren't ready to say it then." Her mouth trembled.

"I wasn't even ready to say it three hours ago. But talking to my mother—" His voice cracked. "She made me see how precious love is, and no matter what happens, you are my godsend, Rayn. You are the emerald-eyed enchantress in my dreams."

"And you are my knight in shining armor."

Without another word, Shadoe lifted her off the floor and kissed her. Their kiss was salty, and sweet as sorrow and joy merged into a wave of passion that pervaded every thread of Rayn's being, every measured beat of her heart. She felt his fingers possessively roam the length of her, then return to weave within her tresses. Rayn pressed closer, and his arms tightened about her so she thought she'd break. When at last he gently released her, Rayn refused to let go.

"Heaven is closer than I ever imagined," Shadoe sighed against her cheek.

"And hell is just outside this door," Galahad's serious inflection interrupted them.

Shadoe turned but kept his arm about Rayn's waist. "Your gift of timing hasn't changed, friend."

Galahad ducked his head beneath the low archway and smirked. "Well, at least you married the brat."

"Aye, he has indeed, brother." Rayn held Galahad's smile a moment, then turned solemn. "We're ready."

Shadoe stopped her. "First we pray, wife."

Galahad nodded and left them.

"We've not much time, my love," Rayn whispered.

"We don't need time, My Queen; we need God." His tone was firm.

Rayn submitted—something she had promised Niamh to do. And this time, at least, it seemed to take surprisingly less effort than she had anticipated. Holding hands, they went down on their knees.

Shadoe spoke for them. "Abba Father, the great I Am, hear your children's plea. Send your angels to stand between the Pendragon legions and those of your enemies. Let all decisions in this battle against evil be done in thy name and with thy blessing. No matter who the victor is, we ask that thy will be fulfilled. Protect my beloved Rayn and keep her in the palm of thy mighty hand. One thing more, Lord God, soften her mulish nature. Amen."

Rayn was about to comment on Shadoe's last request, but Galahad returned and ushered them out. As she and Shadoe entered the hall, Rayn realized that Galahad had been right. Hell was here. Armed knights and warriors of all supportive clans hastened in every direction. Many of the chieftains had left; even now some exited the doors. The outside racket was so loud it penetrated the caer's walls.

Shadoe escorted Rayn to the dais.

"Silence," Tristam shouted.

When the quiet came, Shadoe lifted their hands high in unison. The audience cheered. His powerful baritone boomed over the chaos. "Who will fight with us against the Saxons of Morgause and the incoming Scotti?"

Rayn looked at Shadoe. He'd said Morgause instead of Mordred. What did he mean? A frightening silence ensued. Rayn looked at the spectators. Almost two hundred warriors reverently stared at them. The men looked as startled by Shadoe's declaration as she felt, especially about the Scotti. Not one questioned his revelation.

"I am with you, Pendragon!" Caithest walked forward and bowed.

One after another, the chieftains came forth and pledged their clans' fidelity. Within minutes, battle strategies were being discussed. The order and calmness among the usually argumentative clansmen defied logic. As the orders were being decided upon and implemented, Rayn realized Shadoe and her father had long had these chieftains in their corner. Everything that happened today had been ceremony, tradition, prophecy fulfilled. Exhausted and heartsick, Rayn slumped into the queen's chair and slept.

Chapter Thirty-One

THE SENTRIES WERE RIGHT. Mordred had moved north but not across Hadrian's Wall. He made camp eight miles southeast of the wall, ten miles closer to the demesne of Camelot, which was just north of the Roman wall. The Saxon King Hengist sided with Mordred. Shadoe assumed that the minor clans' union with the Pendragons had influenced Hengist's decision. He had tried for more than a year to conquer the western Celt and Briton clans. He had almost succeeded, until now.

Within twelve hours, Pendragon infantry and light cavalry marched to join the other clans' troops, two miles from Hadrian's Wall. By noon of the second day, their numbers surpassed Shadoe's expectations. Although the tribes of Pictland had yet to arrive, Shadoe knew they would come. Pendragon envoys had been sent to Mordred's camp, and an understanding reached. The battlefield would be the same as it had been seventeen years before.

For all his knowledge of Roman and Celtic warfare, Shadoe knew the Celts and Picts were more comfortable attacking in small knots. Nor were they comfortable on horseback, which worked to Shadoe's advantage since there was a shortage of war-horses. Instead, they preferred guerilla tactics and the dense wooded terrain that resembled their homeland. Thus, Shadoe and Lancelot decided to give Caithest free rein with the Celt clans. By nightfall, Caithest would occupy the forest that Mordred would enter before breaching the open, rugged fields. That would give Shadoe an advantage—he hoped.

Weary in body and mind, Shadoe crossed the threshold of his tent. Halfway across the earthen floor, he slung Excalibur on a stake within arm's reach of his fur-padded pallet. A servant had dug a small pit and set a fire. Gray puffs of smoke billowed through a vent cut into the cloth roof.

Tonight would be his only night to sleep, perhaps his last. Shadoe insisted his tent be set back from the rest. Lancelot had argued that, as high king, Shadoe needed heavy protection. Tonight, Shadoe insisted on his privacy if for no other reason than to pray and meditate upon God and his beloved Rayn.

Concerned for her welfare, Shadoe had commanded Rayn to stay back. She'd agreed. Nor did she question his order that every man, woman, and child be moved off Wind's Haven and out of the city of Ayr. He'd insisted they move into the hills north of Ayr and that Caer Camelot be vacated and the gates locked. Nay, she'd not argued a word.

While he tugged off his boots, Shadoe focused on Rayn. She had woven herself into every fiber of his heart, mind, and soul. Since the wedding, they'd not had a moment alone—mayhap poetic justice. What Shadoe desired most, he might never experience: making love to his godsend, Rayn.

More than ever he felt grateful for the pledge Merlin had extracted from him sixteen months before. Scripture said that once God forgave a sin, he literally forgot that sin and buried it in the deepest ocean.

Shadoe now clung to that promise and had put his carnal indiscretions behind him. He felt renewed, washed as clean as the virgin wool he slept upon. He could no longer see the faces of those women or imagine their caresses or pleasured sighs. Shadoe saw but one face, felt one caress, and heard one pleasured sigh, Rayn's. Yet he worried. After all of their stolen moments and passionate embraces, doubt squirmed its way into his heart. Did Rayn desire him as much as he desired her?

Closing his eyes, he imagined Rayn's long, silky fingers grasp his hand and urge him toward her. Shadoe turned and gazed into the smoldering fire and saw a ribbon of blue among crimson tresses.

"Oh, my beloved enchantress! Were it but possible to touch you with my thoughts, let you know my heart and my fervor for you. I'd beg thee come, Emerald Rose, come to me here now, tonight."

A vulture screeched on the brisk air, jarring Shadoe back to reality. Even now Morgause seemed to mock him. Well, she might take Camelot, but the harpy would never have Emerald Rose Rayn. Never.

Shadoe knew not how much time had elapsed while he prayed that God would protect and rule among his people in this controversy. But weary, he stripped down to his breechclout. He shivered. Autumn's air hinted of the coming winter. He slipped beneath the pile of furs but remained chilled and alone. Only one person could fill the cold void. Rayn.

He envisioned the first day he'd spied her in the stone pool of Loch Lady, a white wet chemise hugging her sensuous curves. He saw her burnished curls cascading about her captivating green eyes, freckled face, and firm bosom. Shadoe's blood seared at the thought of her, and he pressed his musings elsewhere but to no avail. Praying for sleep, he fell into a fitful slumber and dreamt of his enchantress, Rayn.

∽

Shadoe jolted awake. He'd not flinched a muscle, but his heart thudded fiercely against his ribs. The fire had been stoked and now cast shadows on the tent's walls. Shadoe couldn't believe his keen senses had not detected the first footfall. He'd known before that sound, sensed her invisible essences like lovers do. The tent door flapped softly. Autumn air tinged with honeysuckle oil tickled his nostrils. Turning the slightest degree, Shadoe eyed Excalibur. Fire glow reflected off the jeweled hilt. The staff of Aaron leaned against the stake.

Shadoe blinked and sat upright. Poised before the fire, her unclothed beauty robed in crimson curls that swung past the lush curve of her hips, stood his enchantress. Shadoe drew a sharp breath. *Please don't let this be a dream.*

"You are not dreaming, husband." Rayn glided toward him like a misty apparition.

Rayn had not meant to awaken her husband. Her plan had been to slip beneath his covers and sleep in his arms. That alone would have been enough—for now. Rayn had dodged hundreds of sleeping soldiers and armed sentries undiscovered, but one step within Shadoe's tent and he'd roused. Indeed, he was the Merdyn's son.

Still fearing she was an apparition, Shadoe didn't move or speak. Rayn knelt and pressed her hot palm to his upper torso. Her fingertips toyed with the tensed muscles and sparse hairs across his chest. Shadoe trembled from her touch and marveled at her enchantment. *What if she's Morgause?* He tried to remain impassive, but his body betrayed him.

Desperate, he closed his hand about her fine-boned wrist, while her magic fingers blazed a smoldering fire across his ribs.

"You're at Camelot," he choked out, becoming lost in her smile, her scent, and her touch.

"Am I? Is that where you desire me to be, Sire?"

"Nay, my enchantress." *How could this be? I no more than wished Rayn here and . . .* Her sweet perfumed hair tumbled across his face and chest. Shadoe reached out, intertwining her silky tendrils with blunt fingers, while his right hand cradled her fine-chiseled chin. Shadoe looked wonderingly into her lovely face. He examined her button nose, her widow's peak, and the delicate vein between her burnished arched brows. He had memorized every freckle, every laugh line, every facet of her body he'd ever been allowed to see. Joy lit within him.

"You disobeyed me, wife," he snarled, feigning anger.

Her mouth trembled. Her lashes fanned her crimson-stained cheeks, and she lowered her head at his reprisal. "Forgive me, husband. I couldn't abide being without you. I thought you'd be pleased. I thought to hear you call me, thought you wanted . . . me." She pulled away as if to leave.

Shadoe held her possessively in place. "Glory! I want you more than the air I breathe! I thought you'd gone daft when you didn't argue my order to stay home."

"Whist, really?" Her eyes burned like emeralds. Her pouting mouth spooned into a smile, revealing pearled teeth.

"Aye," his husky voice exposed his ardor.

"Is not my home wherever you are, Shadoe un Hollo Tors?"

"Aye. Now come to our marriage bed, wife." Shadoe tossed the coverlet of furs aside and drew her to him. The corners of Shadoe's generous mouth curved ever so slightly, roguishly. His amber gleam lured her like a sparkling jewel. Accepting his invitation, she slid between the furs and into his muscle-taut arms. Her chilled limbs relished his masculine warmth as his strapping, lean body molded into hers. When their thirsting lips melded, she felt his breath hitch and a low rumble escape his chest. Rayn's hands sifted through his hair, and she tugged the faded blue ribbon that had replaced the leather thong at his neck. His dark thick locks were freed. Delirious with need of him, she rose up and kissed his brow, temples, and the cleft of his strong jaw.

"Oh, my beloved brat," he growled and recaptured Rayn's mouth.

The tender teasing of his hands stirred intense pleasure within her. Willingly, she surrendered body and heart to this strong, gentle man whose every caress whispered his passionate love for her. Rayn moved with Shadoe in the intimate, beautiful dance Yahweh had long ordained a husband and wife to share. Never had she thought love could be so glorious. From this moment on, God willing, Rayn was home.

∽

Trumpets blared! Men shouted!

"Rayn, wake-up!" Shadoe untangled himself from her embrace and leapt to his feet.

She bolted upright. Dawn had not yet broken. Clutching the furs to her breasts she looked about in alarm. "What is it?" She reached for her chemise.

"Trouble!" Shadoe pitched her garments into her lap, and then added her mail-shirt and staff.

The tent door flapped open and Perceval rushed in. When he spotted Rayn beneath Shadoe's furs, his astonishment lasted a second. He sent her a wicked grin, and then addressed Shadoe.

"Hengist rides toward the wall," Perceval announced.

"With Mordred?" Shadoe tugged on his leathers.

"Aye. But Mordred divided his army into four cohorts moving about a mile apart from Hengist."

"Toward the wall as well?" Shadoe caught up Excalibur.

"Aye." Perceval glanced at Rayn, who sheepishly grinned as she pulled her clothes on beneath the covers.

"I thought you ordered our queen to stay home?" The knight scratched his red-whiskered jaw.

"Humph, and I thought you knew her so well," Shadoe snorted.

"Enough!" Rayn groused, but a smile touched her eyes.

"Oh, I know her alright. Tristam lost the bet and owes me a piece of silver." Perceval winked at Rayn as she tied back her curls and tucked them into her cap.

"Whist! Now I'm the subject of bets, am I?" she muttered, tugging on her breeches beneath the furs.

"Aye, you've been for years, my Queen, and I'm the richer for it." Perceval chuckled.

Shadoe wanted to laugh, but serious matters pressed him. First, his wife. Noting she was nearly dressed, he exited the tent with Perceval. "I need a moment with Rayn. You must not tell Lancelot she's here."

"Aye, he'd die of distress if he knew." Perceval nodded.

"I know." Shadoe scowled at his friend. "Find Rayn's mare and then round up fifty of our best to escort her to safety. I want you with her."

Perceval agreed and took off. Drawing a breath of resolve, Shadoe sent up a desperate prayer and entered his tent. Rayn had just finished fastening her short sword to her waist.

"I know the wall well, husband. I'll take foot soldiers and cavalry southeast toward—"

"You will return to the hills with Percy." He moved upon her so fast she hadn't a chance to divert his fast claim to her forearms.

"Don't jest, Shadoe. Da is ill. You need me." She jerked free of his left hand.

"I need you alive. We all do." He captured her firm-set jaw and forced her stubborn gaze to his. "Our success greatly depends upon the Pendragon cohorts and the Celt and Briton clans' loyalty to you as the Pendragon. Above all, you must remain alive and out of harm's way."

"Whist! My place is on the front line at your side for I am a warrior queen, I am!"

"You will obey me, brat!" Shadoe demanded.

"On this matter I—"

A flaming arrow hit their tent.

"What the—" Shadoe snatched up his gear and dragged Rayn out of the burning tent. Arrows flew into the camp from all directions, setting alight tents and supplies. Within seconds, the entire camp blazed in the breaching dawn. Unarmed men fell about them.

Rayn clutched Shadoe's sleeve. "I don't understand. How did they break through?"

"We've a traitor among us!" Shadoe broke off an arrow from a cart. "This is a Briton arrow." He fingered the precise fletching. "No doubt, Prince Laxton, scion of Can un Scye."

Rayn gaped at his quick conclusion. "But he pledged his clan's loyalty!"

"Aye, and Galahad saw him with one of Mordred's men shortly after your coronation. Now stay put, love." Shadoe stood and shouted orders at his bowmen shooting at the unseen enemy.

Mayhem exploded through the camp. The stench of burning flesh turned Rayn's stomach. One warrior engulfed in flames fled past her. Rayn's instinct was to go after him, but she reluctantly obeyed Shadoe. Saxon riders attempted to storm the Pendragon camp. Celt and Britons pushed them back. Crouched behind the cart, Rayn saw Lancelot emerge from his tent.

"God be merciful!" Lancelot's voice roared above the clamor. He looked at Shadoe and spotted Rayn. Dodging arrows, he made his way toward her.

"Da!" Rayn motioned him to stay back. A Saxon rider leaped the camp's perimeter and galloped through, knocking over the cart and Rayn with it. Her staff flew out of her reach as she rolled, but not quickly enough. Her left foot was pinned by the tumbling cart. Searing pain shot through her ankle. Sword drawn, the rider thrust his blade at her.

Lancelot leaped between her and the Saxon's sword. Rayn felt the weight of her father collapse on her and heard his painful cry. Overhead the Saxon jerked his bloody blade free. Before he could slay Rayn, someone knocked him from his horse. Shadoe brandished Excalibur and plunged the great blade into the Saxon's heart. Coming to Rayn's aid, Shadoe rolled Lancelot off from her. Galahad arrived and lifted the cart off her foot. Order had replaced chaos. Meantime, the Saxons were being forced back by the great number of Celts and Britons who had come to the Pendragons' rescue.

"Are you all right?" Shadoe pulled her into his embrace.

"Aye." Even as pain shot through her ankle, she limped to her father and fell to her knees. Lancelot lay on his side, blood trickling from his mouth.

"Da!" Rayn eased his head into her lap.

"Dau-ghter?" Lancelot touched her tears.

"Aye, Da, I'm here."

He coughed. "You never . . . did listen well."

"Oh, Da, I'm so sorry I—"

Lancelot shook his head. "'Tis all right. . . . You love him. . . . I'm glad!"

Shadoe examined Lancelot's wound, and Rayn turned pleading eyes upon her husband. His grief-veiled eyes met hers as he shook his head. Shadoe and Galahad knelt beside the great knight. His eyes dimming, Lancelot smiled lovingly at each of them, then looked to Shadoe.

"You were right, Shadoe. No man . . . can redeem the past. But the present . . . and future . . . belong to both of you." He placed Rayn's hand in Shadoe's. Releasing one last breath, Lancelot's head rolled back in Rayn's lap.

"Nooooo!" she wailed and drew her father to her. Shadoe and Galahad embraced her.

About them dawn broke. Their swords and clothes spattered with blood, Tristam and Perceval knelt and paid tribute to their friend, neither holding back their sorrow.

For several minutes, the world spun in slow motion. For Rayn, life came to an unbearable stop. Cradling Lancelot, she wept as she'd never wept before. Not even Merlin's departure had torn her heart so wretchedly as Lancelot's death. Lancelot du Lac, the bravest knight of the Round Table, had been so much more. He had been Rayn's appointed guardian, confidant, friend, and most of all, her father in this world.

They were now surrounded by warriors, both Celt and Briton, who knelt in tribute to the departed Lancelot. Rayn felt Galahad's strong grip on her forearm, felt his tremors of remorse. She was eternally grateful that her brother and father had spent the last few months together.

Willfully surfacing from her shock, Rayn realized that as she cradled Lancelot, Shadoe held her, rocking her like a child. His strength, compassion, and love overwhelmed her. She felt his whiskered jaw against her cheek, and his tears mingled with hers.

When Tristam signaled for Lancelot's remains to be taken away, Shadoe drew her to her feet. They embraced, and then urgent resolve took hold of Rayn. This was war! Lancelot would not stand about grieving, even over her. She eased from Shadoe and snatched up her staff. Rayn found her mare and untied her breastplate, leather jerkin, and shield from the pommel.

Shadoe was on her. "What do you think you're doing?"

Rayn turned about, jaw locked, eyes tearless. "Taking Da's place, I am."

"Your death won't bring Lance back."

"I know. But other than during his last battle, my mother always fought beside Arthur. I'll do the same, I will. I *will* fight with you, husband!"

Despite Shadoe's disfavor, Rayn got her way. She commanded Lancelot's legion, and within the hour, the Pendragon Britons charged forth to war.

∽

Leading their army of Saxons and Jutes, Morgause rode astride her white stallion. She glanced at her son alongside her. "You are different, Mordred."

"Am I now?"

"Aye. You are more sure of yourself."

"Is that not what you've always wanted, Mother?"

He met her wary gaze and held it firm, something he'd dared not do in the past. He reined the shudder threatening to crack his confident demeanor since he now saw Morgause for the demonic creature she had become. The cloud of deceit had been lifted; he saw everything with new eyes—his eyes. He saw that she knew her demons no longer controlled him.

Mordred realized whatever had happened between him and Shadoe in that alleyway was the cause for this new insight. He'd not outwardly admitted it, but Mordred felt gratitude to his half brother. For the first time in two decades, Mordred controlled his thoughts and actions. Not that Morgause still couldn't influence him, but he had the will to resist her, and that clearly unhinged her. She hadn't confronted him, however, until now.

What was it she feared? Surely not him. Yet who else? Unless it was the one supernatural being he'd dared not think about in her presence. Yahweh?

"Yes," she said quietly, jolting him from his revelation. "'Tis what I want."

He nodded and looked away.

"You still want to rule with me, scion?" She reached over and patted his wrist with a talon-like hand, her long yellow nails digging into his flesh.

Mordred glanced down to see what he'd loathed. She was either about to shape-shift, or her ability to conceal her true nature was becoming harder to control.

"Of course, Mother." He dared not think differently, and certainly he couldn't review his plan to defeat her. She'd know. But his heart, he realized, she could not touch. Hence he tried to think with his heart and the hatred for Morgause that flooded it. In time, he would have his revenge. Meanwhile, something new and inviting knocked at his heart, and with it came a peace he'd yet to fully comprehend or experience. Mordred sensed he needed to open his heart's door to let this loving presence enter. He also knew to do so meant his plan for revenge would be squelched. That was one thing he wasn't about to relinquish.

As he urged his commanders on toward the field of battle, a breathless rider galloped up to him.

"Sire, our flank was wheeling through the woods at your command. Then in an instant Celts were all about us!"

∽

Shadoe's knowledge of his half brother's tactical maneuvers proved profitable even before the battle began. Mordred's plan for his flanks to occupy the wood that encompassed the battlefield was squelched. Clad lightly in their new design called chainmaille, Caithest's war bands struck Mordred and Hengist fast and hard. The Saxons, trained to fight in the open, were encumbered with their long swords and shields among the thick bracken and trees. This onslaught left the Saxons with heavy casualties and running amok. They would no sooner escape one trap only to be waylaid by another. And more oft than not, fleeing in fright from the Celt's painted faces and wild, maniac war cries.

Even at the Britons' arrival, the Celts continued their ambushes, upsetting Mordred's organized legion. Shadoe didn't have to hunt down Prince Laxton. The defector had been beheaded by his father Can un Scye. The proud chieftain did not take treason lightly, especially from his son.

While Shadoe dwelt on family, he prayed God had given his half brother a new heart. But when the factions met on the battlefield, Mordred sat in the forefront astride his black war-horse. Morgause sat at his right on her white stallion, and Hengist to his left on a large chestnut war-horse.

The Picts had yet to surface. Caithest had already done a great work in taking a large force out of the way. But in plain truth, Shadoe was greatly outnumbered. He also realized, though, that the key strategist was not Mordred, but Hengist; and Hengist had one flaw. Saxon pride. Shadoe knew the Saxon's war tactics were no match for his Roman-based strategy and, above all, his God.

Galahad, Tristam, and Perceval led separate cohorts of the Roman-crafted army. Beside him, Rayn sat high in her saddle, her demeanor no longer of a daughter who'd lost her father but strong and deter-mined. She had painted her face, looking every bit the strong-willed Pict shield maiden. Reaching over, he encircled the hand that gripped her Roman pommel. "Rayn?"

She turned her winsome face and smiled. The love that coursed be-tween them made words unnecessary; they didn't even share a *Breath of Eden* thought. In unison, they urged their horses out now, riding in front of the line.

"Almighty God protects us!" Rayn shouted repeatedly to their warriors.

The men loudly chanted her prayer and beat swords on shields.

Shadoe raised his hand and signaled the troops.

Pipers blew a shrill battlefield chant that for centuries had frozen the blood of the foes of Roman legions. Across the rugged terrain, Saxon arrows arched through the autumn air. Closing in blocks, the men of Camelot dropped to a knee and raised their shields to deflect the arrows.

Briton archers, arranged to the right and left of the infantry, returned flight for flight, and the forces of Mordred made their first charge.

Shadoe feared that the fortification of men who had trained, but never been in battle, would not hold. But these men were fighting for their wives, children, and lands and to pay back the past crimes against their families. Unlike Mordred's and Hengist's soldiers, these men were fired with a need for retribution. And they would have it.

Never had Shadoe engaged in such a fierce battle. Men fell like tumbling blocks. Within two hours, both the Briton and Saxon cavalries had become scattered remnants. The skirmish continued, most of it in hand-to-hand combat. No more than scant minutes passed between waves. When the Picts arrived, their savage cries and painted naked bodies sent hundreds of Mordred's men fleeing right into the Celts' eager hands. Victory seemed close. Then Hengist charged forth with his Saxon raiders.

War was hell!

His hair matted to his head, cold sweat streamed between Shadoe's ribs. Beyond exhaustion, he relied upon discipline to replace fear. Memories of Merlin's repeatedly walking him through paces of self-defense had fused every fiber of sinew and bone. He reacted before being attacked. Wield, thrust, twist, jerk, and when necessary, duck.

Shadoe pulled Excalibur from a Saxon's belly and turned on another. Beside him, Rayn fought with the bravado of a seasoned warrior. Other than a few cuts and bruises, she'd managed to stay unscathed. He winked at her, and they continued to fight, guarding each other's backs. A flurry of Saxon arrows rained overhead. Shadoe rolled behind a boulder to find himself without Rayn and pinned down by Saxons. By the time he'd slain them, the arrows had stopped. His left arm injured, Shadoe called out for Rayn. She was gone.

∽๑∾

Rayn had no idea how she had gotten separated from Shadoe. Mounting her horse, she searched for him. Instead, she encountered Mordred. To her ire, the man smiled upon her and rode off. Rayn tried to pursue him, but the enemy blocked her path. Breaking backs and necks with her staff, slicing limbs with her sword, Rayn barely had time to catch her breath. Cries of the living and dying became the unholy song of the savage arena.

Come midday, Morgause's demonic voice rasped above the din. Rayn spotted her on a knoll above the battlefield and recognized the sorceress's druid chant. Morgause had cast a spell. Minutes later, a ghastly smoke descended south of Rayn over Tristam's cohort. A wounded Celt told Rayn that Tristam's men were crumbling to the sod, wheezing for breath. When Rayn reached his cohort, Tristam was dead. Only moments before, a mighty wind had blown down from the highlands and extinguished the poisonous air. Rayn knew the wind was God's breath, but too late for Tristam. Personal loss steeled her heart. *Why Tristam?*

She called to Tristam's piper and had him blow the signal to pull the ranks. These more seasoned warriors began fighting their way back together. Rayn then told the piper to blow the charge and led them out toward the rocks where she had seen Morgause. Bareback on a white stallion and wielding a blood-drenched pike in one hand, Morgause charged Rayn.

The young queen brandished her sword at the sorceress but instead swatted air.

Morgause cackled. "You missed, Warrior Queen."

Rayn turned her mare about to find three likenesses of Morgause. Worse yet, not one of Rayn's fellow warriors seemed to see what she saw. Despite the cold, the witch wore a sheer white palla decorated with the blood of her victims. Morgause's long blond hair fanned about her like wildfire. Her beauty was hypnotic. No doubt, those who'd died on her pike had died smiling. Rayn forced herself to look away.

"Which one am I? Or am I even here, brat? 'Tis one of Shadoe's endearments, is it not?" Morgause goaded. "Or do you prefer *my enchantress?*"

Although unnerved by Morgause's intimate knowledge about Shadoe, Rayn's faith and warrior nature sharpened. She galloped toward the apparition on the right and swung her staff. Striking air, Rayn almost toppled from her saddle.

"Shadoe's dead! Slain by my scion. Sliced in half with Excalibur!"

"Noooo!" Rayn screamed and aimed for the next Morgause. That witch evaporated.

"Surrender, Pendragon!"

"Never!" Rayn brought her mare about and faced the last apparition.

Pike raised, Morgause rushed her. Rayn watched the oncoming specter with hypnotic calm.

"Rayn!" The call shattered Morgause's spell. Rayn twisted to her right. On foot, Perceval tore after Morgause. The knight took aim and sliced the sorceress's right shoulder. With a blood-curdling wail, Morgause pierced the knight below his chest plate, then vanished.

Clutching his belly, Perceval collapsed.

"Percy!" Rayn swerved to dismount.

A frightening war cry shattered the dusky sky. Hundreds of Scotti rained down on the theater of war. Before Rayn could alight, a Scotti leaped at her. With a blow of his battle-axe, he sliced her mare's throat. Blood spurted. The dapple-gray mare gasped and buckled. Rayn toppled with her steed. Pain exploded in her head. Darkness swallowed Rayn, and she plummeted into a black, cold void.

Chapter Thirty-Two

IN A CLEARING JUST yards from the battle, the brothers faced off. They'd sparred for nearly an hour but had slain more Scotti than made personal strikes.

"It's over, Mordred," Shadoe panted. Braced against a boulder, he kept Excalibur level with his brother's chest.

Dueling with one hand, Mordred's weariness was evident. His chest plate heaved from the effort. "Bah, what's a few Scotti?" he jeered.

"Nothing if we combine troops. Hengist already did."

"Aye. And still you are outnumbered."

"As are you. So join us."

"Mother wouldn't like that." Mordred advanced.

"I don't care about Morgause. You're free of her demons, brother." Shadoe hoped his words were true.

"Aye. It's been a challenge to convince the hag that she still rules my will." He glanced through the solidifying fog. "No doubt she's nearby. She always is."

Worn-out, the men circled each other but watched their backs as the enemy closed in. Mordred moved onto a plot of blood-free earth.

"We are brothers, Mordred. We can unite. Be one."

"Impossible." Mordred lunged with his short sword. He missed.

"Nothing is impossible with God."

"I killed your wife's parents, little brother. She loathes me."

Shadoe's left arm ached fiercely. He wanted to lower his sword, but the determined look on Mordred's sweat-matted face kept Shadoe on guard. "Rayn knows about Morgause's demonic hold over you. She realizes you weren't responsible. I admit it will take some time, but she'll forgive you."

Mordred snorted. "It changes nothing. I murdered. Deceived. I'm a vile, sinful creature."

Maintaining marginal distance, Shadoe grieved. Mordred was a man seeking forgiveness.

"If there was a chance with Iona. . . . She thinks me unsalvageable. Once . . ." His hard features mellowed.

Shadoe had no time to conceal his aggrieved expression. "Mordred—"

"Tell me!" He stalked forward, wielding his blade.

Shadoe held his stand. "I'm sorry, brother. She died three days ago—"

"How?" Mordred swiped at Shadoe's injured arm.

Iron clashed iron.

Shadoe pushed Mordred back. "With my mother, Niamh. Morgause—"

"Morgause, what?" he snarled and advanced.

"She pulled them with her off the caer's mezzanine. Iona died."

"Nooooo!" Mordred screamed and ran past Shadoe into the battle to a rocky hillock.

Shadoe gave him chase. Mordred lunged and swung at every man in reach, even Saxons. His ferocious cries shattered the air. Those within hearing distance of him stopped and stared. The Scotti watched with alarm.

Mordred fell to his knees, dropped his sword, and screeched to the heavens. "Lord God, Yahweh, help me! Forgive this wretched creature!"

Shadoe went down on one knee. His grip on Excalibur slackened. Alert to the advancing Scotti, he clutched Mordred's tremulous shoulder. He gazed compassionately at Mordred's penitent features. The older man had no idea how to receive his Savior. Shadoe advised him, "Ask him inside and to rule your life."

Through violent sobs Mordred cried out, "Jesu, come into my heart—be Lord of my life!"

Looking into his half brother's tear-filled eyes, Shadoe saw and recognized the Mordred of his youth. Mordred was free of guilt, free of Morgause. In this miraculous moment of Mordred's redemption, God's angels stood between them and their enemies.

"God loves you, my brother." Shadoe nodded with reassurance.

"I know." Mordred embraced him and they held tight.

"I love you, Shadoe," Mordred choked out. "Always have."

"And I love you, brother."

"Now, we will join allegiance and force these heathens back into the sea!" Mordred slapped Shadoe's shoulders with his good hand and gestured to stand.

Hoofbeats shattered their sanctuary. A veil of dark evil settled around them. Mordred tore Excalibur from Shadoe's hand and knocked him over. Stunned, Shadoe looked up. With a pike clutched above her head, Morgause bore down upon them. Mordred thrust Excalibur into his mother. A screech ripped from Morgause's lungs. She toppled off her horse and into Mordred's arms.

Shadoe scrambled to his half brother. Shoving Morgause aside, Shadoe reached to pull the spear from Mordred's chest.

"No." Mordred coughed blood. "Let me go . . . home."

Shadoe knelt beside him.

"Is the whore dead?" Mordred struggled to look past Shadoe's shoulder.

"Aye." Shadoe brushed a curl from his brother's clammy face.

Mordred gripped Shadoe's wrist. "Find Rayn, brother. Protect her . . . love her. Camelot will cease . . . if you don't have the Rose—"

His head flopped back. Mordred was dead.

"Until we meet in heaven, my brother." Shadoe closed Mordred's eyes and drew a breath of resolve. He glanced about. Scotti overran the battleground. Saxons, Celts, and Britons fled in unison. Even the vicious Picts appeared outnumbered. Turning, Shadoe took up Excalibur's hilt and pulled the bloody blade from Morgause's belly.

A demonic growl and rancid breath discharged from the creature's lips. Blood gushing from her wound, Morgause bounded to her feet. Although her left arm had been detached from her shoulder, the demon lived. Shadoe met her malevolent yellow orbs. She intended to shape shift. Adrenaline renewed his fatigued limbs.

"To hell with you, Auntie!" With a mighty roar Shadoe struck the mighty sword at Morgause and sliced off her head. Her neck teetered on her shoulders. Disbelief flickered in the hag's eyes. Her head fell with her body but hit the earth first. Shadoe still didn't believe her dead. He held his stance with Excalibur aimed at her heart. God intervened. Lightning shot from the sky, and Morgause's corpse burst into flames. Then a heavenly breath scattered her ashes.

Before Shadoe could collect himself, he spotted a band of Scotti coming straight at him. "Hail, Christian brother!" Galahad scrambled up the hillock and put his spine to Shadoe's.

Swords flourished, the two men turned in unison, counting off a dozen Scotti and more coming.

"Aye, it's about time you cover my backside!" Shadoe winked over his shoulder, thankful for Galahad's appearance.

"Together in Christ!" Galahad shouted.

"To God be the glory!" Shadoe roared, and they charged the enemy.

∽

As her shock ebbed, Rayn surveyed the battlefield of trampled heather, ravaged and painted scarlet with the sacrificial blood of countless warriors. The blood had flowed so profusely, the earth no longer drank of it. The sweet, sickening perfume of death punctuated the stagnant air. Vultures and crows circled and roosted in standing timbers and bushes. Within seconds, bile churned her belly. Clenching her midsection, Rayn vomited until dry heaves made her breathless and weak.

For the longest while, she huddled on the scarlet sod, her knees pulled to her chest as she cradled herself in empty solace. A few feet away lay Perceval's lifeless body. He'd gone home to Jesu. Her mare's fatal fall had saved Rayn's life. To the enemy, it had appeared Rayn had been pinned and died beneath the weight of the slaughtered horse. When she had come around, Rayn realized the mare had shielded her during the battle and kept her warm. She'd no idea how long she had been unconscious: hours, days? No doubt, a great deal of time had passed.

Her helm and cap missing, Rayn patted her chilled head. Half of her braided hair was gone! No doubt a Scotti trophy. At least they'd stopped at her shoulders. She smoothed her shortened curls the best she could and thanked God she still had her head.

Smearing her tears with the back of her hand, Rayn glanced skyward. Wisps of fog drifted across the moorlands. She could hear the roar of the sea less than a mile off. With day glow fading, the dank air had turned frigid. A tattered wolf's hide lay beside her mare. Rayn snatched it up and draped her cold shoulders. Summoning courage, she took her staff, leaned into it, and struggled to her feet. Her limbs had long gone asleep, and it was minutes before the pinpricks stopped.

Even with the support of the staff, pain burned from her left calf to her swollen ankle. She hoped she hadn't broken it. Then again, why care? If a Scotti or Saxon found her, she'd be raped, killed, or taken hostage. Still, her God-given desire to survive overcame her despair, and she limped northwest toward Camelot, toward home.

As she approached the battleground's core, triumphant Scotti collected the bodies of their fallen warriors while pilfering weapons and currency from the dead. Dodging between the nonliving and field bracken, Rayn eluded the adversary. She listened and watched—for signs of life among her slain clansmen, for a familiar face. Shadoe's face. She found neither. Several times Scotti came within view of her, yet somehow she went unnoticed. Halting mid-step, security embraced her. Rayn walked in a circle of light, the Scotti blind to her presence.

Recalling Shadoe's story of escape from Belizar, she anxiously looked about, and although she saw no angels, Rayn knew she was not alone. God escorted her through this valley of death. Her faith soared on wings. *Thank you, Jesu!*

Tears tracked her cheeks, and she trekked until a comfortable distance from Hadrian's Wall. The remnants of war were behind her. The fog deepened. Night settled in. She was no longer guided by God's light. He'd brought her safely past her enemy, and she praised him.

Rayn's ankle throbbed fiercely. She needed to make camp, to rest. Tomorrow would be another matter. Unless she found a horse, she'd be walking. Even with the staff, her ankle would not support her much longer. Rayn chastised herself for not hours ago taking one of the warhorses wandering the battlefield.

Limping on, she suppressed the tremor of her fingers and clutched the talisman beneath her tunic. "What now, my Savior? I am a queen without a people, a daughter without my da, a friend without friends. Most of all, I am a woman without her lover, a wife without her husband, without the godsend you gave to me. And yet I sense he lives."

"Oh, my beloved Shadoe!" her voice quaked. "I love you so much. What am I to do, how am I to go on? Where are you?"

No answer came, least not what she desired. Hooves pounded the sod. Rayn stepped beneath the canopy of an oak and waited. She wondered if her ears deceived her. She heard it again. A rider or riders approached from the south. Saxons or Scotti? Were they on to her? Her right hand flew to her leather sheath. *A fool am I! Weapons everywhere miles back. Here I stand without so much as a sword, I do!*

Leaning against the tree, she removed the six-inch stinger from her waist cinch. Her eyes threatened to tear, and she clutched her only heirloom from her mother. Well, she had the stinger and her staff. They would suffice to secure for her the transportation she needed. Clenching the stinger's blade between her teeth, Rayn surveyed the empty Roman highway. She climbed the tree and straddled the lowest branch.

The fog limited vision to a few yards. Rayn would use it to her advantage, she would. A lone rider she concluded. He would never know what hit him. Minutes passed before she heard the rhythmic clack of hooves on stone. Restricted by the fog, the rider cantered. Rayn's belly knotted. Her mouth dried. Her palms were slick with cold sweat. No matter how many times she'd used a weapon, it was always the same. She had no intention of taking the man's life, but only God knew if he was friend or foe.

The horse snorted, and a large, black silhouette surfaced from the mist. With all her strength Rayn slammed the staff's blunt end against the man's chest. The dull chime of metal resounded. *Demon's dung! He's in chainmaille!*

She heard his grunt of shock as he swayed in the saddle. The warrior grabbed her staff and tugged hard. Set off balance, Rayn dropped on the rider. Encircling her legs about him, she held tight and clutched his head, her fingers going for his eyes. They toppled off the horse and rolled.

A Gaelic curse burned his lips, but the downed man didn't give Rayn an inch. He latched onto her injured ankle. Rayn cried out in pain and buckled. The outlander pulled her toward him and rose to his knees. Rayn's good foot struck him in the groin.

An agonizing grunt burst from his lungs. The stranger clutched his lower abdomen. "Glory, brat! Is that how you greet your battle-weary husband?"

Her stinger arched to strike, Rayn dropped it and scurried onto her knees to him. "Shadoe?"

"Aye," he rasped with a lopsided smile as he gripped his vitals, and then spying her shortened hair choked out, "Your—prize—gone!"

A prayer of thanks rang heavenward from Rayn's heart. She knew that voice, knew that smile. "'Twill grow back." With wild abandon she fell on Shadoe, knocking him down.

"My arm!" Shadoe winced.

"Whist! Sorry, I am." She crawled off from him.

"Don't you dare!" he growled. Snatching her to him, Shadoe sought Rayn's mouth with a fervor that miraculously numbed her senses, including the pain from her throbbing ankle.

Chapter Thirty-Three

SHADOE AND RAYN RODE through the night, lurking in the dense timbers whenever they spotted bands of Scotti. They knew the battle was lost. The Scotti had seen to that. There were no Pendragon warriors to cheer home on the morrow. Nor would there be any immediate Saxon invasions. The Celts and Britons had fled south, leaving the lowlands unguarded. Shadoe relayed to Rayn what he knew: that the Picts would regroup to defend their lands against the Scotti from the Isle of Eire. Thankful to be together, they didn't question God's plans. And although they didn't discuss it, Rayn knew in her heart the demesne of Camelot would be no more.

At dawn, they reached the moorlands that melded into the smoldering ruins of Ayr. Frost carpeted the terrain but could not blot out the fires and the pungent scent of death. The high stone walls built to protect the Pendragon clan were rubble.

Rayn gasped at the devastation. "Thank our Lord God most everyone left." She turned to Shadoe. "You knew this would happen."

He solemnly nodded. "I felt it strongly."

"We should search for survivors, we should."

"There aren't any," he said with a finality that sent a shiver through her.

Destrier pranced nervously and snorted. Shadoe and Rayn turned in the saddle. Echo bounded out from beneath a clump of Birchwood. Rayn moved to dismount.

Shadoe restrained her. "Wait!" Behind Echo, a large gray wolf cleared the timber. Its ears back, hackles raised, the wild creature growled at their presence.

"It would seem Echo has a mate," Shadoe said softly.

Rayn nodded, delighted and saddened at the prospect.

Echo ran over to her male companion and submissively licked the wolf's muzzle.

"It would also appear she's got the submissive part right." Shadoe chuckled.

Rayn pinched Shadoe's waist. He smirked at her. The male wolf returned Echo's affection. Rayn smiled, recalling that wolves mate for life. So Echo had found her life companion. Rayn and Shadoe watched them for the longest while. When the wolves turned to leave, Echo looked back as if to say farewell. Rayn sniffed tears and waved goodbye to another lady who'd touched her life. Shadoe hugged Rayn to him. She could only fathom the escapades Shadoe and Echo had shared. A moment later, he turned Destrier about, and they galloped to the bay's shore, toward Caer Camelot.

The weather was the oddest Rayn had ever witnessed. Although the damp air barely stirred on shore, across the bay, the heavens blazed with emerald spirals of light and gigantic pewter clouds. An ethereal tempest churned the dark seas to swells of thirty or more feet.

Rayn alighted from Destrier and limped to where the causeway from the shoreline was submerged beneath the cresting seas. Beyond the sinking road, the Isle of Wind's Haven and Caer Camelot became tangled with tendrils of shimmering green light from the imminent storm. She feared Morgause had resurrected and cast a spell upon Wind's Haven. Rayn realized that like Ayris, Camelot was about to vanish.

"'Tis fading away, it is!"

Shadoe dismounted and stood behind her. Tenderly, he drew her into his embrace and pressed his lips to her cropped hair. "Aye, so 'twas ordained."

"You knew?" She turned in his arms.

"'Twas an insight God gave to me."

"But what purpose will it serve to take our home?"

He kissed the tears from her cheeks. "It was never ours, Rayn. But I vow that Wind's Haven and Caer Camelot will be returned to our descendants and will be the birthplace of greatness and of righteousness."

"But God is destroying it, he is." She looked back at Wind's Haven.

"Mayhap, or he's just moving it," he gestured to the sea. "Among the isles of southern Caledonia."

Hoping that was so, Rayn stared at the isle, which became harder to discern amidst the thickening mist. "What of Merlin's scrolls?"

"I have them." He gestured to his satchels slung over his saddle. "At least the ones he asked me to save."

Rayn took comfort in the shelter of Shadoe's arms, and they watched as a green cloak fell across the majestic tors and vales of the Isle of Wind's Haven. Shadoe's jaw trembled against her brow, and his tears wet her temple. Reaching up, she caressed his blue-shadowed face. Shadoe took her hand and pressed it to his lips. For all his lack of sentimentality, it gave her comfort to know he, too, would miss Camelot.

"Da said that although you loved Caer Camelot, you said it was nothing more than cold stones, that the love of God and family warmed those stones and Camelot would forever live on in your heart."

"Aye." He held her tighter.

"Do you still believe that?"

He nodded against her brow. "More than ever, my beloved enchantress."

Rayn could not suppress a shudder of loss and regret.

"We must leave now." He brushed a tendril from her tear-stained face.

"But we can stay and rebuild Ayr, we can."

He shook his head and noted the approaching storm. "If we stay, we will encounter the effects of the tempest."

"Will we vanish?"

"Nay." He chuckled. "But we will forget the truth." He led her to the dunes where Destrier anxiously pranced. "All that will be remembered of Arthur, Guenevere, and Camelot will be no more than folklore. God brought us together for a purpose, Rayn, and someday it will be revealed to us and to our children."

Rayn's thoughts came full circle. "What of my brother, Galahad?" she fearfully asked. "Have I lost him, too?"

Shadoe smiled. "Nay, Galahad's quite alive. I told him not to return. God willing, he will meet us in Tintagel. With Mordred and Morgause dead, their army has deserted the caer."

"Another revelation, husband?" She arched a brow and frowned.

Shadoe gave a sheepish shrug. "We'll make it our home." He offered a crooked smile.

"But how shall we make a livelihood?"

"Doing what my father did after he vacated his stewardship. I will write psalms of praise to our Lord, and ballads of the lost splendor of Camelot, while you, my dearest brat, do what you do best."

"And what is that, Milord Bard?"

"Be the simple godly lass you are and love me well."

"Whist! I can submit to that, I can." She giggled.

"Best you start trying." He lifted her into his arms and kissed her deeply. Wrapping her arms about his neck, Rayn molded with his lean hardness and savored their oneness. At last she'd found her godsend. At last, she had the unfathomable love that Merlin had promised would be hers.

Even when Shadoe's lips left hers, he clung possessively to her. "You will always be my princess, Rayn. But remember, we wear the crowns of the greatest kingdom of all . . . heaven."

Comforted, Rayn smiled for Shadoe; she could do nothing less.

The storm fast approaching, Shadoe swung himself onto Destrier and then lifted Rayn up into the saddle before him. He directed the Arab away from the inward-bound storm and turned eastward.

"Let's go home, my princess."

"Aye, my apprentice." She smiled, then looked one last time upon Wind's Haven and Caer Camelot. Miraculously, the moment Wind's Haven vanished, so did her depression.

Rayn pressed her palm to the Emerald Rose of Avalon. Accepting God's destiny, she acknowledged that the former rock of her security, Caer Camelot, had been a mere substitute for what she now possessed. Camelot's majestic soaring pillars and massive stone walls had been replaced by something far more tangible. Love. Turning her face eastward, Rayn nestled against Shadoe's chest. Even with the rough, steady rhythm of Destrier's hooves beneath them, she felt the quake in Shadoe's chest. Both would always harbor their memories of this mystical place called Camelot. But the real Camelot lived within their hearts.

Feeling Shadoe's strong arm about her waist, divine revelation embraced Rayn. God had answered her prayer. She a simple lass, and Shadoe a humble bard, would be together forever.

Epilogue

THE BARD STOOD and stretched to relieve his arthritic bones. Some of the youth praised his story. Others mocked him. Still with a share of civility, they bade him farewell. One youth lingered. Slighter than the other lordlings, his faded green tunic and bracchae were threadbare. Although he had sat apart from the assembly, he'd appeared keenly interested. Bone-weary, the bard hobbled away.

"Sire?" the stripling called out.

Halting, the lyricist turned his head and impatiently arched a brow. "Aye?"

The youth hesitated, then rushed forward. "I believe every word you spoke, Milord."

"And why is that?" he challenged.

The freckle-faced lad valiantly met his scowl. "Because you spoke of me, you did."

He chortled. "Oh, you are Shadoe un Hollo Tors, aye?"

The stripling's fine-boned features stained crimson. "'Course not, Sire. But the blood of Ayris surges in me veins, it does. A descendant of Arthur Pendragon, I am." He stuck out his flat chest with the pride of a young cock.

Grat-Telor drew a ragged breath and released it slowly. "And with what evidence do you make such an absurd claim?"

"Because of this." He reached between the folds of the bard's tattered, black wool cloak, and then grasped the talisman concealed there. His amber eyes went round as the moon, as if surprised by his find. Still he held tight to the amulet. "'Tis the Emerald Rose of Avalon, it is."

Grat-Telor's weary gaze lowered to the brilliant emerald nestled against the star-shaped bed of diamonds. "You think so, aye?"

"Aye," the plucky youth confirmed. "And you are Shadoe un Hollo Tors, the Pendragon."

"Really?" The bard's gnarled fingers clamped about the youth's grip. Their gazes locked. Grat-Telor smirked.

The brash lad's head bobbed with confidence.

"Do you realize how old that would make me?"

The lad released the amulet and rolled back his slight shoulders. "Ancient, I'm told. O' course not as old as Methuselah. It is the lineage of Ayris that has allowed your longevity, it has."

"If I am whom you say, then mayhap you are my progeny?" he mocked.

"Aye. And you, Sir Shadoe, are my great-great-great—"

Unimpressed, Grat-Telor silenced him with a hand gesture. "So convince me of your claim, lad."

The boy scratched his smooth freckled chin. "Since a wee bairn, I've heard the very account you told, Sire . . . but not as eloquently or in as much detail as you have done this day. Still, you left out vital events, you did."

"I did?" Grat-Telor yawned and leaned on his staff.

"You didn't mention Merlin's scrolls were copies of Jerome's Latin texts of the holy Book, and that you and Lady Rayn gave them to Galahad. Or that Lady Rayn birthed twins—a lad and a lass. Each bairn bore the mark of the Pendragon Rose."

"Impressed, I am."

The stripling grew bolder. "In your narrative, you fought against the Scotti, but years later you were high steward to my granda King Bridei of Dal Riada and an intimate friend to the teacher priest

Columba. Why, Lady Rayn taught Columba to speak the ⌐
tongue."

Grat-Telor tipped his hand in dismissal. "So I was, and so she
but you could have heard that anywhere."

The lad agreed reluctantly. Then as if looking upon something ⌐
cred, he eyed the walking staff. "According to our clan, this is the sta⌐
of Aaron, brother to Moses. The staff performed miracles and drew
water from the stone. The sacred staff was with the Ark of the Covenant. The ark was saved and went to Ayris, and your ancestors managed to save the staff before God's wrath swept Ayris away.

"'Tis also said you found the Isle of Wind's Haven again. There, almost a hundred years ago, you laid your beloved Rayn to rest beside
her parents beneath the chapel's ruins. You then hacked off part of the
staff and planted it at the gates of Caer Camelot. A great tree sprouted
forth. To this day, its dense branches shield Splendor Lost from the
eyes of the unworthy. The isle has been renamed Arran."

Grat-Telor straightened as best he could and huffed. "'Twas but the
dead limb of a tree. Nothing more, lad!"

"But—"

"Yahweh alone performed those miracles and drew water from the
stone!"

The youth waggled his cap-crowned head. "I know, but—"

His voice stern, Grat-Telor tapped the boy's head with a blunt finger. "Think before you speak, scion, for every word should glorify our
Creator."

Again, he sincerely nodded, although his tone was defiant. "What of
my birthright?"

"What of it?" The bard gestured to take his leave.

"But do you not wish to pass on the legacy of Ayris to your descendants?" Exasperation tensed his youthful features.

Grat-Telor reached out to the youth's brow and traced a fingertip
down the vertical vein that was tension roused. "That I do." He chuckled. "But I'm too old and too weary to play games with a brazen child."

449

Pictish

did,

...i you don't believe me, Sire?"

...ew the legacy of your lineage you'd know you

...e birthright."

...r?"

...st of inheritance stems from the woman's namesake, not

...nus, unless you have a sister, well. . . ."

...o living kin," he insisted sadly. "Died from the blood fever, they

...e been pursuing you more than a year. My home is Arran, it is."

...ou journeyed all this way on your own?"

"Aye." He jutted out a willful chin. "With me war-horse." He gestured to a puny black mare grazing on straw grass.

With a grunt, Grat-Telor took up his staff and hobbled toward the ruins where the sound of the surf-buffeted cliffs was deafening. The lad gave him chase, and the mare trotted behind. Arriving at the barren bluff, he found the bard had vanished.

The lad called out, "Lord Grat-Telor, High Steward, King Pendragon, come back. Please, let me explain." He walked in a circle, seeing no one. On his second round, he bumped into the bard's chest.

"Explain what?" Grat-Telor startled him, and he leaped back, wide-eyed.

"Where . . . How . . . ?" The stripling's eyes sparked with fascination at the mysterious reappearance of the bard.

"It's but a slight of hand." Grat-Telor shrugged. "What is so important, aye?"

The youth removed his cap, allowing a wealth of burnished curls to tumble free. "A lass I am, Sir."

Grat-Telor's eyes twinkled. "So you are, Meria Rose un Arran."

"You know my name!"

"Aye, always did. I ventured after you when I heard of family. But you were gone—busy chasing after me."

"But I—"

Grat-Telor slipped a finger beneath her open jaw and shut it. "A princess does not stand about with her mouth ajar, Lady."

Meria nodded and stared.

"Nor do they gape." He turned and trekked inland.

"Oh, I never gape, Lord." She hastened after him, tripping over scattered stone remnants of Caer Tintagel.

"And cease calling me Lord."

"What shall I call you, Sire?"

"Shadoe will suffice."

Catching up her mare's reins, Meria tramped beside Shadoe, who now walked with the gait of youth.

"Does this mean you'll mentor me?"

He turned and looked her over with a skeptical expression. "So, brat, how did you journey this far unscathed?"

"With Yahweh . . ." She reached beneath her jerkin's collar and unfastened a leather thong and scabbard. "And me mum's stinger." Meria handed over a tarnished, gold-stemmed dagger, the aged blade flint-worn. "It's not much, but has served me well, it has." She smiled with pride.

Shadoe traced a fingertip along the familiar worn hilt. Tears rimmed his eyes. "Aye, that it has, brat." He returned the stinger. Gently, Shadoe held Meria's face and looked into her fervent gaze. "Who owns you, Meria Rose un Arran?"

"The Christ Jesu." Her voice cracked with emotion. "Me Lord and Creator."

"He is our Shepherd."

"And we his sheep," she affirmed reverently.

"Aye." Shadoe lowered his tremulous hands and turned about to conceal his joy and the tear that burned his cheek. Stooping, he uprooted a golden cluster of herbs and then scowled at the puzzlement of his new ward. "Name the plant, lass." He shook the bouquet at her.

"Whist! How should I know?" She snorted when he shoved the bouquet in her hands.

"'Tis Woad. And after proper treatment the leaves produce a blue dye that—"

"You mean I must learn herbal lore?" Meria groused as she scuffed her toes in the sod.

He huffed. "You will learn everything necessary to—"

"Demon's dung! Next you'll be teaching me to weave . . . or worse, be a lady. I refuse to prance about in gowns and . . ." She ranted on as if queen of the glen.

Awestruck, Shadoe gawked at his bratty progeny. Divine revelation embraced his soul. *Ooh, Sweet Jesu, you can't be serious? Wait! Don't answer that!*

THE TRUTH

Oh, Isle of bright Pendragon might
Pay heed to this bard's song.
Tho' tides of folklore span yer shores
One truth doth linger on.
From the sowed seeds of Ayris,
Two hearts of Celtic fire
Arose to join as one,
And challenged heaven's foes.

I, a knight in tarnished mail
And she a thorny rose,
Godsends before time e'er was
Bound in body, heart, and soul.

Thus I, the endmost of ancient blood
To fulfill the promise told,
Did prick my flesh upon her thorns;
Then and only then,
Laid claim to the heart of
My beloved Emerald Rose.

—THE STEWARD CHRONICLES,
Shadoe un Hollo Tors

Author's Notes

THIS BOOK WOULD NOT have been conceived or written had God's hand not been upon me to do so. The amazing destinations he led me to contain gems such as the staff of Aaron, the bond between the Stewarts of Scotland and the Isle of Arran, my fictional Loch Lady Falls and the real Glenashdale Falls, and King's Cave, all of which remain miracles in and of themselves. I did not consciously possess this knowledge when I created the characters, setting, and plot. Further evidence that God is sovereign and the creator of everything good that we imagine.

Legend of the Emerald Rose is pure fantasy. It is depicted, however, within a context historically accurate from mid to late A.D. 400 when the real Lucius Artorius Castus, from whom the Arthurian legends emerged, perhaps lived. Therefore, the lifestyle is the darkest of the Dark Ages after Rome deserted the Isle of Might, leaving a Romano-Briton Christian influence on an otherwise pagan Celtic culture.

Whether Artorius existed will, no doubt, remain one of those great unsolved mysteries. Because I believe all legend is based on truth, I think Artorius did live, although probably not in the romantic context we choose to portray him, least of all as a king.

Where he existed also remains an enigma. For centuries, the English, Welsh, and Scots have laid claim to Arthur Pendragon and the lost splendor of Camelot. Oh, to be so popular!

My decision to place Camelot and the Pendragons in Caledonia was an easy choice. My maiden name, Holloway, is of Romano-Briton origin, long established in Great Britain and Ireland. Still, I always felt an inexplicable kinship with Scotland. During my historical research, I learned about Holloways in Scotland.

My research into the Arthurian legend of southwestern Caledonia proved as believable as the assertion that Arthur lived in southeastern Britannia. The evidence that Arthur waged war against the Irish Scotti and Caledonian Picts only seemed logical if he lived within their grasp. Southwestern Caledonia made sense to me. It was also common for a high king to have various fortresses such as Camelot, Belizar, Tintagel, and Glastonbury scattered across his realm. Conversely, it is no secret to Arthurian fans that I blended the Welsh and Scottish traditions.

As for identifying the battle in which Arthur died, I decided to leave that to the reader's imagination. The Welsh historian Nennius records twelve great battles during Arthur's time. Most historians have argued that is too great a number for one man's lifetime. Others, however, suggest that Arthur campaigned around the Isle of Might, defending the Romano-Briton cause against the Saxon invaders. So, it is possible he participated in many battles.

No matter the lack of battle names within *Legend of the Emerald Rose*, the Irish Scotti did engage the Celts and Saxons around the time period presented. Some historians suggest a Saxon, Scotti, and Pictish alliance against Arthur. The Welsh tradition indicates this battle took place in the area of the Scottish border. I simply played with those alliances.

I'm thankful for the opportunity to suggest to the faithful followers of the Arthurian legend that the love story of Arthur and Guenevere, as well as of Merlin and Niamh, did not end with the lost splendor of Camelot. As Grat-Telor would say, "'Twas only the beginning."